KING
SOLOMON'S
MINES

Henry Rider Haggard

COLLINS
CLASSICS

Harper Press
An imprint of HarperCollins*Publishers*
77–85 Fulham Palace Road
Hammersmith
London W6 8JB

This edition published 2010

A catalogue record for this book is available from the British Library

ISBN-13: 978-0-00-735090-2

Printed and bound in Great Britain by Clays Ltd, St Ives plc

Mixed Sources
Product group from well-managed
forests and other controlled sources
www.fsc.org Cert no. SW-COC-001806
© 1996 Forest Stewardship Council

FSC is a non-profit international organisation established to promote the
responsible management of the world's forests. Products carrying
the FSC label are independently certified to assure consumers that
they come from forests that are managed to meet the social,
economic and ecological needs of present and future generations.

Find out more about HarperCollins and the environment at
www.harpercollins.co.uk/green

Life & Times section © Gerard Cheshire
Classic Literature: Words and Phrases adapted from
Collins English Dictionary
Typesetting in Kalix by Palimpsest Book Production Limited,
Grangemouth, Stirlingshire

10 9 8 7 6 5 4 3 2 1

History of Collins

In 1819, Millworker William Collins from Glasgow, Scotland, set up a company for printing and publishing pamphlets, sermons, hymn books and prayer books. That company was Collins and was to mark the birth of HarperCollins Publishers as we know it today. The long tradition of Collins dictionary publishing can be traced back to the first dictionary William published in 1824, *Greek and English Lexicon*. Indeed, from 1840 onwards, he began to produce illustrated dictionaries and even obtained a licence to print and publish the Bible.

Soon after, William published the first Collins novel, *Ready Reckoner*, however it was the time of the Long Depression, where harvests were poor, prices were high, potato crops had failed and violence was erupting in Europe. As a result, many factories across the country were forced to close down and William chose to retire in 1846, partly due to the hardships he was facing.

Aged 30, William's son, William II took over the business. A keen humanitarian with a warm heart and a generous spirit, William II was truly 'Victorian' in his outlook. He introduced new, up-to-date steam presses and published affordable editions of Shakespeare's works and *Pilgrim's Progress*, making them available to the masses for the first time. A new demand for educational books meant that success came with the publication of travel books, scientific books, encyclopaedias and dictionaries. This demand to be educated led to the later publication of atlases and Collins also held the monopoly on scripture writing at the time.

In the 1860s Collins began to expand and diversify and the idea of 'books for the millions' was developed. Affordable editions of classical literature were published and in 1903 Collins introduced 10 titles in their Collins Handy Illustrated Pocket Novels. These proved so popular that a few years later this had increased to an output of 50 volumes, selling nearly half a million in their year of publication. In the same year, The Everyman's Library was also instituted, with the idea of publishing an affordable library of the most important classical works, biographies, religious and philosophical treatments, plays, poems, travel and adventure. This series eclipsed all competition at the time and the introduction of paperback books in the 1950s helped to open that market and marked a high point in the industry.

HarperCollins is and has always been a champion of the classics and the current Collins Classics series follows in this tradition – publishing classical literature that is affordable and available to all. Beautifully packaged, highly collectible and intended to be reread and enjoyed at every opportunity.

Life & Times

About the Author

Henry Rider Haggard was born into a large and well-to-do family in Norfolk, England. At the age of 19 he went to the Cape Colony, later to become South Africa. He lived on the African continent for seven years, having married and begun a family. He remained living in England from 1882 until his death in 1925.

Haggard's writing career began as soon as he returned to Britain. He became a prolific novelist and never retired. His most famous novel is *King Solomon's Mines*, published in 1885. He published a less well known sequel in 1887, titled *Allan Quartermain*. Haggard was naturally given to writing adventure type stories, of which he wrote over 70. Allan Quartermain featured in a number of other titles, including *Allan and the Holy Flower* (1915) and *Allan and the Ice Gods*, published posthumously in 1927.

Many of his stories are fables of one kind or another. This was indicative of the Victorian missionary mindset, which viewed native peoples as primitive and in need of salvation through indoctrination with Christianity and its moral and ethical precepts. In essence it was fundamental racism that established the notion that white Europeans were superior to other human types. This was largely because European civilizations had evolved markedly over centuries, while aboriginal populations around the world had largely remained in stasis. The result was that Europeans perceived them as living lifestyles that they themselves had left behind millennia ago.

Evidently Haggard's own experiences in Africa had also shaped his views of the native peoples. They were either enemies to be attacked and killed or allies to be led and ordered in battle. The white man was always considered superior, whatever the situation. Haggard was, however, a humanist and showed some empathy for his non-European characters – more than many writers of his period, despite the Victorian stereotype.

Fundamentally, Haggard was a supreme story teller, as opposed to literary novelist, and he managed to maintain a high standard of ideas and prose across his 43-year career. It seems fair to say that he lived vicariously through writing his books as much as his readership did by reading them, always finding somewhere new to explore and seeking adventure through his characters.

King Solomon's Mines

In 1871, Henry Morton Stanley, a Welsh journalist, succeeded in locating the whereabouts of David Livingstone, a Scottish missionary and explorer who had been incommunicado in darkest Africa for some years, having been on a quest to find the source of the River Nile. At that time much of Africa was still uncharted and mysterious, giving rise to ideas that the deepest and darkest regions were somehow lost in time; primal and primitive.

It was against this backdrop that Henry Rider Haggard wrote his seminal novel *King Solomon's Mines* (1885), which invented the literary genre now described as 'lost world'. In 1912 Arthur Conan Doyle published a novel titled *The Lost World*, which is where the phrase describing the genre was coined. *King Solomon's Mines* introduced the concept of there being isolated worlds within the wider world. As such they are closed systems that the central characters manage to enter and eventually exit to tell their story. As a literary devise the 'lost world' scenario has served very well ever since Rider Haggard conceived of it.

Rider Haggard was a well educated man and, in addition to his knowledge of Stanley and Livingstone, he also knew of the conquest of the Spanish conquistador, Hernán Cortés, who had taken control of the Aztec Empire in Mexico, 1519, with very few men by cultivating an impression of invincibility and playing on the Aztec's superstitions and beliefs. It is in a similar vein that Rider Haggard's central characters manage to avoid death at the hands of natives on their quest into the African interior.

Having survived various life threatening ordeals on their way, the party of explorers eventually arrives in a 'lost valley' called

Kukuanaland, which is ruled over by a dictatorial king named Twala. The scenario is inadvertently portentous of despotic rulers that will come and go in the 20th century. A native, named Umbopa, is singled out for execution, but the central character, Allan Quartermain, manages to save his life. Umbopa then turns out to be Ignosi, the rightful heir to the throne of Kukuanaland. A civil war then ensues, in which Twala is killed, so that Ignosi becomes king.

Twala's former advisor, Gagool, then leads the explorers to King Solomon's Mines, which are caves within a mountain, containing a hoard of treasure. Gagool then triggers a mechanism to trap the party inside. Following several days of incarceration an escape route is found and the Europeans manage to free themselves, their pockets filled with treasures. They eventually find their way back to England as wealthy men.

In essence the story is one of triumph over self inflicted adversity, in the true spirit of the real life English explorer. The phrase 'nothing ventured, nothing gained' sums up the ethos by which such men, and occasionally women embarked on their epic journeys into the unknown. It struck a chord with the reader because it was a way of living vicariously. One could visit dangerous places in the mind, whilst sitting comfortably by the fire and it made little difference whether the story was fact or fiction, or somewhere in between.

KING
SOLOMON'S
MINES

CONTENTS

AUTHOR'S INTRODUCTION

Now that this book is printed, and about to be given to the world, a sense of its shortcomings, both in style and contents, weighs very heavily upon me. As regards the latter, I can only say that it does not pretend to be a full account of everything we did and saw. There are many things connected with our journey into Kukuanaland that I should have liked to dwell upon at length, to which, as it is, I have scarcely alluded. Amongst these are the curious legends which I collected about the chain armour that saved us from destruction in the great battle of Loo, and also as to the 'Silent Ones' or Colossi at the mouth of the stalactite cave. Again, if I had given way to my own impulses, I should have wished to go into the differences, some of which are to my mind very suggestive, between the Zulu and Kukuana dialects. Also a few pages might have been devoted profitably to the consideration of the indigenous flora and fauna of Kukuanaland.[1] Then there remains the most interesting subject – that, as it is, has only been touched on incidentally – of the magnificent system of military organisation in force in that country, which, in my opinion, is much superior to that inaugurated by Chaka in Zululand, inasmuch as it permits of even more rapid mobilisation, and does not necessitate the employment of the pernicious system of forced celibacy.

[1] I discovered eight varieties of antelope, with which I was previously totally unacquainted, and many new species of plants, for the most part of the bulbous tribe. – A.Q.

Lastly, I have scarcely spoken of the domestic and family customs of the Kukuanas, many of which are exceedingly quaint, or of their proficiency in the art of smelting and welding metals. This science they carry to considerable perfection, of which a good example is to be seen in their 'tollas,' or heavy throwing knives, the backs of these weapons being made of hammered iron, and the edges of beautiful steel welded with great skill on to the iron frames.

The fact of the matter is, I thought, with Sir Henry Curtis and Captain Good, that the best plan would be to tell my story in a plain, straightforward manner, and to leave these matters to be dealt with subsequently in whatever way ultimately may appear to be desirable. In the meanwhile I shall, of course, be delighted to give all information in my power to anybody interested in such things.

And now it only remains for me to offer apologies for my blunt way of writing. I can but say in excuse of it that I am more accustomed to handle a rifle than a pen, and cannot make any pretence to the grand literary flights and flourishes which I see in novels – for sometimes I like to read a novel. I suppose they – the flights and flourishes – are desirable, and I regret not being able to supply them. At the same time I cannot help thinking that simple things are always the most impressive, and that books are easier to understand when – like the Bible – they are written in plain language, though perhaps I have no right to set up an opinion on such a matter. 'A sharp spear,' runs the Kukuana saying, 'needs no polish'; and on the same principle I venture to hope that a true story, however strange it may be, does not require to be decked out in fine words.

Allan Quatermain

CHAPTER 1

I Meet Sir Henry Curtis

It is a curious thing that at my age – I shall never see sixty again – I should find myself taking up a pen to try to write a history. I wonder what sort of a history it will be when I have finished it, if ever I come to the end of the trip! I have done a good many things in my life, which seems a long one to me, owing to my having begun work so young, perhaps. At an age when other boys are at school I was earning my living in the old Colony and Natal. I have been trading, hunting, fighting, or exploring ever since. And yet it is only eight months ago that I made my pile. It is a big pile now that I have got it – I don't yet know how big – but I do not think I would go through the last fifteen or sixteen months again for it; no, not if I knew that I should come out safe at the end, pile and all. But then I am a timid man, and dislike violence; moreover, I am almost sick of adventure. I wonder why I am going to write this book; it is not in my line. I am not a literary man, though very devoted to the Old Testament and also to the 'Ingoldsby Legends.' Let me try to set down my reasons, just to see if I have any.

First reason: Because Sir Henry Curtis and Captain John Good asked me.

Second reason: Because I am laid up here at Durban with the pain in my left leg. Ever since that confounded lion got hold of me

I have been liable to this trouble, and being rather bad just now, it makes me limp more than ever. There must be some poison in a lion's teeth, otherwise how is it that when your wounds are healed they break out again, generally, mark you, at the same time of year that you got your mauling? It is a hard thing when one has shot sixty-five lions or more, as I have in the course of my life, that the sixty-sixth should chew your leg like a quid of tobacco. It breaks the routine of the thing, and putting other considerations aside, I am an orderly man and don't like that. This is by the way.

Third reason: Because I want my boy Harry, who is over there at the hospital in London studying to become a doctor, to have something to amuse him and keep him out of mischief for a week or so. Hospital work must sometimes pall and grow rather dull, for even of cutting up dead bodies there may come satiety, and as this history will not be dull, whatever else it may be, it will put a little life into things for a day or two while Harry is reading of our adventures.

Fourth reason and last: Because I am going to tell the strangest story that I remember. It may seem a queer thing to say, especially considering that there is no woman in it – except Foulata. Stop though! there is Gagaoola, if she was a woman and not a fiend. But she was a hundred at least, and therefore not marriageable, so I don't count her. At any rate, I can safely say that there is not a *petticoat* in the whole history.

Well, I had better come to the yoke. It is a stiff place, and I feel as though I were bogged up to the axle. But *'sutjes, sutjes,'* as the Boers say – I am sure I don't know how they spell it – softly does it. A strong team will come through at last, that is if they are not too poor. You can never do anything with poor oxen. Now to make a start.

I, Allan Quatermain, of Durban, Natal, Gentleman, make oath and say – That's how I headed my deposition before the magistrate about poor Khiva's and Ventvogel's sad deaths; but somehow it doesn't seem quite the right way to begin a book. And, besides, am I a gentleman? What is a gentleman? I don't quite know, and yet I have had to do with niggers – no, I will scratch out that word 'niggers,' for I do not like it: I've known natives who *are*, and so you will say, Harry, my boy, before you have done with this tale, and I have known mean whites with lots of money and fresh out from home, too, who *are not*.

At any rate, I was born a gentleman, though I have been nothing but a poor travelling trader and hunter all my life. Whether I have remained so I know not, you must judge of that. Heaven knows I've tried. I have killed many men in my time, yet I have never slain wantonly or stained my hand in innocent blood, but only in self-defence. The Almighty gave us our lives, and I suppose He meant us to defend them, at least I have always acted on that, and I hope it will not be brought up against me when my clock strikes. There, there, it is a cruel and wicked world, and for a timid man I have been mixed up in a deal of fighting. I cannot tell the rights of it, but at any rate I have never stolen, though once I cheated a Kafir out of a herd of cattle. But then he had done me a dirty turn, and it has troubled me ever since into the bargain.

Well, it is eighteen months or so ago since first I met Sir Henry Curtis and Captain Good. It was in this way. I had been up elephant hunting beyond Bamangwato, and had met with bad luck. Everything went wrong that trip, and to top up with I got the fever badly. So soon as I was well enough I trekked down to the Diamond Fields, sold such ivory as I had, together with my wagon and oxen, discharged my hunters, and took the post-cart to the Cape. After spending a week in Cape Town finding that they overcharged me at the hotel, and having seen everything there was to see, including the botanical gardens, which seem to me likely to confer a great benefit on the country, and the new Houses of Parliament, which I expect will do nothing of the sort, I determined to go back to Natal by the *Dunkeld*, then lying at the docks waiting for the *Edinburgh Castle* due in from England. I took my berth and went aboard, and that afternoon the Natal passengers from the *Edinburgh Castle* transhipped, and we weighed and put out to sea.

Among these passengers who came on board were two who excited my curiosity. One, a gentleman of about thirty, was perhaps the biggest-chested and longest-armed man I ever saw. He had yellow hair, a thick yellow beard, clear-cut features, and large grey eyes set deep in his head. I never saw a finer-looking man, and somehow he reminded me of an ancient Dane. Not that I know much of ancient Danes, though I knew a modern Dane who did me out of ten pounds; but I remember once seeing a picture of some of those gentry, who, I take it, were a kind of white Zulus. They were drinking out of big horns, and their long hair hung down their backs. As I looked at my friend standing there by the companion-ladder, I thought that if he only let his grow a little, put one of those chain shirts on to his great shoulders, and took hold of a battle-axe and a horn mug, he might have sat as a model for that picture. By the way it is a curious thing, and just shows how the blood will out, I discovered afterwards that Sir Henry Curtis, for that was the big man's name, is of Danish blood.[1] Also he reminded me strongly of somebody else, but at the time I could not remember who it was.

The other man, who stood talking to Sir Henry, was stout and dark, and of quite a different cut. I suspected at once that he was a naval officer; I don't know why, but it is difficult to mistake a navy man. I have gone shooting trips with several of them in the course of my life, and they have always proved themselves the best and bravest and nicest fellows I ever met, though sadly given, some of them, to the use of profane language. I asked a page or two back, what is a gentleman? I'll answer the question now: a Royal Naval officer is, in a general sort of way, though of course there may be a black sheep among them here and there. I fancy it is just the wide seas and the breath of God's winds that wash their hearts and blow the bitterness out of their minds and make them what men ought to be.

---

[1] Mr Quatermain's ideas about ancient Danes seem to be rather confused; we have always understood that they were dark-haired people. Probably he was thinking of Saxons. – *Editor.*

Well, to return, I proved right again; I ascertained that the dark man *was* a naval officer, a lieutenant of thirty-one, who, after seventeen years' service, had been turned out of her Majesty's employ with the barren honour of a commander's rank, because it was impossible that he should be promoted. This is what people who serve the Queen have to expect: to be shot out into the cold world to find a living just when they are beginning really to understand their work, and to reach the prime of life. I suppose they don't mind it, for but my own part I had rather earn my bread as a hunter. One's halfpence are as scarce perhaps, but you do not get so many kicks.

The officer's name I found out – by referring to the passengers' list – was Good – Captain John Good. He was broad, of medium height, dark, stout, and rather a curious man to look at. He was so very neat and so very clean-shaved, and he always wore an eyeglass in his right eye. It seemed to grow there, for it had no string, and he never took it out except to wipe it. At first I thought he used to sleep in it, but afterwards I found that this was a mistake. He put it in his trousers pocket when he went to bed, together with his false teeth, of which he had two beautiful sets that, my own being none of the best, have often caused me to break the tenth commandment. But I am anticipating.

Soon after we had got under way evening closed in, and brought with it very dirty weather. A keen breeze sprung up off land, and a kind of aggravated Scotch mist soon drove everybody from the deck. As for the *Dunkeld*, she is a flat-bottomed punt, and going up light as she was, she rolled very heavily. It almost seemed as though she would go right over, but she never did. It was quite impossible to walk about, so I stood near the engines where it was warm, and amused myself with watching the pendulum, which was fixed opposite to me, swinging backwards and forwards as the vessel rolled, and marking the angle she touched at each lurch.

'That pendulum's wrong; it is not properly weighted,' suddenly said a somewhat testy voice at my shoulder. Looking round I saw the naval officer whom I had noticed when the passengers came aboard.

'Indeed, now what makes you think so?' I asked.

'Think so. I don't think at all. Why there' – as she righted herself after a roll – 'if the ship had really rolled to the degree that thing pointed to, then she would never have rolled again, that's all. But it is just like these merchant skippers, they always are so confoundedly careless.'

Just then the dinner-bell rang, and I was not sorry, for it is a dreadful thing to have to listen to an officer of the Royal Navy when he gets on to that subject. I only know one worse thing, and it is to hear a merchant skipper express his candid opinion of officers of the Royal Navy.

Captain Good and I went down to dinner together, and there we found Sir Henry Curtis already seated. He and Captain Good were placed together, and I sat opposite to them. The captain and I soon fell into talk about shooting and what not; he asking me many questions, for he is very inquisitive about all sorts of things, and I answering them as well as I could. Presently he got on to elephants.

'Ah, sir,' called out somebody who was sitting near me,' you've reached the right man for that; Hunter Quatermain should be able to tell you about elephants if anybody can.'

Sir Henry, who had been sitting quite quiet listening to our talk, started visibly.

'Excuse me, sir,' he said, leaning forward across the table, and speaking in a low deep voice, a very suitable voice, it seemed to me, to come out of those great lungs.

'Excuse me, sir, but is your name Allan Quatermain?'

I said that it was.

The big man made no further remark, but I heard him mutter 'fortunate' into his beard.

Presently dinner came to an end, and as we were leaving the saloon Sir Henry strolled up and asked me if I would come into his cabin to smoke a pipe. I accepted, and he led the way to the *Dunkeld* deck cabin, and a very good cabin it is. It had been two cabins, but when Sir Garnet Wolseley or one of those big swells went down the coast in the *Dunkeld*, they knocked away the partition and have never put it up again. There was a sofa in the cabin, and a little table in front of it. Sir Henry sent the steward for a bottle of whisky, and the three of us sat down and lit our pipes.

'Mr Quatermain,' said Sir Henry Curtis, when the man had brought the whisky and lit the lamp, 'the year before last about this time, you were, I believe, at a place called Bamangwato, to the north of the Transvaal.'

'I was,' I answered, rather surprised that this gentleman should be so well acquainted with my movements, which were not, so far as I was aware, considered of general interest.

'You were trading there, were you not?' put in Captain Good, in his quick way.

'I was. I took up a wagon-load of goods, made a camp outside the settlement, and stopped till I had sold them.'

Sir Henry was sitting opposite to me in a Madeira chair, his arms leaning on the table. He now looked up, fixing his large grey eyes full upon my face. There was a curious anxiety in them, I thought.

'Did you happen to meet a man called Neville there?'

'Oh, yes; he outspanned alongside of me for a fortnight to rest his oxen before going on to the interior. I had a letter from a lawyer a few months back, asking me if I knew what had become of him, which I answered to the best of my ability at the time.'

'Yes,' said Sir Henry, 'your letter was forwarded to me. You said in it that the gentleman called Neville left Bamangwato at the beginning of May in a wagon with a driver, a voorlooper, and a Kafir hunter called Jim, announcing his intention of trekking if possible as far as Inyati, the extreme trading post in the Matabele country, where he would sell his wagon and proceed on foot. You also said that he did sell his wagon, for six months afterwards you saw the wagon in the possession of a Portuguese trader, who told you that he had bought it at Inyati from a white man whose name he had forgotten, and that he believed the white man with the native servant had started off for the interior on a shooting trip.'

'Yes.'

Then came a pause.

'Mr Quatermain,' said Sir Henry suddenly, 'I suppose you know or can guess nothing more of the reasons of my – of Mr Neville's journey to the northward, or as to what point that journey was directed?'

'I heard something,' I answered, and stopped. The subject was one which I did not care to discuss.

Sir Henry and Captain Good looked at each other, and Captain Good nodded.

'Mr Quatermain,' went on the former, 'I am going to tell you a story, and ask your advice, and perhaps your assistance. The agent who forwarded me your letter told me that I might rely upon it implicitly, as you were, he said, well known and universally respected in Natal, and especially noted for your discretion.'

I bowed and drank some whisky and water to hide my confusion, for I am a modest man – and Sir Henry went on.

'Mr Neville was my brother.'

'Oh,' I said, starting, for now I knew of whom Sir Henry had reminded me when first I saw him. His brother was a much smaller man and had a dark beard, but now that I thought of it, he possessed eyes of the same shade of grey and with the same keen look in them: the features too were not unlike.

'He was,' went on Sir Henry, 'my only and younger brother, and till five years ago I do not suppose that we were ever a month away from each other. But just about five years ago a misfortune befell us, as sometimes does happen in families. We quarrelled bitterly, and I behaved unjustly to my brother in my anger.'

Here Captain Good nodded his head vigorously to himself. The ship gave a big roll just then, so that the looking-glass, which was fixed opposite us to starboard, was for a moment nearly over our heads, and as I was sitting with my hands in my pockets and staring upwards, I could see him nodding like anything.

'As I daresay you know,' went on Sir Henry, 'if a man dies intestate, and has no property but land, real property it is called in England, it all descends to his eldest son. It so happened that just at the time when we quarrelled our father died intestate. He had put off making his will until it was too late. The result was that my brother, who had not been brought up to any profession, was left without a penny. Of course it would have been my duty to provide for him, but at the time the quarrel between us was so bitter that I did not – to my shame I say it (and he sighed deeply) – offer to do anything. It was not that I grudged him justice, but I waited for him to make advances and he made none. I am sorry to trouble you with all this, Mr Quatermain, but I must make things clear, eh, Good?'

'Quite so, quite so,' said the captain. 'Mr Quatermain will, I am sure, keep this history to himself.'

'Of course,' said I, for I rather pride myself on my discretion, for which, as Sir Henry had heard, I have some repute.

'Well,' went on Sir Henry, 'my brother had a few hundred pounds to his account at the time. Without saying anything to me he drew out this paltry sum, and, having adopted the name of Neville, started off for South Africa in the wild hope of making a fortune. This I learnt afterwards. Some three years passed, and I heard nothing of my brother, though I wrote several times. Doubtless the letters never reached him. But as time went on I grew more and more troubled about him. I found out, Mr Quatermain, that blood is thicker than water.'

'That's true,' said I, thinking of my boy Harry.

'I found out, Mr Quatermain, that I would have given half my fortune to know that my brother George, the only relation I possess, was safe and well, and that I should see him again.'

'But you never did, Curtis,' jerked out Captain Good, glancing at the big man's face.

'Well, Mr Quatermain, as time went on I became more and more anxious to find out if my brother was alive or dead, and if alive to get him home again. I set inquiries on foot, and your letter was one of the results. So far as it went it was satisfactory, for it showed that till lately George was alive, but it did not go far enough. So, to cut a long story short, I made up my mind to come out and look for him myself, and Captain Good was so kind as to come with me.'

'Yes,' said the captain; 'nothing else to do, you see. Turned out by my Lords of the Admiralty to starve on half pay. And now perhaps, sir, you will tell us what you know of the gentleman called Neville.'

CHAPTER 2

The Legend of Solomon's Mines

'What was it that you heard about my brother's journey at Bamangwato?' asked Sir Henry, as I paused to fill my pipe before replying to Captain Good.

'I heard this,' I answered,' and I have never mentioned it to a soul till to-day. I heard that he was starting for Solomon's Mines.'

'Solomon's Mines!' ejaculated both my hearers at once. 'Where are they?'

'I don't know,' I said; 'I know where they are said to be. Once I saw the peaks of the mountains that border them, but there were a hundred and thirty miles of desert between me and them, and I am not aware that any white man ever got across it save one. But perhaps the best thing I can do is to tell you the legend of Solomon's Mines, as I know it, you passing your word not to reveal anything I tell you without my permission. Do you agree to that? I have my reasons for asking.'

Sir Henry nodded, and Captain Good replied, 'Certainly, certainly.'

'Well,' I began, 'as you may guess, generally speaking, elephant hunters are a rough set of men, who do not trouble themselves with much beyond the facts of life and the ways of Kafirs. But here and there you meet a man who takes the trouble to collect traditions from the natives, and tries to make out a little piece of the history

HENRY RIDER HAGGARD

of this dark land. It was such a one as this who first told me the
legend of Solomon's Mines, now a matter of nearly thirty years ago.
That was when I was on my first elephant hunt in the Matabele
country. His name was Evans, and he was killed the following year,
poor fellow, by a wounded buffalo, and lies buried near the Zambesi
Falls. I was telling Evans one night, I remember, of some wonderful
workings I had found whilst hunting koodoo and eland in what is
now the Lydenburg district of the Transvaal. I see they have come
across these workings again lately in prospecting for gold, but I knew
of them years ago. There is a great wide wagon road cut out of the
solid rock, and leading to the mouth of the working or gallery. Inside
the mouth of this gallery are stacks of gold quartz piled up ready for
roasting, which shows that the workers, whoever they were, must
have left in a hurry. Also, about twenty paces in, the gallery is built
across, and a beautiful bit of masonry it is.

"'Ay,' said Evans, "but I will spin you a queerer yarn than
that"; and he went on to tell me how he had found in the far interior a ruined city, which he believed to be the Ophir of the Bible,
and, by the way, other more learned men have said the same long
since poor Evans's time. I was, I remember, listening open-eared to
all these wonders, for I was young at the time, and this story of an
ancient civilisation and of the treasures which those old Jewish or
Phoenician adventurers used to extract from a country long since
lapsed into the darkest barbarism took a great hold upon my imagination, when suddenly he said to me. "Lad, did you ever hear of
the Suliman Mountains up to the north-west of the Mashukulumbwe
country?" I told him I never had. "Ah, well," he said, "that is where
Solomon really had his mines, his diamond mines, I mean."

"'How do you know that?" I asked.

"'Know it! why, what is 'Suliman' but a corruption of Solomon?[1]
Besides, an old Isanusi or witch doctress up in the Manica country told
me all about it. She said that the people who lived across those mountains were a 'branch' of the Zulus, speaking a dialect of Zulu, but finer
and bigger men even; that there lived among them great wizards, who

[1]Suliman is the Arabic form of Solomon. – *Editor.*
14

had learnt their art from white men when 'all the world was dark,' and who had the secret of a wonderful mine of 'bright stones.'"

'Well, I laughed at this story at the time, though it interested me, for the Diamond Fields were not discovered then, but poor Evans went off and was killed, and for twenty years I never thought any more of the matter. However, just twenty years afterwards – and that is a long time, gentlemen; an elephant hunter does not often live for twenty years at his business – I heard something more definite about Suliman's Mountains and the country which lies behind them. I was up beyond the Manica country, at a place called Sitanda's Kraal, and a miserable place it was, for a man could get nothing to eat, and there was but little game about. I had an attack of fever, and was in a bad way generally, when one day a Portugee arrived with a single companion – a half-breed. Now I know your low-class Delagoa Portugee well. There is no greater devil unhung in a general way, battening as he does upon human agony and flesh in the shape of slaves. But this was quite a different type of man to the mean fellows whom I had been accustomed to meet; indeed, in appearance he reminded me more of the polite doms I have read about for he was tall and thin, with large dark eyes, and curling grey mustachios. We talked together a little, for he could speak broken English, and I understood a little Portuguese, and he told me that his name was José Silvestre, and that he had a place near Delagoa Bay. When he went on next day with his half-breed companion, he said "Good-bye," taking off his hat quite in the old style. "Good-bye, señor," he said; "if ever we meet again I shall be the richest man in the world, and I will remember you." I laughed a little – I was too weak to laugh much – and watched him strike out for the great desert to the west, wondering if he were mad, or what he thought he was going to find there.

'A week passed, and I got the better of my fever. One evening I was sitting on the ground in front of the little tent I had with me, chewing the last leg of a miserable fowl I had bought from a native for a bit of cloth worth twenty fowls, and staring at the hot red sun sinking down over the desert, when suddenly I saw a figure, apparently that of a European, for it wore a coat, on the slope of the rising ground opposite to me, about three hundred yards away. The figure crept along on its hands and knees, then it got up and staggered forward a few yards on its legs, only to fall and crawl again. Seeing that it must be some-body in distress, I sent one of my hunters to help him, and presently he arrived, and who do you suppose it turned out to be?'

'José Silvestre, of course,' said Captain Good.

'Yes, José Silvestre, or rather his skeleton and a little skin. His face was bright yellow with bilious fever, and his large dark eyes stood nearly out of his head, for all the flesh had gone. There was nothing but yellow parchment-like skin, white hair, and the gaunt bones sticking up beneath.

'"Water! for the sake of Christ, water!" he moaned and I saw that his lips were cracked, and his tongue, which protruded between them, was swollen and blackish.

'I gave him water with a little milk in it, and he drank it in great gulps, two quarts or so, without stopping. I would not let him have any more. Then the fever took him again, and he fell down and began to rave about Suliman's Mountains, and the diamonds, and the desert. I carried him into the tent and did what I could for him, which was little enough; but I saw how it must end. About eleven o'clock he grew quieter, and I lay down for a little rest and went to sleep. At dawn I woke again, and in the half light saw Silvestre sitting up, a strange, gaunt form, and gazing out towards the desert. Presently the first ray of the sun shot right across the wide plain before us till it reached the far-away crest of one of the tallest of the Suliman Mountains more than a hundred miles away.

'"There it is!" cried the dying man in Portuguese, and pointing with his long, thin arm, "but I shall never reach it, never. No one will ever reach it!"

'Suddenly he paused, and seemed to take a resolution. "Friend," he said, turning towards me, "are you there? My eyes grow dark."

'"Yes," I said; "yes, lie down now, and rest."

'"Ay," he answered, "I shall rest soon, I have time to rest –

all eternity. Listen, I am dying! You have been good to me. I will give you the writing. Perhaps you will get there if you can live to pass the desert, which has killed my poor servant and me."

'Then he groped in his shirt and brought out what I thought was a Boer tobacco pouch made of the skin of the Swart-vet-pens or sable antelope. It was fastened with a little strip of hide, what we call a rimpi, and this he tried to loose, but could not. He handed it to me. "Untie it," he said. I did so, and extracted a bit of torn yellow linen, on which something was written in rusty letters. Inside this rag was a paper.

'Then he went on feebly, for he was growing weak: "The paper has all that is on the linen. It took me years to read. Listen: my ancestor, a political refugee from Lisbon, and one of the first Portuguese who landed on these shores, wrote that when he was dying on those mountains which no white foot ever pressed before or since. His name was José da Silvestra, and he lived three hundred years ago. His slave, who waited for him on this side of the mountains, found him dead, and brought the writing home to Delagoa. It has been in the family ever since, but none have cared to read it, till at last I did. And I have lost my life over it, another may succeed, and become the richest man in the world – the richest man in the world. Only give it to no one, señor; go yourself!"

'Then he began to wander again, and in an hour it was all over.

'God rest him! he died very quietly, and I buried him deep, with big boulders on his breast; so I do not think that the jackals can have dug him up. Then I came away.'

'Ay, but the document?' said Sir Henry, in a tone of deep interest.

'Yes, the document; what was in it?' added the captain.

'Well, gentlemen, if you like I will tell you. I have never showed it to anybody yet except to a drunken old Portuguese trader who translated it for me, and had forgotten all about it by the next morning. The original rag is at my home in Durban, together with poor Dom José's translation, but I have the English rendering in my pocket-book, and a facsimile of the map, if it can be called a map. Here it is.'

'I, José da Silvestra, who am now dying of hunger in the little cave where no snow is on the north side of the nipple of the southernmost of the two mountains I have named Sheba's Breasts, write this in the year 1590 with a cleft bone upon a remnant of my raiment, my blood being the ink. If my slave should find it when he comes, and should bring it to Delagoa, let my friend (name illegible) bring the matter to the knowledge of the king, that he may send an army which, if they live through the desert and the mountains, and can overcome the brave Kukuanes and their devilish arts, to which end many priests should be brought, will make him the richest king since Solomon. With my own eyes have I seen the countless diamonds stored in Solomon's treasure chamber behind the white Death; but through the treachery of Gagool the witch-finder I might bring nought away, scarcely my life. Let him who comes follow the map, and climb the snow of Sheba's left breast till he reaches the nipple, on the north side of which is the great road Solomon made, from whence three days' journey to the King's Palace. Let him kill Gagool. Pray for my soul. Farewell.

José da Silvestra.'[2]

When I had finished reading the above, and shown the copy of the map, drawn by the dying hand of the old Dom with his blood for ink, there followed a silence of astonishment.

'Well,' said Captain Good,' I have been round the world twice,

[2]Eu José da Silvestra que estou morrendo de fome ná pequena cova onde não ha neve ao lado norte do bico mais ao sul das duas montanhas que chamei seio de Sheba; escrevo isto no anno 1590; escrevo isto com um pedaço d'ôsso n'um farrapo de minha roupa e com sangue meu por tinta; se o meu escravo dér com isto quando venha ao levar para Lourenzo Marquez, que o meu amigo – leve a cousa ao conhecimento d' El Rei, para que possa mandar um exercito que, se desfiler pelo deserto e pelas montanhas e mesmo sobrepujar os bravos Kukuanes e suas artes diabolicas, pelo que se deviam trazer muitos padres Fara o Rei mais rico depois de Salomão.

and put in at most ports, but may I be hung for a mutineer if ever I heard a yarn like this out of a story book, or in it either, for the matter of that.'

'It is a queer tale, Mr Quatermain,' said Sir Henry. 'I suppose you are not hoaxing us? It is, I know, sometimes thought allowable to take in a greenhorn.'

'If you think that, Sir Henry,' I said, much put out, and pocketing my paper – for I do not like to be thought one of those silly fellows who consider it witty to tell lies, and who are for ever boasting to newcomers of extraordinary hunting adventures which never happened – 'if you think that, why, there is an end to the matter,' and I rose to go.

Sir Henry laid his large hand on my shoulder. 'Sit down, Mr Quatermain,' he said, 'I beg your pardon; I see very well you do not wish to deceive us, but the story sounded so strange that I could hardly believe it.'

'You shall see the original map and writing when we reach Durban,' I answered, somewhat mollified, for really when I came to consider the question it was scarcely wonderful that he should doubt my good faith.

'But,' I went on, 'I have not told you about your brother. I knew the man Jim who was with him. He was a Bechuana by birth, a good hunter, and for a native a very clever man. That morning on which Mr Neville was starting I saw Jim standing by my wagon and cutting up tobacco on the disselboom.

'"Jim," said I, "where are you off to this trip? Is it elephants?"

'"No, Baas," he answered, "we are after something worth much more than ivory."

'"And what might that be?" I said, for I was curious. "Is it gold?"

_____
Com meus proprios olhos vé os di amantes sem conto guardados nas camaras do thesouro de Salomão a traz da morte branca, mas pela traição de Gagoal a feiticeira achadora, nada podeira levar, e apenas a minha vida. Quem vier siga o mappa a trepe pela neve de Sheba peito à esquerda até chegar ao bica, do lado norte do qual està a grande estrada do Salomão por elle feita, donde ha tres dias de jornada até ao Palacio do Rei. Mate Gagoal. Reze por minha alma. Adeos.
José da Silvestra.

'"No, Baas, something worth more than gold," and he grinned.

'I asked no more questions, for I did not like to lower my dignity by seeming inquisitive, but I was puzzled. Presently Jim finished cutting his tobacco.

'"Baas," said he.

'I took no notice.

'"Baas," said he again.

'"Eh, boy, what is it?" I asked.

'"Baas, we are going after diamonds."

'"Diamonds! why, then, you are steering in the wrong direction; you should head for the Fields."

'"Baas, have you ever heard of Suliman's Berg?" – that is, Solomon's Mountains, Sir Henry.

'"Ay!"

'"Have you ever heard of the diamonds there?"

'"I have heard a foolish story, Jim."

'"It is no story, Baas. Once I knew a woman who came from there, and reached Natal with her child, she told me: – she is dead now."

'"Your master will feed the aasvögels" – that is, vultures – "Jim, if he tries to reach Suliman's country, and so will you if they can get any pickings off your worthless old carcass," said I.

'He grinned. "Mayhap, Baas. Man must die; I'd rather like to try a new country myself; the elephants are getting worked out about here."

'"Ah! my boy," I said, "you wait till the 'pale old man' gets a grip of your yellow throat, and then we shall hear what sort of a tune you sing."

'Half an hour after that I saw Neville's wagon move off. Presently Jim came back running. "Good-bye, Baas," he said. 'I didn't like to start without bidding you good-bye, for I daresay you are right, and that we shall never trek south again.'

'"Is your master really going to Suliman's Berg, Jim, or are you lying?"

'"No," he answered, "he is going. He told me he was bound

to make his fortune somehow, or try to; so he might as well have a fling for the diamonds."

'Oh!' I said; "wait a bit, Jim; will you take a note to your master, Jim, and promise not to give it to him till you reach Inyati?" which was some hundred miles off.

'"Yes, Baas."

'So I took a scrap of paper, and wrote on it, "Let him who comes . . . climb the snow of Sheba's left breast, till he reaches the nipple, on the north side of which is Solomon's great road."

'"Now, Jim," I said, "when you give this to your master, tell him he had better follow the advice on it implicitly. You are not to give it to him now, because I don't want him back asking me questions which I won't answer. Now be off, you idle fellow, the wagon is nearly out of sight."

'Jim took the note and went, and that is all I know about your brother, Sir Henry; but I am much afraid—'

'Mr Quatermain,' said Sir Henry, 'I am going to look for my brother; I am going to trace him to Suliman's Mountains, and over them if necessary, till I find him, or until I know that he is dead. Will you come with me?'

I am, as I think I have said, a cautious man, indeed a timid one, and this suggestion frightened me. It seemed to me that to undertake such a journey would be to go to certain death, and putting other considerations aside, as I had a son to support, I could not afford to die just then.

'No, thank you, Sir Henry, I think I had rather not,' I answered. 'I am too old for wild-goose chases of that sort, and we should only end up like my poor friend Silvestre. I have a son dependent on me, so I cannot afford to risk my life foolishly.'

Both Sir Henry and Captain Good looked very disappointed.

'Mr Quatermain,' said the former, 'I am well off, and I am bent upon this business. You may put the remuneration for your services at whatever figure you like in reason, and it shall be paid over to you before we start. Moreover, I will arrange in the event of anything untoward happening to us or to you, that your son shall be suitably provided for. You will see from this offer how necessary I think your presence. Also, if by chance we should reach this place and find diamonds, they shall belong to you and Good equally. I do not want them. But of course that promise is worth nothing at all, though the same thing would apply to any ivory we may get. You may pretty well make your own terms with me, Mr Quatermain; and of course I shall pay all expenses.'

'Sir Henry,' said I, 'this is about the most liberal proposal I ever had; one not to be sneezed at by a poor hunter and trader. But the job is the biggest I have come across, and I must take time to think it over. I will give you my answer before we get to Durban.'

'Very good,' answered Sir Henry.

Then I said good night and turned in, and dreamt about poor long-dead Silvestre and the diamonds.

CHAPTER 3

Umbopa Enters our Service

It takes from four to five days, according to the speed of the vessel and the state of the weather, to run up from the Cape to Durban. Sometimes, if the landing is bad at East London, where they have not yet made that wonderful harbour they talk so much of, and sink such a mint of money in, a ship is delayed for twenty-four hours before the cargo boats can get out to take off the goods. But on this occasion we had not to wait at all, for there were no breakers on the Bar to speak of, and the tugs came out at once with the long strings of ugly flat-bottomed boats behind them, into which the packages were bundled with a crash. It did not matter what they might be, over they went slapbang; whether they contained china or woollen goods they met with the same treatment. I saw one case holding four dozen of champagne smashed all to bits, and there was the champagne fizzing and boiling about in the bottom of the dirty cargo boat. It was a wicked waste, and evidently so the Kafirs in the boat thought, for they found a couple of unbroken bottles, and knocking off the necks drank the contents. But they had not allowed for the expansion caused by the fizz in the wine, and, feeling themselves swelling, rolled about in the bottom of the boat, calling out that the good liquor was 'tagati' – that is, bewitched. I spoke to them from the vessel, and told them it was the white man's strongest medicine, and that they were as good as dead men. Those Kafirs went to the shore in a very great fright, and I do not think that they will touch champagne again.

Well, all the time that we were steaming up to Natal I was thinking over Sir Henry Curtis's offer. We did not speak any more on the subject for a day or two, though I told them many hunting yarns, all true ones. There is no need to tell lies about hunting, for so many curious things happen within the knowledge of a man whose business it is to hunt; but this is by the way.

At last, one beautiful evening in January, which is our hottest month, we steamed past the coast of Natal expecting to make Durban Point by sunset. It is a lovely coast all along from East London, with its red sandhills and wide sweeps of vivid green, dotted here and there, with Kafir kraals, and bordered by a ribbon of white surf, which spouts up in pillars of foam where it hits the rocks. But just before you come to Durban there is a peculiar richness about the landscape. There are the sheer kloofs cut in the hills by the rushing rains of centuries, down which the rivers sparkle; there are the deep green of the bush, growing as God planted it, and the other greens of the mealie gardens and the sugar patches, while now and again a white house, smiling out at the placid sea, puts a finish and gives an air of homeliness to the scene. For to my mind, however beautiful a view may be, it requires the presence of man to make it complete, but perhaps that is because I have lived so much in the wilderness, and therefore know the value of civilisation, though to be sure it drives away the game. The Garden of Eden, no doubt, looked fair before man was, but I always think that it must have been fairer when Eve adorned it.

To return, we had miscalculated a little, and the sun was well down before we dropped anchor off the Point, and heard the gun which told the good folks of Durban that the English mail was in. It was too late to think of getting over the bar that night, so we went comfortably to dinner, after seeing the mails carried off in the lifeboat.

When we came up again the moon was out, and shining so brightly over sea and shore that she almost paled the quick, large flashes from the lighthouse. From the shore floated sweet spicy odours that always remind me of hymns and missionaries, and in the windows of the houses on the Berea sparkled a hundred lights. From a large brig lying near also came the music of the sailors as they worked at getting the anchor up in order to be ready for the wind. Altogether it was a perfect night, such a night as you sometimes get in Southern Africa, and it threw a garment of peace over everybody as the moon threw a garment of silver over everything. Even the great bulldog, belonging to a sporting passenger, seemed to yield to its gentle influences, and forgetting his yearning to come to close quarters with a baboon in its cage of the fo'c'sle, snored heavily at the door of the cabin, dreaming no doubt that he had finished it, and happy in his dream.

We three – that is, Sir Henry Curtis, Captain Good, and myself – went and sat by the wheel, and were quiet for a while.

'Well, Mr Quatermain,' said Sir Henry presently, 'have you been thinking about my proposals?'

'Ay,' echoed Captain Good, 'what do you think of them, Mr Quatermain? I hope that you are going to give us the pleasure of your company so far as Solomon's Mines, or wherever the gentleman you knew as Neville may have got to.'

I rose and knocked out my pipe before I answered. I had not made up my mind, and wanted an additional moment to decide. Before the burning tobacco had fallen into the sea I had decided; just that little extra second did the trick. It is often the way when you have been bothering a long time over a thing.

'Yes, gentlemen,' I said, sitting down again, 'I will go, and by your leave I will tell you why, and on what conditions. First for the terms which I ask.

'1. You are to pay all expenses, and any ivory or other valuables we may get is to be divided between Captain Good and myself.

'2. That you give me £500 for my services on the trip before we start, I undertaking to serve you faithfully till you choose to abandon the enterprise or till we succeed, or disaster overtakes us.

'3. That before we trek you execute a deed agreeing, in the event of my death or disablement, to pay my boy Harry, who is studying medicine over there in London, at Guy's Hospital, a sum of £200 a year for five years, by which time he ought to be able to earn a living for himself if he is worth his salt. That is all, I think, and I daresay you will say quite enough too.'

'No,' answered Sir Henry, 'I accept very gladly. I am bent upon this project, and would pay more than that for your help, considering the peculiar and exclusive knowledge which you possess.'

'Pity I did not ask it, then, but I won't go back on my word. And now that I have got my terms I will give you my reasons for making up my mind to go. First of all, gentlemen, I have been observing you both for the last few days, and if you will not think me impertinent I may say that I like you, and believe that we shall come up well to the yoke together. That is something, let me remark, when one has a long journey like this before one.

'And now as to the journey itself, I tell you flatly, Sir Henry and Captain Good, that I do not think it probable we can come out of it alive, that is, if we attempt to cross the Suliman Mountains. What was the fate of the old Dom da Silvestra three hundred years ago? What was the fate of his descendant twenty years ago? What has been your brother's fate? I tell you frankly, gentlemen, that as their fates were so I believe ours will be.'

I paused to watch the effect of my words. Captain Good looked a little uncomfortable, but Sir Henry's face did not change. 'We must take our chance,' he said.

'You may perhaps wonder,' I went on, 'why, if I think this, I, who am, as I told you, a timid man, should undertake such a journey. It is for two reasons. First, I am a fatalist, and believe that my time is appointed to come without reference to my own movements and will, and that if I am to go to Suliman's Mountains to be killed, I shall go there and shall be killed. God Almighty, no doubt, knows

His mind about me, so I need not trouble on that point. Secondly, I am a poor man. For nearly forty years I have hunted and traded, but I have never made more than a living. Well, gentlemen; I don't know if you are aware that the average life of an elephant hunter from the time he takes to the trade is between four and five years. So you see I have lived through about seven generations of my class, and I should think that my time cannot be far off, anyway. Now, if anything were to happen to me in the ordinary course of business, by the time my debts are paid there would be nothing left to support my son Harry whilst he was getting in the way of earning his bread, whereas now he will be set up for five years. There is the whole affair in a nutshell.'

'Mr Quatermain,' said Sir Henry, who had been giving me his most serious attention, 'your motives for undertaking an enterprise which you believe can only end in disaster reflect a great deal of credit on you. Whether or not you are right, of course time and the event alone can show. But whether you are right or wrong, I may as well tell you at once that I am going through with it to the end, sweet or bitter. If we are to be knocked on the head, all I have to say is, that I hope we get a little shooting first, eh, Good?'

'Yes, yes,' put in the captain. 'We have all three of us been accustomed to face danger, and to hold our lives in our hands in various ways, so it is no good turning back now. And so I vote we go down to the saloon and take an observation just for luck, you know.' And we did – through the bottom of a tumbler.

Next day we went ashore, and I put up Sir Henry and Captain Good at the little grey shanty I have built on the Berea, which I call my home. There are only three rooms and a kitchen in it, and it is constructed of green brick with a galvanised iron roof, but there is a good garden with the best loquot trees in it that I know, and some nice young mangoes, of which I hope great things. The curator of the botanical gardens gave them to me. It is looked after by an old hunter of mine named Jack, whose thigh was so badly broken by a buffalo cow in Sikukuni's country that he will never hunt again. But he can potter about and garden, being a Griqua by birth. You will never persuade a Zulu to take much interest in gardening. It is a peaceful art, and peaceful arts are not in his line.

Sir Henry and Good slept in a tent pitched in my little grove of orange trees at the end of the garden, for there was no room for them in the house. What with the smell of the bloom, and the sight of the green and golden fruit – in Durban you will see all three on the tree together – I daresay it is a pleasant place enough, for we have few mosquitoes here on the Berea, unless there happens to come an unusually heavy rain.

Well, to get on – for if I do not, Harry, you will be tired of my story before ever we fetch up at Suliman's Mountains – having once made up my mind to go I set about making the necessary preparations. First I secured the deed from Sir Henry, providing for you, my boy, in case of accidents. There was some difficulty about its legal execution, as Sir Henry was a stranger here, and the property to be charged is over the water; but is was ultimately got over with the help of a lawyer, who charged £20 for the job – a price that I thought outrageous. Then I pocketed my cheque for £500.

Having paid this tribute to my bump of caution, I purchased a wagon and a span of oxen on Sir Henry's behalf, and beauties they were. It was a twenty-two-foot wagon with iron axles, very strong, very light, and built throughout of stink-wood; not quite a new one, having been to the Diamond Fields and back, but, in my opinion, all the better for that, for I could see that the wood was well seasoned. If anything is going to give in a wagon, or if there is green wood in it, it will show out on the first trip. This particular vehicle was what we call a 'half-tented' wagon, that is to say, only covered in over and after twelve feet, leaving all the front part free for the necessaries we had to carry with us. In this after part were a hide 'cartle,' or bed, on which two people could sleep, also racks for rifles, and many other little conveniences. I gave £125 for it, and think that it was cheap at the price.

Then I bought a beautiful team of twenty Zulu oxen, which I had kept my eye on for a year or two. Sixteen oxen is the usual number for a team, but I took four extra to allow for casualties. These Zulu cattle are small and light, not more than half the size of the Africander oxen, which are generally used for transport purposes; but they will live where the Africanders would starve, and with a moderate load can make five miles a day better going, being quicker and not so liable to become footsore. What is more, this lot were thoroughly 'salted,' that is, they had worked all over South Africa, and so had become proof, comparatively speaking, against red water, which so frequently destroys whole teams of oxen when they get on to strange 'veld' or grass country. As for 'lung sick,' which is a dreadful form of pneumonia, very prevalent in this country, they had all been inoculated against it. This is done by cutting a slit in the tail of an ox, and binding in a piece of the diseased lung of an animal which has died of the sickness. The result is that the ox sickens, takes the disease in a mild form, which causes its tail to drop off, as a rule about a foot from the root, and becomes proof against future attacks. It seems cruel to rob the animal of his tail, especially in a country where there are so many flies, but it is better to sacrifice the tail and keep the ox than to lose both tail and ox, for a tail without an ox is not much good, except to dust with. Still it does look odd to trek along behind twenty stumps, where there ought to be tails. It seems as though Nature had made a trifling mistake, and stuck the stern ornaments of a lot of prize bull-dogs on to the rumps of the oxen.

Next came the question of provisioning and medicines, one which required the most careful consideration, for what we had to do was to avoid lumbering the wagon, and yet to take everything absolutely necessary. Fortunately, it turned out that Good is a bit of a doctor, having at some period in his previous career managed to pass through a course of medical and surgical instruction, which he has more or less kept up. He is not, of course, qualified, but he knows more about it than many a man who can write M.D. after his name, as we found out afterwards, and he had a splendid travelling medicine chest and a set of instruments. Whilst we were at Durban he cut off a Kafir's big toe in a way which it was a pleasure to see. But he was quite nonplussed when the Kafir, who had sat stolidly watching the operation, asked him to put on another, saying that a 'white one' would do at a pinch.

There remained, when these questions were satisfactorily settled, two further important points for consideration, namely, that of arms, and that of servants. As to the arms I cannot do better than put down a list of those which we finally decided on from among the ample store that Sir Henry had brought with him from England, and those which I owned. I copy it from my pocket-book, where I made the entry at the time.

'Three heavy breech-loading double-eight elephant guns, weighing about fifteen pounds each, to carry a charge of eleven drachms of black powder.' Two of these were by a well-known London firm, most excellent makers, but I do not know by whom mine, which is not so highly finished, was made. I have used it on several trips, and shot a good many elephants with it, and it has always proved a most superior weapon, thoroughly to be relied on.

'Three double-500 Expresses, constructed to stand a charge of six drachms,' sweet weapons, and admirable for medium-sized game, such as eland or sable antelope, or for men, especially in an open country and with the semi-hollow bullet.

'One double No. 12 central-fire Keeper's shot-gun, full choke both barrels.' This gun proved of the greatest service to us afterwards in shooting birds for the pot.

'Three Winchester repeating rifles (not carbines), spare guns.

'Three single-action Colt's revolvers, with the heavier or American pattern of cartridge.'

This was our total armament, and doubtless the reader will observe that the weapons of each class were of the same make and calibre, so that the cartridges were interchangeable, a very important point. I make no apology for detailing it at length, as every experienced hunter will know how vital a proper supply of guns and ammunition is to the success of an expedition.

Now as to the men who were to go with us. After much consultation, we decided that their number should be limited to five, namely, a driver, a leader, and three servants.

The driver and leader I found without much difficulty, two Zulus, named respectively Goza and Tom; but to get the servants proved a more difficult matter. It was necessary that they should be thoroughly trustworthy and brave men, as in a business of this sort our lives might depend upon their conduct. At last I secured two, one a Hottentot called Ventvögel, or 'windbird,' and one a little Zulu named Khiva, who had the merit of speaking English perfectly. Ventvögel I had known before, he was one of the most perfect 'spoorers,' that is, game trackers, I ever had to do with, and tough as whipcord. He never seemed to tire. But he had one failing, so common with his race – drink. Put him within reach of a bottle of gin and you could not trust him. However, as we were going beyond the region of grog-shops this little weakness of his did not so much matter.

Having secured these two men I looked in vain for a third to suit my purpose, so we determined to start without one, trusting to luck to find a suitable man on our way up country. But, as it happened, on the evening before the day we had fixed for our departure the Zulu Khiva informed me that a Kafir was waiting to see me. Accordingly, when we had done dinner, for we were at table at the time, I told Khiva to bring him in. Presently a tall, handsome-looking man, somewhere about thirty years of age, and very light-coloured for a Zulu, entered, and, lifting his knob-stick by way of salute, squatted himself down in the corner on his haunches, and sat silent. I did not take any notice of him for a while, for it is a great mistake to do so. If you rush into conversation at once, a Zulu is apt to think you a person of little dignity or consequence. I observed, however, that he was a 'Keshla' or ringed man; that is, he wore on his head the black ring, made of a species of gum polished with fat and worked up in the hair, which is usually assumed by

Zulus on attaining a certain age or dignity. Also it struck me that his face was familiar to me.

'Well,' I said at last, 'what is your name?'

'Umbopa,' answered the man in a slow, deep voice.

'I have seen your face before.'

'Yes; the Inkosi, the chief, my father, saw my face at the place of the Little Hand' – that is Isandhlwana – ' on the day before the battle.'

Then I remembered. I was one of Lord Chelmsford's guides in that unlucky Zulu War, and took part in the battle, which I had the good fortune to survive. I will say nothing about it here, indeed the subject is painful to, me. On the day before it happened, however, I fell into conversation with this man, who held some small command among the native auxiliaries, and he had expressed to me his doubts as to the safety of the camp. At the time I told him to hold his tongue, and leave such matters to wiser heads; but afterwards I thought of his words.

'I remember,' I said; 'what is it you want?'

'It is this, "Macumazahn". (That is my Kafir name, and means the man who gets up in the middle of the night, or, in vulgar English, he who keeps his eyes open.) I hear that you go on a great expedition far into the North with the white chiefs from over the water. Is it a true word?'

'It is.'

'I hear that you go even to the Lukanga River, a moon's journey beyond the Manick country. Is this so also, "Macumazahn"?'

'Why do you ask whither we go? What is it to you?' I answered suspiciously, for the objects of our journey had been kept a dead secret.

'It is this, O white men, that if indeed you travel so far I would travel with you.'

There was a certain assumption of dignity in the man's mode of speech, and especially in his use of the words 'O white men,' instead of 'O Inkosis,' or chiefs, which struck me.

'You forget yourself a little,' I said. 'Your words run out

unawares. That is not the way to speak. What is your name, and where is your kraal? Tell us, that we may know with whom we have to deal.'

'My name is Umbopa. I am of the Zulu people, yet not of them. The house of my tribe is in the far North; it was left behind when the Zulus came down here a "thousand years ago," long before Chaka reigned in Zulu-land. I have no kraal. I have wandered for many years. I came from the North as a child to Zululand. I was Cetewayo's man in the Nkomabakosi Regiment, serving under the great captain, Umslopogaasi of the Axe,[1] who taught my hands to fight. Afterwards I ran away from Zululand and came to Natal because I wanted to see the white man's ways. Next I fought against Cetewayo in the war. Since then I have been working in Natal. Now I am tired, and would go North again. Here is not my place. I want no money, but I am a brave man and well worth my place and meat. I have spoken.'

I was rather puzzled by this man and his way of speech. It was evident to me from his manner that in the main he was telling the truth, but somehow he seemed different from the ordinary run of Zulus, and I rather mistrusted his offer to come without pay. Being in a difficulty, I translated his words to Sir Henry and Good, and asked them their opinion.

Sir Henry told me to ask him to stand up. Umbopa did so, at the same time slipping off the long military greatcoat which he wore, and revealing himself naked except for the mocha round his centre and a necklace of lions' claws. Certainly he was a magnificent looking man; I never saw a finer native. Standing about six foot three high, he was broad in proportion, and very shapely. In that light, too, his skin looked scarcely more than dark except here and there where deep black scars marked old assegai wounds. Sir Henry walked up to him and looked into his proud, handsome face.

[1] For the history of Umslopogaasi and his Axe, the reader is referred to the books called 'Allan Quatermain' and 'Nada the Lily.' – *Editor*

'They make a good pair, don't they?' said Good; 'one as big as the other.'

'I like your looks, Mr Umbopa, and I will take you as my servant,' said Sir Henry in English.

Umbopa evidently understood him, for he answered in Zulu, 'It is well'; and then added, with a glance at the white man's great stature and breadth.

'We are men, thou and I.'

CHAPTER 4

An Elephant Hunt

Now I do not propose to narrate at full length all the incidents of our long trek up to Sitanda's Kraal, near the junction of the Lakanga and Kalukwe Rivers. It was a journey of more than a thousand miles from Durban, the last three hundred or so of which we had to make on foot, owing to the frequent presence of the dreadful 'tsetse' fly, whose bite is fatal to all animals except donkeys and men.

We left Durban at the end of January, and it was in the second week of May that we camped near Sitanda's Kraal. Our adventures on the way were many and various, but as they are of the sort which befall every African hunter – with one exception to be presently detailed – I shall not set them down here, lest I should render this history too wearisome.

At Inyati, the outlying trading station in the Matabele country, of which Lobengula (a great and cruel scoundrel) is king, with many regrets we parted from our comfortable wagon. Only twelve oxen remained to us out of the beautiful span of twenty which I had bought at Durban. One we lost from the bite of a cobra, three had perished from 'poverty' and the want of water, one starved and the other three died from eating the poisonous herb called 'tulip.' Five more sickened from this cause, but we managed to cure them with doses of an infusion made by boiling down the tulip leaves. If administered in time this is a very effective antidote.

The wagon and oxen we left in the immediate charge of Goza and Tom, our driver and leader, both trustworthy boys, requesting a worthy Scotch missionary who lived in this distant place to keep an eye to them. Then, accompanied by Umbopa, Khiva, Ventvögel, and half a dozen bearers whom we hired on the spot, we started off on foot upon our wild quest. I remember we were all a little silent on the occasion of this departure, and I think that each of us was wondering if we should ever see our wagon again; for my part I never expected to do so. For a while we tramped on in silence, till Umbopa, who was marching in front, broke into a Zulu chant about how some brave men, tired of life and the tameness of things, started off into a vast wilderness to find new ones or die, and how, lo and behold! when they had travelled far into the wilderness they discovered that it was not a wilderness at all, but a beautiful place full of young wives and fat cattle, of game to hunt, and enemies to kill.

Then we all laughed and took it for a good omen. Umbopa was a cheerful savage, in a dignified sort of way, when he was not suffering from one of his fits of brooding, and he had a wonderful knack of keeping up our spirits. We all grew very fond of him.

And now for the one adventure to which I am going to treat myself, for I do dearly love a hunting yarn.

About a fortnight's march from Inyati we came across a peculiarly beautiful bit of well-watered woodland country. The kloofs in the hills were covered with dense bush, 'idoro' bush as the natives call it, and in some places with the 'wachteen-beche,' or 'wait-a-little thorn,' and there were great quantities of the lovely 'machabell' tree, laden with refreshing yellow fruit having enormous stones. This tree is the elephant's favourite food, and there were not wanting signs that the great brutes had been about, for not only was their spoor frequent, but in many places the trees were broken down and even uprooted. The elephant is a destructive feeder.

One evening, after a long day's march, we came to a spot of great loveliness. At the foot of a bush-clad hill lay a dry river-bed, in which, however, were to be found pools of crystal water all trodden round with the hoof-prints of game. Facing this hill was a park-like plain, where grew clumps of flat-topped mimosa, varied with occasional glossy-leaved machabells, and all round stretched the sea of pathless, silent bush.

As we emerged into this river-bed path suddenly we started a troop of tall giraffes, which galloped, or rather sailed off, with their strange gait, their tails screwed up over their backs, and their hooves rattling like castanets. They were about three hundred yards from us, and therefore practically out of shot, but Good, who was walking ahead, and who had an Express loaded with solid ball in his hand, could not resist temptation. Lifting his gun, he let drive at the last, a young cow. By some extraordinary chance the ball struck it full on the back of the neck, shattering the spinal column, and that giraffe went rolling head over heels just like a rabbit. I never saw a more curious thing.

'Curse it!' said Good – for I am sorry to say he had a habit of using strong language when excited – contracted, no doubt, in the course of his nautical career; 'curse it! I've killed him.'

'*Ou*, Bougwan,' ejaculated the Kafirs; '*ou! ou!*'

They called Good 'Bougwan,' or Glass-Eye, because of his eye-glass.

'Oh, "Bougwan"!' re-echoed Sir Henry and I; and from that day Good's reputation as a marvellous shot was established, at any rate among the Kafirs. Really he was a bad one, but whenever he missed we overlooked it for the sake of that giraffe.

Having set some of the 'boys' to cut off the best of the giraffe meat, we went to work to build a 'scherm' near one of the pools and about a hundred yards to its right. This is done by cutting a quantity of thorn bushes and piling them in the shape of a circular hedge. Then the space enclosed is smoothed, and dry tambouke grass, if obtainable, is made into a bed in the centre, and a fire or fires lighted.

By the time the 'scherm' was finished the moon peeped up, and our dinners of giraffe steaks and roasted marrow-bones were ready. How we enjoyed those marrow-bones, though it was rather a job to crack them! I know of no greater luxury than giraffe marrow, unless it is elephant's heart, and we had that on the morrow. We ate our simple meal by the light of the moon, pausing at times to thank Good for his wonderful shot; then we began to smoke and yarn, and a curious picture we must have made squatting there round the fire. I, with my short grizzled hair sticking up straight, and Sir Henry with his yellow locks, which were getting rather long, made rather a contrast, especially as I am thin, and short, and dark, weighing only nine stone and a half, and Sir Henry is tall, and broad, and fair, and weighs fifteen. But perhaps the most curious-looking of the three, taking all the circumstances of the case into consideration, was Captain John Good, R.N. There he sat upon a leather bag, looking just as though he had come in from a comfortable day's shooting in a civilised country, absolutely clean, tidy and well dressed. He wore a shooting suit of brown tweed, with a hat to match, and neat gaiters. As usual, he was beautifully shaved, his eye-glass and his false teeth appeared to be in perfect order, and altogether he looked the neatest man I ever had to do with in the wilderness. He even sported a collar, of which he had a supply, made of white gutta-percha.

'You see, they weigh so little,' he said to me innocently, when I expressed my astonishment at the fact; 'and I always like to turn out like a gentleman.' Ah! if he could have foreseen the future and the raiment prepared for him.

Well, there we three sat yarning away in the beautiful moonlight, and watching the Kafirs a few yards off sucking their intoxicating 'daccha' from a pipe of which the mouthpiece was made of the horn of an eland, till one by one they rolled themselves up in their blankets and went to sleep by the fire. That is, all except Umbopa, who was a little apart, his chin resting on his hand, and thinking deeply. I noticed that he never mixed much with the other Kafirs.

Presently, from the depths of the bush behind us came a loud '*woof woof!*' 'That's a lion,' said I, and we all started up to listen. Hardly had we done so, when from the pool, about a hundred yards off, we heard the strident trumpeting of an elephant. '*Indlovu! Indlovu!*' 'Elephant! Elephant!' whispered the Kafirs, and a few minutes afterwards we saw a succession of vast shadowy forms moving slowly from the direction of the water towards the bush.

Up jumped Good, burning for slaughter, and thinking, perhaps, that it was as easy to kill elephant as he had found it to shoot giraffe, but I caught him by the arm and pulled him down.

'It's no good,' I whispered, 'let them go.'

'It seems that we are in a paradise of game. I vote we stop here a day or two, and have a go at them,' said Sir Henry presently.

I was rather surprised, for hitherto Sir Henry had always been for pushing forward as fast as possible, more especially since we ascertained at Inyati that about two years ago an Englishman of the name of Neville *had* sold his wagon there, and gone on up country. But I suppose his hunter instincts got the better of him for a while.

Good jumped at the idea, for he was longing to have a shot at those elephants. So, to speak the truth, did I, for it went against my conscience to let such a herd as that escape without a pull at them.

'All right, my hearties,' said I. 'I think we want a little recreation. And now let's turn in, for we ought to be off by dawn, and then perhaps we may catch them feeding before they move on.'

The others agreed and we proceeded to make our preparations. Good took off his clothes, shook them, put his eye-glass and his false teeth into his trousers pocket, and folding each article neatly, placed them out of the dew under a corner of his mackintosh sheet. Sir Henry and I contented ourselves with rougher arrangements, and soon were curled up in our blankets, and dropping off into the dreamless sleep that rewards the traveller.

Going, going, go – What was that?

Suddenly from the direction of the water came sounds of violent scuffling, and next instant there broke upon our ears a succession of the most awful roars. There was no mistaking their origin;

only a lion could make such a noise as that. We all jumped up and looked towards the water, in the direction of which we saw a confused mass, yellow and black in colour, staggering and struggling towards us. We seized our rifles, and slipping on our veldschoens, that is shoes made of untanned hide, ran out of the scherm. By this time the mass had fallen, and was rolling over and over on the ground, and when we reached the spot it struggled no longer, but lay quite still.

Now we saw what it was. On the grass there lay a sable antelope bull – the most beautiful of all the African antelopes – quite dead, and transfixed by its great curved horns was a magnificent black-maned lion, also dead. Evidently what had happened was this: The sable antelope had come down to drink at the pool where the lion – no doubt the same which we had heard – was lying in wait. While the antelope drank, the lion had sprung upon him, only to be received upon the sharp curved horns and transfixed. Once before I saw a similar thing happen. Then the lion, unable to free himself, had torn and bitten at the back and neck of the bull, which, maddened with fear and pain, had rushed on until it dropped dead.

As soon as we had examined the beasts sufficiently we called the Kafirs, and between us managed to drag their carcasses up to the scherm. After that we went in and lay down, to wake no more till dawn.

With the first light we were up and making ready for the fray. We took with us the three eight-bore rifles, a good supply of ammunition, and our large water-bottles, filled with weak cold tea, which I have always found the best stuff to shoot on. After swallowing a little breakfast we started, Umbopa, Khiva, and Ventvögel accompanying us. The other Kafirs we left with instructions to skin the lion and the sable antelope, and to cut up the latter.

We had no difficulty in finding the broad elephant trail, which Ventvögel, after examination, pronounced to have been made by between twenty and thirty elephants, most of them full-grown bulls. But the herd had moved on some way during the night, and it was nine o'clock, and already very hot, before, by the broken trees, bruised leaves and bark, and smoking droppings, we knew that we could not be far from them.

Presently we caught sight of the herd, which numbered, as Ventvögel had said, between twenty and thirty, standing in a hollow, having finished their morning meal, and flapping their great ears. It was a splendid sight, for they were only about two hundred yards from us. Taking a handful of dry grass, I threw it into the air to see how the wind was; for if once they winded us I knew they would be off before we could get a shot. Finding that, if anything, it blew from the elephants to us, we crept on stealthily, and thanks to the cover managed to get within forty yards or so of the great brutes. Just in front of us, and broadside on, stood three splendid bulls, on of them with enormous tusks. I whispered to the others that I would take the middle one; Sir Henry covering the elephant to the left, and Good the bull with the big tusks.

'Now,' I whispered.

Boom! boom! boom! went the three heavy rifles, and down came Sir Henry's elephant dead as a hammer, shot right through the heart. Mine fell on to its knees, and I thought that he was going to die, but in another moment he was up and off, tearing along straight past me. As he went I gave him the second barrel in the ribs, and this brought him down in good earnest. Hastily slipping in two fresh cartridges I ran close up to him, and a ball through the brain put an end to the poor brute's struggles. Then I turned to see how Good had fared with the big bull, which I had heard screaming with rage and pain as I gave mine its quietus. On reaching the captain I found him in a great state of excitement. It appeared that on receiving the bullet the bull had turned and come straight for his assailant, who had barely time to get out of his way, and then charged on blindly past him, in the direction of our encampment. Meanwhile the herd had crashed off in wild alarm in the other direction.

For a while we debated whether to go after the wounded bull or to follow the herd, and finally deciding for the latter alternative, departed, thinking that we had seen the last of those big tusks.

I have often wished since that we had. It was easy work to follow the elephants, for they had left a trail like a carriage road behind them, crushing down the thick bush in their furious flight as though it were tambouki grass.

But to come up with them was another matter, and we had struggled on under the broiling sun for over two hours before we found them. With the exception of one bull, they were standing together, and I could see, from their unquiet way and the manner in which they kept lifting their trunks to test the air, that they were on the look-out for mischief. The solitary bull stood fifty yards or so to this side of the herd, over which he was evidently keeping sentry, and about sixty yards from us. Thinking that he would see or wind us, and that it would probably start them off again if we tried to get nearer, especially as the ground was rather open, we all aimed at this bull, and at my whispered word we fired. The three shots took effect, and down he went, dead. Again the herd started, but unfortunately for them about a hundred yards farther on was a nullah, or dried-out water track, with steep banks, a place very much resembling the one where the Prince Imperial was killed in Zululand. Into this the elephants plunged, and when we reached the edge we found them struggling in wild confusion to get up the other bank, filling the air with their screams, and trumpeting as they pushed one another aside in their selfish panic, just like so many human beings. Now was our opportunity, and firing as quickly as we could load, we killed five of the poor beasts, and no doubt should have bagged the whole herd, had they not suddenly given up their attempts to climb the bank and rushed headlong down the nullah. We were too tired to follow them, and perhaps also a little sick of slaughter, eight elephants being a pretty good bag for one day.

So after we were rested a little, and the Kafirs had cut out the hearts of two of the dead elephants for supper, we started homewards, very well pleased with our day's work, having made up our minds to send the bearers on the morrow to chop away the tusks.

Shortly after we re-passed the spot where Good had wounded

the patriarchal bull we came across a herd of eland, but did not shoot at them, as we had plenty of meat. They trotted past us, and then stopped behind a little patch of bush about a hundred yards away, wheeling round to look at us. As Good was anxious to get a near view of them, never having seen an eland close, he handed his rifle to Umbopa, and, followed by Khiva, strolled up to the patch of bush. We sat down and waited for him, not sorry of the excuse for a little rest.

The sun was just going down in its reddest glory, and Sir Henry and I were admiring the lovely scene, when suddenly we heard an elephant trumpet, and saw its huge and rushing form with uplifted trunk and tail silhouetted against the great fiery globe of the sun. Next second we saw something else, and that was Good and Khiva tearing back towards us with the wounded bull – for it was he – charging after them. For a moment we did not dare to fire – though at that distance it would have been of little use if we had done so – for fear of hitting one of them. The next a dreadful thing happened – Good fell a victim to his passion for civilised dress. Had he consented to discard his trousers and gaiters like the rest of us, and to hunt in a flannel shirt and a pair of veldschoens, it would have been all right. But as it was, his trousers cumbered him in that desperate race, and presently, when he was about sixty yards from us, his boot, polished by the dry grass, slipped, and down he went on his face right in front of the elephant.

We gave a gasp, for we knew that he must die, and ran as hard as we could towards him. In three seconds it had ended, but not as we thought. Khiva, the Zulu boy, saw his master fall, and brave lad as he was, turned and flung his assegai straight into the elephant's face. It stuck in his trunk.

With a scream of pain, the brute seized the poor Zulu, hurled him to earth, and placing one huge foot on to his body about the middle, twined its trunk round his upper part and *tore him in two*.

We rushed up mad with horror, and fired again and again, till presently the elephant fell upon the fragments of the Zulu.

As for Good, he rose and wrung his hands over the brave man

who had given his life to save him, and, though I am an old hand, I felt a lump grow in my throat. Umbopa stood contemplating the huge dead elephant and the mangled remains of poor Khiva.

'Ah, well,' he said presently, 'he is dead, but he died like a man!'

CHAPTER 5

Our March into the Desert

We had killed nine elephants, and it took us two days to cut out the tusks, and having brought them into camp, to bury them carefully in the sand under a large tree, which made a conspicuous mark for miles round. It was a wonderfully fine lot of ivory. I never saw a better, averaging as it did between forty and fifty pounds a tusk. The tusks of the great bull that killed poor Khiva scaled one hundred and seventy pounds the pair, so nearly as we could judge.

As for Khiva himself, we buried what remained of him in an ant-bear hole, together with an assegai to protect himself on his journey to a better world. On the third day we marched again, hoping that we might live to return to dig up our buried ivory, and in due course, after a long and wearisome tramp, and many adventures which I have not space to detail, we reached Sitanda's Kraal, near the Lukanga River, the real starting-point of our expedition. Very well do I recollect our arrival at that place. To the right was a scattered native settlement with a few stone cattle kraals and some cultivated lands down by the water, where these savages grew their scanty supply of grain, and beyond it stretched great tracts of waving 'veld' covering with tall grass, over which herds of smaller game were wandering. To the left lay the vast desert. This spot appears to be the outpost of the fertile country, and it would be difficult to

45

say to what natural causes such an abrupt change in the character of the soil is due. But so it is.

Just below our encampment flowed a little stream, on the farther side of which is a stony slope, the same down which, twenty years before, I had seen poor Silvestre creeping back after his attempt to reach Solomon's Mines. Beyond that slope begins the waterless desert, covered with a species of karoo shrub.

It was evening when we pitched our camp, and the red ball of the sun was sinking into the desert, sending glorious rays of many-coloured light flying over all its vast expanse. Leaving Good to superintend the arrangement of our little camp, I took Sir Henry with me, and walking to the top of the slope opposite, we gazed across the sandy waste. The air was very clear, and far, far away, I could distinguish the faint blue outlines of the Suliman Berg, here and there capped with white.

'There,' I said, 'there is the wall round Solomon's Mines, but God knows if we shall ever climb it.'

'My brother should be there, and if he is, I shall reach him somehow,' said Sir Henry, in that tone of quiet confidence which marked the man.

'I hope so,' I answered, and turned to go back to the camp, when I saw that we were not alone. Behind us, also gazing earnestly towards the far-off mountains, stood the great Kafir Umbopa.

The Zulu spoke when he saw that I had observed him, addressing Sir Henry, to whom he had attached himself.

'Is it to that land that thou wouldst journey, Incubu?' (a native word meaning an elephant and the Zulu name given to Sir Henry by the Kafirs), he said, pointing towards the mountains with his broad assegai.

I asked him sharply what he meant by addressing his master in that familiar way. It is very well for natives to have a name for one among themselves, but it is not decent that they should call a white man by their heathenish appellations to his face. The Zulu laughed a quiet little laugh which angered me.

'How dost thou know that I am not the equal of the Inkosi whom I serve?' he said. ' He is of a royal house, no doubt; one can see it in his size and by his mien; so, mayhap, am I. At least I am as great a man. Be my mouth, O Macumazahn, and say my words to the Inkoos Incubu, my master, for I would speak to him and to thee.'

I was wroth with the man, for I am not accustomed to be talked to in that way by Kafirs, but somehow he impressed me. Besides, I was curious to know what he had to say. So I translated, expressing my opinion at the same time that he was an impudent fellow, and that his swagger was outrageous.

'Yes, Umbopa,' answered Sir Henry 'I would journey there.'

'The desert is wide and there is no water in it, the mountains are high and covered with snow, and man cannot say what lies beyond them behind the place where the sun sets; how shalt thou come thither, Incubu, and wherefore dost thou go?'

I translated again.

'Tell him,' answered Sir Henry, 'that I go because I believe that a man of my blood, my brother, has gone there before me, and I journey to seek him.'

'That is so, Incubu; a Hottentot I met on the road told me that a white man went out into the desert two years ago towards those mountains with one servant, a hunter. They never came back.'

'How do you know it was my brother?' asked Sir Henry.

'Nay, I know not. But the Hottentot, when I asked what the white man was like, said that he had thine eyes and a black beard. He said, too, that the name of the hunter with him was Jim; that he was a Bechuana hunter and wore clothes.'

'There is no doubt about it,' said I; 'I knew Jim well.'

Sir Henry nodded. 'I was sure of it,' he said. 'If George set his mind upon a thing he generally did it. It was always so from his boyhood. If he meant to cross the Suliman Berg he has crossed it, unless some accident overtook him, and we must look for him on the other side.'

Umbopa understood English, though he rarely spoke it.

'It is a far journey, Incubu,' he put in, and I translated his remark.

'Yes,' answered Sir Henry, 'it is far. But there is no journey upon this earth that a man may not make if he sets his heart to it. There is nothing, Umbopa, that he cannot do. There are no mountains he may not climb, there are no deserts he cannot cross, save a mountain and a desert of which you are spared the knowledge, if love leads him and he holds his life in his hand counting it as nothing, ready to keep it or lose it as Heaven above may order.'

I translated.

'Great words, my father,' answered the Zulu – I always called him a Zulu, though he was not really one – 'great swelling words fit to fill the mouth of a man. Thou art right, my father Incubu. Listen! what is life? It is a feather, it is the seed of the grass, blown hither and thither, sometimes multiplying itself and dying in the act, sometimes carried hence into the heavens. But if that seed be good and heavy it may perchance travel a little way on the road it wills. It is well to try and journey one's road and to fight with the air. Man must die. At the worst he can but die a little sooner. I will go with thee across the desert and over the mountains, unless perchance I fall to the ground on the way, my father.'

He paused awhile, and then went on with one of those strange bursts of rhetorical eloquence that Zulus sometimes indulge in, which to my mind, full though they are of vain repetition, show that the race is by no means devoid of poetic instinct and of intellectual power.

'What is life? Tell me, O white men, who are wise, who know the secrets of the world, and of the world of stars, and the world that lies above and around the stars; who flash your words from afar without a voice; tell me, white men, the secret of our life – whither it goes and whence it comes!

'You cannot answer me; you know not. Listen, I will answer. Out of the dark we came, into the dark we go. Like a storm-driven bird at night we fly out of the Nowhere; for a moment our wings are seen in the light of the fire, and, lo! we are gone again into the Nowhere. Life is nothing. Life is all. It is the Hand with which we hold off Death. It is the glow-worm that shines in the night-time and is black in the morning; it is the white breath of the oxen in winter; it is the little shadow that runs across the grass and loses itself at sunset'

'You are a strange man,' said Sir Henry, when he had ceased.

Umbopa laughed. 'It seems to me that we are much alike, Incubu. Perhaps *I* seek a brother over the mountains.'

I looked at him suspiciously. 'What dost thou mean?' I asked; 'what dost thou know of those mountains?'

'A little; a very little. There is a strange land yonder, a land of witchcraft and beautiful things; a land of brave people, and of trees, and streams, and snowy peaks, and of a great white road. I have heard of it. But what is the good of talking? It grows dark. Those who live to see will see.'

Again I looked at him doubtfully. The man knew too much.

'You need not fear me, Macumazahn,' he said, interpreting my looks. 'I dig no holes for you to fall in. I make no plots. If ever we cross those mountains behind the sun I will tell what I know. But Death sits upon them. Be wise and turn back. Go and hunt elephants, my masters. I have spoken.'

And without another word he lifted his spear in salutation, and returned towards the camp, where shortly afterwards we found him cleaning a gun like any other Kafir.

'That is an odd man,' said Sir Henry.

'Yes,' answered I, 'too odd by half. I don't like his little ways. He knows something, and will not speak out. But I suppose it is no use quarrelling with him. We are in for a curious trip, and a mysterious Zulu won't make much difference one way or another.'

Next day we made our arrangements for starting. Of course it was impossible to drag our heavy elephant rifles and other kit with us across the desert, so, dismissing our bearers, we made an arrange-ment with an old native who had a kraal close by to take care of them till we returned. It went to my heart to leave such things as those sweet tools to the tender mercies of an old thief of a savage whose greedy eyes I could see gloating over them. But I took some precautions.

First of all I loaded all the rifles, placing them at full cock, and informed him that if he touched them they would go off. He tried the experiment instantly with my eight-bore, and it did go off, and blew a hole right through one of his oxen, which were just then being driven up to the kraal, to say nothing of knocking him head over heels with the recoil. He got up considerably startled, and not at all pleased at the loss of the ox, for which he had the impudence to ask me to pay. After that, nothing would induce him to touch the guns again.

'Put the live devils out of the way up there in the thatch,' he said, 'or they will murder us all.'

Then I told him that, when we came back, if one of those things were missing I would kill him and his people by witchcraft; and if we died and he tried to steal the rifles I would come to haunt him and turn his cattle mad and his milk sour till life was a weariness, and would make the devils in the guns jump out and talk to him in a way he did not like, and generally gave him a good idea of judgment to come. After that he promised to look after them as though they were his father's spirit. He was a very superstitious old Kafir and a great villain.

Having thus disposed of our superfluous gear we arranged the kit, we five – Sir Henry, Good, myself, Umbopa, and the Hottentot Ventvögel – were to take with us on our journey. It was small enough, but do what we would we could not get its weight down under about forty pounds a man. This is what it consisted of: –

Three express rifles and two hundred rounds of ammunition.

The two Winchester repeating rifles (for Umbopa and Ventvögel), with two hundred rounds of cartridge.

Three 'Colt' revolvers and sixty rounds of cartridge.

Five Cochrane's water-bottles, each holding four pints.

Five blankets.

Twenty-five pounds' weight of biltong – *i.e.* sun-dried game flesh.

Ten pounds' weight of best mixed beads for gifts.

A selection of medicine, including an ounce of quinine, and one or two small surgical instruments.

Our knives, a few sundries, such as a compass, matches, a pocket filter, tobacco, a trowel, a bottle of brandy, and the clothes we stood in.

This was our total equipment, a small one indeed for such a venture, but we dare not attempt to carry more. Indeed, that load was a heavy one per man with which to travel across the burning desert, for in such places every additional ounce tells. But we could not see our way to reducing the amount. There was nothing taken but what was absolutely necessary.

With great difficulty, and by the promise of a present of a good hunting-knife each, I succeeded in persuading three wretched natives from the village to come with us for the first stage, twenty miles, and to carry large gourds holding a gallon of water apiece. My object was to enable us to refill our water-bottles after the first night's march, for we determined to start in the cool of the evening. I gave out to these natives that we were going to shoot ostriches, with which the desert abounded. They jabbered and shrugged their shoulders, saying that we were mad and should perish of thirst, which I must say seemed probable. Still being desirous of obtaining the knives, which were almost unknown treasures up there, they consented to come, having probably reflected that, after all, our subsequent extinction would be no affair of theirs.

All next day we rested and slept, and at sunset ate a hearty meal of fresh beef washed down with tea, the last, as Good remarked sadly, we were likely to drink for many a long day. Then, having made our final preparations, we lay down and waited for the moon to rise. At last, about nine o'clock, up she came in all her glory, flooding the wild country with light, and throwing a silver sheen on the expanse of rolling desert before us, which looked as solemn and quiet and as alien to man as the star-studded firmament above. We rose up, and in a few minutes were ready, and yet we hesitated a little, as human nature is prone to hesitate on the threshold of an irrevocable step. We three white men stood by ourselves. Umbopa, assegai in hand and a rifle slung across his shoulders, looked out fixedly across the desert a few paces ahead of us; while the hired natives, with the gourds of water, and Ventvögel, were gathered in a little knot behind.

'Gentlemen,' said Sir Henry presently, in his deep voice, 'we are going on about as strange a journey as men can make in this world. It is very doubtful if we can succeed in it. But we are three men who will stand together for good or for evil to the last. Now, before we start let us for a moment pray to the Power who shapes the destinies of men, and who ages since has marked out our paths, that it may please Him to direct our steps in accordance with His will.'

Taking off his hat, for the space of a minute or so, he covered his face with his hands, and Good and I did likewise.

I do not say that I am a first-rate praying man – few hunters are; and as for Sir Henry, I never heard him speak like that before, and only once since, though deep down in his heart I believe that he is very religious. Good, too, is pious, though apt to swear. Anyhow, I do not remember, excepting on one, no, two occasions, ever putting up a better prayer in my life than I did during that minute, and somehow I felt the happier for it. Our future was so completely unknown, and I think that the unknown and the awful always bring a man nearer to his Maker.

'And now,' said Sir Henry, '*trek!*'

So we started.

We had nothing to guide ourselves by except the distant mountains and old José da Silvestra's chart, which, considering that it was drawn by a dying and half-distraught man on a fragment of linen three centuries ago, was not a very satisfactory sort of thing to work with. Still, our sole hope of success depended upon it, such as it was. If we failed in finding that pool of bad water which the old Dom marked as being situated in the middle of the desert, about sixty miles from our starting-point, and as far from the mountains, in all probability we must perish miserably of thirst. But to my mind the chances of our finding it in that great sea of sand and karoo scrub seemed almost infinitesimal. Even supposing that da Silvestra had marked the pool correctly, what was there to prevent its having been dried up by the sun generations ago, or trampled in by game, or filled with the drifting sand?

On we tramped silently as shades through the night and in the heavy sand. The karoo bushes caught our feet and retarded us, and the sand worked into our veldschoens and Good's shooting-boots, so that every few miles we had to stop and empty them. Still the night kept fairly cool, though the atmosphere was thick and heavy, giving a sort of creamy feel to the air, and we made fair progress. It was very silent and lonely there in the desert, oppressively so indeed. Good felt this, and once began to whistle 'The Girl I left behind me,' but the notes sounded lugubrious in that vast place, and he gave it up.

Shortly afterwards a little incident occurred which, though it startled us at the time, gave rise to a laugh. Good was leading, as the holder of the compass, which, being a sailor, of course he understood thoroughly, and we were toiling along in single file behind him, when suddenly we heard a half-smothered exclamation, and he vanished. Next second there arose all around us a most extraordinary hubbub; snorts, groans, and wild sounds of rushing feet. In the faint light, too, we could descry dim, galloping forms half-hidden by wreaths of sand. The natives threw down their loads and prepared to bolt, then remembering that there was nowhere to run to, they cast themselves upon the ground and howled something about ghosts. As for Sir Henry and myself, we stood amazed; nor was our amazement lessened when we perceived the form of Good careering off in the direction of the mountains, apparently mounted on the back of a horse and halloaing wildly. In another second he threw up his arms, and we heard him come to the earth with a thud.

Then I saw what had happened; we had stumbled upon a herd of sleeping quagga, on to the back of one of which Good had actually had fallen, whereupon the brute naturally got up and made off with him. Calling out to the others that it was all right, I ran towards Good, much afraid lest he should be hurt, but to my great relief, I found him sitting in the sand, his eye-glass still fixed firmly in his eye, rather shaken and very much frightened, but not in any way injured.

After this we travelled on without any further misadventure till about one o'clock, when we called a halt, and having drunk a little water, not much, for water was precious, and rested for half an hour, we started again.

On, on we went, till at last the east began to blush like the cheek of a girl. Next appeared faint rays of primrose light, that changed presently to golden bars, through which the dawn glided out across the desert. The stars grew pale and paler still, till at last they vanished; the golden moon waxed wan, and her mountain ridges stood out against her sickly face like the bones on the cheek of a dying man. Then came spear upon spear of light flashing far away across the boundless wilderness, piercing and firing the veils of mist, till the desert was draped in a tremulous golden glow, and it was day.

Still we did not halt, though by this time we should have been glad enough to do so, for we knew that when once the sun was fully up it would be almost impossible for us to travel. At length, about an hour later, we spied a little pile of boulders rising out of the plain, and to this we dragged ourselves. As luck would have it, here we found an overhanging slab of rock carpeted beneath with smooth sand, which afforded a most grateful shelter from the heat. Underneath this we crept, and each of us having drunk some water and eaten a bit of biltong, we lay down and soon were sound asleep.

It was three o'clock in the afternoon before we woke, to find our bearers preparing to return. They had seen enough of the desert already, and no number of knives would have tempted them to come a step farther. So we took a hearty drink, and having emptied our water-bottles, filled them up again from the gourds that they had brought with them. Then we watched them depart on their twenty miles' tramp home.

At half-past four we started again. It was lonely and desolate work, for with the exception of a few ostriches there was not a single living creature to be seen on all the vast expanse of sandy plains. Evidently it was too dry for game, and with the exception of a deadly-looking cobra or two we saw no reptiles. One insect, however, we found abundant, and that was the common or house fly. On they came, 'not as single spies but in battalions,' as I think the Old Testament[1] says somewhere. The house fly is a most extra-ordinary insect. Go where you will you find him, and so it must have been always. I have seen him enclosed in amber, which is, I was told, quite half a million years old, looking exactly like his descendant of to-day, and I have little doubt that when the last man lies dying on the earth he will be buzzing round – if this event should happen to occur in summer – watching for an opportunity to settle on his nose.

At sunset we halted, waiting for the moon to rise. At last she came up, beautiful and serene as ever, and, with one halt about two o'clock in the morning, we trudged on wearily through the night, till at last the welcome sun put a period to our labours. We drank a little and flung ourselves down on the sand, thor-oughly tired out, and soon were all asleep. There was no need to set a watch, for we had nothing to fear from anybody or anything in that vast untenanted plain. Our only enemies were heat, thirst, and flies, but far rather would I have faced any danger from man or beast than that awful trinity. This time we were not so lucky as to find a sheltering rock to guard us from the glare of the sun, with the result that about seven o'clock we woke up experiencing

---

[1]Readers must beware of accepting Mr Quatermain's references as accurate, as, it has been found, some are prone to do. Although his reading evidently was limited, the impression produced by it upon his mind was mixed. Thus to him the Old Testament and Shakespeare were interchangeable authorities. – *Editor*.

the exact sensations one would attribute to a beefsteak on a grid-iron. We were literally being baked through and through. The burning sun seemed to be sucking our very blood out of us. We sat up and gasped.

'Phew,' said I, grabbing at the halo of flies which buzzed cheer-fully round my head. The heat did not affect *them*.

'My word!' exclaimed Sir Henry.

'It is devilish hot!' echoed Good.

It was hot, indeed, and there was not a bit of shelter to be found. Look where we would there were no rocks or trees, nothing but an unending glare, rendered dazzling by the heated air that danced over the surface of the desert as it dances over a cooking stove.

'What is to be done?' asked Sir Henry; 'we can't stand this for long.'

We looked at each other blankly.

'I have it,' said Good, 'we must dig a hole, get in it, and cover ourselves with the karoo bushes.'

It did not seem a very promising suggestion, but at least it was better than nothing, so we set to work, and, with the trowel we had brought with us and the help of our hands, in about an hour we succeeded in delving out a patch of ground some ten feet long by twelve wide to the depth of two feet. Then we cut a quan-tity of low scrub with our hunting-knives, and, creeping into the hole, pulled it over all of us, with the exception of Ventvögel, on whom, being a Hottentot, the heat had no particular effect. This gave us some slight shelter from the burning rays of the sun, but the atmosphere in that amateur grave can be better imagined than described. The Black Hole of Calcutta must have been a fool to it; indeed, to this moment I do not know how we lived through the day. There we lay panting, and every now and again mois-tening our lips from our scanty supply of water. Had we followed our inclinations we should have finished all we possessed in the first two hours, but we were forced to exercise the most rigid care, for if our water failed us we knew that very soon we must perish miserably.

But everything has an end, if only you live long enough to see it, and somehow that miserable day wore on towards evening. About three o'clock in the afternoon we determined that we could bear it no longer. It would be better to die walking than to be killed slowly by heat and thirst in this dreadful pit. So taking each of us a little drink from our fast diminishing supply of water, now warmed to about the same temperature as a man's blood, we staggered forward.

We had now covered some fifty miles of wilderness. If the reader will refer to the rough copy and translation of old da Silvestra's map, he will see that the desert is marked as measuring forty leagues across, and the ' pan bad water,' is set down as being about in the middle of it. Now forty leagues is one hundred and twenty miles, consequently we ought at the most to be within twelve or fifteen miles of the water if any should really exist.

Through the afternoon we crept slowly and painfully along, scarcely doing more than a mile and a half in an hour. At sunset we rested again, waiting for the moon, and after drinking a little managed to get some sleep.

Before we lay down, Umbopa pointed out to us a slight and indistinct hillock on a flat surface of the plain about eight miles away. At the distance it looked like an ant-hill, and as I was dropping off to sleep I fell to wondering what it could be.

With the moon we marched again, feeling dreadfully exhausted, and suffering tortures from thirst and prickly heat. Nobody who has not felt it can know what we went through. We walked no longer, we staggered, now and again falling from exhaustion, and being obliged to call a halt every hour or so. We had scarcely energy left in us to speak. Up to this Good had chatted and joked, for he is a merry fellow; but now he had not a jest in him.

At last, about two o'clock, utterly worn out in body and mind, we came to the foot of the queer hill, or sand koppie, which at first sight resembled a gigantic ant-heap about a hundred feet high, covering at its base nearly two acres of ground.

Here we halted, and driven to it by our desperate thirst, sucked down our last drops of water. We had but half a pint a head, and each of us could have drunk a gallon.

Then we lay down. Just as I was dropping off to sleep I heard Umbopa remark to himself in Zulu –

'If we cannot find water we shall all be dead before the moon rises to-morrow.'

I shuddered, hot as it was. The near prospect of such an awful death is not pleasant, but even the thought of it could not keep me from sleeping.

CHAPTER 6

Water! Water!

Two hours later, that is, about four o'clock, I woke up, for so soon as the first heavy demand of bodily fatigue had been satisfied, the torturing thirst from which I was suffering asserted itself. I could sleep no more. I had been dreaming that I was bathing in a running stream, with green banks and trees upon them, and I awoke to find myself in this arid wilderness, and to remember, as Umbopa had said, that if we did not find water this day we must perish miserably. No human creature could live long without water in that heat. I sat up and rubbed my grimy face with my dry and horny hands, as my lips and eyelids were stuck together, and it was only after some friction and with an effort that I was able to open them. It was not far from dawn, but there was none of the bright feel of dawn in the air, which was thick with a hot murkiness that I cannot describe. The others were still sleeping.

Presently it began to grow light enough to read, so I drew out a little pocket copy of the 'Ingoldsby Legends' which I had brought with me, and read 'The Jackdaw of Rheims.' When I got to where

> 'A nice little boy held a golden ewer,
> Embossed, and filled with water so pure.
> As any that flows between Rheims and Namur.'

I literally smacked my cracking lips, or rather tried to smack them. The mere thought of that pure water made me mad. If the Cardinal had been there with his bell, book, and candle, I would have whipped in and drunk his water up; yes, even if he had filled it already with the suds of soap 'worthy of washing the hands of the Pope,' and I knew that the whole concentrated curse of the Catholic Church should fall upon me for so doing. I almost think that I must have been a little light-headed with thirst, weariness and the want of food; for I fell to thinking how astonished the Cardinal and his nice little boy and the jackdaw would have looked to see a burnt up, brown-eyed, grizzly-haired little elephant hunter suddenly bound between them, put his dirty face into the basin, and swallow every drop of the precious water. The idea amused me so much that I laughed, or rather cackled aloud, which woke the others, and they began to rub their dirty faces and to drag *their* gummed-up lips and eyelids apart.

As soon as we were all well awake we began to discuss the situation, which was serious enough. Not a drop of water was left. We turned the bottles upside down, and licked their tops, but it was a failure; they were dry as a bone. Good, who had charge of the flask of brandy, got it out and looked at it longingly; but Sir Henry promptly took it away from him, for to drink raw spirit would only have been to precipitate the end.

'If we do not find water we shall die,' he said.

'If we can trust to the old Dom's map there should be some about,' I said; but nobody seemed to derive much satisfaction from this remark. It was so evident that no great faith could be put in the map. Now it was gradually growing light, and as we sat staring blankly at each other, I observed the Hottentot Ventvögel rise and begin to walk about with his eyes on the ground. Presently he stopped short, and uttering a guttural exclamation, pointed to the earth.

'What is it?' Good exclaimed; and rising simultaneously we went to where Ventvögel was standing staring at the sand.

'Well,' I said, 'it is fresh springbok spoor; what of it?'

'Springbucks do not go far from water,' the Hottentot answered in Dutch.

'No,' I answered, 'I forgot; and thank God for it.'

This new discovery put new life into us; for it is wonderful, when a man is in a desperate position, how he catches at the slightest hope, and feels almost happy. On a dark night a single star is better than nothing.

Meanwhile Ventvögel was lifting his snub nose, and sniffing the hot air for all the world like an old Impala ram who scents danger. Presently he spoke again.

'I *smell* water,' he said.

Then we felt quite jubilant, for we knew what a wonderful instinct these wild-bred men possess.

Just at that moment the sun came up gloriously, and revealed so grand a sight to our astonished eyes that for a moment or two we even forgot our thirst.

There, not more than forty or fifty miles from us, glittering like silver in the early rays of the morning sun, soared Sheba's Breasts; and stretching away for hundreds of miles on either side of them ran the great Suliman Berg. Now that, sitting here, I attempt to describe the extraordinary grandeur and beauty of that sight, language seems to fail me. I am impotent even at its memory. Before us, rose two enormous mountains, the like of which are not, I believe, to be seen in Africa, if indeed there are any to match them in the world, measuring, each of them, at least fifteen thousand feet in height, standing not more than a dozen miles apart, linked together by a precipitous cliff of rock, and towering in awful white solemnity straight into the sky. These mountains, placed thus, like the pillars of a gigantic gateway, are shaped after the fashion of a woman's breasts, and at times the mists and shadows beneath them take the form of a recumbent woman, veiled mysteriously in sleep. Their bases swell gently from the plain, looking at that distance perfectly round and smooth; and upon the top of each is a vast hillock covered with snow, exactly corresponding to the nipple on the female breast.

The stretch of cliff that connects them appears to be some thousands of feet in height, and perfectly precipitous, and on each flank of them, so far as the eye can reach, extend similar lines of cliff, broken only here and there by flat table-topped mountains, something like the world-famed one at Cape Town; a formation, by the way, that is very common in Africa.

To describe the comprehensive grandeur of that view is beyond my powers. There was something so inexpressibly solemn and over-powering about those huge volcanoes – for doubtless they are extinct volcanoes – that it quite awed us. For a while the morning lights played upon the snow and the brown and swelling masses beneath, and then, as though to veil the majestic sight from our curious eyes, strange vapours and clouds gathered and increased around the mountains, till presently we could only trace their pure and gigantic outlines, showing ghost-like through that fleecy envelope. Indeed, as we afterwards discovered, usually they were wrapped in this gauze-like mist, which doubtless accounted for our not having seen them more clearly before.

Sheba's Breasts had scarcely vanished into cloud-clad privacy, before our thirst – literally a burning question – reasserted itself.

It was all very well for Ventvögel to say that he smelt water, but we could see no signs of it, look which way we would. So far as the eye might reach there was nothing but arid sweltering sand and karoo scrub. We walked round the hillock and gazed about anxiously on the other side, but it was the same story, not a drop of water could be found; there was no indication of a pan, a pool, or a spring.

'You are a fool,' I said angrily to Ventvögel; 'there is no water.' But still he lifted his ugly snub nose and sniffed.

'I smell it, Baas,' he answered; 'it is somewhere in the air.'

'Yes,' I said, 'no doubt it is in the clouds, and about two months hence it will fall and wash our bones.'

Sir Henry stroked his yellow beard thoughtfully. 'Perhaps it is on the top of the hill,' he suggested.

'Rot,' said Good; 'whoever heard of water being found at the top of a hill!'

'Let us go and look,' I put in, and hopelessly enough we scrambled up the sandy sides of the hillock, Umbopa leading. Presently he stopped as though he was petrified.

'*Nanzia amanzi!*' that is, 'Here is water!' he cried with a loud voice.

We rushed up to him, and there, sure enough, in a deep cut or indentation on the very top of the sand koppie, was an undoubted pool of water. How it came to be in such a strange place we did not stop to inquire, nor did we hesitate at its black and unpleasant appearance. It was water, or a good imitation of it, and that was enough for us. We gave a bound and a rush, and in another second we were all down on our stomachs sucking up the uninviting fluid as though it were nectar fit for the gods. Heavens, how we did drink! Then when we had done drinking we tore off our clothes and sat down in the pool, absorbing the moisture through our parched skins. You, Harry my boy, who have only to turn on a couple of taps to summon 'hot' and 'cold' from an unseen, vasty cistern, can have little idea of the luxury of that muddy wallow in brackish tepid water.

After a while we rose from it, refreshed indeed, and fell to on our ' biltong,' of which we had scarcely been able to touch a mouthful for twenty-four hours, and ate our fill. Then we smoked a pipe, and lay down by the side of that blessed pool, under the overhanging shadow of its bank, and slept till noon.

All that day we rested there by the water, thanking our stars that we had been lucky enough to find it, bad as it was, and not forgetting to render a due share of gratitude to the shade of the long-departed da Silvestra, who had set its position down so accurately on the tail of his shirt. The wonderful thing to us was that the pan should have lasted so long, and the only way in which I can account for this is on the supposition that it is fed by some spring deep down in the sand.

Having filled both ourselves and our water-bottles as full as possible, in far better spirits we started off again with the moon. That night we covered nearly five-and-twenty miles; but, needless to say, found no more water, though we were lucky enough on the following day to get a little shade behind some ant-heaps. When the sun rose, and, for awhile, cleared away the mysterious mists, Suliman's Berg with the two majestic Breasts, now only about twenty miles off, seemed to be towering right above us, and looked grander than ever. At the approach of evening we marched again, and, to cut a long story short, by daylight next morning found ourselves upon the lowest slopes of Sheba's left Breast, for which we had been steadily steering. By this time our water was exhausted once more, and we were suffering severely from thirst, nor indeed could we see any chance of relieving it till we reached the snow-line far, far above us. After resting an hour or two, driven to it by our torturing thirst, we went on, toiling painfully in the burning heat up the lava slopes, for we found that the huge base of the mountain was composed entirely of lava beds belched from the bowels of the earth in some far past age.

By eleven o'clock we were utterly exhausted, and generally speaking, in a very bad state indeed. The lava clinker, over which we must drag ourselves, though smooth compared with some clinker I have heard of, such as that on the Island of Ascension, for instance, was yet rough enough to make our feet very sore, and this, together with our other miseries, had pretty well finished us. A few hundred yards above us were some large lumps of lava, and towards these we steered with the intention of lying down beneath their shade. We reached them, and to our surprise, so far as we had a capacity for surprise left in us, on a little plateau or ridge close by we saw that the clinker was covered with a dense green growth. Evidently soil formed of decomposed lava had rested there, and in due course had become the receptacle of seeds deposited by birds. But we did not take much further interest in the green growth, for one cannot live on grass like Nebuchadnezzar. That requires a special dispensation of Providence and peculiar digestive organs.

So we sat down under the rocks and groaned, and for one I wished heartily that we had never started on this fool's errand. As we were sitting there I saw Umbopa get up and hobble towards the patch of green, and a few minutes afterwards, to my great astonishment, I perceived that usually very dignified individual dancing and shouting like a maniac, and waving something green. Off we all scrambled towards him as fast as our wearied limbs would carry us, hoping that he had found water.

'What is it, Umbopa, son of a fool?' I shouted in Zulu.

'It is food and water, Macumazahn,' and again he waved the green thing.

Then I saw what he had found. It was a melon. We had hit upon a patch of wild melons, thousands of them, and dead ripe.

'Melons!' I yelled to Good, who was next me; and another minute his false teeth were fixed in one of them.

I think that we ate about six each before we had done, and poor fruit as they were, I doubt if I ever thought anything nicer.

But melons are not very nutritious, and when we had satisfied our thirst with their pulpy substance, and put a stock to cool by the simple process of cutting them in two and setting them end on in the hot sun to grow cold by evaporation, we began to feel exceedingly hungry. We had still some biltong left, but our stomachs turned from biltong, and besides, we were obliged to be very sparing of it, for we could not say when we should find more food. Just at this moment a lucky thing chanced. Looking across the desert I saw a flock of about ten large birds flying straight towards us.

'*Skit, Baas, skit!*' 'Shoot, master, shoot!' whispered the Hottentot, throwing himself on his face, an example which we all followed.

Then I saw that the birds were a flock of *pauw* or bustards, and that they would pass within fifty yards of my head. Taking one of the repeating Winchesters, I waited till they were nearly over us, and then jumped to my feet. On seeing me the *pauw* bunched up together, as I expected that they would, and I fired two shots straight into the thick of them, and, as luck would have it, brought one down, a fine fellow, that weighed about twenty pounds. In half an hour we had a fire made of dry melon stalks, and he was toasting over it, and we made such a feed as we had not tasted for a week. We ate that *pauw*; nothing was left of him but his leg-bones and his beak, and we felt not a little the better afterwards.

That night we went on again with the moon, carrying as many melons as we could with us. As we ascended we found the air grow cooler and cooler, which was a great relief to us, and at dawn, so far as we could judge, we were not more than about a dozen miles from the snow-line. Here we discovered more melons, and so had no longer any anxiety about water, for we knew that we should soon get plenty of snow. But the ascent had now become very precipitous, and we made slow progress, not more than a mile an hour. Also that night we ate our last morsel of biltong. As yet, with the exception of the *pauw*, we had seen no living thing on the mountain, nor had we come across a single spring or stream of water which struck us as very odd, considering the expanse of snow above us, which must, we thought, melt sometimes. But as we afterwards discovered, owing to a cause which it is quite beyond my power to explain, all the streams flowed down upon the north side of the mountains.

Now we began to grow very anxious about food. We had escaped death by thirst, but it seemed probable that it was only to die of hunger. The events of the next three miserable days are best described by copying the entries made at the time in my notebook.

'21st May. – Started 11 a.m., finding the atmosphere quite cold enough to travel by day, and carrying some water-melons with us. Struggled on all day, but found no more melons, having evidently passed out of their district. Saw no game of any sort. Halted for the night at sundown, having had no food for many hours. Suffered much during the night from cold.

'22nd. – Started at sunrise again, feeling very faint and

weak. Only made about five miles all day; found some patches of snow, of which we ate, but nothing else. Camped at night under the edge of a great plateau. Gold bitter. Drank a little brandy each, and huddled ourselves together, each wrapped up in his blanket, to keep ourselves alive. Are now suffering frightfully from starvation and weariness. Thought that Ventvögel would have died during the night.

'23rd. – Struggled forward once more as soon as the sun was well up, and had thawed our limbs a little. We are now in a dreadful plight, and I fear that unless we get food this will be our last day's journey. But little brandy left. Good, Sir Henry, and Umbopa bear up wonderfully, but Ventvögel is in a very bad way. Like most Hottentots, he cannot stand cold. Pangs of hunger not so bad, but have a sort of numb feeling about the stomach. Others say the same. We are now on a level with the precipitous chain, or wall of lava, linking the two breasts, and the view is glorious. Behind us the glowing desert rolls away to the horizon, and before us lie miles of smooth hard snow almost level, but swelling gently upwards, out of the centre of which the nipple of the mountain, that appears to be some miles in circumference, rises about four thousand feet into the sky. Not a living thing is to be seen. God help us; I fear that our time has come.'

And now I will drop the journal, partly because it is not very interesting reading; also what follows requires telling rather more fully.

All that day – the 23rd May – we struggled slowly up the incline of snow, lying down from time to time to rest. A strange gaunt crew we must have looked, while, laden as we were, we dragged our weary feet over the dazzling plain, glaring round us with hungry eyes. Not that there was much use in glaring, for we could see nothing to eat. We did not accomplish more than seven miles that day. Just before sunset we found ourselves exactly under the nipple of Sheba's left Breast, which towered thousands of feet into the air, a vast smooth hillock of frozen snow. Weak as we were, we could not but appreciate the wonderful scene, made even more splendid by the flying rays of light from the setting sun, which here and there stained the snow blood-red, and crowned the great dome above us with a diadem of glory.

'I say,' gasped Good, presently, 'we ought to be somewhere near that cave the old gentleman wrote about.'

'Yes,' said I, 'if there is a cave.'

'Come, Quatermain,' groaned Sir Henry, 'don't talk like that; I have every faith in the Dom; remember the water! We shall find the place soon.'

'If we don't find it before dark we are dead men, that is all about it,' was my consolatory reply.

For the next ten minutes we trudged in silence, when suddenly Umbopa, who was marching along beside me, wrapped in his blanket, and with a leather belt strapped so tightly round his stomach, to 'make his hunger small' as he said, that his waist looked like a girl's, caught me by the arm.

'Look!' he said, pointing towards the springing slope of the nipple.

I followed his glance, and some two hundred yards from us perceived what appeared to be a hole in the snow.

'It is the cave,' said Umbopa.

We made the best of our way to the spot, and found sure enough that the hole was the mouth of a cavern, no doubt the same as that of which da Silvestra wrote. We were not too soon, for just as we reached shelter the sun went down with startling rapidity, leaving the world nearly dark, for in these latitudes there is but little twilight. So we crept into the cave, which did not appear to be very big, and huddling ourselves together for warmth, swallowed what remained of our brandy – barely a mouthful each – and tried to forget our miseries in sleep. But the cold was too intense to allow us to do so, for I am convinced that at this great altitude the thermometer cannot have marked less than fourteen or fifteen degrees below freezing point. What such a temperature meant to us, enervated as we were by hardship, want of food, and the great heat of the desert, the reader may imagine better than I can describe. Suffice it to say that it was something as near death from exposure as I have ever felt. There we sat for hour after hour through the still and bitter night, feeling the frost wander round and nip us now in the finger, now in the foot, now in the face. In vain did we huddle up closer and closer; there was no warmth in our miserable starved carcasses. Sometimes one of us would drop into an uneasy slumber for a few minutes, but we could not sleep much, and perhaps this was fortunate, for if we had I doubt if we should ever have woke again. Indeed, I believe that it was only by force of will that we kept ourselves alive at all.

Not very long before dawn I heard the Hottentot Ventvögel, whose teeth had been chattering all night like castanets, give a deep sigh. Then his teeth stopped chattering. I did not think anything of it at the time, concluding that he had gone to sleep. His back was resting against mine, and it seemed to grow colder and colder, till at last it felt like ice.

At length the air began to grow grey with light, then golden arrows sped across the snow, and at last the glorious sun peeped above the lava wall and looked in upon our half-frozen forms. Also it looked upon Ventvögel, sitting there amongst us, *stone dead*. No wonder his back felt cold, poor fellow. He had died when I heard him sigh, and was now frozen almost stiff. Shocked beyond measure, we dragged ourselves from the corpse – how strange is that horror we mortals have of the companionship of a dead body – and left it sitting there, its arms clasped about its knees.

By this time the sunlight was pouring its cold rays, for here they were cold, straight into the mouth of the cave. Suddenly I heard an exclamation of fear from someone, and turned my head.

This was what I saw: Sitting at the end of the cavern – it was not more than twenty feet long – was another form, of which the head rested on the chest and the long arms hung down. I stared at it, and saw that this too was a *dead man*, and what was more, a white man.

The others saw also, and the sight proved too much for our shattered nerves. One and all we scrambled out of that cave as fast as our half-frozen limbs would carry us.

CHAPTER 7

Solomon's Road

Outside the cavern we halted, feeling rather foolish.

'I am going back,' said Sir Henry.

'Why?' asked Good.

'Because it has struck me that – what we saw – may be my brother.'

This was a new idea, and we re-entered the place to put it to the proof. After the bright light outside, our eyes, weak as they were with staring at the snow, could not pierce the gloom of the cave for a while. Presently, however, they grew accustomed to the semi-darkness, and we advanced towards the dead man.

Sir Henry knelt down and peered into his face.

'Thank God,' he said, with a sigh of relief, 'it is *not* my brother,'

Then I drew near and looked. The body was that of a tall man in middle life with aquiline features, grizzled hair, and a long black moustache. The skin was perfectly yellow, and stretched tightly over the bones. Its clothing, with the exception of what seemed to be the remains of a woollen pair of hose, had been removed, leaving the skeleton-like frame naked. Round the neck of the corpse, which was frozen perfectly stiff, hung a yellow ivory crucifix.

'Who on earth can it be?' said I.

'Can't you guess?' asked Good.

I shook my head.

'Why, the old Dom, José da Silvestra, of course – who else?'

'Impossible,' I gasped; 'he died three hundred years ago.'

'And what is there to prevent him from lasting for three thousand years in this atmosphere, I should like to know?' asked Good. 'If only the temperature is sufficiently low, flesh and blood will keep fresh as New Zealand mutton for ever, and Heavens knows it is cold enough here. The sun never gets in here; no animal comes here to tear or destroy. No doubt his slave, of whom he speaks on the writing, took off his clothes and left him. He could not have buried him alone. Look!' he went on, stooping down to pick up a queerly-shaped bone scraped at the end into a sharp point, 'here is the "cleft bone" that Silvestra used to draw the map with.'

We gazed for a moment astonished, forgetting our own miseries in this extraordinary and, as it seemed to us, semi-miraculous sight.

'Ay,' said Sir Henry, 'and this is where he got his ink from,' and he pointed to a small wound on the Dom's left arm. 'Did ever a man see such a thing before?'

There was no longer any doubt about the matter, which for my own part, I confess, perfectly appalled me. There he sat, the dead man, whose directions, written some ten generations ago, had led us to this spot. Here in my own hand was the rude pen with which he had written them, and about his neck hung the crucifix that his dying lips had kissed. Gazing at him, my imagination could reconstruct the last scene of the drama, the traveller dying of cold and starvation, yet striving to convey to the world the great secret which he had discovered: – the awful loneliness of his death, of which the evidence sat before us. It even seemed to me that I could trace in his strongly-marked features a likeness to those of my poor friend Silvestre his descendant, who had died twenty years before in my arms, but perhaps that was fancy. At any rate, there he sat, a sad memento of the fate that so often overtakes those who would penetrate into the unknown; and there doubtless he will still sit, crowned with the dread majesty of death, for centuries yet unborn, to startle the eyes of wanderers like ourselves, if ever any such should come again to invade his loneliness. The thing over-powered us, already almost perished as we were with cold and hunger.

'Let us go,' said Sir Henry, in a low voice; 'stay, we will give him a companion,' and lifting up the dead body of the Hottentot Ventvögel, he placed it near to that of the old Dom. Then he stooped, and with a jerk broke the rotten string of the crucifix which hung round da Silvestra's neck, for his fingers were too cold to attempt to unfasten it. I believe that he has it still. I took the bone pen, and it is before me as I write – sometimes I use it to sign my name.

Then leaving these two, the proud white man of a past age, and the poor Hottentot, to keep their eternal vigil in the midst of the eternal snows, we crept out of the cave into the welcome sunshine and resumed our path, wondering in our hearts how many hours it would be before we were even as they are.

When we had walked about half a mile we came to the edge of the plateau, for the nipple of the mountain does not rise out of its exact centre, though from the desert side it had seemed to do so. What lay before us we could not see, for the landscape was wreathed in billows of morning fog. Presently, however, the higher layers of mist cleared a little, and revealed, at the end of the long slope of snow, a patch of green grass, some five hundred yards beneath us, through which a stream was running. Nor was this all. By the stream basking in the bright sun stood and lay a group of from ten to fifteen *large antelopes* – at that distance we could not see of what species.

The sight filled us with an unreasoning joy. If only we could get it, there was food in plenty. But the question was how to do so. The beasts were fully six hundred yards off, a very long shot, and one not to be depended on when our lives hung upon the results.

Rapidly we discussed the advisability of trying to stalk the game, but in the end dismissed it reluctantly. To begin with, the wind was not favourable, and further, we must certainly be perceived, however careful we were, against the blinding back-ground of snow, which we should be obliged to traverse.

'Well, we must have a try from where we are,' said Sir Henry. 'Which shall it be, Quatermain, the repeating rifles or the expresses?'

Here again was a question. The Winchester repeaters – of which we had two, Umbopa carrying poor Ventvogel's as well as his own – were sighted up to a thousand yards, whereas the expresses were only sighted to three hundred and fifty, beyond which distance shooting with them was more or less guesswork. On the other hand, if they did hit, the express bullets, being 'expanding,' were much more likely to bring the game down. It was a knotty point, but I made up my mind that we must risk it and use the expresses.

'Let each of us take the buck opposite to him. Aim well at the point of the shoulder and high up,' said I; 'and Umbopa, do you give the word, so that we may all fire together.'

Then came a pause, each of us aiming his level best, as indeed a man is likely to do when he knows that life itself depends upon the shot.

'Fire,' said Umbopa in Zulu, and at almost the same instant the three rifles rang out loudly; three clouds of smoke hung for a moment before us, and a hundred echoes went flying over the silent snow. Presently the smoke cleared, and revealed – oh, joy! – a great buck lying on its back and kicking furiously in its death agony. We gave a yell of triumph – we were saved – we should not starve. Weak as we were, we rushed down the intervening slope of snow, and in ten minutes from the time of shooting, that animal's heart and liver were lying before us. But now a new difficulty arose, we had no fuel, and therefore could make no fire to cook them. We gazed at each other in dismay.

'Starving men should not be fanciful,' said Good, 'we must eat raw meat.'

There was no other way out of the dilemma, and our gnawing hunger made the proposition less distasteful than it would other-wise have been. So we took the heart and liver and buried them for a few minutes in a patch of snow to cool them. Then we washed them in the ice-cold water of the stream, and lastly ate them greedily. It sounds horrible enough, but honestly, I never tasted anything so good as that raw meat. In a quarter of an hour we were changed men. Our life and vigour came back to us, our feeble pulses grew strong again, and the blood went coursing through our veins. But mindful of the results of over-feeding on starved stomachs, we were careful not to eat too much, stopping whilst we were still hungry.

'Thank Heaven!' said Sir Henry; 'that brute has saved our lives. What is it, Quatermain?'

I rose and went to look at the antelope, for I was not certain. It was about the size of a donkey, with large curved horns. I had never seen one like it before; the species was new to me. It was brown in colour, with faint red stripes, and grew a thick coat. I afterwards discovered that the natives of that wonderful country call these bucks '*inco*' They are very rare, and only found at a great altitude where no other game will live. This animal was fairly hit up in the shoulder, though whose bullet knocked it over we could not, of course, discover. I believe that Good, mindful of his marvellous shot at the giraffe, secretly set it down to his own prowess, and we did not contradict him.

We had been so busy satisfying our hunger that hitherto we had not found time to look about us. But now, having set Umbopa to cut off as much of the best meat as we were likely to be able to carry, we began to inspect our surroundings. The mist had cleared away, for it was eight o'clock, and the sun had sucked it up, so we were able to take in all the country before us at a glance. I know not how to describe the glorious panorama which unfolded itself to our gaze. I have never seen anything like it before, nor shall, I suppose, again.

Behind and over us towered Sheba's snowy Breasts, and below, some five thousand feet beneath where we stood, lay league on league of the most lovely champaign country. Here were dense patches of lofty forest, there a great river wound its silvery way. To the left stretched a vast expanse of rich, undulating veld or grass land, whereon we could just make out countless herds of game or cattle, at that distance we could not tell which. This expanse appeared to be ringed in by a wall of distant mountains. To the right the country was more or less mountainous; that is, solitary hills stood up from its level, with stretches of cultivated land between, amongst which we could see groups of dome-shaped huts. The landscape lay before us as a map, wherein rivers flashed like silver snakes, and Alp-like peaks crowned with wildly twisted snow wreaths rose in grandeur, whilst over all was the glad sunlight and the breath of Nature's happy life.

Two curious things struck us as we gazed. First, that the country before us must lie at least three thousand feet higher than the desert we had crossed, and secondly, that all the rivers flowed from south to north. As we had painful reason to know, there was no water upon the southern side of the vast range on which we stood, but on the northern face were many streams, most of which appeared to unite with the great river we could see winding away farther than our eyes could follow.

We sat down for a while and gazed in silence at this wonderful view. Presently Sir Henry spoke.

'Isn't there something on the map about Solomon's Great Road?' he said.

I nodded, for I was still gazing out over the far country.

'Well, look; there it is!' and he pointed a little to our right.

Good and I looked accordingly, and there, winding away towards the plain was what appeared to be a wide turnpike road. We had not seen it at first because, on reaching the plain, it turned behind some broken country. We did not say anything, at least, not much, we were beginning to lose the sense of wonder. Somehow it did not seem particularly unnatural that we should find a sort of Roman road in this strange land. We accepted the fact, that was all.

'Well,' said Good, 'it must be quite near us if we cut off to the right. Hadn't we better be making a start?'

This was sound advice, and as soon as we had washed our faces and hands in the stream we acted on it. For a mile or more we made our way over boulders and across patches of snow, till suddenly, on reaching the top of the little rise, we found the road at our feet. It was a splendid road cut out of the solid rock, at least fifty feet wide, and apparently well kept; though the odd thing was that it seemed to begin there. We walked down and stood on it, but one single hundred paces behind us, in the direction of Sheba's Breasts, it vanished, the entire surface of the mountain being strewn with boulders interspersed with patches of snow.

'What do you make of this, Quatermain?' asked Sir Henry.

I shook my head, I could make nothing of the thing.

'I have it!' said Good; 'the road no doubt ran right over the range and across the desert on the other side, but the sand there has covered it up, and above us it has been obliterated by some volcanic eruption of molten lava.'

This seemed a good suggestion; at any rate, we accepted it, and proceeded down the mountain. It proved a very different business travelling along down hill on that magnificent pathway with full stomachs from what it was travelling up hill over the snow quite starved and almost frozen. Indeed, had it not been for melancholy recollections of poor Ventvogel's sad fate, and of that grim cave where he kept company with the old Dom, we should have felt positively cheerful, notwithstanding the sense of unknown dangers before us. Every mile we walked the atmosphere grew softer and balmier, and the country before us shone with a yet more luminous beauty. As for the road itself, I never saw such an engineering work, though Sir Henry said that the great road over the St Gothard in Switzerland is very similar. No difficulty had been too great for the Old World engineer who laid it out. At one place we came to a ravine three hundred feet broad and at least a hundred deep. This vast gulf was actually filled in with huge blocks of dressed stone, having arches pierced through them at the bottom for a waterway, over which the road went on sublimely. At another place it was cut in zigzags out of the side of the precipice five hundred feet deep, and in a third it tunnelled through the base of an intervening ridge, a space of thirty yards or more.

Here we noticed that the sides of the tunnel were covered with quaint sculptures, mostly of mailed figures driving in chariots. One, which was exceedingly beautiful, represented a whole battle scene with a convoy of captives being marched off in the distance.

'Well,' said Sir Henry, after inspecting this ancient work of art, 'it is very well to call this Solomon's Road, but my humble opinion is that the Egyptians had been here before Solomon's people ever set foot on it. If this isn't Egyptian or Phoenician handiwork, I must say that it is very like it.'

By midday we had advanced sufficiently down the mountain to reach the region where wood was to be met with. First we came to scattered bushes which grew more and more frequent, till at last we found the road winding through a vast grove of silver trees similar to those which are to be seen on the slopes of Table Mountain at Cape Town. I had never before met with them in all my wanderings, except at the Cape, and their appearance here astonished me greatly.

'Ah!' said Good, surveying these shining-leaved trees with evident enthusiasm, 'here is lots of wood, let us stop and cook some dinner; I have about digested that raw heart.'

Nobody objected to this, so leaving the road we made our way to a stream which was babbling away not far off, and soon had a goodly fire of dry boughs blazing. Cutting off some substantial hunks from the flesh of the *inco* which we had brought with us, we proceeded to toast them on the end of sharp sticks, as one sees the Kafirs do, and ate them with relish. After filling ourselves, we lit our pipes and gave ourselves up to enjoyment that, compared with the hardships we had recently undergone, seemed almost heavenly.

The brook, of which the banks were clothed with dense masses of a gigantic species of maidenhair fern interspersed with feathery tufts of wild asparagus, sung merrily at our side, the soft air murmured through the foliage of the silver trees, doves cooed around, and bright-winged birds flashed like living gems from bough to bough. It was a Paradise.

The magic of the place combined with an overwhelming sense of dangers left behind, and of the promised land reached at last, seemed to charm us into silence. Sir Henry and Umbopa sat conversing in a mixture of broken English and Kitchen Zulu in a low voice, but earnestly enough, and I lay, with my eyes half shut, upon that fragrant bed of fern and watched them.

Presently I missed Good and looked to see what had become of him. Soon I observed him sitting by the bank of the stream, in which he had been bathing. He had nothing on but his flannel shirt, and his natural habits of extreme neatness having reasserted themselves, he was actively employed in making a most elaborate toilet. He had washed his gutta-percha collar, had thoroughly shaken out his trousers, coat and waistcoat, and was now folding them up neatly till he was ready to put them on, shaking his head sadly as he scanned the numerous rents and tears in them, which naturally had resulted from our frightful journey. Then he took his boots, scrubbed them with a handful of fern, and finally rubbed them over with a piece of fat, which he had carefully saved from the *inco* meat, till they looked, comparatively speaking, respectable. Having inspected them judicially through his eye-glass, he put the boots on and began a fresh operation. From a little bag that he carried he produced a pocket-comb in which was fixed a tiny looking-glass, and in this he surveyed himself. Apparently he was not satisfied, for he proceeded to do his hair with great care. Then came a pause whilst he again contemplated the effect; still it was not satisfactory. He felt his chin, on which the accumulated scrub of a ten days' beard was flourishing.

'Surely,' thought I, 'he is not going to try to shave.' But so it was. Taking the piece of fat with which he had greased his boots, Good washed it thoroughly in the stream. Then diving again into the bag he brought out a little pocket razor with a guard to it, such as are bought by people who are afraid of cutting themselves, or by those about to undertake a sea voyage. Then he rubbed his face and chin vigorously with the fat and began. Evidently it proved a painful process, for he groaned very much over it, and I was convulsed with inward laughter as I watched him struggling with that stubbly beard. It seemed so very odd that a man should take the trouble to shave himself with a piece of fat in such a place and in our circumstances. At last he succeeded in getting the hair off the right side of his face and chin, when suddenly I, who was watching, became conscious of a flash of light that passed just by his head.

Good sprang up with a profane exclamation (if it had not been a safety razor he would certainly have cut his throat), and so did I, without the exclamation, and this was what I saw. Standing not more than twenty paces from where I was, and ten from Good, were a group of men. They were very tall and copper coloured, and some of them wore great plumes of black feathers and short cloaks of leopard skins; this was all I noticed at the moment. In front of them stood a youth of about seventeen, his hand still raised and his body bent forward in the attitude of a Grecian statue of a spear thrower. Evidently the flash of light had been caused by a weapon which he had hurled.

As I looked an old solder-like man stepped forward out of the group, and catching the youth by the arm said something to him. Then they advanced upon us.

Sir Henry, Good, and Umbopa by this time had seized their rifles and lifted them threateningly. The party of natives still came on. It struck me that they could not know what rifles were, or they would not have treated them with such contempt.

'Put down your guns!' I halloed to the others, seeing that our only chance of safety lay in conciliation. They obeyed, and walking to the front I addressed the elderly man who had checked the youth.

'Greeting,' I said in Zulu, not knowing what language to use. To my surprise I was understood.

'Greeting,' answered the man, not, indeed, in the same tongue, but in a dialect so closely allied to it that neither Umbopa nor myself had any difficulty in understanding him. Indeed, as we afterwards found out, the language spoken by this people is an old-fashioned form of the Zulu tongue, bearing about the same relationship to it that the English of Chaucer does to the English of the nineteenth century.

'Whence come you?' he went on, 'who are you? And why are the faces of three of you white, and the face of the fourth as the face of our mother's sons?' and he pointed to Umbopa. I looked at Umbopa as he said it, and it flashed across me that he was right. The face of Umbopa was like the faces of the men before me, and so was his great form like their forms. But I had not time to reflect on this coincidence.

'We are strangers, and come in peace,' I answered, speaking very slowly, so that he might understand me, 'and this man is our servant.'

'Ye lie,' he answered; 'no strangers can cross the mountains where all things perish. But what do your lies matter? If ye are strangers then ye must die, for no strangers may live in the land of the Kukuanas. It is the king's law. Prepare then to die, O strangers!'

I was slightly staggered at this, more especially as I saw the hands of some of the men steal down to their sides, where hung on each what looked to me like a large and heavy knife.

'What does that beggar say?' asked Good.

'He says we are going to be killed,' I answered grimly.

'Oh, Lord!' groaned Good; and, as was his way when perplexed, he put his hand to his false teeth, dragging the top set down and allowing them to fly back to his jaw with a snap. It was a most fortunate move, for next second the dignified crowd of Kukuanas uttered a simultaneous yell of horror, and bolted back some yards.

'What's up?' said I.

'It's his teeth,' whispered Sir Henry excitedly. 'He moved them. Take them out, Good, take them out!'

He obeyed, slipping the set into the sleeve of his flannel shirt.

In another second curiosity had overcome fear, and the men advanced slowly. Apparently they had now forgotten their amiable intention of killing us.

'How it is, O strangers,' asked the old man solemnly, 'that this fat man (pointing to Good, who was clad in nothing but boots and a flannel shirt, and had only half finished his shaving), whose body is clothed, and whose legs are bare, who grows hair on one side of his sickly face and not on the other, and who wears one shining and transparent eye – how is it, I ask, that he has teeth which move of themselves, coming away from the jaws and returning of their own will?'

'Open your mouth,' I said to Good, who promptly curled up

his lips and grinned at the old gentleman like an angry dog, revealing to his astonished gaze two thin red lines of gum as utterly innocent of ivories as is a new-born elephant. The audience gasped.

'Where are his teeth?' they shouted; 'with our eyes we saw them.'

Turning his head slowly and with a gesture of ineffable contempt, Good swept his hand across his mouth. Then he grinned again, and lo, there were two rows of lovely teeth.

Now the young man who had flung the knife threw himself down on the grass and gave vent to a prolonged howl of terror; and as for the old gentleman, his knees knocked together with fear.

'I see that ye are spirits,' he said falteringly; 'did ever man born of woman have hair on one side of his face and not on the other, or a round and transparent eye, or teeth which moved and melted away and grew again? Pardon us, O my lords.'

Here was luck indeed, and, needless to say, I jumped at the chance.

'It is granted,' I said with an imperial smile. 'Nay, ye shall know the truth. We come from another world, though we are men such as ye; we come,' I went on, 'from the biggest star that shines at night.'

'Oh! oh!' groaned the chorus of astonished aborigines.

'Yes,' I went on, 'we do, indeed'; and again I smiled benignly, as I uttered that amazing lie. 'We come to stay with you a little while, and to bless you by our sojourn. Ye will see, O friends, that I have prepared myself for this visit by the learning of your language.'

'It is so, it is so,' said the chorus.

'Only, my lord,' put in the old gentleman, 'thou hast learnt it very badly.'

I cast an indignant glance at him, and he quailed.

'Now, friends,' I continued, 'ye might think that after so long a journey we should find it in our hearts to avenge such a reception, mayhap to strike cold in death the impious hand that – that, in short – threw a knife at the head of him whose teeth come and go.'

'Spare him, my lords,' said the old man in supplication; 'he is the king's son, and I am his uncle. If anything befalls him his blood will be required at my hands.'

'Yes, that is certainly so,' put in the young man with great emphasis.

'Ye may perhaps doubt our power to avenge,' I went on heedless of this by-play. 'Stay, I will show you. Here, thou dog and slave (addressing Umbopa in a savage tone), give me the magic tube that speaks;' and I tipped a wink towards my express rifle.

Umbopa rose to the occasion. With something as nearly resembling a grin as I have ever seen on his dignified face he handed me the gun.

'It is here, O Lord of Lords,' he said with a deep obeisance.

Now just before I asked for the rifle I had perceived a little *klipspringer* antelope standing on a mass of rock about seventy yards away, and determined to risk the shot.

'Ye see that buck,' I said, pointing the animal out to the party before me. 'Tell me, is it possible for man born of woman to kill it from here with a noise?'

'It is not possible, my lord,' answered the old man.

'Yet shall I kill it,' I said quietly.

The old man smiled. 'That my lord cannot do,' he answered.

I raised the rifle and covered the buck. It was a small animal, and one which a man might well be excused for missing, but I knew that it would not do to miss.

I drew a deep breath, and slowly pressed on the trigger. The buck stood still as a stone.

'Bang! thud!' The antelope sprang in the air and fell on the rock dead as a door nail.

A simultaneous groan of terror burst from the group before us.

'If you want meat,' I remarked coolly, 'go fetch that buck.'

The old man made a sign; one of his followers departed, and presently returned bearing the *klipspringer*. I noticed with satisfaction that I had hit it fairly behind the shoulder. They gathered round the poor creature's body, gazing at the bullet-hole in consternation.

'Ye see,' I said, 'I do not speak empty words.'

There was no answer.

'If ye yet doubt our power,' I went on. 'let one of you go stand upon that rock that I may make him as this buck.'

None of them seemed at all inclined to take the hint till at last the king's son spoke.

'It is well said. Do thou, my uncle, go stand upon the rock. It is but a buck that the magic has killed. Surely it cannot kill a man.'

The old gentleman did not take the suggestion in good part. Indeed, he seemed hurt.

'No! no!' he ejaculated hastily, 'my old eyes have seen enough. These are wizards, indeed. Let us bring them to the king. Yet if any should wish a further proof, let *him* stand upon the rock, that the magic tube may speak with him.'

There was a most general and hasty expression of dissent.

'Let not good magic be wasted on our poor bodies,' said one; 'we are satisfied. All the witchcraft of our people cannot show the like of this.'

'It is so,' remarked the old gentleman, in a tone of intense relief; 'without any doubt it is so. Listen, children of the Stars, children of the shining Eye and the movable Teeth, who roar out in thunder and slay from afar. I am Infadoos, son of Kafa, once king of the Kukuana people. This youth is Scragga.'

'He nearly scragged me,' murmured Good.

'Scragga, son of Twala, the great king – Twala, husband of a thousand wives, chief and lord paramount of the Kukuanas, keeper of the great Road, terror of his enemies, student of the Black Arts, leader of a hundred thousand warriors, Twala the One-eyed, the Black, the Terrible.'

'So,' said I superciliously, 'lead us then to Twala. We do not talk with low people and underlings.'

'It is well, my lords, we will lead you; but the way is long. We are hunting three days' journey from the place of the king. But let my lords have patience, and we will lead them.'

'So be it,' I said carelessly; 'all time is before us, for we do not

die. We are ready; lead on. But Infadoos, and thou Scragga, beware!
Play us no monkey tricks, set for us no foxes' snares, for before your
brains of mud have thought of them we shall know and avenge. The
light from the transparent eye of him with the bare legs and the
half-haired face shall destroy you, and go through your land; his
vanishing teeth shall fix themselves fast in you and eat you up, you
and your wives and children; the magic tubes shall argue with you
loudly, and make you as sieves. Beware!'

This magnificent address did not fail of its effect; indeed, it
might almost have been spared, so deeply were our friends already
impressed with our powers.

The old man made a deep obeisance, and murmured the words,
'*Koom*! *Koom*!' which I afterwards discovered was their royal salute,
corresponding to the *Bayete* of the Zulus, and turning, addressed
his followers. These at once proceeded to lay hold of all our goods
and chattels, in order to bear them for us, excepting only the guns,
which they would on no account touch. They even seized Good's
clothes, that, as the reader may remember, were neatly folded up
beside him.

He saw and made a dive for them, and a loud altercation
ensued.

'Let not my lord of the transparent Eye and the melting Teeth
touch them,' said the old man. 'Surely his slave shall carry the
things.'

'But I want to put 'em on!' roared Good, in nervous English.
Umbopa translated.

'Nay, my lord,' answered Infadoos; 'would my lord cover up
his beautiful white legs (although he is so dark Good has a singu-
larly white skin) from the eyes of his servants? Have we offended
my lord that he should do such a thing?'

Here I nearly exploded with laughing; and meanwhile one of
the men started on with the garments.

'Damn it!' roared Good, 'that black villain has got my trousers.'

'Look here, Good,' said Sir Henry; 'you have appeared in this
country in a certain character, and you must live up to it. It will

never do for you to put on trousers again. Henceforth you must exist in a flannel shirt, a pair of boots, and an eye-glass.'

'Yes,' I said, 'and with whiskers on one side of your face and not on the other. If you change any of these things the people will think that we are impostors. I am very sorry for you, but, seriously, you must. If once they begin to suspect us our lives will not be worth a brass farthing.'

'Do you really think so?' asked Good gloomily.

'I do, indeed. Your "beautiful white legs" and your eye-glass are now *the* features of our party, and as Sir Henry says, you must live up to them. Be thankful that you have got your boots on, and that the air is warm.'

Good sighed, and said no more, but it took him a fortnight to become accustomed to his new and scant attire.

CHAPTER 8

We Enter Kukuanaland

All that afternoon we travelled along the magnificent roadway, which trended steadily in a north-westerly direction. Infadoos and Scragga walked with us, but their followers marched about one hundred paces ahead.

'Infadoos,' I said at length, 'who made this road?'

'It was made, my lord, of old time, none know how or when, not even the wise woman Gagool, who has lived for generations. We are not old enough to remember its making. None can fashion such roads now, but the king suffers no grass to grow upon it.'

'And whose are the writings on the wall of the caves through which we have passed on the road?' I asked referring to the Egyptian-like sculptures that we had seen.

'My lord, the hands that made the road wrote the wonderful writings. We know not who wrote them.'

'When did the Kukuana people come into this country?'

'My lord, the race came down hither like the breath of a storm ten thousand thousand moons ago, from the great lands which lie there beyond,' and he pointed to the north. 'They could travel no farther because of the high mountains which ring in the land, so say the old voices of our fathers that have descended to us the children, and so says Gagool, the wise woman, the smeller-out of witches,' and again he pointed to the snow-clad peaks. 'The country, too, was good, so they settled here and grew strong and powerful, and now our numbers are like the sea sand, and when Twala the king calls up his regiments their plumes cover the plain so far as the eye of man can reach.'

'And if the land is walled in with mountains, who is there for the regiments to fight with?'

'Nay, my lord, the country is open there towards the north, and now and again warriors sweep down upon us in clouds from a land we know not, and we slay them. It is the third part of the life of a man since there was a war. Many thousands died in it, but we destroyed those who came to eat us up. So since then there has been no war.'

'Your warriors must grow weary of resting on their spears, Infadoos.'

'My lord, there was one war, just after we destroyed the people that came down upon us, but it was a civil war; dog ate dog.'

'How was that?'

'My lord, the king, my half-brother, had a brother born at the same birth, and of the same woman. It is not our custom, my lord, to suffer twins to live; the weaker must always die. But the mother of the king hid away the feebler child, which was born the last, for her heart yearned over it, and that child is Twala the king. I am his brother, born of another wife.'

'Well?'

'My lord, Kafa, our father, died when we came to manhood, and my brother Imotu was made king in his place, and for a space reigned and had a son by his favourite wife. When the babe was three years old, just after the great war, during which no man could sow or reap, a famine came upon the land, and the people murmured because of the famine, and looked round like a starved lion for something to rend. Then it was that Gagool, the wise and terrible woman, who does not die, made a proclamation to the people, saying, "The king Imotu is no king." And at the time Imotu was sick with a wound, and lay in his kraal not able to move.

'Then Gagool went into the hut and led out Twala, my half-brother, and twin brother to the king, whom she had hidden among the caves and rocks since he was born, and stripping the *"moocha"* (waist-cloth) off his loins, showed the people of the Kukuanas the mark of the sacred snake coiled round his middle, wherewith the eldest son of the king is marked at birth, and cried out loud, "Behold your king whom I have saved for you even to this day!"

'Now the people being mad with hunger, and altogether bereft of reason and the knowledge of truth, cried out – *"The King! The king!"* but I knew that it was not so, for Imotu my brother was the elder of the twins, and our lawful king. Then just as the tumult was at its height Imotu the king, though he was very sick, crawled from his hut holding his wife by the hand, and followed by his little son Ignosi – that is, by interpretation, the Lightning.

'"What is this noise?" he asked. "Why cry ye *The king! The king!*"

'Then Twala, his own brother, born of the same woman, and in the same hour, ran to him, and taking him by the hair, stabbed him through the heart with his knife. And the people being fickle, and ever ready to worship the rising sun, clapped their hands and cried, "*Twala is king!* Now we know that Twala is king!"'

'And what became of Imotu's wife and her son Ignosi? Did Twala kill them too?'

'Nay, my lord. When she saw that her lord was dead the queen seized the child with a cry and ran away. Two days afterwards she came to a kraal very hungry, and none would give her milk or food, now that her lord the king was dead, for all men hate the unfortunate. But at nightfall a little child, a girl, crept out and brought her corn to eat, and she blessed the child, and went on towards the mountains with her boy before the sun rose again. There she must have perished, for none have seen her since, nor the child Ignosi.'

'Then if this child Ignosi had lived he would be the true king of the Kukuana people?'

'That is so, my lord; the sacred snake is round his middle. If he lives he is king; but, alas! he is long dead.'

'See, my lord,' and Infadoos pointed to a vast collection of huts surrounded by a fence, which was in its turn encircled by a great ditch, that lay on the plain beneath us. 'That is the kraal where the wife of Imotu was last seen with the child Ignosi. It is there that we shall sleep to-night, if, indeed,' he added doubtfully, 'my lords sleep at all upon this earth.'

'When we are among the Kukuanas, my good friend Infadoos, we do as the Kukuanas do,' I said majestically, and turned round quickly to address Good, who was tramping along sullenly behind, his mind fully occupied with unsatisfactory attempts to prevent his flannel shirt from flapping in the evening breeze. To my astonishment I butted into Umbopa, who was walking along immediately behind me, and very evidently had been listening with the greatest interest to my conversation with Infadoos The expression on his face was most curious, and gave. me the idea of a man who was struggling with partial success to bring something long ago forgotten back into his mind.

All this while we had been pressing on at a good rate towards the undulating plain beneath us. The mountains we had crossed now loomed high above our heads, and Sheba's Breasts were veiled modestly in diaphanous wreaths of mist. As we went the country grew more and more lovely. The vegetation was luxuriant, without being tropical; the sun was bright and warm, but not burning; and a gracious breeze blew softly along the odorous slopes of the mountains. Indeed, this new land was little less than an earthly paradise; in beauty, in natural wealth, and in climate I have never seen its like. The Transvaal is a fine country in parts, but it is nothing to Kukuana-land.

So soon as we started, Infadoos had despatched a runner to warn the people of the kraal, which, by the way, was in his military command, of our arrival. This man had departed at an extraordinary speed, which Infadoos informed me he would keep up all the way, as running was an exercise much practised among his people.

The result of this message now became apparent. When we arrived within two miles of the kraal we could see that company after company of men were issuing from its gates and marching towards us.

Sir Henry laid his hand upon my arm, and remarked that it looked as though we were going to meet with a warm reception. Something in his tone attracted Infadoos' attention.

'Let not my lords be afraid,' he said hastily, 'for in my breast there dwells no guile. This regiment is one under my command, and comes out by my orders to greet you.'

I nodded easily, though I was not quite easy in my mind.

About half a mile from the gates of this kraal is a long stretch of rising ground sloping gently upwards from the road, and here the companies formed. It was a splendid sight to see them, each company about three hundred strong, charging swiftly up the rise, with flashing spears and waving plumes, to take their appointed place. By the time we reached the slope twelve such companies, or in all three thousand six hundred men, had passed out and taken up their positions along the road.

Presently we came to the first company, and were able to gaze in astonishment on the most magnificent set of warriors that I have ever seen. They were all men of mature age, mostly veterans of about forty, and not one of them was under six feet in height, whilst many stood six feet three or four. They wore upon their heads heavy black plumes of Sakaboola feathers, like those which adorned our guides. About their waists and beneath the right knees were bound circlets of white ox tails, while in their left hands they carried round shields measuring about twenty inches across. These shields are very curious. The framework is made of an iron plate beaten out thin, over which is stretched milk-white ox-hide.

The weapons that each man bore were simple, but most effective, consisting of a short and very heavy two-edged spear with a wooden shaft, the blade being about six inches across at the widest part. These spears are not used for throwing, but like the Zulu *'bangwan,'* or stabbing assegai, are for close quarters only, when the wound inflicted by them is terrible. In addition to his *bangwan* every man carried three large and heavy knives, each knife weighing about two pounds. One knife was fixed in the ox-tail girdle, and the other two at the back of the round shield. These knives, which are called 'tollas' by the Kukuanas, take the place of the throwing assegai of the Zulus. The Kukuana warriors can cast them with great accuracy to a distance of fifty yards, and it is their custom on charging to hurl a volley of them at the enemy as they come to close quarters.

Each company remained still as a collection of bronze statues till we were opposite to it. Then at a signal given by its commanding officer, who, distinguished by a leopard-skin cloak, stood some places in front, every spear was raised into the air, and from three hundred throats sprang forth with a sudden roar the royal salute of 'Koom.' So soon as we had passed, the company formed up behind us and followed us towards the kraal, till at last the whole regiment of the 'Greys' – thus called from their white shields – the crack corps of the Kukuana people, was marching in our rear with a tread that shook the ground.

At length, branching off from Solomon's Great Road, we came to the wide fosse surrounding the kraal, which is at least a mile round, and fenced with a strong palisade of piles formed of the trunks of trees. At the gateway this fosse is spanned by a primitive drawbridge, which was let down by the guard to allow us to pass in. The kraal is exceedingly well laid out. Through the centre runs a wide pathway intersected at right angles by other pathways so arranged as to cut the huts into square blocks, each block being the quarters of a company. The huts are dome-shaped, and built, like those of the Zulus, of a frame-work of wattle, beautifully thatched with grass; but, unlike the Zulu huts, they have doorways through which men can walk. Also they are much larger, and surrounded by a veranda about six feet wide, beautifully paved with powdered lime trodden hard.

All along each side of this wide pathway that pierces the kraal were ranged hundreds of women, brought out by curiosity to look at us. These women, for a native race, are exceedingly handsome. They are tall and graceful, and their figures are wonderfully fine. The hair, though short, is rather curly than woolly, the features are frequently aquiline, and the lips are not unpleasantly thick, as is the case among most African races. But what struck us most was their exceedingly quiet and dignified air. They were as well-bred in their way as the *habituées* of a fashionable drawing-room, and in this respect they differ from Zulu women and their cousins the Masai who inhabit the district behind Zanzibar. Their curiosity had brought them out to see us, but they allowed no rude expressions of astonishment or savage criticism to pass their lips as we trudged wearily in front of them. Not even when old Infadoos with a surreptitious motion of his hand pointed out the crowning wonder of poor Good's 'beautiful white legs,' did they suffer the feelings of intense admiration which evidently mastered their minds to find expression. They fixed their dark eyes upon this new and snowy loveliness, for, as I think I have said, Good's skin is exceedingly white, and that was all. But it was quite enough for Good, who is modest by nature.

When we reached the centre of the kraal, Infadoos halted at the door of a large hut, which was surrounded at a distance by a circle of smaller ones.

'Enter, Sons of the Stars,' he said in a magniloquent voice, 'and deign to rest awhile in our humble habitations. A little food shall be brought to you, so that ye may have no need to draw your belt tight from hunger; some honey and some milk, and an ox or two, and a few sheep; not much, my lords, but still a little food.'

'It is good,' said I. 'Infadoos, we are weary with travelling through realms of air; now let us rest.'

Accordingly we entered into the hut, which we found amply prepared for our comfort. Couches of tanned skins were spread for us to lie on, and water was placed for us to wash in.

Presently we heard a shouting outside, and stepping to the door, saw a line of damsels bearing milk and roasted mealies, and honey in a pot. Behind these was some youths driving a fat young ox. We received the gifts, and then one of the young men drew a knife from his girdle and dexterously cut the ox's throat. In ten minutes it was dead, skinned, and jointed. The best of the meat was then cut off for us, and the rest, in the name of our party, I presented to the warriors round us, who took it and distributed the 'white lords' gift.'

Umbopa set to work, with the assistance of an extremely prepossessing young woman, to boil our portion in a large earthenware pot over a fire which was built outside the hut, and when it was nearly ready we sent a message to Infadoos, and asked him and Scragga, the king's son, to join us.

Presently they came, and sitting down upon little stools, of which there were several about the hut, for the Kukuanas do not in general squat upon their haunches like the Zulus, they helped us to get through our dinner. The old gentleman was most affable and polite, but it struck me that the young one regarded us with doubt. Together with the rest of the party, he had been overawed by our white appearance and by our magic properties; but it seemed to me that, on discovering that we ate, drank, and slept like other mortals, his awe was beginning to wear off, and to be replaced by a sullen suspicion – which made me feel rather uncomfortable.

In the course of our meals Sir Henry suggested to me that it might be well to try to discover if our hosts knew anything of his brother's fate, or if they had ever seen or heard of him; but, on the whole, I thought that it would be wiser to say nothing of the matter at this time. It was difficult to explain a relative lost from 'the Stars.'

After supper we produced our pipes and lit them; a proceeding which filled Infadoos and Scragga with astonishment. The Kukuanas were evidently unacquainted with the divine delights of tobacco-smoke. The herb is grown among them extensively; but, like the Zulus, they use it for snuff only, and quite failed to identify it in its new form.

Presently I asked Infadoos when we were to proceed on our journey, and was delighted to learn that preparations had been made for us to leave on the following morning, messengers having already departed to inform Twala the king of our coming.

It appeared that Twala was at his principal place, known as Loo, making ready for the great annual feast which was to be held in the first week of June. At this gathering all the regiments, with the exception of certain detachments left behind for garrison purposes, are brought up and paraded before the king; and the great annual witch-hunt, of which more by-and-by, is held.

We were to start at dawn; and Infadoos, who was to accompany us, expected that we should reach Loo on the night of the second day, unless we were detained by accident or by swollen rivers.

When they had given us this information our visitors bade us good night; and, having arranged to watch turn and turn about, three of us flung ourselves down and slept the sweet sleep of the weary, whilst the fourth sat up on the look-out for possible treachery.

CHAPTER 9

Twala the King

It will not be necessary for me to detail at length the incidents of our journey to Loo. It took two full days' travelling along Solomon's Great Road, which pursued its even course right into the heart of Kukuanaland. Suffice it to say that as we went the country seemed to grow richer and richer, and the kraal, with their wide surrounding belts of cultivation, more and more numerous. They were all built upon the same principles as the first camp which we had reached, and were guarded by ample garrisons of troops. Indeed, in Kukuanaland, as among the Germans, the Zulus, and the Masai, every able-bodied man is a soldier, so that the whole force of the nation is available for its wars, offensive or defensive. As we travelled we were overtaken by thousands of warriors hurrying up to Loo to be present at the great annual review and festival, and more splendid troops I never saw.

At sunset on the second day, we stopped to rest awhile upon the summit of some heights over which the road ran, and there on a beautiful and fertile plain before us lay Loo itself. For a native town it is an enormous place, quite five miles round, I should say, with outlying kraals projecting from it, that serve on grand occasions as cantonments for the regiments, and a curious horseshoe-shaped hill, with which we were destined to become better acquainted, about two miles to the north. It is beautifully situated, and through the centre of the kraal, dividing it into two portions, runs a river, which appeared to be bridged in several places, the same indeed that we had seen from the slopes of Sheba's Breasts. Sixty or seventy miles away three great snow-capped mountains, placed at the points of a triangle, started out of the level plain. The conformation of these mountains is unlike that of Sheba's Breasts, being sheer and precipitous, instead of smooth and rounded.

Infadoos saw us looking at them, and volunteered a remark.

'The road ends there,' he said, pointing to these mountains which are known among the Kukuanas as the 'Three Witches.'

'Why does it end?' I asked.

'Who knows?' he answered with a shrug; 'the mountains are full of caves, and there is a great pit between them. It is there that the wise men of old time used to go to get whatever it was they came for to this country, and now it is there that our kings are buried in the Place of Death.'

'What was it they came for?' I asked eagerly.

'Nay, I know not. My lords who have dropped from the stars should know,' he answered with a quick look. Evidently he knew more than he chose to say.

'Yes,' I went on, 'you are right; in the Stars we learn many things. I have heard, for instance, that the wise men of old came to these mountains to find bright stones, pretty playthings, and yellow iron.'

'My lord is wise,' he answered coldly; 'I am but a child and cannot talk with my lord on such matters. My lord must speak with Gagool the old, at the king's place, who is wise as my lord,' and he went away.

So soon as he was gone I turned to the others, and pointed out the mountains. 'There are Solomon's diamond mines,' I said.

Umbopa was standing with them, apparently plunged in one of the fits of abstraction which were common to him, and caught my words.

'Yes, Macumazahn,' he put in, in Zulu, 'the diamonds are surely there, and you shall have them, since you white men are so fond of toys and money.'

'How dost thou know that, Umbopa?' I asked sharply, for I did not like his mysterious ways.

He laughed. 'I dreamed it in the night, white men,' he said. Then he turned on his heel and went.

'Now what,' said Sir Henry, 'is our black friend driving at? He knows more than he chooses to say, that is clear. By the way, Quatermain, has he heard anything of – of my brother?

'Nothing; he has asked everyone he became friendly with, but they declare that no white man has ever been seen in the country before.'

'Do you suppose that he got here at all?' suggested Good; 'we have only fetched up by a miracle; is it likely he could have reached it without the map?'

'I don't know,' said Sir Henry gloomily, 'but somehow I think that I shall find him.'

Slowly the sun sank, then sudden darkness rushed down on the land like a tangible thing. There was no breathing-space between the day and night, no soft transformation scene, for in these latitudes twilight does not exist. The change from day to night is as quick and as absolute as the change from life to death. The sun sank and the world was wreathed in shadows. But not for long, for see in the west there is a glow, then come rays of silver light, and at last the full and glorious moon lights up the plain and shoots its gleaming arrows far and wide, filling the earth with a faint refulgence.

We stood and watched the lovely sight, whilst the stars grew pale before this chastened majesty, and felt our hearts lifted up in the presence of a beauty that I cannot describe. Mine has been a rough life, but there are a few things for which I am thankful to have lived, and one of them is to have seen that moon shine over Kukuana-land.

Presently our meditations were broken in upon by our polite friend Infadoos.

'If my lords are rested we will journey on to Loo, where a hut is made ready for my lords to-night. The moon is now bright, so that we shall not fall by the way.'

We assented, and in an hour's time were at the outskirts of the town, of which the extent, mapped out as it was by thousands of camp fires, appeared absolutely endless. Indeed, Good, who is always fond of a bad joke, christened it 'Unlimited Loo.' Soon we came to a moat with a drawbridge, where we were met by the rattling of arms and the hoarse challenge of a sentry. Infadoos gave some password that I could not catch, which was met with a salute, and we marched on through the central street of the great grass city. After nearly half an hour's tramp, past endless lines of huts, Infadoos halted at last by the gate of a little group of huts which surrounded a small courtyard of powdered limestone, and informed us that these were to be our 'poor' quarters.

We entered, and found that a hut had been assigned to each of us. These huts were superior to any that we had yet seen, and in each was a most comfortable bed made of tanned skins, spread upon mattresses of aromatic grass. Food too was ready for us, and so soon as we had washed ourselves with water, which stood ready in earthenware jars, some young women of handsome appearance brought us roasted meats, and mealie cobs daintily served on wooden platters, and presented them to us with deep obeisances.

We ate and drank, and then, the beds having been all moved into one hut by our request, a precaution at which the amiable young ladies smiled, we flung ourselves down to sleep, thoroughly wearied with our long journey.

When we woke it was to find the sun high in the heavens, and our female attendants, who did not seem to be troubled by any false shame, already standing inside the hut, having been ordered to attend and help us to 'make ready.'

'Make ready, indeed,' growled Good; 'when one has only a flannel shirt and a pair of boots, that does not take long. I wish you would ask them for my trousers, Quatermain.'

I asked accordingly, but was informed that these sacred relics had already been taken to the king who would see us in the forenoon.

Having requested the young ladies to step outside, somewhat to their astonishment and disappointment, we proceeded to make the best toilet of which the circumstances admitted. Good even went the length of again shaving the right side of his face; the left, on which now appeared a very fair crop of whiskers, we impressed upon him he must on no account touch. Curtis and I were contented with a good wash and combing our hair. Sir Henry's yellow locks were now almost upon his shoulders, and he looked more like an ancient Dane than ever, while my grizzled scrub was fully an inch long, instead of half an inch, which in a general way I considered my maximum length.

By the time that we had eaten our breakfasts, and smoked a pipe, a message was brought to us by Infadoos himself to the effect that Twala the king was ready to see us, if we would be pleased to come.

We remarked in reply that we should prefer to wait till the sun was a little higher, we were yet weary with our journey, &c., &c. It is always well, when dealing with uncivilised people, not to be in too great a hurry. They are apt to mistake politeness for awe or servility. So although we were quite as anxious to see Twala as Twala could be to see us, we sat down and waited for an hour, employing the interval in preparing such presents as our slender stock of goods permitted – namely, the Winchester rifle which had been used by poor Ventvögel, and some beads. The rifle and ammunition we determined to present to his royal highness, and the beads were for his wives and courtiers. We had already given a few to Infadoos and Scragga, and found that they were delighted with them, never having seen such things before. At length we declared that we were ready, and guided by Infadoos, started off to the audience, Umbopa carrying the rifle and beads.

After walking a few hundred yards we came to an enclosure, something like that surrounding the huts which had been allotted to us, only fifty times as big, for it could not have covered less than six or seven acres of ground. All round the outside fence stood a row of huts, which were the habitations of the king's wives. Exactly opposite the gateway, on the farther side of the open space, was a very large hut, built by itself, in which his majesty resided. All the rest was open ground; that is to say, it would have been open had it not been filled by company after company of warriors, who were mustered there to the number of seven or eight thousand. These men stood still as statues as we advanced through them, and it would be impossible to give an adequate idea of the grandeur of the spectacle which they presented, with their waving plumes, their glancing spears, and iron-backed ox-hide shields.

The space in front of the large hut was empty, but before it were placed several stools. On three of these at a sign from Infadoos, we seated ourselves, Umbopa standing behind us. As for Infadoos, he took up a position by the door of the hut. So we waited for ten minutes or more in the midst of a dead silence, but conscious that we were the object of the concentrated gaze of some eight thousand pairs of eyes. It was a somewhat trying ordeal, but we went through it as best we could. At length the door of the hut opened, and a gigantic figure, having a splendid tiger-skin karross flung over its shoulders, stepped out, followed by the boy Scragga, and what appeared to us to be a withered-up monkey, wrapped in a fur cloak. The figure seated itself upon a stool, Scragga took his stand behind it, and the withered-up monkey crept on all fours into the shade of the hut and squatted down.

Still there was silence.

Then the gigantic figure slipped off the karross and stood up before us, a truly alarming spectacle. It was that of an enormous man with the most entirely repulsive countenance we had ever beheld. This man's lips were thick as a negro's, the nose was flat, he had but one gleaming black eye, for the other was represented by a hollow in the face, and his whole expression was cruel and sensual to a degree. From the large head rose a magnificent plume of white ostrich feathers, his body was clad in a shirt of shining chain armour, whilst round the waist and right knee were the usual circlets of white ox-tails. In his right hand he held a huge spear, about the neck was a thick torque of gold, and bound on the fore-head shone a single and enormous uncut diamond.

Still there was silence; but not for long. Presently this man, whom we rightly guessed to be the king, raised the great javelin in his hand. Instantly eight thousand spears were lifted in answer, and from eight thousand throats rang out the royal salute of *'Koom'* Three times this was repeated, and each time the earth shook with the noise, that can only be compared to the deepest notes of thunder.

'Be humble, O people!' piped out a thin voice which seemed to come from the monkey in the shade, 'it is the king!'

'It is the king!' boomed the answer from eight thousand throats. *'Be humble, O people, it is the king!'*

Then there was silence again – dead silence. Presently, however, it was broken. A soldier on our left dropped his shield, which fell with a clatter to the limestone flooring.

Twala turned his one fierce eye in the direction of the noise.

'Come hither, thou,' he said, in a cold voice.

A fine young man stepped out of the ranks, and stood before him.

'It was thy shield that fell, thou awkward dog. Wilt thou make me a reproach in the eyes of these strangers from the Stars? What has thou to say for thyself?'

We saw the poor fellow turn pale under his dusky skin.

'It was by chance, O Calf of the Black Cow,' he murmured.

'Then it is a chance for which thou must pay. Thou hast made me foolish; prepare for death.'

'I am the king's ox,' was the low answer.

'Scragga,' roared the king, 'let me see how thou canst use thy spear. Kill me this blundering fool.'

Scragga stepped forward with an ill-favoured grin, and lifted his spear. The poor victim covered his eyes with his hand and stood still. As for us, we were petrified with horror.

'Once, twice,' he waved the spear and then struck, ah! right home – the spear stood out a foot behind the soldier's back. He flung up his hands and dropped dead. From the multitude about us rose something like a murmur, it rolled round and round, and died away. The tragedy was finished; there lay the corpse, and we had not yet realised that it had been enacted. Sir Henry sprang up and swore a great oath, then, overpowered by the sense of silence, sat down again.

'The thrust was a good one,' said the king; 'take him away.'

Four men stepped out of the ranks, and lifting the body of the murdered man, carried it thence.

'Cover up the bloodstains, yes, cover them up,' piped the thin voice that proceeded from the monkey-like figure; 'the king's word is spoken, the king's doom is done!'

Thereupon a girl came forward from behind the hut, bearing a jar filled with powdered lime, which she scattered over the red mark, blotting it from sight.

Sir Henry meanwhile was boiling with rage at what had happened; indeed, it was with difficulty that we could keep him still.

'Sit down, for heaven's sake,' I whispered; 'our lives depend on it.'

He yielded and remained quiet.

Twala sat silent until the traces of the tragedy had been removed, then he addressed us.

'White people,' he said, 'who come hither, whence I know not, and why I know not, greeting.'

'Greeting Twala, King of the Kukuanas,' I answered.

'White people, whence come ye, and what seek ye?'

'We come from the Stars, ask us not how. We come to see this land.'

'Ye journey from far to see a little thing. And that man with you,' pointing to Umbopa, 'does he also come from the Stars?'

'Even so; there are people of thy colour in the heavens above; but ask not of matters too high for thee, Twala the king.'

'Ye speak with a loud voice, people of the Stars,' Twala answered in a tone which I scarcely liked. 'Remember that the Stars are far off, and ye are here. How if I make you as him whom they bore away?'

I laughed out loud, though there was little laughter in my heart.

'O king,' I said, 'be careful, walk warily over hot stones, lest thou shouldst burn thy feet; hold the spear by the handle lest thou shouldst cut thy hands. Touch but one hair of our heads, and destruction shall come upon thee. What, have not these' – pointing to Infadoos and Scragga, who, young villain that he was, was employed in cleaning the blood of the soldier off his spear? – ' told thee what manner of men we are? Hast thou seen the like of us?' and I pointed to Good, feeling quite sure that he had never seen anybody before in the least resembling the Captain as he then appeared.

'It is true, I have not,' said the king, surveying Good with intense interest.

'Have they not told thee how we strike with death from afar?' I went on.

'They have told me, but I believe them not. Let me see you kill. Kill me a man among those who stand yonder' – and he pointed to the opposite side of the kraal – 'and I will believe.'

'Nay,' I answered; 'we shed no blood of men except in just punishment. Yet if thou wilt see, bid thy servants drive an ox through the kraal gates, and before he has run twenty paces I will strike him dead.'

'Nay,' laughed the king, 'kill me a man and I will believe.'

'Good, O king, so be it,' I answered coolly; 'do thou walk across the open space and before thy feet reach the gate thou shalt be dead; or if thou wilt not, send thy son Scragga' (whom at that moment it would have given me much pleasure to shoot).

On hearing this suggestion Scragga uttered a sort of howl, and bolted into the hut.

Twala frowned majestically; the suggestion did not please him.

'Let a young ox be driven in,' he said.

Two men at once departed, running swiftly.

'Now, Sir Henry,' said I, 'do you shoot. I want to show this ruffian that I am not the only magician of the party, and we can't trust Good.'

Sir Henry accordingly took his 'express,' and made ready.

'I hope I shall make a good shot,' he groaned.

'You must,' I answered. 'If you miss with the first barrel, let him have the second. Sight for one hundred and fifty yards, and wait till the beast turns broadside on.'

Then came a pause, until presently we caught sight of an ox running straight for the kraal gate. It came on through the gate, then, catching sight of the vast concourse of people, stopped stupidly, turned round, and bellowed.

'Now's your time,' I whispered.

Up went the rifle.

Bang! *thud!* and the ox was kicking on his back, shot in the ribs. The semi-hollow bullet had done its work well, and a sigh of astonishment went up from the assembled thousands.

I turned round coolly –

'Have I lied, O king?'

'Nay, white man, it is the truth,' was the somewhat awed answer.

'Listen, Twala,' I went on. 'Thou hast seen. Now know we come in peace, not in war. See,' and I held up the Winchester repeater; 'here is a hollow staff that shall enable thee to kill even as we kill, only I lay this charm upon it, thou shalt kill no man with it. If thou liftest it against a man, it shall kill thee. Stay, I will show thee. Bid a soldier step forty paces and place the shaft of a spear in the ground so that the flat blade looks towards us.'

In a few seconds it was done.

'Now, see, I will break yonder spear.'

Taking a careful sight I fired. The bullet struck the flat of the spear, and shattered the blade into fragments.

Again the sigh of astonishment went up.

'Now, Twala, we give this magic tube to thee. By-and-by I will show thee how to use it; but beware how thou turnest the magic of the Stars against a man of earth,' and I handed him the rifle.

The king took it very gingerly and laid it down at his feet. As he did so I observed the wizened, monkey-like figure creeping from the shadow of the hut. It crept on all fours, but when it reached the place where the king sat it rose upon its feet, and throwing the furry covering from its face, revealed a most extraordinary and weird countenance. Apparently it was that of a woman of great age so shrunken that in size it seemed little larger than the face of a year-old child, but made up of countless deep and yellow wrinkles. Set among these wrinkles was a sunken slit that represented the mouth, beneath which the chin curved outwards to a point. There was no nose to speak of; indeed, the visage might have been taken for that of a sun-dried corpse, had it not been for a pair of large black eyes, still full of fire and intelligence, which gleamed and played under the snow-white eyebrows, and the projecting parchment-coloured skull, like jewels in a charnel-house. The head itself was perfectly bare, and yellow in hue, while the naked wrinkled scalp moved and contracted like the head of a cobra.

The figure to which this fearful countenance belonged, a countenance so fearful indeed that it caused a shiver of fear to pass through us as we gazed on it, stood still for a moment. Then suddenly it projected a skinny claw armed with nails nearly an inch long, and laying it on the shoulder of Twala the king, began to speak in a thin and piercing voice –

'Listen, O king! Listen, O warriors! Listen, O mountains and plains and rivers, home of the Kukuana race! Listen, O stars and sun, O rain and storm and mist! Listen, O men and matrons, O youths and maidens and O ye babes unborn! Listen, all things that live and must die! Listen, all dead things that shall live again – again to die! Listen, the spirit of life is in me, and I prophesy. I prophesy! I prophesy!'

The words died away in a faint wail, and dread seemed to seize upon the hearts of all who heard them, including our own. This old woman was very terrible.

'*Blood! blood! blood!* rivers of blood; blood everywhere. I see it, I smell it, I taste it – it is salt; it runs red upon the ground, it rains down from the skies.

'*Footsteps! footsteps! footsteps!* the tread of the white man coming from afar. It shakes the earth; the earth trembles before her master.

'Blood is good, the red blood is bright; there is no smell like the smell of new-shed blood. The lions shall lap it, and roar, the vultures shall wash their wings in it and shriek with joy.

'I am old! I am old! I have seen much blood; *ha, ha!* but I shall see more ere I die, and be merry. How old am I, think ye? Your grandfathers knew me, and *their* fathers knew me, and *their* fathers' fathers' fathers. I have seen the white man and his desires. I am old, but the mountains are older than I. Who made the great road, tell me? Who wrote the pictures on the rocks, tell me? Who reared up the three Silent Ones yonder, that gaze across the pit, tell me?' and she pointed towards the three precipitous mountains which we had noticed on the previous night.

'Ye know not, but I know. It was a white people who were before ye are, who shall be when ye are not, who shall eat you up and destroy you. *Yea, yea, yea!*

'And what came they for, the White Ones, the Terrible Ones, the skilled in magic and all learning, the strong, the unswerving? What is that bright stone upon thy forehead, O king? Whose hands made the iron garments upon thy breast, O king? Ye know not, but I know. I the Old One, I the Wise One, I the *Isanusi*, the Witch doctress!'

Then she turned her bald vulture-head towards us.

'What seek ye, white men of the Stars – ah, yes, of the Stars? Do ye seek a lost one? Ye shall not find him here. He is not here. Never for ages upon ages has a white foot pressed this land; never save once, and I remember that he left it but to die. Ye come for bright stones; I know it – I know it; ye shall find them when the blood is dry; but shall ye return whence ye came, or shall ye stop with me? *Ha! ha! ha!*

'And thou, thou with the dark skin and the proud bearing,' and she pointed her skinny fingers at Umbopa, 'who are *thou*, and what seekest *thou*? Not stones that shine, not yellow metal that gleams, these thou leavest to "white men from the Stars," Methinks I know thee; methinks I can smell the smell of the blood in thy heart. Strip off the girdle—'

Here the features of this extraordinary creature became convulsed, and she fell to the ground foaming in an epileptic fit, and was carried into the hut.

The king rose up trembling, and waved his hand. Instantly the regiments began to file off, and in ten minutes, save for ourselves, the king, and a few attendants, the great space was left empty.

'White people,' he said, 'it passes in my mind to kill you. Gagool has spoken strange words. What say ye?' I laughed. 'Be careful, O king, we are not easy to slay. Thou hast seen the fate of the ox; wouldst thou be as the ox is?'

The king frowned. 'It is not well to threaten a king.'

'We threaten not; we speak what is true. Try to kill us, O king, and learn.'

The great savage put his hand to his forehead and thought.

'Go in peace,' he said at length. 'To-night is the great dance. Ye shall see it. Fear not that I shall set a snare for you. To-morrow I will think.'

'It is well, O king,' I answered unconcernedly, and then, accompanied by Infadoos, we rose and went back to our kraal.

CHAPTER 10

The Witch-Hunt

On reaching our hut I motioned to Infadoos to enter with us.

'Now, Infadoos,' I said, 'we would speak with thee.'

'Let my lords say on.'

'It seems to us, Infadoos, that Twala the king is a cruel man.'

'It is so, my lords. Alas! the land cries out because of his cruelties. To-night ye shall see. It is the great witch-hunt, and many will be smelt out as wizards and slain. No man's life is safe. If the king covets a man's cattle, or a man's wife, or if he fears a man that he should excite a rebellion against him, then Gagool, whom ye saw, or some of the witch-finding women that she has taught, will smell that man out as a wizard, and he will be killed. Many must die before the moon grows pale to-night. It is ever so. Perhaps I too shall be killed. As yet I have been spared because I am skilled in war, and beloved by the soldiers; but I know not how long I have to live. The land groans at the wickedness of Twala the king; it is wearied of him and his red ways.'

'Then why is it, Infadoos, that the people do not cast him down?'

'Nay, my lords, he is the king, and if he were killed Scragga would reign in his place, and the heart of Scragga is blacker than the heart of Twala his father. If Scragga were king his yoke upon our neck would be heavier than the yoke of Twala. If Imotu had never been slain, or if Ignosi his son had lived, it might have been otherwise; but they are both dead.'

'How knowest thou that Ignosi is dead?' said a voice behind us. We looked round astonished to see who spoke. It was Umbopa.

'What meanest thou, boy?' asked Infadoos; 'who told thee to speak?'

'Listen, Infadoos,' was the answer, 'and I will tell thee a story. Years ago the king Imotu was killed in this country and his wife fled with the boy Ignosi. Is it not so?'

'It is so.'

'It was said that the woman and her son died upon the mountains. Is it not so?'

'It is even so.'

'Well, it came to pass that the mother and the boy Ignosi did not die. They crossed the mountains, and were led by a tribe of wandering desert men across the sands beyond, till at last they came to water and grass and trees again.'

'How knowest thou this?'

'Listen. They travelled on and on, many months' journey till they reached a land where a people called the Amazulu, who also are of the Kukuana stock, live by war, and with them they tarried many years, till at length the mother died. Then the son Ignosi became a wanderer again, and journeyed into a land of wonders, where white people live, and for many more years he learned the wisdom of the white people.'

'It is a pretty story,' said Infadoos, incredulously.

'For years he lived there working as a servant and a soldier, but holding in his heart all that his mother had told him of his own place, and casting about in his mind to find how he might journey thither to see his people and his father's house before he died. For long years he lived and waited, and at last the time came, as it comes ever to him who can wait, and he met certain white men who would seek the unknown land, and joined himself to them. The white men started and travelled on and on seeking for one who is lost.

They crossed the burning desert, they crossed the snow-clad mountains, and at last reached the land of the Kukuanas, and there they found *thee*, O Infadoos.'

'Surely thou art mad to talk thus,' exclaimed the astonished old soldier.

'Thou thinkest so; see I, will show thee, O my uncle.
I am Ignosi, rightful king of the Kukuanas!'

Then with a single movement Umbopa slipped off his 'moocha' or girdle, and stood naked before us.

'Look,' he said; 'what is this?' and he pointed to the picture of a great snake tattooed in blue round his middle, its tail disappearing into its open mouth just above where the thighs are set into the body.

Infadoos looked, his eyes starting nearly out of his head. Then he fell upon his knees.

'Koom! Koom!' he ejaculated; 'it is my brother's son; it is the king.'

'Did I not tell thee so, my uncle? Rise; I am not yet the king, but with thy help, and with the help of these brave white men who are my friends, I shall be. Yet the old witch Gagool was right, the land will run with blood first, and hers shall run with it, if she has any and can die, for she killed my father with her words, and drove my mother forth. And now, Infadoos, choose thou. Wilt thou lay thy hands between my hands and be my man? Will thou share the dangers that lie before me, and help me to overthrow this tyrant and murderer, or wilt thou not? Choose thou.'

The old man put his hand to his head and thought. Then he rose, and advancing to where Umbopa, or rather Ignosi, stood, he knelt before him and took his hand.

'Ignosi, rightful king of the Kukuanas, I lay my hand between thy hands, and am thy man till death. When thou wast a babe I dandled thee upon my knees, now shall my old arm strike for thee and freedom.'

'It is well, Infadoos; if I conquer, thou shalt be the greatest man in my kingdom after the king. If I fail, thou canst only die, and death is not far off from thee. Rise, my uncle.

'And ye, white men, will ye help me? What have I to offer you! The white stones! If I conquer and can find them, ye shall have as many as ye can carry hence. Will that suffice you?'

I translated this remark.

'Tell him,' answered Sir Henry, 'that he mistakes an Englishman. Wealth is good, and if it comes in our way we will take; but a gentleman does not sell himself for wealth. Still, speaking for myself, I say this. I have always liked Umbopa, and so far as lies in me I will stand by him in this business. It will be very pleasant to me to try to square matters with that cruel devil Twala. What do you say, Good, and you, Quatermain?'

'Well,' said Good, 'to adopt the language of hyperbole, in which all these people seem to indulge, you can tell him that a row is surely good, and warms the cockles of the heart, and, in short, that so far as I am concerned I'm his boy. My only stipulation is that he allows me to wear trousers.'

I translated the substance of these answers.

'It is well, my friends,' said Ignosi, late Umbopa. 'But what sayest thou, Macumazahn, art thou also with me, old Watcher-by-night, cleverer than a wounded buffalo?'

I thought awhile and scratched my head.

'Umbopa, or Ignosi,' I said, 'I don't like revolutions. I am a man of peace, and a bit of a coward' – here Umbopa smiled – 'but, on the other hand, I stick to my friends, Ignosi. You have stuck to us and played the part of a man, and I will stick to you. But mind you, I am a trader, and have to make my living, so I accept your offer about those diamonds in case we should ever be in a position to avail ourselves of it. Another thing: we came, as you know, to look for Incubu's (Sir Henry's) lost brother. You must help us to find him.'

'That I will do,' answered Ignsoi. 'Stay, Infadoos, by the sign of the snake about my middle, tell me the truth. Has any white man to thy knowledge set his foot within the land?'

'None, O Ignosi.'

'If any white man had been seen or heard of, wouldst thou have known?'

'I should certainly have known.'

'Thou hearest, Incubu,' said Ignosi to Sir Henry; 'he has not been here.'

'Well, well,' said Sir Henry, with a sigh; 'there it is; I suppose that he never got so far. Poor fellow, poor fellow! So it has all been for nothing. God's will be done.'

'Now for business,' I put in, anxious to escape from a painful subject. 'It is very well to be a king by right divine, Ignosi, but how dost thou propose to become a king indeed?'

'Nay, I know not. Infadoos, hast thou a plan?'

'Ignosi, Son of the Lightning,' answered his uncle, 'to-night is the great dance and witch-hunt. Many must be smelt out and perish, and in the hearts of many others there will be grief and anguish and fury against the king Twala. When the dance is over, then I will speak to some of the great chiefs, who in turn, if I can win them over, will speak to their regiments. I shall speak to the chiefs softly at first, and bring them to see that thou art indeed the king, and I think that by to-morrow's light thou wilt have twenty thousand spears at thy command. And now I must go and think, and hear, and make ready. After the dance is done, if I am yet alive, and we are all alive, I will meet thee here, and we can talk. At the best there must be war.'

At this moment our conference was interrupted by the cry that messengers had come from the king. Advancing to the door of the hut we ordered that they should be admitted, and presently three men entered, each bearing a shining shirt of chain armour, and a magnificent battle-axe.

'The gifts of my lord the king to the white men from the Stars!' said a herald who came with them.

'We thank the king,' I answered; 'withdraw.'

The men went, and we examined the armour with great interest. It was the most wonderful chain work that any of us had ever seen. A whole coat fell together so closely that it formed a mass of links scarcely too big to be covered with both hands.

'Do you make these things in this country, Infadoos?' I asked; 'they are very beautiful.'

'Nay, my lord, they came down to us from our fore-fathers. We know not who made them, and there are few left[1]. None but those of royal blood may be clad in them. They are magic coats through which no spear can pass, and those who wear them are well-nigh safe in the battle. The king is well pleased or much afraid, or he would not have sent you these garments of steel. Clothe yourselves in them to-night, my lords.'

The remainder of that day we spent quietly, resting and talking over the situation, which was sufficiently exciting. At last the sun went down, the thousand watch fires glowed out, and through the darkness we heard the tramp of many feet and the clashing of hundreds of spears, as the regiments passed to their appointed places to be ready for the great dance. Then the full moon shone out in splendour, and as we stood watching her rays, Infadoos arrived, clad in his war dress, and accompanied by a guard of twenty men to escort us to the dance. As he recommended, we had already donned the shirts of chain armour which the king had sent us, putting them on under our ordinary clothing, and finding to our surprise that they were neither very heavy nor uncomfortable. These steel shirts, which evidently had been made for men of a very large stature, hung somewhat loosely upon Good and myself, but Sir Henry's fitted his magnificent frame like a glove. Then strapping our revolvers round our waists, and taking in our hands the battle-axes which the king had sent with the armour, we started.

On arriving at the great kraal, where we had that morning been received by the king, we found that it was closely packed with some twenty thousand men arranged round it in regiments. These regiments were in turn divided into companies, and between each company ran a little path to allow space for the witch-finders to pass up and down. Anything more imposing than the sight that was

---

[1] In the Soudan swords and coats of mail are still worn by Arabs, whose ancestors must have stripped them from the bodies of Crusaders. – Editor.

presented by this vast and orderly concourse of armed men it is impossible to conceive. There they stood perfectly silent, and the moon poured her light upon the forest of their raised spears, upon their majestic forms, waving plumes, and the harmonious shading of their various-coloured shields. Wherever we looked were lines upon lines of dim faces surmounted by range upon range of shimmering spears.

'Surely,' I said to Infadoos, 'the whole army is here?'

'Nay, Macumazahn,' he answered, 'but a third of it. One third part is present at this dance each year, another third is mustered outside in case there should be trouble when the killing begins, ten thousand more garrison the outposts round Loo, and the rest watch at the kraals in the country. Thou seest it is a great people.'

'They are very silent,' remarked Good; and indeed the intense stillness among such a vast concourse of living men was almost overpowering.

'What says Bougwan?' asked Infadoos.

I translated.

'Those over whom the shadow of Death is hovering are silent,' he answered grimly.

'Will many be killed?'

'Very many.'

'It seems,' I said to the others, 'that we are going to assist at a gladiatorial show arranged regardless of expense.'

Sir Henry shivered, and Good said he wished that we could get out of it.

'Tell me,' I asked Infadoos, 'are we in danger?'

'I know not, my lords, I trust not; but do not seem afraid. If ye live through the night all may go well with you. The soldiers murmur against the king.'

All this while we had been advancing steadily towards the centre of the open space, in the midst of which were placed some stools. As we proceeded we perceived another small party coming from the direction of the royal hut.

'It is the king Twala, Scragga his son, and Gagool the old; and see, with them are those who slay,' said Infadoos, pointing to a little group of about a dozen gigantic and savage-looking men, armed with spears in one hand and heavy kerries in the other.

The king seated himself upon the centre stool, Gagool crouched at his feet, and the others stood behind him.

'Greeting, white lords,' Twala cried as, we came up; 'be seated, waste not precious time – the night is all too short for the deeds that must be done. Ye come in a good hour, and shall see a glorious spectacle. Look round, white lords; look round,' and he rolled his one wicked eye from regiment to regiment. 'Can the Stars show you such a sight as this? See how they shake in their wickedness, all those who have evil in their hearts and fear the judgment of "Heaven above."'

'Begin! begin!' piped Gagool, in her thin piercing voice; 'the hyenas are hungry, they howl for food. *Begin! begin!'*

Then for a moment there was intense stillness, made horrible by a presage of what was to come.

The king lifted his spear, and suddenly twenty thousand feet were raised, as though they belonged to one man, and brought down with a stamp upon the earth. This was repeated three times, causing the solid ground to shake and tremble. Then from a far point of the circle a solitary voice began a wailing song, of which the refrain ran something as follows: –

'What is the lot of man born of woman?'

Back came the answer rolling out from every throat in that vast company –

'Death!'

Gradually, however, the song was taken up by company after company, till the whole armed multitude were singing it, and I could no longer follow the words, except in so far as they appeared to represent various phases of human passions, fears, and joys. Now it seemed to be a love song, now a majestic swelling war chant, and last of all a death dirge ending suddenly in one heart-breaking wail that went echoing and rolling away in a volume of blood-curdling sound.

Again silence fell upon the place, and again it was broken by the king lifting his hand. Instantly we heard a pattering of feet, and from out of the masses of warriors strange and awful figures appeared running towards us. As they drew near we saw that these were women, most of them aged, for their white hair, ornamented with small bladders taken from fish, streamed out behind them. Their faces were painted in stripes of white and yellow; down their backs hung snake-skins, and round their waists rattled circlets of human bones, while each held a small forked wand in her shrivelled hand. In all there were ten of them. When they arrived in front of us they halted, and one of them, pointing with her wand towards the crouching figure of Gagool, cried out –

'Mother, Old Mother, we are here.'

'*Good! good! good!*' answered that aged Iniquity. 'Are your eyes keen, *Isanusis* [witch doctoresses], ye seers in dark places?'

'Mother, they are keen.'

'*Good! good! good!* Are your ears open, *Isanusis*, ye who hear words that come not from the tongue?'

'Mother, they are open.'

'*Good! good! good!* Are your senses awake, *Isanusis* – can ye smell blood, can ye purge the land of the wicked ones who compass evil against the king and against their neighbours? Are ye ready to do the justice of "Heaven above," ye whom I have taught, ye who have eaten of the bread of my wisdom, and drunk of the water of my magic?'

'Mother, we can.'

'Then go! Tarry not, ye vultures; see, the slayers' – pointing to the ominous group of executioners behind – 'make sharp their spears; the white men from afar are hungry to see. *Go!*'

With a wild yell Gagool's horrid ministers broke away in every direction, like fragments from a shell, the dry bones round their waists rattling as they ran, and headed for various points of the dense human circle. We could not watch them all, so we fixed our eyes upon the *Isanusi* nearest to us. When she came to within a few paces of the warriors she halted and began to dance wildly, turning round and round with an almost incredible rapidity, and shrieking out sentences such as 'I smell him, the evildoer!' 'He is near, he who poisoned his mother!' 'I hear the thoughts of him who thought evil of the king!'

Quicker and quicker she danced, till she lashed herself into such a frenzy of excitement that the foam flew in flecks from her gnashing jaws, till her eyes seemed to start from her head, and her flesh to quiver visibly. Suddenly she stopped dead and stiffened all over, like a pointer dog when he scents game, and then with outstretched wand she began to creep stealthily towards the soldiers before her. It seemed to us that as she came their stoicism gave way, and that they shrank from her. As for ourselves, we followed her movements with a horrible fascination. Presently, still creeping and crouching like a dog, the *Isanusi* was before them. Then she halted and pointed, and again crept on a pace or two.

Suddenly the end came. With a shriek she sprang in and touched a tall warrior with her forked wand. Instantly two of his comrades, those standing immediately next to him, seized the doomed man, each by one arm, and advanced with him towards the king.

He did not resist, but we saw that he dragged his limbs as though they were paralysed, and that his fingers, from which the spear had fallen, were limp like those of a man newly dead.

As he came, two of the villainous executioners stepped forward to meet him. Presently they met, and the executioners turned round, looking towards the king as though for orders.

'*Kill!*' said the king.

'*Kill!*' squeaked Gagool.

'*Kill!*' re-echoed Scragga, with a hollow chuckle.

Almost before the words were uttered the horrible deed was done. One man had driven his spear into the victim's heart, and to make assurance doubly sure, the other had dashed out his brains with a great club.

'*One,*' counted Twala the king, just like a black Madame Defarge, as Good said, and the body was dragged a few paces away and stretched out.

Hardly was the thing done before another poor wretch was brought up, like an ox to the slaughter. This time we could see, from the leopard-skin cloak which he wore, that the man was a person of rank. Again the awful syllables were spoken, and the victim fell dead.

'*Two,*' counted the king.

And so the deadly game went on, till about a hundred bodies were stretched in rows behind us. I have heard of the gladiatorial shows of the Caesars, and of the Spanish bull-fights, but I take the liberty of doubting if either of them could be half so horrible as this Kukuana witch-hunt. Gladiatorial shows and Spanish bull-fights at any rate contributed to the public amusement, which certainly was not the case here. The most confirmed sensation-monger would fight shy of sensation if he knew that it was well on the cards that he would, in his own proper person, be the subject of the next 'event.'

Once we rose and tried to remonstrate, but were sternly repressed by Twala.

'Let the law take its course, white men. These dogs are magicians and evil-doers; it is well that they should die,' was the only answer vouchsafed to us.

About half-past ten there was a pause. The witch-finders gathered themselves together, apparently exhausted with their bloody work, and we thought that the performance was done with. But it was not so, for presently, to our surprise, the ancient woman, Gagool, rose from her crouching position, and supporting herself with a stick, staggered off into the open space. It was an extraordinary sight to see this frightful, vulture-headed old creature, bent nearly double with extreme age, gather strength by degrees, until at last she rushed about almost as actively as her ill-omened pupils. To and fro she ran, chanting to herself, till suddenly she made a dash at a tall man standing in front of one of the regiments, and touched him. As she did this a sort of groan went up from the regiment which evidently he commanded.

But two if its officers seized him all the same, and brought him up for execution. We learned afterwards that he was a man of great wealth and importance, being indeed a cousin of the king.

He was slain and Twala counted one hundred and three. Then Gagool again sprang to and fro, gradually drawing nearer and nearer to ourselves.

'Hang me if I don't believe she is going to try her games on us,' ejaculated Good in horror.

'Nonsense!' said Sir Henry.

As for myself, when I saw the old fiend dancing nearer and nearer, my heart positively sank into my boots. I glanced behind us at the long rows of corpses, and shivered.

Nearer and nearer waltzed Gagool looking for all the world like an animated crooked stick or comma, her horrid eyes gleaming and glowing with a most unholy lustre.

Nearer she came, and yet nearer, every creature in that vast assemblage watching her movements with intense anxiety. At last she stood still and pointed.

'Which is it to be?' asked Sir Henry to himself.

In a moment all doubts were set at rest, for the old hag had rushed in and touched Umbopa, alias Ignosi, on the shoulder.

'I smell him out,' she shrieked. 'Kill him, kill him, he is full of evil; kill him, the stranger, before blood flows for him. Slay him, O king.'

There was a pause, of which I instantly took advantage.

'O king,' I called out, rising from my seat, 'this man is the servant of thy guests, he is their dog; whosoever sheds the blood of our dog sheds our blood. By the sacred law of hospitality I claim protection for him.'

'Gagool, old mother of the witch-finders, has smelt him out; he must die, white man,' was the sullen answer.

'Nay, he shall not die,' I replied; 'he who tries to touch him shall die indeed.'

'Seize him!' roared Twala to the executioners, who stood round red to the eyes with the blood of their victims.

They advanced towards us, and then hesitated. As for Ignosi, he clutched his spear, and raised it as though determined to sell his life dearly.

'Stand back, ye dogs!' I shouted, 'if ye would see to-morrow's light. Touch one hair of his head and your king dies,' and I covered Twala with my revolver. Sir Henry and Good also drew their pistols, Sir Henry pointing his at the leading executioner, who was advancing to carry out the sentence, and Good taking a deliberate aim at Gagool.

Twala winced perceptibly as my barrel came in a line with his broad chest.

'Well,' I said, 'what is it to be, Twala?'

Then he spoke.

'Put away your magic tubes,' he said; 'ye have adjured me in the name of hospitality, and for that reason, but not from fear of what ye can do, I spare him. Go in peace.'

'It is well,' I answered unconcernedly; 'we are weary of slaughter and would sleep. Is the dance ended?'

'It is ended,' Twala answered sulkily. 'Let these dead dogs,' pointing to the long row of corpses, 'be flung out to the hyenas and the vultures,' and he lifted his spear.

Instantly the regiments began to defile through the kraal gateway in perfect silence, a fatigue party only remaining behind to drag away the corpses of those who had been sacrificed.

Then we rose also, and making our salaam to his majesty, which he hardly deigned to acknowledge, we departed to our huts.

'Well,' said Sir Henry, as we sat down, having first lit a lamp of the sort used by the Kukuanas, of which the wick is made from the fibre of a species of palm-leaf, and the oil from clarified hippopotamus fat. 'Well, I feel uncommonly inclined to be sick.'

'If I had any doubts about helping Umbopa to rebel against that that infernal blackguard,' put in Good, 'they are gone now. It was as much as I could do to sit still while that slaughter was going on. I tried to keep my eyes shut, but they would open just at the wrong time. I wonder where Infadoos is. Umbopa, my friend, you ought to be grateful to us; your skin came near to having an air-hole made in it.'

'I am grateful, Bougwan,' was Umbopa's answer, when I had translated, ' and I shall not forget. As for Infadoos, he will be here by-and-by. We must wait.'

So we lit our pipes and waited.

CHAPTER 11

We Give a Sign

For a long while – two hours, I should think – we sat there in silence, being too much overwhelmed by the recollection of the horrors we had seen to talk. At last, just as we were thinking of turning in – for the night drew nigh to dawn – we heard a sound of steps. Then came the challenge of a sentry posted at the kraal gate, which apparently was answered, though not in an audible tone, for the steps still advanced. In another second Infadoos had entered the hut, followed by some half-dozen stately-looking chiefs.

'My lords,' he said, 'I have come according to my word. My lords and Ignosi, rightful king of the Kukuanas, I have brought with me these men,' pointing to the row of chiefs, 'who are great men among us, having each one of them the command of three thousand soldiers, that live but to do their bidding, under the king's. I have told them of what I have seen, and what my ears have heard. Now let them also behold the sacred snake around thee, and hear thy story, Ignosi, that they may say whether or no they will make cause with thee against Twala the king.'

By the way of answer Ignosi again stripped off his girdle, and exhibited the snake tattooed about him. Each chief in turn drew near and examined the sign by the dim light of the lamp, and without saying a word passed on to the other side.

Then Ignosi resumed his moocha, and addressing them, repeated the history he had detailed in the morning.

'Now ye have heard, chiefs,' said Infadoos, when he had done, 'what say ye; will ye stand by this man and help him to his fathers' throne, or will ye not? The land cries out against Twala, and the blood of the people flows like the waters in spring. Ye have seen to-night. Two other chiefs there were with whom I had it in my mind to speak, and where are they now? The hyenas howl over their corpses. Soon shall ye be as they are if ye strike not. Choose then, my brothers.'

The eldest of the six men, a short, thick-set warrior, with white hair, stepped forward a pace and answered –

'Thy words are true, Infadoos; the land cries out. My own brother is among those who died to-night; but this is a great matter and the thing is hard to believe. How know we that if we lift our spears it may not be for a cheat and a liar? It is a great matter, I say, of which none can see the end. For of this be sure, blood will flow in rivers before the deed is done; many will still cleave to the king, for men worship the sun that still shines bright in the heavens, rather than that which has not risen. These white men from the Stars, their magic is great, and Ignosi is under the cover of their wing. If he be indeed the rightful king, let them give us a sign, and let the people have a sign, that all may see. So shall men cleave to us, knowing of a truth that the white man's magic is with them.'

'Ye have the sign of the snake,' I answered.

'My lord, it is not enough. The snake may have been placed there since the man's childhood. Show us a sign, and it will suffice. But we will not move without a sign.'

The others gave a decided assent, and I turned in perplexity to Sir Henry and Good, and explained the situation.

'I think that I have it,' said Good, exultingly; 'ask them to give us a moment to think.'

I did so, and the chiefs withdrew. So soon as they had gone Good went to the little box where he kept his medicines unlocked it, and took out a notebook, in the fly-leaves of which was an almanack. 'Now look here, you fellows, isn't to-morrow the 4th of June?' he said.

We had kept a careful note of the days, so were able to answer that it was.

'Very good; then here we have it – "4th June, total eclipse of the moon commences at 8.15 Greenwich time, visible in Teneriffe – *South Africa*, etc." There's a sign for you. Tell them we will darken the moon to-morrow night.'

The idea was a splendid one; indeed, the only weak spot about it was a fear lest Good's almanack might be incorrect. If we made a false prophecy on such a subject, our prestige would be gone for ever, and so would Ignosi's chance of the throne of the Kukuanas.

'Suppose that the almanack is wrong,' suggested Sir Henry to Good, who was busily employed in working out something on a blank page of the book.

'I see no reason to suppose anything of the sort,' was his answer. 'Eclipses always come up to time; at least that is my experience of them, and it especially states that this one will be visible in South Africa. I have worked out the reckonings as well as I can, without knowing our exact position; and I make out that the eclipse should begin here about ten o'clock to-morrow night, and last until half-past twelve. For an hour and a half or so there should be almost total darkness.'

'Well,' said Sir Henry, 'I suppose we had better risk it.'

I acquiesced, though doubtfully, for eclipses are queer cattle to deal with – it might be a cloudy night, for instance, or our dates might be wrong – and sent Umbopa to summon the chiefs back. Presently they came, and I addressed them thus –

'Great men of the Kukuanas, and thou Infadoos, listen. We love not to show our powers, for to do so is to interfere with the course of nature, and to plunge the world into fear and confusion. But since this matter is a great one, and as we are angered against the king because of the slaughter we have seen, and because of the act of the *Isanusi* Gagool, who would have put our friend Ignosi to death, we have determined to break a rule, and to give such a sign as all men may see. Come hither;' and I led them to the door of the hut and pointed to the red ball of the moon. 'What see ye there?'

'We see the sinking moon,' answered the spokesman of the party.

'It is so. Now tell me, can any mortal man put out that moon before the hour of setting, and bring the curtain of black night down on to the land?'

The chief laughed a little at the question.

'No, my lord, that no man can do. The moon is stronger than man who looks on her, nor can she vary in her courses.'

'Ye say so. Yet I tell you that to-morrow night, about two hours before midnight, we will cause the moon to be eaten up for a space of an hour and the half of an hour. Yes, deep darkness shall cover the earth, and it shall be for a sign that Ignosi is indeed king of the Kukuanas. If we do this thing, will ye be satisfied?'

'Yea, my lords,' answered the old chief with a smile which was reflected on the faces of his companions; '*if* ye do this thing, we will be satisfied indeed.'

'It shall be done; we three, Incubu, Bougwan, and Macumazahn, have said it, and it shall be done. Dost thou hear, Infadoos?'

'I hear, my lord, but it is a wonderful thing that ye promise, to put out the moon, the mother of the world, when she is at her full.'

'Yet shall we do it, Infadoos.'

'It is well, my lords. To-day, two hours after sunset, Twala will send for my lords to witness the Girls' Dance, and one hour after the dance begins the girl whom Twala thinks the fairest shall be killed by Scragga, the king's son, as a sacrifice to the silent Stone Ones, who sit and keep watch by the mountains yonder,' and he pointed towards the three strange-looking peaks where Solomon's Road was supposed to end. 'Then let my lords darken the moon, and save the maiden's life, and the people will believe indeed.'

'Ay,' said the old chief, still smiling a little, 'the people will believe indeed.'

'Two miles from Loo,' went on Infadoos, 'there is a hill curved like a new moon, a stronghold, where are stationed my regiment, and three other regiments which these chiefs command. This morning we will make a plan whereby two or three other regiments may be moved there also. Then, if in truth my lords can darken the moon, in the darkness I will take my lords by the hand and lead them out of Loo to this place, where they shall be safe, and thence we can make war upon Twala the king.'

'It is good,' said I. 'Now let us sleep awhile and to make ready our magic.'

Infadoos rose, and, having saluted us, departed with the chiefs.

'My friends,' said Ignosi, so soon as they were gone, 'can ye do this wonderful thing, or were ye speaking empty words to the captains?'

'We believe that we can do it, Umbopa – Ignosi, I mean.'

'It is strange,' he answered, 'and had ye not been Englishmen I would not have believed it; but I have learned that English "gentlemen" tell no lies. If we live through the matter, be sure that I will repay you.'

'Ignosi,' said Sir Henry, 'promise me one thing.'

'I will promise, Incubu, my friend, even before I hear it,' answered the big man with a smile. 'What is it?'

'This: that if ever you come to be king of this people you will do away with the smelling out of wizards such as we saw last night; and that the killing of men without trial shall no longer take place in the land.'

Ignosi thought for a moment after I had translated this request, and then answered –

'The ways of black people are not as the ways of white men, Incubu, nor do we value life so highly. Yet I will promise. If it be in my power to hold them back, the witch-finders shall hunt no more, nor shall any man die the death without trial and judgment.'

'That's a bargain, then,' said Sir Henry; 'and now let us get a little rest.'

Thoroughly wearied out, we were soon sound asleep, and slept till Ignosi woke us about eleven o'clock. Then we rose, washed, and ate a hearty breakfast. After that we went outside the hut and walked about, amusing ourselves with examining the structure of the Kukuana huts and observing the customs of the women.

'I hope that eclipse will come off,' said Sir Henry presently.

'If it does not it will soon be all up with us,' I answered mournfully; 'for so sure as we are living men some of those chiefs will tell the whole story to the king. Then there will be another sort of eclipse, and one that we shall certainly not like.'

Returning to the hut we ate some dinner, and passed the rest of the day in receiving visits of ceremony and curiosity. At length the sun set, and we enjoyed a couple of hours of such quiet as our melancholy forebodings would allow to us. Finally, about half-past eight, a messenger came from Twala to bid us to the great annual 'Dance of Girls' which was about to be celebrated.

Hastily we put on the chain shirts that the king had sent us, and taking our rifles and ammunition with us, so as to have them handy in case we must fly, as suggested by Infadoos, we started boldly enough, though with inward fear and trembling. The great space in front of the king's kraal bore a very different appearance from that which it had presented on the previous evening. In place of the grim ranks of serried warriors were company after company of Kukuana girls, not overdressed, so far as clothing went, but each crowned with a wreath of flowers, and holding a palm leaf in one hand and a white arum lily in the other. In the centre of the open moonlit space sat Twala the king, with old Gagool at his feet, attended by Infadoos, the boy Scragga, and twelve guards. There were also present about a score of chiefs, amongst whom I recognised most of our friends of the night before.

Twala greeted us with much apparent cordiality, though I saw him fix his one eye viciously on Umbopa.

'Welcome, white men from the Stars,' he said; ' this is another sight from that which your eyes gazed on by the light of last night's moon, but it is not so good a sight. Girls are pleasant, and were it not for such as these,' and he pointed round him, 'we should none of us be here this day; but men are better. Kisses and the tender words of women are sweet, but the sound of the clashing of the spears of warriors, and the smell of men's blood, are sweeter far! Would ye have wives from among our people, white men? If so, choose the fairest here, and ye shall have them, as many as ye will,' and he paused for an answer.

The prospect did not seem to be without attractions for Good, who, like most sailors, is of a susceptible nature. But being elderly and wise, I foresaw the endless complications that anything of the sort would involve, for women bring trouble so surely as the night follows the day, and put in a hasty answer –

'Thanks to thee, O King, but we white men wed only with white women like ourselves. Your maidens are fair, but they are not for us!'

The king laughed. 'It is well. In our land there is a proverb which runs, "Women's eyes are always bright, whatever the colour," and another that says, "Love her who is present, for be sure she who is absent is false to thee." But perhaps these things are not so in the Stars. In a land where men are white all things are possible. So be it, white men; the girls will not go begging! Welcome again; and welcome, too, thou black one; if Gagool here had won her way, thou wouldst have been stiff and cold by now. It is lucky for thee that thou too camest from the stars; ha! ha!'

'I can kill thee before thou killest me, O King,' was Ignosi's calm answer, 'and thou shalt be stiff before my limbs cease to bend.'

Twala started. 'Thou speakest boldly, boy,' he replied angrily; 'presume not too far.'

'He may well be bold in whose lips are truth. The truth is a sharp spear which flies home and misses not. It is a message from "the Stars," O King.'

Twala scowled, and his one eye gleamed fiercely, but he said nothing more.

'Let the dance begin,' he cried.

Then the flower-crowned girls sprang forward in companies, singing a sweet song and waving the delicate palms and white lilies. On they danced, looking faint and spiritual in the soft, sad light of the risen moon; now whirling round and round, now meeting in mimic warfare; swaying, eddying here and there, coming forward, falling back in an ordered confusion delightful to witness. At last they paused, and a beautiful young woman sprang out of the ranks and began to pirouette in front of us with a grace and vigour which would have put most ballet girls to shame. At length she retired exhausted, and another took her place, then another and another, but none of them, either in grace, skill, or personal attractions, came up to the first.

When the chosen girls had all danced, the king lifted his hand.

'Which deem ye the fairest, white men?' he asked.

'The first,' said I unthinkingly. Next second I regretted it, for I remembered that Infadoos had told us that the fairest woman must be offered up as a sacrifice.

'Then is my mind as your minds, and my eyes are as your eyes. She is the fairest! and a sorry thing it is for her, since she must die!'

'*Ay, must die!*' piped out Gagool, casting a quick glance in the direction of the poor girl, who, as yet ignorant of the awful fate in store for her, was standing some ten yards off in front of a company of maidens, engaged in nervously picking a flower from her wreath to pieces, petal by petal.

'Why, O King?' said I, restraining my indignation with difficulty. 'The girl has danced well, and pleased us; she is fair too; it would be hard to reward her with death.'

Twala laughed as he answered –

'It is our custom, and the Shapes who sit in stone yonder,' and he pointed towards the three distant peaks, 'must have their due. Did I fail to put the fairest girl to death to-day, misfortune would fall upon me and my house. Thus runs the prophecy of my people: "If the king offer not a sacrifice of a fair girl, on the day of the Dance of Maidens, to the Old Ones who sit and watch on the mountains, then shall he fall, and his House." Look ye, white men, my brother who reigned before me offered not the sacrifice, because of the tears of the woman, and he fell, and his House, and I reign in his stead. It is finished; she must die!' Then turning to the guards – 'Bring her hither. Scragga, make sharp thy spear.'

Two of the men stepped forward, and as they advanced, the girl, for the first time realising her impending fate, screamed aloud and turned to fly. But the strong hands caught her fast, and brought her, struggling and weeping before us.

'What is thy name, girl?' piped Gagool. 'What! wilt thou not answer! Shall the king's son do his work at once?'

At this hint, Scragga, looking more evil than ever, advanced a step and lifted his great spear, and at that moment I saw Good's hand creep to his revolver. The poor girl caught the faint glint of steel through her tears, and it sobered her anguish. She ceased struggling, and clasping her hands convulsively, stood shuddering from head to foot.

'See,' cried Scragga in high glee, 'she shrinks from the sight of my little plaything even before she has tasted it,' and he tapped the broad blade of his spear.

'If ever I get the chance you shall pay for that, you young hound!' I heard Good mutter beneath his breath.

'Now that thou art quiet, give us thy name, my dear. Come, speak out, and fear not,' said Gagool in mockery.

'Oh, mother,' answered the girl, in trembling accents, 'my name is Foulata, of the house of Suko. Oh, mother, why must I die? I have done no wrong!'

'Be comforted,' went on the old woman in her hateful tone of mockery. 'Thou must die, indeed, as a sacrifice to the Old Ones who sit yonder,' and she pointed to the peaks. 'It is better to sleep in the night than to toil in the daytime; it is better to die than to live, and thou shalt die by the royal hand of the king's own son.'

The girl Foulata wrung her hands in anguish, and cried out aloud, 'Oh, cruel! and I so young! What have I done that I should never again see the sun rise out of the night, or the stars come following on his track in the evening, that I may no more gather flowers when the dew is heavy, or listen to the laughing of the waters? Woe is me, that I shall never see my father's hut again, nor feel my mother's kiss, nor tend the lamb that is sick! Woe is me, that no lover shall put his arm around me and look into my eyes, nor shall men children be born of me! Oh, cruel, cruel!'

And again she wrung her hands and turned her tearstained, flower-crowned face to Heaven, looking so lovely in her despair – for she was indeed a beautiful woman – that assuredly the sight of her would have melted the hearts of any less cruel than were the three fiends before us. Prince Arthur's appeal to the ruffians who came to blind him was not more touching than that of this savage girl.

Still it did not move Gagool or Gagool's master, though I saw signs of pity among the guards behind, and on the faces of the chiefs. As for Good, he gave a fierce snort of indignation, and made a motion as though to go to her assistance. With all a woman's quickness, the doomed girl interpreted what was passing in his mind. By a sudden movement she flung herself before him, and clasped his 'beautiful white legs' with her hands.

'Oh, white father from the Stars!' she cried, 'throw over me the mantle of protection; let me creep into the shadow of thy strength, that I may be saved. Oh, keep me from these cruel men and from the mercies of Gagool!'

'All right, my hearty, I'll look after you,' sang out Good, in nervous Saxon. 'Come, get up, there's a good girl,' and he stooped and caught her hand.

Twala turned and motioned to his son, who advanced with his spear lifted.

'Now's your time,' whispered Sir Henry to me; 'what are you waiting for?'

'I am waiting for that eclipse,' I answered; 'I have had my eye on the moon for the last half-hour, and I never saw it look healthier.'

'Well, you must risk it now, or the girl will be killed. Twala is losing patience.'

Recognising the force of the argument, and having cast one more despairing look at the bright face of the moon; for never did the most ardent astronomer with a theory to prove await a celestial event with such anxiety, I stepped with all the dignity that I could command between the prostrate girl and the advancing spear of Scragga.

'King,' I said, 'it shall not be; we will not endure this thing; let the girl go in safety.'

Twala rose from his seat in wrath and astonishment, and from the chiefs and serried ranks of maidens who had closed in slowly upon us in anticipation of the tragedy came a murmur of amazement.

'*Shall not be!* thou white dog, that yappest at the lion in his cave; *shall not be!* art thou mad? Be careful, lest this chicken's fate should overtake thee, and those with thee. How canst thou save her or thyself? Who art thou that thou settest thyself between me and my will? Back, I say. Scragga, kill her! Ho, guards! seize these men.'

At his words armed men ran swiftly from behind the hut, where they had evidently been placed before-hand.

Sir Henry, Good, and Umbopa ranged themselves alongside of me, and lifted their rifles.

'Stop!' I shouted boldly, though at the moment my heart was in my boots. 'Stop! we, the white men from the Stars, say that it shall not be. Come but one pace nearer, and we will put out the moon like a wind-blown lamp, as we who dwell in her House can do, and plunge the land in darkness. Dare to disobey, and ye shall taste of our magic.'

My threat produced an effect; the men halted, and Scragga stood still before us, his spear lifted.

'Hear him! hear him!' piped Gagool; 'hear the liar who says he will put out the moon like a lamp. Let him do it and the girl shall be spared. Yes, let him do it, or die by the girl, he and those with him.'

I glanced up at the moon despairingly, and now to my intense joy and relief saw that we – or rather the almanack – had made no mistake. On the edge of the great orb lay a faint rim of shadow, while a smoky shade grew and gathered upon its bright surface. Never shall I forget that supreme, that superb moment of relief.

Then I lifted my hand solemnly towards the sky, an example

which Sir Henry and Good followed, and quoted a line or two from the 'Ingoldsby Legends' at it in the most impressive tones that I could command. Sir Henry followed suit with a verse out of the Old Testament, and something about Balbus building a wall, in Latin, whilst Good addressed the Queen of Night in a volume of the most classical bad language which he could think of.

Slowly the penumbra, the shadow of a shadow, crept on over the bright surface, and as it crept I heard deep gasps of fear rising from the multitude around.

'Look, O King!' I cried; 'look, Gagool! Look, chiefs and people and women, and see if the white men from the Stars keep their word, or if they be but empty liars!

'The moon grows black before your eyes; soon there will be darkness – ay, darkness in the hour of the full moon. Ye have asked for a sign; it is given to you. Grow dark, O Moon! withdraw thy light, thou pure and holy One; bring the proud heart of usurping murderers to the dust, and eat up the world with shadows.'

A groan of terror burst from the onlookers. Some stood petrified with dread, others threw themselves upon their knees and cried aloud. As for the king, he sat still and turned pale beneath his dusky skin. Only Gagool kept her courage.

'It will pass,' she cried; 'I have often seen the like before; no man can put out the moon; lose not heart; sit still – the shadow will pass.'

'Wait, and ye shall see,' I replied, hopping with excitement. 'O Moon! Moon! Moon! wherefore art thou so cold and fickle?' This appropriate quotation I took from the pages of a popular romance that I chanced to have read recently. Yet now I come to think of it, it was ungrateful to abuse the Lady of the Heavens –

> That orbéd maiden with white fire laden
> Whom mortals call the moon –

who was showing herself to be the truest of friends to us, however she may have behaved to the impassioned lover in the novel. Then I added: 'Keep it up, Good, I can't remember any more poetry. Curse away, there's a good fellow.'

Good responded nobly to this tax upon his inventive faculties. Never before had I the faintest conception of the breadth and depth and height of a naval officer's objurgatory powers. For ten minutes he went on in several languages without stopping, and he scarcely ever repeated himself.

Meanwhile the dark ring crept on, while all that great assembly fixed their eyes upon the sky and stared and stared in fascinated silence. Strange and unholy shadows encroached upon the moon-light; an ominous quiet filled the place. Everything grew still as death. Slowly and in the midst of this most solemn silence the minutes sped away, and while they sped the full moon passed deeper and deeper into the shadow of the earth, as the inky segment of its circle slid in awful majesty across the lunar craters. The great pale orb seemed to draw near and to grow in size. She turned a coppery hue, then that portion of her surface which was unobscured as yet, grew grey and ashen, and at length, as totality approached, her mountains and her plains were to be seen glowing luridly through a crimson gloom.

On, yet on, crept the ring of darkness; it was now more than half across the blood-red orb. The air grew thick, and still more deeply tinged with dusky crimson. On, yet on, till we could scarcely see the fierce faces of the group before us. No sound rose now from the spectators, and at last Good stopped swearing.

'The moon is dying – the white wizards have killed the moon,' yelled the prince Scragga at last. 'We shall perish in the dark.' Then animated by fear or fury, or by both, he lifted his spear and drove it with all his force at Sir Henry's breast. But he forgot the mail shirts that the king had given us, which we wore beneath our clothing. The steel rebounded harmless, and before he could repeat the blow Curtis had snatched the spear from his hand and sent it straight through him. Scragga dropped dead.

At the sight, and driven mad with fear of the gathering darkness, and of the unholy shadow which, as they believed was swallowing the moon, the companies of girls broke up in wild confusion, and ran screeching for the gateways. Nor did the panic stop there. The king himself, followed by his guards, some of the chiefs, and Gagool, who hobbled away after them with marvellous alacrity, fled for the huts. Thus in another minute we ourselves, the intended victim Foulata, Infadoos, and most of the chiefs who had interviewed us on the previous night, were left alone upon the scene, together with the dead body of Scragga, Twala's son.

'Chiefs,' I said, 'we have given you the sign. If ye are satisfied, let us fly swiftly to the place of which ye spoke. The charm cannot now be stopped. It will work for an hour and the half of an hour. Let us cover ourselves with the darkness.'

'Come,' said Infadoos, turning to go, an example which was followed by the awed captains, ourselves, and the girl Foulata, whom Good took by the arm.

Before we reached the gate of the kraal the moon went out utterly, and from every quarter of the firmament stars rushed forth into the inky sky.

Holding each other by the hand we stumbled on through the darkness.

CHAPTER 12

Before the Battle

Luckily for us, Infadoos and the chiefs knew all the paths of the great town perfectly, so that we passed by side-ways unmolested, and notwithstanding the gloom we made fair progress.

For an hour or more we journeyed on, till at length the eclipse began to pass, and that edge of the moon which had disappeared the first became again visible. Suddenly, as we watched, there burst from it a silver streak of light, accompanied by a wondrous ruddy glow, which hung upon the blackness of the sky like a celestial lamp. A wild and lovely sight it was. In another five minutes the stars began to fade, and there was sufficient light to see our whereabouts. We then discovered that we were clear of the town of Loo, and approaching a large flat-topped hill, measuring some two miles in circumference. This hill, which is of a formation common in South Africa, is not very high; indeed, its greatest elevation is scarcely more than two hundred feet, but it is shaped like a horseshoe, and its sides are rather precipitous and strewn with boulders. On the grass table-land at its summit is ample camping-ground, which had been utilised as a military cantonment of no mean strength. Its ordinary garrison was one regiment of three thousand men, but as we toiled up the steep side of the mountain, in the returning moonlight we perceived that there were several of such regiments encamped there.

Reaching the table-land at last, we found crowds of men roused from their sleep, shivering with fear and huddled up together in the utmost consternation at the natural phenomenon which they were witnessing. Passing through these without a word, we gained a hut in the centre of the ground. Here we were astonished to find two men waiting, laden with our few goods and chattels, which of course we had been obliged to leave behind in our hasty flight.

'I sent for them,' explained Infadoos; 'also for these,' and he lifted up Good's long-lost trousers.

With an exclamation of rapturous delight Good sprang at them, and instantly proceeded to put them on.

'Surely my lord will not hide his beautiful white legs!' exclaimed Infadoos regretfully.

But Good persisted, and once only did the Kukuana people get the chance of seeing his beautiful legs again. Good is a very modest man. Henceforward they had to satisfy their aesthetic longings with his one whisker, his transparent eye, and his movable teeth.

Still gazing with fond remembrance at Good's trousers, Infadoos next informed us that he had commanded the regiments to muster so soon as the day broke, in order to explain to them fully the origin and circumstances of the rebellion which was decided on by the chiefs, and to introduce to them the rightful heir to the throne, Ignosi.

Accordingly, when the sun was up, the troops – in all some twenty thousand men, and the flower of the Kukuana army – mustered on a large open space to which we went. The men were drawn up in the three sides of a dense square, and presented a magnificent spectacle. We took our station on the open side of the square, and were speedily surrounded by all the principal chiefs and officers.

These, after silence had been proclaimed, Infadoos proceeded to address. He narrated to them in vigorous and graceful language – for, like most Kukuanas of high rank, he was a born orator – the history of Ignosi's father, and of how he had been basely murdered by Twala the king, and his wife and child driven out to starve. Then he pointed out that the people suffered and groaned under Twala's cruel rule, instancing the proceedings of the previous night, when, under pretence of their being evildoers, many of the noblest in the land had been dragged forth and wickedly done to death. Next he went on to say that the white lords from the Stars, looking down upon their country, had perceived its trouble, and determined, at great personal inconvenience, to alleviate its lot: That they had accordingly taken the real king of the Kukuanas, Ignosi, who was languishing in exile, by the hand, and led him over the mountains: That they had seen the wickedness of Twala's doings, and for a sign to the wavering, and to save the life of the girl Foulata, actually, by the exercise of their high magic, had put out the moon and slain the young fiend Scragga; and that they were prepared to stand by them, to assist them to overthrow Twala, and to set up the rightful king, Ignosi, in his place.

He finished his discourse amidst a murmur of approbation. Then Ignosi stepped forward and began to speak. Having reiterated all that Infadoos his uncle had said, he concluded with a powerful speech in these words: –

'O chiefs, captains, soldiers, and people, ye have heard my words. Now must ye make choice between me and him who sits upon my throne, the uncle who killed his brother, and hunted his brother's child forth to die in the cold and the night. That I am indeed the king these' – pointing to the chiefs – 'can tell you, for they have seen the snake about my middle. If I were not the king, would these white men be on my side with all their magic? Tremble, chiefs, captains, soldiers, and people! Is not the darkness they have brought upon the land to confound Twala and cover our flight, darkness even in the hour of the full moon, yet before your eyes?'

'It is,' answered the soldiers.

'I am the king; I say to you, I am the king,' went on Ignosi, drawing up his great stature to its full, and lifting the broad-bladed battle-axe above his head. 'If there be any man among you who says that it is not so, let him stand forth and I will fight him now, and his blood shall be a red token that I tell you true. Let him stand forth, I say;' and he shook the great axe till it flashed in the sunlight.

As nobody seemed inclined to respond to this heroic version of 'Dilly, Dilly, come and be killed,' our late henchman proceeded with his address.

'I am indeed the king, and should ye stand by my side in the battle, if I win the day ye shall go with me to victory and honour. I will give you oxen and wives, and ye shall take place of all the regiments; and if ye fall, I will fall with you.

'Behold, I give you this promise also, that when I sit upon the seat of my fathers, bloodshed shall cease in the land. No longer shall ye cry for justice to find slaughter, no longer shall the witch-finder hunt you out so that ye may be slain without a cause. No man shall die save he who offends against the laws. The "eating up" of your kraals shall cease; each one of you shall sleep secure in his own hut and fear nought, and justice shall walk blindfold throughout the land. Have ye chosen, chiefs, captains, soldiers, and people?'

'We have chosen, O king,' came back the answer.

'It is well. Turn your heads and see how Twala's messengers go forth from the great town, east and west, and north and south, to gather a mighty army to slay me and you, and these my friends and protectors. To-morrow, or perchance the next day, he will come against us with all who are faithful to him. Then I shall see the man who is indeed my man, the man who fears not to die for his cause; and I tell you that he shall not be forgotten in the time of spoil. I have spoken, O chiefs, captains, soldiers, and people. Now go to your huts and make you ready for war.'

There was a pause, till presently one of the chiefs lifted his hand, and out rolled the royal salute, '*Koom.*' It was a sign that the soldiers accepted Ignosi as their king. Then they marched off in battalions.

Half an hour afterwards we held a council of war, at which all the commanders of regiments were present. It was evident to us that before very long we should be attacked in overwhelming force. Indeed, from our point of vantage on the hill we could see troops mustering, and runners going forth from Loo in every direction, doubtless to summon soldiers to the king's assistance. We had on our side about twenty thousand men, composed of seven of the best regiments in the country. Twala, so Infadoos and the chiefs calculated, had at least thirty to thirty-five thousand on whom he could rely at present assembled in Loo, and they thought that by midday on the morrow he would be able to gather another five thousand or more to his aid. It was, of course, possible that some of the troops would desert and come over to us, but it was a not contingency which could be reckoned on. Meanwhile, it was clear that active preparations were being made by Twala to subdue us. Already strong bodies of armed men were patrolling round and round the foot of the hill; also there were other signs of coming assault.

Infadoos and the chiefs, however, were of opinion that no attack would take place that day, which would be devoted to preparation and to the removal by every available means of the moral effect produced upon the minds of the soldiery by the supposed magical darkening of the moon. The onslaught would be on the morrow, they said, and they proved to be right.

Meanwhile we set to work to strengthen the position in all ways possible. Almost every man was turned out, and in the course of the day, which seemed far too short, much was done. The paths up the hill – that was rather a sanatorium than a fortress, being used generally as the camping place of regiments suffering from recent service in unhealthy portions of the country – were carefully blocked with masses of stones, and every other approach was made as impregnable as time would allow. Piles of boulders were collected at various spots to be rolled down upon an advancing enemy, stations were appointed to the different regiments, and all preparation was made which our joint ingenuity could suggest.

Just before sundown, as we rested after our toil, we perceived a small company of men advancing towards us from the direction of Loo, one of whom bore a palm leaf in his hand for a sign that he came as a herald.

As he drew near, Ignosi, Infadoos, one or two chiefs and

ourselves went down to the foot of the mountain to meet him. He was a gallant-looking fellow, wearing the regulation leopard-skin cloak.

'Greeting!' he cried, as he came; 'the king's greeting to those who make unholy war against the king; the lion's greeting to the jackals that snarl around his heels.'

'Speak,' I said.

'These are the king's words. Surrender to the king's mercy ere a worse thing befall you. Already the shoulder has been torn from the black bull, and the king drives him bleeding about the camp.'[1]

'What are Twala's terms?' I asked from curiosity.

'His terms are merciful, worthy of a great king. These are the words of Twala, the one-eyed, the mighty, the husband of a thousand wives, lord of the Kukuanas, keeper of the Great Road (Solomon's Road), beloved of the Strange Ones who sit in silence at the mountains yonder (the Three Witches), Calf of the Black Cow, Elephant whose tread shakes the earth, Terror of the evil-doer, Ostrich whose feet devour the desert, huge One, black One, wise One, King from generation to generation! these are the words of Twala: "I will have mercy and be satisfied with a little blood. One in every ten shall die, the rest shall go free; but the white man Incubu, who slew Scragga my son, and the black man his servant, who pretends to my throne, and Infadoos my brother, who brews rebellion against me, these shall die by torture as an offering to the Silent Ones." Such are the merciful words of Twala.'

After consulting with the others a little, I answered him in a loud voice, so that the soldiers might hear, thus –

'Go back, thou dog, to Twala, who sent thee, and say that we, Ignosi, veritable king of the Kukuanas, Incubu, Bougwan, and Macumazahn, the wise ones from the Stars, who make dark the moon, Infadoos, of the royal house, and the chiefs, captains, and

[1] This cruel custom is not confined to the Kukuanas, but is not uncommon amongst Africans tribe on the occasion of the outbreak of war or any other important public event. – A.Q.

people here gathered, make answer and say, "That we will not surrender; that before the sun has gone down twice, Twala's corpse shall stiffen at Twala's gate, and Ignosi, whose father Twala slew, shall reign in his stead." Now go, ere we whip thee away, and beware how thou dost lift a hand against such as we are.'

The herald laughed loudly. 'Ye frighten not men with such swelling words,' he cried out. 'Show yourselves as bold to-morrow, O ye who darken the moon. Be bold, fight, and be merry, before the crows pick your bones till they are whiter than your faces. Farewell; perhaps we may meet in the fight; fly not to the Stars, but wait for me, I pray, white men.'

With this shaft of sarcasm he retired, and almost immediately the sun sank.

That night was a busy one, for weary as we were, so far as was possible by the moonlight all preparations for the morrow's fight were continued, and messengers were constantly coming and going from the place where we sat in council. At last, about an hour after midnight, everything that could be done was done, and the camp, save for the occasional challenge of a sentry, sank into silence. Sir Henry and I, accompanied by Ignosi and one of the chiefs, descended the hill and made a round of the pickets. As we went, suddenly, from all sorts of unexpected places, spears gleamed out in the moonlight, only to vanish again when we uttered the password. It was clear to us that none were sleeping at their posts. Then we returned, picking our way warily through thousands of sleeping warriors, many of whom were taking their last earthly rest.

The moonlight flickering along their spears, played upon their features and made them ghastly; the chilly night wind tossed their tall and hearse-like plumes. There they lay in wild confusion, with arms outstretched and twisted limbs; their stern, stalwart forms looking weird and unhuman in the moonlight.

'How many of these do you suppose will be alive at this time to-morrow?' asked Sir Henry.

I shook my head and looked again at the sleeping men, and to my tired yet excited imagination it seemed as though Death had already touched them. My mind's eye singled out those who were sealed to slaughter, and there rushed in upon my heart a great sense of the mystery of human life, and an overwhelming sorrow at its futility and sadness. To-night these thousands slept their healthy sleep, tomorrow they, and many others with them, ourselves perhaps among them, would be stiffening in the cold; their wives would be widows, their children fatherless, and their place know them no more for ever. Only the old moon would shine on serenely, the night wind would stir the grasses, and the wide earth would take its rest, even as it did aeons before we were, and will do aeons after we have been forgotten.

Yet man dies not whilst the world, at once his mother and his monument, remains. His name is lost, indeed, but the breath he breathed still stirs the pine-tops on the mountains, the sound of the words he spoke yet echoes on through space; the thoughts his brain gave birth to we have inherited to-day; his passions are our cause of life; the joys and sorrows that he knew are our familiar friends – the end from which he fled aghast will surely overtake us also!

Truly the universe is full of ghosts, not sheeted, churchyard spectres, but the inextinguishable elements of individual life, which having once been, can never *die*, though they blend and change, and change again for ever.

All sorts of reflections of this nature passed through my mind – for as I grow older I regret to say that a detestable habit of thinking seems to be getting a hold of me – while I stood and stared at those grim yet fantastic lines of warriors, sleeping, as their saying goes, 'upon their spears.'

'Curtis,' I said, 'I am in a condition of pitiable fear.'

Sir Henry stroked his yellow beard and laughed, as he answered –

'I have heard you make that sort of remark before, Quatermain.'

'Well, I mean it now. Do you know, I very much doubt if one of us will be alive to-morrow night. We shall be attacked in over-whelming force, and it is quite a chance if we can hold this place.'

'We'll give a good account of some of them, at any rate. Look here, Quatermain, this business is nasty, and one with which, properly speaking, we ought not to be mixed up, but we are in for it, so we must make the best of our job. Speaking personally, I had rather be killed fighting than any other way, and now that there seems little chance of our finding my poor brother, it makes the idea easier to me. But fortune favours the brave, and we may succeed. Anyway, the battle will be awful, and having a reputation to keep up, we shall need to be in the thick of the thing.'

He made this last remark in a mournful voice, but there was a gleam in his eye which belied its melancholy. I have an idea that Sir Henry Curtis actually likes fighting.

After this we went to sleep for a couple of hours or so.

Just about dawn we were awakened by Infadoos, who came to say that great activity was to be observed in Loo, and that parties of the king's skirmishers were driving in our outposts.

We rose and dressed ourselves for the fray, each putting on his chain armour shirt, for which garments at the present juncture we felt exceedingly thankful. Sir Henry went the whole length about the matter, and dressed himself like a native warrior. 'When you are in Kukuanaland, do as the Kukuanas do,' he remarked, as he drew the shining steel over his broad breast, which it fitted like a glove. Nor did he stop there. At his request Infadoos had provided him with a complete set of native war uniform. Round his throat he fastened the leopard-skin cloak of a commanding officer, on his brows he bound the plume of black ostrich feathers worn only by generals of high rank, and about his middle a magnificent moocha of white ox-tails. A pair of sandals, a leglet of goat's hair, a heavy battle-axe with a rhinoceros-horn handle, a round iron shield covered with white ox-hide, and the regulation number of *tollas,* or throwing-knives, made up his equipment, to which, however, he added his revolver. The dress was, no doubt, a savage one, but I am bound to say that I seldom saw a finer sight than Sir Henry Curtis presented in this guise. It showed off his magnificent physique to the greatest advantage, and when Ignosi arrived presently, arrayed in a similar costume, I thought to myself that I had never before seen two such splendid men.

As for Good and myself, the armour did not suit us well. To begin with, Good insisted upon wearing his newfound trousers, and a stout, short gentleman with an eyeglass, and one half of his face shaved, arrayed in a mail shirt, carefully tucked into a very seedy pair of corduroys, looks more remarkable than imposing. In my case, the chain shirt being too big for me, I put it on over all my clothes, which caused it to bulge in a somewhat ungainly fashion. I discarded my trousers, however, retaining only my veldschoens, having determined to go into battle with bare legs, in order to be the lighter for running, in case it became necessary to retire quickly. The mail coat, a spear, a shield that I did not know how to use, a couple of *tollas*, a revolver, and a huge plume, which I pinned into the top of my shooting hat, in order to give a bloodthirsty finish to my appearance, completed my modest equipment. In addition to all these articles, of course, we had our rifles, but as ammunition was scarce, and as they would be useless in case of a charge, we arranged that they should be carried behind us by bearers.

When at length we had equipped ourselves, we swallowed some food hastily, and then started out to see how things were going on. At one point in the tableland of the mountain, there was a little koppie of brown stone, which served the double purpose of headquarters and of a conning tower. Here we found Infadoos surrounded by his own regiment, the Greys, which was undoubtedly the finest in the Kukuana army, and the same that we had first seen at the outlying kraal. This regiment, now three thousand five hundred strong, was being held in reserve, and the men were lying down on the grass in companies, and watching the king's forces creep out of Loo in long ant-like columns. There seemed to be no end to the length of these columns – three in all, and each of them numbering, as we judged, at least eleven or twelve thousand men.

As soon as they were clear of the town the regiments formed up. Then one body marched off to the right, one to the left, and the third came on slowly towards us.

'Ah,' said Infadoos, 'they are going to attack us on three sides at once.'

This seemed rather serious news, for our position on the top of the mountain, which measured a mile and a half in circumference, being an extended one, it was important to us to concentrate our comparatively small defending force as much as possible. But since it was impossible for us to dictate in what way we should be assailed, we had to make the best of it, and accordingly sent orders to the various regiments to prepare to receive the separate onslaughts.

CHAPTER 13

The Attack

Slowly, and without the slightest appearance of haste or excitement, the three columns crept on. When within about five hundred yards of us, the main or centre column halted at the root of a tongue of open plain which ran up into the hill, to give time to the other divisions to circumvent our position, which was shaped more or less in the form of a horseshoe, with its two points facing towards the town of Loo. The object of this manoeuvre was that the threefold assault should be delivered simultaneously.

'Oh, for a Gatling!' groaned Good, as he contemplated the serried phalanxes beneath us. 'I would clear that plain in twenty minutes.'

'We have not got one, so it is no use yearning for it; but suppose you try a shot, Quatermain,' said Sir Henry.

'See how near you can go to that tall fellow who appears to be in command. Two to one you miss him, and an even sovereign, to be honestly paid if ever we get out of this, that you don't drop the bullet within five yards.'

This piqued me, so, loading the Express with solid ball, I waited till my friend walked some ten yards out from his force, in order to get a better view of our position, accompanied only by an orderly; then, lying down and resting the Express upon a rock, I covered him. The rifle, like all Expresses, was only sighted to three hundred and fifty yards, so to allow for the drop in trajectory I took him half-way down the neck, which ought, I calculated, to find him in the chest. He stood quite still and gave me every opportunity, but whether it was the excitement or the wind, or the fact of the man being a long shot, I don't know, but this was what happened. Getting dead on, as I thought, and taking a fine sight, I pressed. When the puff of smoke had cleared away, to my disgust, I saw my man standing unharmed, whilst his orderly, who was at least three paces to the left, was stretched upon the ground apparently dead. Turning swiftly, the officer I had aimed at began to run towards his men in evident alarm.

'Bravo, Quatermain!' sang out Good; 'you've frightened him.'

This made me very angry, for, if possible to avoid it, I hate to miss in public. When a man is master of only one art he likes to keep up his reputation in that art. Moved quite out of myself at my failure, I did a rash thing. Rapidly covering the general as he ran, I let drive with the second barrel. Instantly the poor man threw up his arms, and fell forward on to his face. This time I had made no mistake; and – I say it as a proof of how little we think of others when our own safety, pride, and reputation are in question – I was brute enough to feel delighted at the sight.

The regiments who had seen the feat cheered wildly at this exhibition of the white man's magic, which they took as an omen of success, while the force the general had belonged to – which, indeed, as we ascertained afterwards, he had commanded – fell back in confusion. Sir Henry and Good now took up their rifles and began to fire, the latter industriously 'browning' the dense mass before him with a Winchester repeater, and I also had another shot or two, with the result, so far as we could judge, that we put some six or eight men *hors de combat* before they were out of range.

Just as we stopped firing there came an ominous roar from our far right, then a similar roar rose on our left. The two other divisions were engaging us.

At the sound, the mass of men before us opened out a little, and advanced towards the hill and up the spit of bare grass land at a slow trot, singing a deep-throated song as they ran. We kept up a steady fire from our rifles as they came, Ignosi joining in occasionally, and accounted for several men, but of course we produced no more effect upon that mighty rush of armed humanity than he who throws pebbles does on the breaking wave.

On they came, with a shout and the clashing of spears; now they were driving in the pickets we had placed among the rocks at the foot of the hill. After that the advance was a little slower, for though as yet we had offered no serious opposition, the attacking forces must climb up hill, and they came slowly to save their breath. Our first line of defence was about half-way down the side of the slope, our second fifty yards farther back, while our third occupied the edge of the plateau.

On they stormed, shouting their war-cry, 'Twala! Twala! Chiele! Chiele!' (Twala! Twala! Smite! Smite!). 'Ignosi! Ignosi! Chiele! Chiele!' answered our people. They were quite close now, and the *tollas*, or throwing-knives, began to flash backwards and forwards, and now with an awful yell the battle closed in.

To and fro swayed the mass of struggling warriors, men falling fast as leaves in an autumn wind; but before long the superior weight of the attacking force began to tell, and our first line of defence was slowly pressed back, till it merged into the second. Here the struggle was very fierce, but again our people were driven back and up, till at length, within twenty minutes of the commencement of the fight, our third line came into action.

But by this time the assailants were much exhausted, and besides had lost many men killed and wounded, and to break through that third impenetrable hedge of spears proved beyond their powers. For a while the seething lines of savages swung backwards and forwards, in the fierce ebb and flow of battle, and the issue was doubtful. Sir Henry watched the desperate struggle with a kindling eye, and then without a word he rushed off, followed by Good, and flung himself into the hottest of the fray. As for myself, I stopped where I was.

The soldiers caught sight of his tall form as he plunged into battle, and there rose a cry of –

'*Nanzia Incubu! Nanzia Incubu!*' (Here is the Elephant!) '*Chiele! Chiele!*'

From that moment the end was no longer in doubt. Inch by inch, fighting with splendid gallantry, the attacking force was pressed back down the hillside, till at last it retreated upon its reserves in something like confusion. At that instant, too, a messenger arrived to say that the left attack had been repulsed; and I was just beginning to congratulate myself, believing that the affair was over for the present, when, to our horror, we perceived our men who had been engaged in the right defence being driven towards us across the plain, followed by swarms of the enemy, who had evidently succeeded at this point.

Ignosi, who was standing by me, took in the situation at a glance, and issued a rapid order. Instantly the reserve regiment around us, the Greys, extended itself.

Again Ignosi gave a word of command, which was taken up and repeated by the captains, and in another second, to my intense disgust, I found myself involved in a furious onslaught upon the advancing foe. Getting as much as I could behind Ignosi's huge frame, I made the best of a bad job, and toddled along to be killed as though I liked it. In a minute or two – the time seemed all too short to me – we were plunging through the flying groups of our men, who at once began to re-form behind us, and then I am sure I do not know what happened. All I can remember is a dreadful rolling noise of the meeting of shields, and the sudden apparition of a huge ruffian, whose eyes seemed literally to be starting out of his head, making straight at me with a bloody spear. But – I say it with pride – I rose – or rather sank – to the occasion. It was one before which most people would have collapsed once and for all. Seeing that if I stood where I was I must be killed, as the horrid apparition came I flung myself down in front of him so cleverly that, being unable to stop himself, he took a header right over my prostrate form. Before he could rise again, *I* had risen and settled the matter from behind with my revolver.

Shortly after this somebody knocked me down, and I remember no more of that charge.

When I came to I found myself back at the koppie, with Good bending over me holding some water in a gourd.

'How do you feel, old fellow?' he asked anxiously.

I got up and shook myself before replying.

'Pretty well, thank you,' I answered.

'Thank Heaven! When I saw them carry you in, I felt quite sick; I thought that you were done for.'

'Not this time, my boy. I fancy I only got a rap on the head, which knocked me stupid. How has it ended?'

'They are repulsed at every point for a while. The loss is dreadfully heavy; we have quite two thousand killed and wounded, and they must have lost three. Look, there's a sight!' and he pointed to long lines of men advancing by fours.

In the centre of every group of four, and being borne by it, was a kind of hide tray, of which a Kukuana force always carries a quantity, with a loop for a handle at each corner. On these trays – and their number seemed endless – lay wounded men, who as they arrived were hastily examined by the medicine men, of whom ten were attached to a regiment. If the wound was not of a fatal character the sufferer was taken away and attended to as carefully as circumstances would allow. But if, on the other hand, the injured man's condition proved hopeless, what followed was very dreadful, though doubtless it may have been the truest mercy. One of the doctors, under pretence of carrying out an examination, swiftly opened an artery with a sharp knife, and in a minute or two the sufferer expired painlessly. There were many cases that day in which this was done. In fact, it was done in the majority of cases when the wound was in the body, for the gash made by the entry of the enormously broad spears used by the Kukuanas generally rendered recovery impossible. In most instances the poor sufferers were already unconscious, and in others the fatal 'nick' of the artery was inflicted so swiftly and painlessly that they did not seem to notice it. Still it was a ghastly sight, and one from which we were glad to escape. Indeed, I never remember anything of the kind that affected me more than seeing those gallant soldiers thus put out of pain by the red-handed medicine men, except, indeed, on one occasion when, after an attack, I saw a force of Swazis burying their hopelessly wounded *alive*.

Hurrying from this dreadful scene to the farther side of the koppie, we found Sir Henry, who still held a battle-axe in his hand, Ignosi, Infadoos, and one or two of the chiefs in deep consultation.

'Thank Heaven, here you are, Quatermain! I can't quite make out what Ignosi wants to do. It seems that though we have beaten off the attack. Twala is now receiving large reinforcements, and is showing a disposition to invest us, with a view of starving us out.'

'That's awkward.'

'Yes; especially as Infadoos says that the water supply has given out.'

'My lord, that is so,' said Infadoos; 'the spring cannot supply the wants of so great a multitude, and it is failing rapidly. Before night we shall all be thirsty. Listen, Macumazahn. Thou art wise, and hast doubtless seen mány wars in the lands from whence thou camest – that is if indeed they make wars in the Stars. Now tell us, what shall we do? Twala has brought up many fresh men to take the place of those who have fallen. Yet Twala has learnt his lesson; the hawk did not think to find the heron ready; but our beak has pierced his breast; he fears to strike at us again. We too are wounded, and he will wait for us to die; he will wind himself round us like a snake round a buck, and fight the fight of "sit down."'

'I hear thee,' I said.

'So, Macumazahn, thou seest we have no water here, and but a little food, and we must choose between these three things – to languish like a starving lion in his den, or to strive to break away towards the north, or' – and here he rose and pointed towards the dense mass of our foes – 'to launch ourselves straight at Twala's throat. Incubu, the great warrior – for to-day he fought like a buffalo in a net, and Twala's soldiers went down before his axe like young corn before the hail; with these eyes I saw it – Incubu says " Charge"; but the Elephant is ever prone to charge. Now what says Macumazahn, the wily old fox, who has seen much, and loves to bite his enemy from behind? The last word is in Ignosi the king, for it is a king's right to speak of war; but let us hear thy voice, O Macumazahn, who watchest by night, and the voice too of him of the transparent eye.'

'What sayest thou, Ignosi?' I asked.

'Nay, my father,' answered our quondam servant, who now, clad as he was in the full panoply of savage war, looked every inch a warrior king, 'do thou speak, and let me, who am but a child in wisdom beside thee, hearken to thy words.'

Thus adjured, after taking hasty counsel with Good and Sir Henry, I delivered my opinion briefly to the effect, that, being trapped, our best chance, especially in view of the failure of our water supply, was to initiate an attack upon Twala's forces. Then I recommended that the attack should be delivered at once, 'before our wounds grew stiff'; also before the sight of Twala's overpowering force caused the hearts of our soldiers 'to wax small like fat before a fire.' Otherwise I pointed out, some of the captains might change their minds, and, making peace with Twala, desert to him, or even betray us into his hands.

This expression of opinion, seemed on the whole, to be favourably received; indeed, among the Kukuanas my utterances met with a respect which has never been accorded to them before or since. But the real decision as to our plans lay with Ignosi, who, since he had been recognised as rightful king, could exercise the almost unbounded rights of sovereignty, including, of course, the final decision on matters of generalship, and it was to him that all eyes were now turned.

At length, after a pause, during which he appeared to be thinking deeply, he spoke.

'Incubu, Macumazahn, and Bougwan, brave white men, and my friends; Infadoos, my uncle, and chiefs; my heart is fixed. I will strike at Twala this day, and set my fortunes on the blow, ay, and my life – my life and your lives also. Listen; thus will I strike. Ye see how the hill curves round like the half-moon, and how the plain runs like a green tongue towards us within the curve?'

'We see,' I answered.

'Good; it is now midday, and the men eat and rest after the toil of battle. When the sun has turned and travelled a little way towards the darkness, let thy regiment, my uncle, advance with one other down to the green tongue; and it shall be that when Twala sees it he will hurl his force at it to crush it. But the spot is narrow, and the regiments can come against thee one at a time only; so may they be destroyed one by one, and the eyes of all Twala's army shall be fixed upon a struggle the like of which has not been seen by living man. And with thee, my uncle, shall go Incubu my friend, that when Twala sees his battle-axe flashing in the first rank of the Greys his heart may grow faint. And I will come with the second regiment, that which follows thee, so that if ye are destroyed, as it might happen, there may yet be a king left to fight for; and with me shall come Macumazahn the wise.'

'It is well, O king,' said Infadoos, apparently contemplating the certainty of the complete annihilation of his regiment with perfect calmness.

Truly, these Kukuanas are a wonderful people. Death has no terrors for them when it is incurred in the course of duty.

'And whilst the eyes of the multitude of Twala's soldiers are thus fixed upon the fight,' went on Ignosi, 'behold, one-third of the men who are left alive to us (*i. e.* about six thousand) shall creep along the right horn of the hill and fall upon the left flank of Twala's force, and one-third shall creep along the left horn and fall upon Twala's right flank. And when I see that the horns are ready to toss Twala, then will I, with the men who remain to me, charge home in Twala's face, and if fortune goes with us the day will be ours, and before Night drives her black oxen from the mountains to the mountains we shall sit in peace at Loo. Now let us eat and make ready; and, Infadoos, do thou prepare, that the plan be carried out without fail; and stay, let my white father Bougwan go with the right horn, that his shining eye may give courage to the captains.'

The arrangements for attack thus briefly indicated were set in motion with a rapidity that spoke well for the perfection of the

Kukuana military system. Within little more than an hour rations had been served out and devoured, the divisions were formed, the scheme of onslaught was explained to the leaders, and the whole force, numbering about eighteen thousand men, was ready to move, with the exception of a guard left in charge of the wounded.

Presently Good came up to Sir Henry and myself.

'Good-bye, you fellows,' he said; 'I am off with the right wing according to orders. So I have come to shake hands, in case we should not meet again, you know,' he added significantly.

We shook hands in silence, and not without the exhibition of as much emotion as Anglo-Saxons are wont to show.

'It is a queer business,' said Sir Henry, his deep voice shaking a little, 'and I confess I never expect to see tomorrow's sun. So far as I can make out, the Greys, with whom I am to go, are to fight until they are wiped out in order to enable the wings to slip round unawares and outflank Twala. Well, so be it; at any rate, it will be a man's death. Good-bye, old fellow. God bless you! I hope you will pull through and live to collar the diamonds; but if you do, take my advice and don't have anything more to do with Pretenders to a Throne!'

In another second Good had wrung us both by the hand and gone. Then Infadoos came up and led off Sir Henry to his place in the forefront of the Greys, whilst, with many misgivings, I departed with Ignosi to my station in the second attacking regiment.

CHAPTER 14

The Last Stand of the Greys

In a few more minutes the regiments destined to carry out the flanking movements had tramped off in silence, keeping carefully under the lee of the rising ground in order to conceal their advance from the keen eyes of Twala's scouts.

Half an hour or more was allowed to elapse between the setting out of the horns or wings of the army before any stir was made by the Greys and their supporting regiments, known as the Buffaloes, which formed its chest, and were destined to bear the brunt of the battle.

Both of these regiments were almost perfectly fresh, and of full strength, the Greys having been in reserve in the morning, and having lost but a small number of men in sweeping back that part of the attack which had proved successful in breaking the line of defence, on the occasion when I charged with them and was stunned for my pains. As for the Buffaloes, they had formed the third line of defence on the left, and since the attacking force at that point had not succeeded in breaking through the second, they had scracely come into action at all.

Infadoos, who was a wary old general, and knew the absolute importance of keeping up the spirits of his men on the eve of such a desperate encounter, employed the pause in addressing his own regiment, the Greys, in poetical language. He explained to them the

157

honour that they were receiving in being set thus in the forefront of the battle, and in having the great white warrior from the Stars to fight with them in their ranks. Also he promised large rewards of cattle and promotion to all who survived, in the event of Ignosi's arms being successful.

I looked down the long lines of waving black plumes and of stern faces beneath them, and sighed to think that within one short hour most, if not all of those magnificent veteran warriors, not a man of whom was under forty years of age, would be laid dead or dying in the dust. It could not be otherwise; with that sagacious recklessness of human life which marks the great general, and often saves his forces and attains his ends, they were being condemned to inevitable slaughter, in order to give their cause and the remainder of the army a chance of success. They were foredoomed to die, and they knew the truth. It was to be their task to engage regiment after regiment of Twala's army on the narrow strip of green beneath us, till they were exterminated, or until the wings found a favourable opportunity for their onslaught. And yet they never hesitated, nor could I detect a sign of fear upon the face of a single warrior. There they stood – going to certain death, about to walk the dreadful bridge of spears, about to quit the blessed light of day, and yet able to contemplate their doom without a tremor. Even at that moment I could not help contrasting their state of mind with my own, which was far from comfortable, and breathing a sigh of envy and admiration. Never before had I seen such an absolute devotion to the idea of duty, and such a complete indifference to its bitter fruits.

'Behold your king!' ended old Infadoos, pointing to Ignosi; 'go fight and fall for him, as is the duty of brave men, and cursed and shameful for ever be the name of him who shrinks from death for his king, or who turns his back to the foe. Chiefs, captains, and soldiers, behold your king! Now do your homage to the sacred Snake, and follow on, that Incubu and I may show you a road to the heart of Twala's host.'

There was a moment's pause, then suddenly a murmur arose from the serried phalanxes before us, a sound like the distant whisper of the sea, caused by the gentle tapping of the handles of six thousand spears against their holder's shields. Slowly it swelled, till its growing volume deepened and widened into a roar of rolling noise, that echoed like thunder against the mountains, and filled the air with heavy waves of sound. Then it decreased, until by faint degrees it died away into nothing, and suddenly out crashed the royal salute.

Ignosi, I thought to myself, might well be a proud man that day, for no Roman emperor ever had such a salutation from gladiators 'about to die.'

Ignosi acknowledged this magnificent act of homage by lifting his battle-axe, and then the Greys filed off in a triple formation, each line containing about one thousand fighting men, exclusive of officers. When the last companies had advanced some five hundred yards, Ignosi put himself at the head of the Buffaloes, which regiment was drawn up in a similar three-fold formation, and gave the word to march. Off we went, I, needless to say, uttering the most heartfelt prayers that I might emerge from that entertainment with a whole skin. Many a queer position have I found myself in, but seldom before in one quite so unpleasant, or one in which my chance of coming off safe was smaller.

By the time that we reached the edge of the plateau the Greys were already half-way down the slope ending in the tongue of grass land that ran up into the bend of the mountain, something as the frog of a horse's foot runs up into the shoe. The excitement in Twala's camp on the plain beyond seemed very great. Regiment after regiment was starting forward at a long swinging trot in order to reach the root of the tongue of land before the attacking force could emerge into the plain of Loo.

This tongue, which was some four hundred yards in depth, even at its root or widest part was not more than six hundred and fifty paces across, while at its tip it scarcely measured ninety. The Greys, who, in passing down the side of the hill and on to the tip of the tongue, had formed into column, on reaching the spot where it broadened out again, reassumed their triple-line formation, and halted dead.

Then we – that is, the Buffaloes – moved down the tip of the tongue and took our stand in reserve, about one hundred yards behind the last line of the Greys, and on slightly higher ground. Meanwhile we had leisure to observe Twala's entire force, which evidently had been reinforced since the morning attack, and could not now, notwithstanding their losses, number fewer than forty thousand, moving swiftly up towards us. But as they drew near the root of the tongue they hesitated, having discovered that only one regiment could advance into the gorge at a time, and that there, some seventy yards from the mouth of it, unassailable except in front, on account of the high walls of boulder-strewn ground on each side, stood the famous regiment of Greys, the pride and glory of the Kukuana army, ready to hold the way against their power as the three Romans once held the bridge against the ranks of Tusculum.

They hesitated, and finally stopped their advance; there was no eagerness to cross spears with these three grim ranks of warriors who stood so firm and ready. Presently, however, a tall general, wearing the customary head-dress of nodding ostrich plumes, appeared, attended by a group of chiefs and orderlies, being, I thought, none other than Twala himself. He gave an order, and the first regiment, raising a shout, charged up towards the Greys, who remained perfectly still and silent till the attacking troops were within forty yards, and a volley of *tollas*, or throwing-knives, came rattling among the ranks.

Then suddenly with a bound and a roar, the Greys sprang forward with uplifted spears, and the regiments met in deadly strife. Next second the roll of the meeting shields came to our ears like the sound of thunder, and the plain seemed to be alive with flashes of light reflected from the shimmering spears. To and fro swung the surging mass of struggling, stabbing humanity, but not for long. Suddenly the attacking lines began to grow thinner, and then with a slow, long heave the Greys passed over them, just as a great wave heaves up its bulk and passes over a sunken ridge. It was done; that regiment was completely destroyed but now the Greys had but two lines left; a third of their number were dead.

Closing up shoulder to shoulder, once more they halted in silence and awaited attack; and I was rejoiced to catch sight of Sir Henry's yellow beard as he moved to and fro arranging the ranks. So he was yet alive!

Meanwhile we moved on to the ground of the encounter, which was cumbered by about four thousand prostrate human beings, dead, dying, and wounded, and literally stained red with blood. Ignosi issued an order, which was rapidly passed down the ranks, to the effect that none of the enemy's wounded were to be killed, and so far as we could see this command was scrupulously carried out. It would have been a shocking sight, if we had found time to think of such things.

But now a second regiment, distinguished by white plumes, kilts, and shields, was moving to the attack of the two thousand remaining Greys, who stood waiting in the same ominous silence as before, till the foe was within thirty yards or so, when they hurled themselves with irresistible force upon them. Again there came the awful roll of the meeting shields, and as we watched the tragedy repeated itself.

But this time the issue was left longer in doubt; indeed, it seemed for awhile almost impossible that the Greys should again prevail. The attacking regiment, which was formed of young men, fought with the utmost fury, and at first seemed by sheer weight to be driving the veterans back. The slaughter was truly awful, hundreds falling every minute; and from among the shouts of the warriors, and the groans of the dying, set to the music of clashing spears, came a continuous hissing undertone of 'S'gee, s'gee,' the note of triumph of each victor as he passed his assegai through and through the body of his fallen foe.

But perfect discipline and steady and unchanging valour can do wonders, and one veteran soldier is worth two young ones, as soon became apparent in the present case. For just when we thought that it was all over with the Greys, and were preparing to take their place so soon as they made room by being destroyed, I heard Sir Henry's deep voice ringing through the din, and caught a glimpse of his circling battle-axe as he waved it high above his plumes. Then came a change; the Greys ceased to give; they stood still as a rock, against which the furious waves of spearmen broke again and again, only to recoil. Presently they began to move once more – forward this time; as they had no firearms there was no smoke, so we could see it all. Another minute and the onslaught grew fainter.

'Ah, these are *men*, indeed; they will conquer again,' called out Ignosi, who was grinding his teeth with excitement at my side. 'See, it is done!'

Suddenly, like puffs of smoke from the mouth of a cannon, the attacking regiment broke away in flying groups, their white head-dresses streaming behind them in the wind, and left their opponents victors, indeed, but, alas! no more a regiment. Of the gallant triple line, which forty minutes before had gone into action three thousand strong, there remained at most some six hundred blood-bespattered men; the rest were under foot. And yet they cheered and waved their spears in triumph, and then, instead of falling back upon us as we expected, they ran forward, for a hundred yards or so, after the flying groups of foemen, took possession of a rising knoll of ground, and, resuming their triple formation, formed a threefold ring around its base. And there, thanks be to Heaven, standing on the top of the mound for a minute, I saw Sir Henry, apparently unharmed, and with him our old friend Infadoos. Then Twala's regiments rolled down upon the doomed band, and once more the battle closed in.

As those who read this history will probably long ago have gathered, I am, to be honest, a bit of a coward, and certainly in no way given to fighting, though somehow it has often been my lot to get into unpleasant positions, and to be obliged to shed man's blood. But I have always hated it, and kept my own blood as undiminished in quantity as possible, sometimes by a judicious use of my heels. At this moment, however, perhaps for the first time in my life, I felt my bosom burn with martial ardour. Warlike fragments from the 'Ingoldsby Legends,' together with numbers of sanguinary verses in the Old Testament, sprang up in my brain like mushrooms in the dark; my blood, which hitherto had been half-frozen with horror, went beating through my veins, and there came upon me a savage desire to kill and spare not. I glanced round at the serried ranks of warriors behind us, and somehow, all in an instant, I began to wonder if my face looked like theirs. There they stood, their heads craned forward over their shields, the hands twitching, the lips apart, the fierce features instinct with the hungry lust of battle, and in the eyes a look like the glare of a bloodhound when after long pursuit he sights his quarry.

Only Ignosi's heart, to judge from his comparative self-possession, seemed, to all appearance, to beat as calmly as ever beneath his leopard-skin cloak, though even *he* still ground his teeth. I could bear it no longer.

'Are we to stand here till we put out roots, Umbopa – Ignosi, I mean – while Twala swallows our brothers yonder?' I asked.

'Nay, Macumazahn,' was the answer; 'see, now is the ripe moment: let us pluck it.'

As he spoke a fresh regiment rushed past the ring upon the little mound, and, wheeling round, attacked it from the hither side.

Then, lifting his battle-axe, Ignosi gave the signal to advance, and, screaming the wild Kukuana war-cry, the Buffaloes charged home with a rush like the rush of the sea.

What followed immediately on this it is out of my power to tell. All I can remember is an irregular yet ordered advance, that seemed to shake the ground; a sudden change of front and forming up on the part of the regiment against which the charge was directed; then an awful shock, a dull roar of voices, and a continuous flashing of spears, seen through a red mist of blood.

When my mind cleared I found myself standing inside the remnant of the Greys near the top of the mound, and just behind no less a person than Sir Henry himself. How I got there I had at the moment no idea, but Sir Henry afterwards told me that I was borne up by the first furious charge of the Buffaloes almost to his feet, and there left, as they in turn were pressed back. Thereon he dashed out of the circle and dragged me into shelter.

As for the fight that followed, who can describe it? Again and again the multitudes surged against our momentarily lessening circle, and again and again we beat them back.

> 'The stubborn spearmen still made good
> The dark impenetrable wood,
> Each stepping where his comrade stood
> The instant that he fell,'
> as someone or other beautifully says.

It was a splendid sight to see those brave battalions come on time after time over the barriers of their dead, sometimes lifting corpses before them to receive our spear thrusts, only to leave their own corpses to swell the rising piles. It was a gallant thing to hear that sturdy old warrior, Infadoos, as cool as though he were on parade, shouting out orders, taunts, and even jests, to keep up the spirit of his few remaining men, and then, as each charge rolled on, to watch him spring to wherever the fighting was thickest, to bear his share in its repulse. And yet more gallant was the vision of Sir Henry, whose ostrich plumes had been shorn off by a spear thrust, so that his long yellow hair streamed out in the breeze behind him. There he stood, the great Northman, for he was nothing else, his hands, his axe, and his armour all red with blood, and none could live before his stroke. Time after time I saw it sweeping down, as some great warrior ventured to give him battle, and as he struck he shouted '*O-hoy! O-hoy!*' like his Berserker forefathers, and the blow went crashing through shield and spear, through headdress, hair, and skull, till at last none would of their own will come near the tall white '*umtagati*,' the wizard, who killed and failed not.

But suddenly there arose a cry of '*Twala, y' Twala*,' and out of the press sprang forward none other than the gigantic one-eyed king himself, also armed with battle-axe and shield, and clad in chain armour.

'Where art thou, Incubu, thou white man, who slewest Scragga my son – see if thou canst slay me!' he shouted, and at the same time hurled a *tolla* straight at Sir Henry, who fortunately saw it coming, and caught it on his shield, which it transfixed, remaining wedged in the iron plate behind the hide.

Then, uttering a cry, Twala sprang straight at Curtis, and with his battle-axe struck him such a blow upon the shield that the mere force and shock of it brought him, strong man as he is, down upon his knees.

But at this time the matter went no further, for that instant there rose from the regiments pressing round us something like a shout of dismay, and on looking up I saw the cause.

To the right and to the left the plain was alive with the plumes of charging warriors. The out-flanking squadrons had come to our relief. The time could not have been better chosen. All Twala's army, as Ignosi predicted would be the case, had fixed their attention on the bloody struggle which was raging round the remnant of the Greys and that of the Buffaloes, who were now carrying on a battle of their own at a little distance, which two regiments had formed the chest of our army. It was not until our horns were about to close upon them that they had dreamed of their approach, for they believed these forces to be hidden in reserve upon the crest of the moon-shaped hill. And now, before they could even assume a proper formation for defence, the outflanking *Impis* had leapt, like greyhounds, on their flanks.

In five minutes the fate of the battle was decided. Taken on both flanks, and dismayed at the awful slaughter inflicted upon them by the Greys and Buffaloes, Twala's regiments broke into flight, and soon the whole plain between us and Loo was scattered with groups of running soldiers making good their retreat. As for the hosts that had so recently surrounded us and the Buffaloes, they melted away as though by magic, and presently we were left standing there like a rock from which the sea has retreated. But what a sight it was! Around us the dead and dying lay in heaped-up masses, and of the gallant Greys there remained but ninety-five men upon their feet. More than three thousand four hundred had fallen in this one regiment, most of them never to rise again.

'Men,' said Infadoos calmly, as between the intervals of binding a wound in his arm he surveyed what remained to him of his corps, 'ye have kept up the reputation of your regiment, and this day's fighting will be well spoken of by your children's children.' Then he turned round and shook Sir Henry Curtis by the hand. 'Thou art a great captain, Incubu,' he said simply; 'I have lived a long life among warriors, and I have known many a brave one, yet have I never seen a man like unto thee.'

At this moment the Buffaloes began to march past our position on the road to Loo, and as they went a message was brought to us from Ignosi requesting Infadoos, Sir Henry, and myself to join him. Accordingly, orders having been issued to the remaining ninety men of the Greys to employ themselves in collecting the wounded, we joined Ignosi, who informed us that he was pressing on to Loo to complete the victory by capturing Twala, if that should be possible. Before we had gone far, suddenly we discovered the figure of Good sitting on an ant-heap about one hundred paces from us. Close beside him was the body of a Kukuana.

'He must be wounded,' said Sir Henry, anxiously. As he made the remark, an untoward thing happened. The dead body of the Kukuana soldier, or rather what had appeared to be his dead body, suddenly sprang up, knocked Good head over heels off the ant-heap, and began to spear him. We rushed forward in terror, and as we drew near we saw the brawny warrior making dig after dig at the prostrate Good, who at each prod jerked all his limbs into the air. Seeing us coming, the Kukuana gave one final and most vicious dig, and with a shout of 'Take that, wizard! ' bolted away. Good did not move, and we concluded that our poor comrade was done for. Sadly we came towards him, and were astonished to find him pale and faint indeed, but with a serene smile upon his face, and his eyeglass still fixed in his eye.

'Capital armour this,' he murmured, on catching sight of our faces bending over him. 'How sold that beggar must have been,' and then he fainted. On examination we discovered that he had been seriously wounded in the leg by a *tolla* in the course of the pursuit, but that the chain armour had prevented his last assailant's spear from doing anything more than bruise him badly. It was a merciful escape. As nothing could be done for him at the moment, he was placed on one of the wicker shields used for the wounded, and carried along with us.

On arriving before the nearest gate of Loo we found one of our regiments watching it in obedience to orders received from Ignosi. The other regiments were in the same way guarding the different exits from the town. The officer in command of this regiment saluted Ignosi as king, and informed him that Twala's army had taken refuge in the town, whither Twala himself had also escaped, but he thought that they were thoroughly demoralised, and would surrender. Thereupon Ignosi, after taking counsel with us, sent forward heralds to each gate ordering the defenders to open, and promising on his royal word life and forgiveness to every soldier who laid down his arms, but saying that if they did not do so, before nightfall he would certainly burn Loo and all within its gates. This message was not without its effect. Half an hour later, amid the shouts and cheers of the Buffaloes, the bridge was dropped across the fosse, and the gates upon the farther side were flung open.

Taking due precautions against treachery, we marched on into the town. All along the roadways stood thousands of dejected warriors, their heads drooping, and their shields and spears at their feet, who, headed by their officers, saluted Ignosi as king as he passed. On we marched, straight to Twala's kraal. When we reached the great space, where a day or two previously we had seen the review and the witch hunt, we found it deserted. No, not quite deserted, for there, on the farther side, in front of his hut, sat Twala himself, with but one attendant – Gagool.

It was a melancholy sight to see him seated thus, his battle-axe and shield by his side, his chin upon his mailed breast, with but one old crone for companion, and notwithstanding his cruelties and misdeeds, a pang of compassion shot through me as I looked upon Twala so 'fallen from his high estate.' Not a soldier of all his armies, not a courtier out of the hundreds who had cringed round him, not even a solitary wife, remained to share his fate or halve the bitterness of his fall. Poor savage! he was learning the lesson which Fate teaches to most of us who live long enough, that the eyes of mankind are blind to the discredited, and that he who is defenceless and undone finds few friends and little mercy. Nor, indeed, in this case did he deserve any.

Filing through the kraal gate, we marched across the open space to where the ex-king sat. When within about fifty yards of him the regiment was halted, and accompanied only by a small guard we advanced towards him, Gagool reviling us bitterly as we came. As we drew near, Twala, for the first time, lifted his plumed head, and fixed his one eye, which seemed to flash with suppressed fury almost as brightly as the great diamond bound round his forehead, upon his successful rival – Ignosi.

'Hail, O king!' he said, with bitter mockery; 'thou who hast eaten of my bread, and now by the aid of the white man's magic hast seduced my regiments and defeated mine army, hail! What fate hast thou for me, O king?'

'The fate thou gavest to my father, whose throne thou hast sat on these many years!' was the stern answer.

'It is good. I will show thee how to die, that thou mayest remember it against thine own time. See, the sun sinks in blood,' and he pointed with his battle-axe towards the setting orb; 'it is well that my sun should go down in its company. And now, O king! I am ready to die, but I crave the boon of the Kukuana royal House[1] to die fighting. Thou canst not refuse it, or even those cowards who fled to-day will hold thee shamed.'

'It is granted. Choose – with whom wilt thou fight? Myself I cannot fight with thee, for the king fights not except in war.'

Twala's sombre eye ran up and down our ranks, and I felt, as for a moment it rested on myself, that the position had developed

---

[1] It is a law amongst the Kukuanas that no man of the direct royal blood can be put to death, unless by his own consent, which is, however, never refused. He is allowed to choose a succession of antagonists, to be approved by the king, with whom he fights, till one of them kills him. – A.Q.

a new horror. What if he chose to begin by fighting *me!* What chance should I have against a desperate savage six feet five high, and broad in proportion? I might as well commit suicide at once. Hastily I made up my mind to decline the combat, even if I were hooted out of Kukuanaland as a consequence. It is, I think, better to be hooted than be quartered with a battle-axe.

Presently Twala spoke.

'Incubu, what sayest thou, shall we end what we began to-day, or shall I call thee coward, white – even to the liver?'

'Nay,' interposed Ignosi hastily; 'thou shalt not fight with Incubu.'

'Not if he is afraid,' said Twala.

Unfortunately Sir Henry understood this remark, and the blood flamed up into his cheeks.

'I will fight him,' he said; 'he shall see if I am afraid.'

'For Heaven's sake,' I entreated, ' don't risk your life against that of a desperate man. Anybody who saw you to-day will know that you are brave enough.'

'I will fight him,' was the sullen answer. 'No living man shall call me a coward. I am ready now!' and he stepped forward and lifted his axe.

I wrung my hands over this absurd piece of Quixotism; but if he was determined on this duel, of course I could not stop him.

'Fight not, my white brother,' said Ignosi, laying his hand affectionately on Sir Henry's arm; 'thou hast fought enough, and if aught befell thee at his hands it would cut my heart in twain.'

'I will fight, Ignosi,' was Sir Henry's answer.

'It is well, Incubu; thou art a brave man. It will be a good fray. Behold, Twala, the Elephant is ready for thee.'

The ex-king laughed savagely, and stepping forward faced Curtis. For a moment they stood thus, and the light of the sinking sun caught their stalwart frames and clothed them both in fire. They were a well-matched pair.

Then they began to circle round each other, their battle-axes raised.

Suddenly Sir Henry sprang forward and struck a fearful blow at Twala, who stepped to one side. So heavy was the stroke that the striker half over-balanced himself, a circumstance of which his antagonist took a prompt advantage. Circling his massive battle-axe round his head, he brought it down with tremendous force. My heart jumped into my mouth; I thought that the affair was already finished. But no; with a quick upward movement of the left arm Sir Henry interposed his shield between himself and the axe, with the result that its outer edge was shorn away, the axe falling on his left shoulder, but not heavily enough to do any serious damage. In another moment Sir Henry got in a second blow, which was also received by Twala upon his shield.

Then followed blow upon blow, that were, in turn, either received upon the shield or avoided. The excitement grew intense; the regiment which was watching the encounter forgot its discipline, and, drawing near, shouted and groaned at every stroke. Just at this time, too, Good, who had been laid upon the ground by me, recovered from his faint, and, sitting up, perceived what was going on, In an instant he was up, and catching hold of my arm, hopped about from place to place on one leg, dragging me after him, and yelling encouragement to Sir Henry –

'Go it, old fellow!' he hallooed. 'That was a good one! Give it him amidships,' and so on.

Presently Sir Henry, having caught a fresh stroke upon his shield, hit out with all his force. The blow cut through Twala's shield and through the tough chain armour behind it, gashing him in the shoulder. With a yell of pain and fury Twala returned the blow with interest, and, such was his strength, shore right through the rhinoceros horn handle of his antagonist's battle-axe, strengthened as it was with bands of steel, wounding Curtis in the face.

A cry of dismay rose from the Buffaloes as our hero's broad axe-head fell to the ground; and Twala, again raising his weapon, flew at him with a shout. I shut my eyes. When I opened them again it was to see Sir Henry's shield lying on the ground, and Sir Henry himself with his great arms twined round Twala's middle. To and fro they swung, hugging each other like bears, straining with all their mighty muscles for dear life, and dearer honour. With a supreme effort Twala swung the Englishman clean off his feet. Down they came together, rolling over and over on the lime paving, Twala striking out at Curtis's head with the battle-axe, and Sir Henry trying to drive the *tolla* he had drawn from his belt through Twala's armour.

It was a mighty struggle, and an awful thing to see.

'Get his axe!' Good yelled; and perhaps our champion heard him.

At any rate, dropping the *tolla*, he snatched at the axe, which was fastened to Twala's wrist by a strip of buffalo hide, and still rolling over and over, they fought for it like wild cats, drawing their breath in heavy gasps. Suddenly the hide string burst, and then, with a great effort, Sir Henry freed himself, the weapon remaining in his hand. Another second and he was upon his feet, the red blood streaming from the wound in his face, and so was Twala. Drawing the heavy *tolla* from his belt, he reeled straight at Curtis and struck him upon the breast. The stab came home true and strong, but whoever it was who made that chain armour understood his art, for it turned the steel. Again Twala struck out with a savage yell; again the sharp knife rebounded, and Sir Henry went staggering back. Once more Twala came on, and as he came our great Englishman gathered himself together, and swinging the big axe round his head with both hands, hit at him with all his force.

There was a shriek of excitement from a thousand throats, and, behold! Twala's head seemed to spring from his shoulders. It fell and came rolling and bounding along the ground toward Ignosi, stopping just at his feet. For a second the corpse stood upright; then with a dull crash it came to the earth, and the gold torque from its neck rolled away across the pavement. As it did so Sir Henry, overpowered by faintness and loss of blood, fell heavily across the body of the dead king.

In a second he was lifted up, and eager hands were pouring water on his face. Another minute and the grey eyes opened wide.

He was not dead.

Now I, just as the sun sank, stepping to where Twala's head lay in the dust, unloosed the diamond from the dead brows, and handed it to Ignosi.

'Take it,' I said, 'lawful king of the Kukuanas – king by birth and victory.'

Ignosi bound the diadem upon his brows. Then advancing, he placed his foot upon the broad chest of his headless foe and broke out into a chant, or rather a paean of triumph, so beautiful, and yet so utterly savage, that I despair of being able to give an adequate version of his words. Once I heard a scholar with a fine voice read aloud from the Greek poet Homer, and I remember that the sound of the rolling lines seemed to make my blood stand still. Ignosi's chant, uttered as it was in a language as beautiful and sonorous as the old Greek, produced exactly the same effect on me, although I was exhausted with toil and many emotions.

'Now' he began, '*now our rebellion is swallowed up in victory, and our evil-doing is justified by strength.*

'*In the morning the oppressors arose and stretched themselves; they bound on their harness and made them ready to war.*

'*They rose up and tossed their spears: the soldiers called to the captains, "Come, lead us" – and the captains cried to the king, "Direct thou the battle."*

'*They laughed in their pride, twenty thousand men, and yet a twenty thousand.*

'*Their plumes covered the valleys as the plumes of a bird cover her nest; they shook their shields and shouted, yea, they shook their shields in the sunlight; they lusted for the battle and were glad.*

'*They came up against me; their strong ones ran swiftly to slay me; they cried "Ha! ha! he is as one already dead"*

'*Then breathed I on them, and my breath was as the breath of a wind, and lo! they were not.*

'*My lightnings pierced them; I licked up their strength with the lightning of my spears; I shook them to the ground with the thunder of my shoutings.*

'*They broke – they scattered – they were gone as the mists of the morning.*

'*They are food for the kites and the foxes, and the place of battle is fat with their blood.*

'*Where are the mighty ones who rose up in the morning?*

'*Where are the proud ones who tossed their spears and cried, "He is as a man already dead"?*

'*They bow their heads, but not in sleep; they are stretched out, but not in sleep.*

'*They are forgotten; they have gone into the blackness; they dwell on the dead moons; yea, others shall lead away their wives, and their children shall remember them no more.*

'*And I! – the king – like an eagle I have found my eyrie.*

'*Behold! far have I flown in the night season, yet have I returned to my young at the daybreak.*

'*Shelter ye under the shadow of my wings, O people, and I will comfort you, and ye shall not be dismayed.*

'*Now is the good time, the time of spoil.*

'*Mine are the cattle on the mountains, mine are the virgins in the kraals.*

'*The winter is overpast with storms, the summer is come with flowers.*

'*Now Evil shall cover up her face, now Mercy and Gladness shall dwell in the land.*

'*Rejoice, rejoice, my people!*

'*Let all the world rejoice in that this tyranny is trodden down, in that I am the king.*'

Ignosi ceased his song, and out of the gathering gloom came back the deep reply –'

'*Thou art the king!*'

Thus was my prophecy to the herald fulfilled, and within the forty-eight hours Twala's headless corpse was stiffening at Twala's gate.

CHAPTER 15

Good Falls Sick

After the fight was ended Sir Henry and Good were carried into Twala's hut, where I joined them. They were both utterly exhausted by exertion and loss of blood, and, indeed, my own condition was little better. I am very wiry, and can stand more fatigue than most men, probably on account of my light weight and long training; but this night I was quite done up, and, as is always the case with me when exhausted, that old wound which the lion gave me began to pain. Also my head was aching violently from the blow I had received in the morning, when I was knocked senseless. Altogether, a more miserable trio than we were that evening it would have been difficult to discover. Our only comfort lay in the reflection that we were exceedingly fortunate to be there to feel miserable, instead of being stretched dead upon the plain, as so many thousands of brave men were that night, who had risen well and strong in the morning.

Somehow, with the assistance of the beautiful Foulata, who, since we had been the means of saving her life, had constituted herself our handmaiden, and especially Good's, we managed to get off the chain shirts, which had certainly saved the lives of two of us that day. As I expected, we found that the flesh underneath was terribly contused, for though the steel links had kept the weapons from entering, they had not prevented them from bruising. Both Sir Henry and Good were a mass of contusions, and I was by no means free. As a remedy Foulata brought us some pounded green leaves, with an aromatic odour, which, when applied as a plaster, gave us considerable relief.

But though the bruises were painful, they did not give us such anxiety as Sir Henry's and Good's wounds. Good had a hole right through the fleshy part of his 'beautiful white leg,' from which he had lost a great deal of blood; and Sir Henry, with other hurts, had a deep cut over the jaw, inflicted by Twala's battle-axe. Luckily, Good is a very decent surgeon, and so soon as his small box of medicines was forthcoming, having thoroughly cleansed the wounds, he managed to stitch up first Sir Henry's and then his own pretty satisfactorily, considering the imperfect light given by the primitive Kukuana lamp in the hut. Afterwards he smeared the injured places plentifully with some antiseptic ointment, of which there was a pot in the little box, and we covered them with the remains of a pocket-handkerchief which we possessed.

Meanwhile Foulata had prepared us some strong broth, for we were too weary to eat. This we swallowed, and then threw ourselves down on the piles of magnificent karrosses, or fur rugs, which were scattered about the dead king's great hut. By a very strange instance of the irony of fate, it was on Twala's own couch, and wrapped in Twala's own particular karross, that Sir Henry, the man who had slain him, slept that night.

I say slept; but after that day's work sleep was indeed difficult. To begin with, in very truth the air was full

'Of farewells to the dying
And mournings for the dead.'

From every direction came the sound of the wailing of women whose husbands, sons, and brothers had perished in the battle. No wonder that they wailed, for over twelve thousand men, or nearly a fifth of the Kukuana army, had been destroyed in that awful struggle. It was heartrending to lie and listen to their cries for those who never would return; and it made me understand the full horror of the work done that day to further man's ambition. Towards midnight, however, the ceaseless crying of the women grew less frequent, till at length the silence was only broken at intervals of a few minutes by a long piercing howl that came from a hut in our immediate rear. This, as I afterwards discovered, proceeded from Gagool 'keening' over the dead king Twala.

After that I got a little fitful sleep, only to wake from time to time with a start, thinking that I was once more an actor in the terrible events of the past twenty-four hours. Now I seemed to see that warrior whom my hand had sent to his account charging at me on the mountain-top; now I was once more in that glorious ring of Greys, which made its immortal stand against all Twala's regiments upon the little mound; and now again I saw Twala's plumed and gory head roll past my feet with gnashing teeth and glaring eye.

At last, somehow or other, the night passed away; but when dawn broke I found that my companions had slept no better than myself. Good, indeed, was in a high fever, and very soon afterwards began to grow lightheaded, and also, to my alarm, to spit blood, the result, no doubt, of some internal injury, inflicted during the desperate efforts made by the Kukuana warrior on the previous day to force his big spear through the chain armour. Sir Henry, however, though he was so sore and stiff that he could scarcely stir, seemed pretty fresh, notwithstanding his wound on the face, which made eating difficult and laughter an impossibility.

About eight o'clock we had a visit from Infadoos, who appeared but little the worse – tough old warrior that he was – for his exertions in the battle, although he informed us that he had been up all night. He shook our hands cordially, and was delighted to see us, but much grieved at Good's condition. I noticed, however, that he addressed Sir Henry with a kind of reverence, as though he were something more than human; and, indeed, as we found out afterwards, the great Englishman was looked on throughout Kukuanaland as a supernatural being. No man, the soldiers said, could have fought as he fought, or at the end of a day of such toil and bloodshed, could have slain Twala, who, in addition to being the king, was supposed to be the strongest warrior in the country, in single combat, shearing through his bull-neck at a stroke. Indeed, that stroke became proverbial in Kukuanaland, and any extraordinary blow or feat of strength was henceforth known as 'Incubu's blow.'

Infadoos told us also that all Twala's regiments had submitted to Ignosi, and that like submissions were beginning to arrive from chiefs in the outlying country. Twala's death at the hands of Sir Henry had put an end to all further chance of disturbance; Scragga had been his only legitimate son, so there was no rival claimant to the throne left alive.

I remarked that Ignosi had swum to power through blood. The old chief shrugged his shoulders. 'Yes,' he answered; 'but the Kukuana people can only be kept cool by letting their blood flow sometimes. Many are killed, indeed, but the women are left, and others must soon grow up to take the places of the fallen. After this the land will be quiet for a while.'

Afterwards, in the course of the morning, we had a short visit from Ignosi, on whose brows the royal diadem was now bound. As I contemplated him advancing with kingly dignity, an obsequious guard following his steps, I could not help recalling to my mind the tall Zulu who had presented himself to us at Durban some few months before, asking to be taken into our service, and reflecting on the strange revolutions of the wheel of fortune.

'Hail, O king!' I said, rising.

'Yes, Macumazahn. King at last, by the might of your three right hands,' was the ready answer.

All was, he said, going on well; and he hoped to arrange a great feast in two weeks' time in order to show himself to the people.

I asked him what he had settled to do with Gagool.

'She is the evil genius of the land,' he answered, 'and I shall kill her and all the witch doctors with her! She has lived so long that none can remember when she was not very old, and she it is who has always trained the witch-hunters, and made the land wicked in the sight of the heavens above.'

'Yet she knows much,' I replied; 'it is easier to destroy knowledge, Ignosi, than to gather it.'

'That is so,' he said thoughtfully. 'She, and she only, knows the secret of the "Three Witches," yonder, whither the great road runs, where the kings are buried, and the Silent Ones sit.'

'Yes, and the diamonds are. Forget not thy promise, Ignosi; thou must lead us to the mines, even if thou hast to spare Gagool alive to show the way.'

'I will not forget, Macumazahn, and I will think on what thou sayest.'

After Ignosi's visit I went to see Good, and found him quite delirious. The fever set up by his wound seemed to have taken a firm hold of his system, and to be complicated with an internal injury. For four or five days his condition was most critical; indeed, I believe firmly that had it not been for Foulata's indefatigable nursing he must have died.

Women are women all the world over, whatever their colour. Yet somehow it seemed curious to watch this dusky beauty bending night and day over the fevered man's couch, and performing all the merciful errands of a sickroom swiftly, gently, and with as fine an instinct as that of a trained hospital nurse. For the first night or two I tried to help her, and so did Sir Henry as soon as his stiffness allowed him to move. But Foulata bore our interference with impatience, and finally insisted upon our leaving him to her, saying that our movements made him restless, which I think was true. Day and night she watched and tended him, giving him his only medicine, a native cooling drink made of milk, in which was infused juice from the bulb of a species of tulip, and keeping the flies from settling on him. I can see the whole picture now as it appeared night after night by the light of our primitive lamp; Good tossing to and fro, his features emaciated, his eyes shining large and luminous, and jabbering nonsense by the yard; and seated on the ground by his side, her back resting against the wall of the hut, the soft-eyed, shapely Kukuana beauty, her face, weary as it was with her long vigil, animated by a look of infinite compassion – or was it something more than compassion?

For two days we thought that he must die, and crept about with heavy hearts.

Only Foulata would not believe it.

'He will live,' she said.

For three hundred yards or more around Twala's chief hut, where the sufferer lay, there was silence; for by the king's order all who lived in the habitations behind it, except Sir Henry and myself, had been removed, lest any noise should come to the sick man's ears. One night, it was the fifth of Good's illness, as was my habit, I went across to see how he was doing before turning in for a few hours.

I entered the hut carefully. The lamp placed upon the floor showed the figure of Good tossing no more, but lying quite still.

So it had come at last! In the bitterness of my heart I gave something like a sob.

'Hush – h – h!' came from the patch of dark shadow behind Good's head.

Then, creeping closer, I saw that he was not dead, but sleeping soundly, with Foulata's taper fingers clasped tightly in his poor white hand. The crisis had passed, and he would live. He slept like that for eighteen hours; and I scarcely like to say it, for fear I should not be believed, but during the entire period did this devoted girl sit by him, fearing that if she moved and drew away her hand it would wake him. What she must have suffered from cramp and weariness, to say nothing of want of food, nobody will ever know; but it is a fact that, when at last he woke, she had to be carried away – her limbs were so stiff that she could not move them.

After the turn had once been taken, Good's recovery was rapid and complete. It was not till he was nearly well that Sir Henry told him of all he owed to Foulata; and when he came to the story of how she sat by his side for eighteen hours, fearing lest by moving she should wake him, the honest sailor's eyes filled with tears. He turned and went straight to the hut where Foulata was preparing the midday meal, for we were back in our old quarters now, taking me with him to interpret in case he could not make his meaning clear to her, though I am bound to say that she understood him marvellously as a rule, considering how extremely limited was his foreign vocabulary.

'Tell her,' said Good, 'that I owe her my life, and that I will never forget her kindness to my dying day.'

I interpreted, and under her dark skin she actually seemed to blush.

Turning to him with one of those swift and graceful motions that in her always reminded me of the flight of a wild bird, Foulata answered softly, glancing at him with her large brown eyes –

'Nay, my lord; my lord forgets! Did he not save my life; am I not my lord's handmaiden?'

It will be noted that the young lady appeared to be oblivious of the share which Sir Henry and myself had taken in her preservation from Twala's clutches. But that is the way of women! I remember others who were just the same. Well, I retired from that little interview sad at heart. I did not like Miss Foulata's soft glances, for I knew the fatal amorous propensities of sailors in general, and of Good in particular.

There are two things in the world, as I have found out, which cannot be prevented: you cannot keep a Zulu from fighting, or a sailor from falling in love upon the slightest provocation! And here the provocation was not slight.

A few days after this last touching occurrence Ignosi held his great 'indaba,' or council, and was formally recognised as king by the 'indunas,' or head men, of Kukuanaland. The spectacle was a most imposing one, including as it did a grand review of troops. On this day the remaining fragments of the Greys were formally paraded, and in the face of the army thanked for their splendid conduct in the great battle. To each man the king made a large present of cattle, promoting them one and all to the rank of officers in the new corps of Greys then in process of formation.

An order was also promulgated throughout the length and breadth of Kukuanaland that, whilst we honoured the country by our presence, we three were to be greeted with the royal salute, and to be treated with the same ceremony and respect that was by custom accorded to the king. Also the power of life and death was publicly conferred upon us. Ignosi, too, in the presence of his people, reaffirmed the promises which he had made, to the effect that no man's blood should be shed without trial, and that witch-hunting should cease in the land.

When the ceremony was over we waited upon Ignosi, and informed him that we were now anxious to investigate the mystery of the mines to which Solomon's Road ran, asking him if he had discovered anything about them.

'My friends,' he answered, 'I have discovered this. It is yonder that the three great figures sit, who here are called the "Silent Ones," and to whom Twala would have offered the girl Foulata as a sacrifice. It is there, too, in a great cave deep in the mountain, that the kings of the land are buried; there ye shall find Twala's body, sitting with those who went before him. There, also, is a deep pit, which, at some time, long-dead men dug out, mayhap for the stones ye speak of, such as I have heard men in Natal tell of at Kimberley. There, too, in the Place of Death is a hidden chamber, secret to all save the king and Gagool. But Twala, who knew it, is dead, and I know it not, nor know I what is in it. Yet there is a legend in the land that once, many generations gone, a white man crossed the mountains, and was led by a woman to the dark chamber and shown the wealth concealed in it. But before he could take it she betrayed him, and he was driven by the king of that day back to the mountains, and since then no man has entered the ancient place.'

'The story is surely true, Ignosi, for on the mountains we found the white man,' I said.

'Yes, we found him. And now I have promised you that if ye can come to that chamber, and the stones are there –'

'The gem upon thy forehead proves that they are there,' I put in, pointing to the great diamond I had taken from Twala's dead brows.

'Mayhap; and if they are there,' he said, 'ye shall have as many as ye can take hence – if indeed ye would leave me, my brothers.'

'First we must find the chamber,' said I.

'There is but one who can show it to thee – Gagool.'

'And if she will not?'

'Then she must die,' said Ignosi sternly. 'I have saved her alive but for this. Stay, she shall choose,' and calling to a messenger he ordered Gagool to be brought before him.

In a few minutes she came, hurried along by two guards, whom she was cursing as she walked.

'Leave her,' said the king to the guards.

So soon as their support was withdrawn, the withered old bundle – for she resembled a bundle more than anything else, out of which her two bright and wicked eyes gleamed like those of a snake – sank in a heap on the floor.

'What will ye with me, Ignosi?' she piped. 'Ye dare not touch me. If ye touch me I will slay you all as ye sit. Beware of my magic.'

'Thy magic could not save Twala, old she-wolf, and it cannot hurt us,' was the answer. 'Listen; I will this of thee, that thou reveal to us the chamber where are the shining stones.'

'Ha! ha!' she piped, 'none know its key but I, and I will never tell it thee. The white devils shall go hence empty-handed.'

'Thou shalt tell me. I will make thee tell me.'

'How, O King? Thou art great, but can thy power wring the truth from a woman?'

'It is difficult, yet will I do so.'

'How, O King?'

'Nay, thus; if thou dost refuse thou shalt slowly die.'

'Die!' she shrieked in terror and fury; 'ye dare not touch me – man, ye know not who I am! How old am I, think ye? I knew your fathers, and their fathers' father's fathers. When the country was young I was here; when the country grows old I shall still be here. I cannot die unless I be killed by chance, for none dare slay me.'

'Yet will I slay thee. See, Gagool, mother of evil, thou art so old that thou canst no longer love thy life. What can life be worth to such a hag as thou, who hast no shape, nor form, nor hair, nor teeth – hast naught, save wickedness and evil eyes? It will be mercy to make an end of thee, Gagool.'

'Thou fool,' shrieked the old fiend, 'thou accursed fool, deemest thou that life is sweet only to the young? It is not so, and naught thou knowest of the heart of man to think it. To the young, indeed, death is sometimes welcome, for the young can feel. They love and suffer, and it wrings them to see their beloved pass to the land of shadows. But the very old feel not, they love not, and, *ha! ha!* they laugh to see another go out into the dark; *ha! ha!* they laugh to see the evil that is done under the stars. All they love is life, the warm, warm sun, and the sweet, sweet air. They are afraid of the cold, afraid of the cold and the dark, *ha! ha! ha!*' and the old hag writhed in ghastly merriment on the ground.

'Cease thine evil talk and answer me,' said Ignosi angrily. 'Wilt thou show the place where the stones are, or wilt thou not? If thou wilt not thou diest, even now,' and he seized a spear and held it over her.

'I will not show it; thou darest not kill me, darest not! He who slays me will be accursed for ever. In life and death woe shall be his bed-fellow.'

Slowly Ignosi brought down the spear till it pricked the prostrate heap of rags.

With a thin scream Gagool sprang to her feet, then fell again and rolled upon the floor.

'Nay, I will show thee. Only let me live on, let me sit in the sun for one more short hundred years and have my meat to suck, and I will show thee.'

'It is well. I thought that I should find a way to reason with thee. To-morrow shalt thou go with Infadoos and my white brothers to the place, and beware how thou failest, for if thou showest it not, then thou shalt slowly die of hunger. I have spoken.'

'I will not fail, Ignosi. I always keep my word – *ha! ha! ha!* Once before a woman showed the chamber to a white man, and, behold! evil befell him,' here her wicked eyes glinted. 'Her name was Gagool also. Perchance I was that woman.'

'Thou liest,' I said, 'that was ten generations gone.'

'Mayhap, mayhap; when one lives long one forgets. Perhaps it was my mother's mother who told me; surely her name was Gagool also. But, mark, ye will find in the place where the bright playthings are a bag of hide full of stones. The man filled that bag, but he never took it away. Evil befell him, I say, evil befell him! Perhaps it was my mother's mother who told me. It will be a merry journey – we can see the bodies of those who died in the battle as we go. Their eyes will be sunk by now, and their ribs will be hollow. *Ha! ha! ha!*

CHAPTER 16

The Place of Death

It was already dark on the third day after the scene described in the previous chapter when we camped in some huts at the foot of the 'Three Witches,' as the triangle of mountains is called to which Solomon's Great Road runs. Our party consisted of our three selves and Foulata, who waited on us – especially on Good – Infadoos, Gagool, who was borne along in a litter, inside which she could be heard muttering and cursing all day long, and a party of guards and attendants. The mountains, or rather the three peaks of the mountain, for their mass was evidently the result of a solitary upheaval, were, as I have said, in the form of a triangle, of which the base was towards us, one peak being on our right, one on our left, and one straight in front of us. Never shall I forget the sight afforded by those three towering peaks in the early sunlight of the following morning.

High, high above us, up into the blue air, soared their twisted snow-wreaths. Beneath the snow-line the peaks were purple with heaths, and so were the wild moors that ran up the slopes towards them. Straight before us the white ribbon of Solomon's Great Road stretched away uphill to the foot of the centre peak, about five miles away, and there stopped. It was its terminus.

I had better leave the feelings of intense excitement with which we set out on our march that morning to the imagination of those who read this history. At last we were drawing near to the wonderful mines that had been the cause of the miserable death of the old Portuguese Dom three centuries ago; of my poor friend, his ill-starred descendant, and also, as we feared, of George Curtis, Sir Henry's brother. Were we destined, after all that we had gone through, to fare any better? Evil befell them, as that old fiend Gagool said; would it also befall us? Somehow, as we were marching up that last stretch of beautiful road, I could not help feeling a little superstitious about the matter, and so I think did Good and Sir Henry.

For an hour and a half or more we tramped on up the heather-fringed way, going so fast in our excitement that the bearers of Gagool's hammock could scarcely keep pace with us, and its occupant piped out to us to stop.

'Walk more slowly, white men,' she said, projecting her hideous, shrivelled countenance between the grass curtains, and fixing her gleaming eyes upon us. 'Why will ye run to meet the evil that shall befall you, ye seekers after treasure?' and she laughed that horrible laugh which always sent a cold shiver down my back, and for a while quite took the enthusiasm out of us.

However, on we went, till we saw before us, and between ourselves and the peak, a vast circular hole with sloping sides, three hundred feet or more in depth, and over half a mile round.

'Can't you guess what that is?' I said to Sir Henry and Good who were staring in astonishment at the awful pit before us.

They shook their heads.

'Then it is clear that you have never seen the diamond diggings at Kimberley. You may depend on it that this is Solomon's Diamond Mine. Look there,' I said, pointing to the strata of stiff blue clay which were yet to be seen among the grass and bushes that clothed the sides of the pit, 'the formation is the same. I'll be bound that if we went down there we should find "pipes" of soapy, brecciated rock. Look, too,' and I pointed to a series of worn, flat slabs of stone that were placed on a gentle slope below the level of a watercourse which in some past age had been cut out of the solid rock; 'if those are not tables once used to wash the "stuff," I'm a Dutchman.'

At the edge of this vast hole, which was none other than the pit marked on the old Dom's map, the Great Road branched into two and circumvented it. In many places, by the way, this surrounding road was built entirely of blocks of stone, apparently with the object of supporting the edges of the pit and preventing falls of reef. Along this path we pressed, driven by curiosity to see what the three towering objects might be which we discerned from the hither side of the great gulf. As we drew nearer we perceived that they were Colossi of some strange sort, and rightly conjectured that before us sat the three 'Silent Ones' that are held in such awe by the Kukuana people. But it was not until we were quite close to them that we recognised the full majesty of these 'Silent Ones.'

There, upon huge pedestals of dark rock, sculptured with rude emblems of the Phallic worship, separated from each other by a distance of forty paces, and looking down the road which crossed some sixty miles of plain to Loo, were three colossal seated forms – two male and one female – each measuring about fifty feet from the crown of its head to the pedestal.

The female form, which was nude, was of great though severe beauty, but unfortunately the features had been injured by centuries of exposure to the weather. Rising from either side of her head were the points of a crescent. The two male Colossi, on the contrary, were draped, and presented a terrifying cast of features, especially the one to our right, which had the face of a devil. That to our left was serene in countenance, but the calm upon it seemed dreadful. It was the calm of that inhuman cruelty, Sir Henry remarked, which the ancients attributed to being potent for good, who could yet watch the sufferings of humanity, if not with rejoicing, at least without sorrow. These three statues form a most awe-inspiring trinity, as they sit there in their solitude, and gaze out across the plain for ever.

Contemplating these 'Silent Ones,' as the Kukuanas call them, an intense curiosity again seized us to know whose were the hands which had shaped them, who it was that had dug the pit and made the road. Whilst I was gazing and wondering, suddenly it occurred to me – being familiar with the Old Testament – that Solomon went astray after strange gods, the names of three of whom I remembered – 'Ashtoreth, the goddess of the Zidonians, Chemosh, the god of the Moabites, and Milcom, the god of the children of Ammon' – and I suggested to my companions that the figures before us might represent these false and exploded divinities.

'Hum,' said Sir Henry, who is a scholar, having taken a high degree in classics at college, 'there may be something in that; Ashtoreth of the Hebrews was the Astarte of the Phoenicians, who were the great traders of Solomon's time. Astarte, who afterwards became the Aphrodite of the Greeks, was represented with horns like the half-moon, and there on the brow of the female figure are distinct horns. Perhaps these Colossi were designed by some Phoenician official who managed the mines. Who can say?'[1]

Before we had finished examining these extraordinary relics of remote antiquity, Infadoos came up, and having saluted the 'Silent Ones' by lifting his spear, asked us if we intended entering the 'Place of Death' at once, or if we would wait till after we had taken food at midday. If we were ready to go at once, Gagool had announced her willingness to guide us. As it was not later than eleven o'clock – driven to it by a burning curiosity – we announced our intention of proceeding instantly, and I suggested that, in case we should be detained in the cave, we should take some food with us.

Accordingly Gagool's litter was brought up, and that witch herself assisted to descend. Meanwhile Foulata, at my request, stored some 'biltong' or dried game-flesh, together with a couple of gourds of water, in a reed-basket with a hinged cover. Straight in front of us, at a distance of some fifty paces from the backs of the Colossi, rose a sheer wall of rock, eighty feet or more in height, that gradually sloped

---

[1] Compare Milton, 'Paradise Lost,' Book i.: –

'With these in troop Came Ashtoreth, whom the Phoenicians called Astarté, Queen of Heaven, with crescent horns; To whose bright image nightly by the moon Sidonian virgins paid their vows and songs.'

upwards till it formed the base of the lofty snow-wreathed peak, which soared into the air three thousand feet above.

As soon as she was lifted from her hammock Gagool cast one evil glare upon us; then, leaning on a stick, she hobbled off towards the face of this wall. We followed her till we came to a narrow portal solidly arched that looked like the opening of a gallery of a mine.

Here Gagool was waiting for us, with a devilish grin upon her horrid face.

'Now, white men from the Stars,' she piped; 'great warriors, Incubu, Bougwan, and Macumazahn the wise, are ye ready? Behold, I am here to do the bidding of my lord the king, and to show you the store of bright stones. *Ha! ha! ha!*'

'We are ready,' I said.

'Good, good. Make strong your hearts to bear what ye shall see. Comest thou too, Infadoos, thou who didst betray thy master?'

Infadoos frowned as he answered –

'Nay, I come not; it is not for me to enter there. But thou, Gagool, curb thy tongue, and beware how thou dealest with my lords. At thy hands will I require them, and if a hair of them be hurt, Gagool, be thou fifty times a witch, thou shalt die. Hearest thou?'

'I hear, Infadoos; I know thee, thou didst ever love big words; when thou wast a babe I remember thou didst threaten thine own mother. That was but the other day. But, fear not, fear not, I live only to do the bidding of the king. I have done the bidding of many kings, Infadoos, till in the end they did mine. *Ha! ha!* I go to look upon their faces once more, and Twala's also! Come on, come on, here is the lamp,' and she drew a large gourd full of oil, and fitted with a rush wick, from under her fur cloak.

'Art thou coming, Foulata?' asked Good in his villainous 'kitchen' Kukuana, in which he had been improving himself under that young lady's tuition.

'I fear, my lord,' the girl answered timidly.

'Then give me the basket.'

'Nay, my lord, whither thou goest there I go also.'

'The deuce you do!' thought I to myself; 'that may be rather awkward if ever we get out of this.'

Without further ado Gagool plunged into the passage, which was wide enough to admit of two walking abreast, and quite dark. We followed the sound of her voice as she piped to us to be swift, in some fear and trembling, which was not allayed by the flutter of a sudden rush of wings.

'Hallo! what's that?' halloed Good; 'somebody hit me in the face.'

'Bats,' said I; 'on you go.'

When, so far as we could judge, we had gone some fifty paces, we perceived that the passage was growing faintly light. Another minute, and we were in perhaps the most wonderful place that the eyes of any living man have beheld.

Let the reader picture to himself the hall of the vastest cathedral he ever stood in, windowless indeed, but dimly lighted from above, presumably by shafts connected with the outer air and driven in the roof, which arched away a hundred feet above our heads, and he will get some idea of the size of the enormous cave in which we found ourselves, with the difference that this cathedral designed by nature was loftier and wider than any built by man.

But its stupendous size was the least of the wonders of the place, for running in rows adown its length were gigantic pillars of what looked like ice, but were, in reality, huge stalactites. It is impossible for me to convey any idea of the overpowering beauty and grandeur of these pillars of white spar, some of which were not less than twenty feet in diameter at the base, and sprang up in lofty and yet delicate beauty, sheer to the distant roof. Others again were in process of formation. On the rock floor there was in these instances what looked, Sir Henry said, exactly like a broken column in an old Grecian temple, whilst high above, depending from the roof, the point of a huge lime icicle could be dimly seen.

Even as we gazed we heard the process going on, for now and again with a tiny splash a drop of water would fall from the far-off icicle on to the column below. On some columns the drops only fell once in two or three minutes, and in these cases it would be an interesting calculation to discover how long, at that rate of dripping, it would take to form a pillar, say eighty feet high by ten in diameter. That the process, in at least one instance, was incalculably slow, the following example will suffice to show. Cut on one of these pillars we discovered the rude likeness of a mummy, by which sat what appeared to be the beast-headed figure of an Egyptian god, doubtless the handiwork of some old-world labourer in the mine. This work of art was executed at the natural height at which an idle fellow, be he Phoenician workman or British cad, is in the habit of trying to immortalise himself at the expense of nature's masterpieces, namely, about five feet from the ground. Yet at the time that we saw it, which *must* have been nearly three thousand years after the date of the execution of the carving, the column was only eight feet high, and was still in process of formation, which gives a rate of growth of a foot to a thousand years, or an inch and a fraction to a century. This we knew because, as we were standing by it, we heard a drop of water fall.

Sometimes the stalagmites below took strange forms, presumably where the dropping of the water had not always been on the same spot. Thus, one huge mass, which must have weighed a hundred tons or so, was in the shape of a pulpit, beautifully fretted over outside with a design that looked like lace. Others resembled strange beasts, and on the sides of the cave were fanlike ivory tracings, such as frost leaves upon a pane.

Out of the vast main aisle there opened here and there smaller caves, exactly, Sir Henry said, as chapels open out of great cathedrals. Some were large, but one or two – and this is a wonderful instance of how nature carries out her handiwork by the same unvarying laws, utterly irrespective of size – were tiny. One little nook, for instance, was no larger than an unusually big doll's house, and yet it might have been a model of the whole place, for the water dropped, tiny icicles of lime hung, and spar columns were forming in just the same way.

We had not, however, enough time to examine this beautiful

cavern so thoroughly as we should have liked to do, since, unfortunately, Gagool seemed to be indifferent to stalactites, and only anxious to get her business over. This annoyed me the more, as I was particularly anxious to discover, if possible, by what system the light was admitted into the cave, and whether it was by the hand of man or by that of nature that this was done; also if the place had been used in any way in ancient times, as seemed probable. However, we consoled ourselves with the idea that we would investigate it thoroughly on our way back, and followed quickly at the heels of our uncanny guide.

On she led us, straight to the top of the mighty, silent cave, where we found another doorway, not arched as the first was, but square at the top, something like the doorways of Egyptian temples.

'Are ye prepared to enter the Place of Death, white men?' asked Gagool, evidently with a view to making us feel uncomfortable.

'Lead on, Macduff,' said Good solemnly, trying to look as though he was not at all alarmed, as indeed we all did except Foulata, who caught Good by the arm for protection.

'This is getting rather ghastly,' said Sir Henry, peeping into the dark doorway. 'Come on, Quatermain – *seniores priores!* We mustn't keep the old lady waiting!' and he politely made way for me to lead the van, for which inwardly I did not bless him.

Tap, tap, went old Gagool's stick down the passage, as she trotted along, chuckling hideously; and still overcome by some unaccountable presentiment of evil, I hung back.

'Come, get on, old fellow,' said Good, 'or we shall lose our fair guide.'

Thus adjured, I started down the passage, and after about twenty paces found myself in a gloomy apartment some fifty feet long, by thirty broad, and twenty high, which in some past age evidently had been hollowed, by hand-labour, out of the mountain. This apartment was not nearly so well lighted as the vast stalactite ante-cave, and at the first glance all I could discern was a massive stone table running down its length, with a colossal white figure at its head, and life-sized white figures all round it. Next I discovered a brown thing, seated on the table in the centre. In another moment my eyes grew accustomed to the light, and I saw what all these things were, and was tailing out of the place as hard as my legs would carry me.

I am not a nervous man in a general way, nor greatly troubled with superstitions, of which I have lived to see the folly. Yet I am free to own that this sight quite upset me, and had it not been that Sir Henry caught me by the collar and held me, I do honestly believe that in another five minutes I should have been outside the stalactite cave, and that a promise of all the diamonds in Kimberley would not have induced me to enter it again. But he held me tight, so I stopped because I could not help myself. Very soon, however, *his* eyes became focused to the light, and he let go of me, and began to mop the perspiration off his forehead. As for Good, he swore feebly, while Foulata threw her arms round his neck and shrieked.

Only Gagool chuckled loud and long.

It *was* a ghastly sight. There at the end of the long stone table, holding in his skeleton fingers a great white spear, sat *Death* himself, shaped in the form of a colossal human skeleton, fifteen feet or more in height. High above his head he held the spear, as though in the act to strike. One bony hand rested on the stone table before him, in the position a man assumes on rising from a seat, whilst his frame was bent forward so that the vertebrae of the neck and the grinning, gleaming skull projected towards us, and fixed its hollow eye-places upon us, the jaws a little open, as though it were about to speak.

'Great heavens!' I exclaimed faintly, at last, 'what can it be?'

'And what are *those things*?' asked Good, pointing to the white company round the table.

'And what on earth is *that thing*?' said Sir Henry, pointing to the brown creature seated on the table.

'*Hee! hee! hee!*' laughed Gagool. 'To those who enter the Hall of the Dead, evil draws near. *Hee! hee! hee! ha! ha!*'

'Come, Incubu, brave in battle, come and see him thou slewest;' and the old creature caught Curtis's coat in her skinny fingers, and led him away towards the table. We followed.

Presently she stopped and pointed at the brown object seated on the table. Sir Henry looked, and started back with an exclamation. No wonder, for there, quite naked, the head which Curtis's battle-axe had shorn from the body resting on its knees, was the gaunt corpse of Twala, the last king of the Kukuanas! Yes, there, the head perched upon the knees, it sat in all its ugliness, the vertebrae projecting a full inch above the level of the shrunken flesh of the neck, for all the world like a black double of Hamilton Tighe.[2] Over the surface of the black corpse was gathered a thin glassy film, that made its appearance yet more appalling. For this we were, at the moment, quite unable to account, till presently we observed that from the roof of the chamber the water fell steadily, *drip! drop! drip!* on to the neck of the dead man, whence it trickled over the entire surface, and finally escaped into the rock through a tiny hole in the table. Then I guessed what the film was – *Twala's body was being transformed into a stalactite!*

A look at the white forms seated on the stone bench which ran round that ghastly board confirmed this view. They were human bodies indeed, or rather they had been human; now they were *stalactites*. This was the way in which the Kukuana people had from time immemorial preserved their royal dead. They petrified them. What the exact system might be, if there was any, beyond the placing of them for a long period of years under the drip, I never discovered, but there they sat, iced over and preserved for ever by the silicious fluid.

Anything more awe-inspiring than the spectacle of this long line of departed royalties (there were twenty-seven of them, the last being Ignosi's father), wrapped, each one, in a shroud of ice-like spar, through which the features could be dimly discovered, and seated round that inhospitable board, with Death himself for a host, it is impossible to imagine. That the practice of thus preserving their kings must have been ancient is very evident from the number, which, allowing for an average reign of fifteen years,

[2]'Now haste ye, my handmaidens, haste and see
How he sits there and glowers with his head on his knee.'

and supposing that every king who reigned was placed here – an improbable thing, as some are sure to have perished in battle far from home – would fix the date of its commencement at four and a quarter centuries ago.

But the colossal Death, who sits at the head of the board, is far older than that, and, unless I am much mistaken, owes his origin to the same artist who designed the three Colossi. He is hewn out of a single stalactite, and, looked at as a work of art, is most admirably conceived and executed. Good, who understands such things, declared that, so far as he could see, the anatomical design of the skeleton is perfect down to the smallest bones.

My own idea is that this terrific object was a freak of fancy on the part of some old-world sculptor, and that its presence had suggested to the Kukuanas the idea of placing their royal dead under its awful presidency. Or perhaps it was set there to frighten away any marauders who might have designs upon the treasure chamber beyond. I cannot say. All I can do is to describe it as it is, and the reader must form his own conclusion.

Such, at any rate, was the White Death and such were the White Dead!

CHAPTER 17

Solomon's Treasure Chamber

While we were engaged in recovering from our fright, and in examining the grisly wonders of the Place of Death, Gagool had been differently occupied. Somehow or other – for she was marvellously active when she chose – she had scrambled on to the great table, and made her way to where our departed friend Twala was placed, under the drip, to see, suggested Good, how he was 'pickling,' or for some dark purpose of her own. Then, after bending down to kiss his icy lips as though in affectionate greeting, she hobbled back, stopping now and again to address a remark, the tenor of which I could not catch, to one or other of the shrouded forms, just as you or I might welcome an old acquaintance. Having gone through this mysterious and horrible ceremony, she squatted herself down on the table immediately under the White Death, and began, so far as I could make out, to offer up prayers. The spectacle of this wicked creature pouring out supplications, evil ones, no doubt, to the arch-enemy of mankind, was so uncanny that it caused us to hasten our inspection.

'Now, Gagool,' said I, in a low voice – somehow one did not dare to speak above a whisper in that place – 'lead us to the chamber.'

The old witch promptly scrambled down from the table.

'My lords are not afraid?' she said, leering up into my face.

'Lead on.'

'Good, my lords;' and she hobbled round to the back of the great Death. 'Here is the chamber; let my lords light the lamp, and enter,' and she placed the gourd full of oil upon the floor, and leaned herself against the side of the cave. I took out a match, of which we had still a few in a box, and lit the rush wick. Then looked for the doorway, but there was nothing before us except the solid rock. Gagool grinned, and said:

'The way is there, my lords. *Ha! ha! ha!*'

'Do not jest with us,' I answered sternly.

'I jest not, my lords. See!' and she pointed to the rock.

As she did so, on holding up the lamp we perceived that a mass of stone was rising slowly from the floor and vanishing into the roof above, where doubtless there is a cavity prepared to receive it. The mass was of the width of a good-sized door, about ten feet high and not less than five feet thick. It must have weighed at least twenty or thirty tons, and was clearly moved upon some simple balance principle of counter-weights, probably the same as that by which the opening and shutting of an ordinary modern window is arranged. How that principle was set in motion, of course, none of us saw; Gagool was careful to avoid this; but I have little doubt that there was some primitive lever, which was moved ever so little by pressure at a secret spot, thereby throwing additional weight on to the hidden counter-balances, and causing the monolith to be lifted from its bed.

Very slowly and gently the great stone raised itself, till at last it had vanished altogether, and a dark hole presented itself to us in the place which the door had filled.

Our excitement was so intense, as we saw the way to Solomon's treasure chamber thrown open at last, that I for one began to tremble and shake. Would it prove a hoax after all, I wondered, or was old da Silvestra right? Were there vast hoards of wealth hidden in that dark place, hoards which would make us the richest men in the whole world? We should know in a minute or two.

'Enter, white men from the Stars,' said Gagool, advancing into the doorway; 'but first hear your servant Gagool the old. The bright stones that ye will see were dug out of the pit over which the Silent Ones are set, and stored here, I know not by whom, for that was done longer ago than even I remember. Only once has this place been entered since the time that those who hid the stones departed in haste, leaving them behind. The report of the treasure went down indeed among the peoples who lived in the country from age to age, but none knew where the chamber was, nor the secret of the door. But it happened that a white man reached this country from over the mountains – perchance he too came from "the Stars" – and was well received by the king of that day. He it is who sits yonder,' and she pointed to the fifth king at the table of the Dead. 'And it came to pass that he and a woman of the country who was with him journeyed to this place, and that by chance, or magic, the woman learnt the secret of the door – a thousand years might ye search, but ye would never find that secret. Then the white man entered with the woman, and found the treasure, and filled with stones the skin of a small goat, which the woman had with her to hold food. Also as he was going from the chamber he took up one more stone, a large one and held it in his hand.'

Here she paused.

'Well,' I asked, breathless with interest as we all were, 'what happened to da Silvestra?'

The old hag started at the mention of the name.

'How knowest thou the dead man's name?' she asked sharply; and then, without waiting for an answer, went on –

'None can tell what happened; but it came about that the white man was frightened, for he flung down the goatskin, with the stones, and fled out with only the one stone in his hand, and that the king seized, and it is the stone which thou, Macumazahn, didst take from Twala's brow.'

'Have none entered here since?' I asked, peering again down the dark passage.

'None, my lords. Only the secret of the door has been kept, and every king has opened it in his day, though he has not entered.

There is a saying, that those who enter there will die within a moon, even as the white man died in the cave upon the mountain, where ye found him, Macumazahn, and therefore the kings do not enter. *Ha! ha!* mine are true words.'

Our eye met as she said it, and I turned sick and cold. How did the old hag know all these things?

'Enter, my lords. If I speak truth, the goat-skin with the stones will lie upon the floor; and if there is truth as to whether it is death to enter here, that ye will learn afterwards. *Ha! ha! ha!*' and she hobbled through the doorway, bearing the light with her; but I confess that once more I hesitated about following.

'Oh, confound it all!' said Good; 'here goes. I am not going to be frightened by that old devil;' and followed by Foulata, who, however, evidently did not at all like the business, for she was shivering with fear, he plunged into the passage after Gagool – an example which we quickly followed.

A few yards down the passage, in the narrow way hewn out of the living rock, Gagool had paused, and was waiting for us.

'See, my lords,' she said, holding the light before her, 'those who stored the treasure here fled in haste, and bethought them to guard against any who should find the secret of the door, but had not the time,' and she pointed to large square blocks of stone, which, to the height of two courses (about two feet three), had been placed across the passage with the object of walling it up. Along the side of the passage were similar blocks ready for use, and, most curious of all, a heap of mortar and a couple of trowels, which tools, so far as we had time to examine them, appeared to be of a similar shape and make to those used by workmen to this day.

Here Foulata, who had been in a state of great fear and agitation throughout, said that she felt faint, and could go no further, but would wait there. Accordingly we set her down on the unfinished wall, placing the basket of provisions by her side, and left her to recover.

Following the passage for about fifteen paces further, we came suddenly to an elaborately painted wooden door. It was standing wide open. Whoever was last there either had not found the time to shut it, or had forgotten to do so.

Across the threshold of this door lay a skin bag, fashioned from a goat-skin, that appeared to he full of pebbles.

'*Hee! hee!* white men,' sniggered Gagool, as the light from the lamp fell upon it. 'What did I tell you, that the white man who came here fled in haste, and dropped the woman's bag – behold it! Look within also and ye will find a water-gourd amongst the stones.'

Good stooped down and lifted it. It was heavy, and jingled.

'By Jove! I believe it's full of diamonds,' he said in an awed whisper; and, indeed, the idea of a small goat-skin full of diamonds is enough to awe anybody.

'Go on,' said Sir Henry impatiently. 'Here, old lady, give me the lamp,' and taking it from Gagool's hand, he stepped through the doorway and held it high above his head.

We pressed in after him, forgetful for the moment of the bag of diamonds, and found ourselves in King Solomon's treasure chamber.

At first, all that the somewhat faint light of the lamp revealed was a lofty room hewn out of the living rock, and apparently not more than fifteen feet square. Next there came into sight, stored one on the other to the arch of the roof a splendid collection of elephant-tusks. How many of them there were we did not know, for of course we could not see to what depth they went back, but there could not have been less than the ends of four or five hundred tusks of the first quality visible to our eyes. There, alone, was enough ivory before us to make a man wealthy for life. Perhaps, I thought, it was from this very store that Solomon drew the raw material for his 'great throne of ivory,' of which 'there was not the like made in any kingdom.'

On the opposite side of the chamber were about a score of wooden boxes, something like Martini-Henry ammunition boxes, only rather larger, and painted red.

'There are the diamonds,' cried I; 'bring the light.'

Sir Henry did so, holding it close to the top box, of which the lid, rendered rotten by time even in that dry place, appeared to have been smashed in, probably by da Silvestra himself. Pushing my hand through the hole in the lid I drew it out full, not of diamonds, but of gold pieces, of a shape that none of us had seen before, and with what looked like Hebrew characters stamped upon them.

'Ah!' I said, replacing the coin, 'we shan't go back empty-handed, anyhow. There must be a couple of thousand pieces in each box, and there are eighteen boxes. I suppose this was the money to pay the workmen and merchants.'

'Well,' put in Good, 'I think that is the lot; I don't see any diamonds, unless the old Portuguese put them all into his bag.'

'Let my lords look yonder where it is darkest, if they would find the stones,' said Gagool, interpreting our looks. 'There my lords will find a nook, and three stone chests in the nook, two sealed and one open.'

Before translating this to Sir Henry, who carried the light, I could not resist asking how she knew these things, if no one had entered the place since the white man, generations ago.

'Ah, Macumazahn, the Watcher by Night,' was the mocking answer, 'ye who dwell in the Stars, do ye not know that some live long, and that some have eyes which can see through rock? *Ha! ha! ha!*'

'Look in that corner, Curtis,' I said, indicating the spot Gagool had pointed out.

'Great heavens! you fellows,' he cried presently, 'see here.'

We hurried up to where he was standing in a nook shaped something like a small bow window. Against the wall of this recess were placed three stone chests, each about two feet square. Two were fitted with stone lids; the lid of the third rested against the side of the chest, which was open.

'*See!*' he repeated hoarsely, holding the lamp over the open chest. We looked, and for a moment could make out nothing, on account of a silvery sheen which dazzled us. When our eyes grew used to it we saw that the chest was three-parts full of uncut diamonds, most of them of considerable size. Stooping, I picked up a handful. Yes, there was no doubt of it, they had the unmistakable soapy feel.

I gasped as I dropped them.

'We are the richest men in the whole world,' I exclaimed. 'Monte Cristo was a fool to us.'

'We shall flood the market with diamonds,' said Good.

'Got to get them there first,' suggested Sir Henry.

We stood still with pale faces and stared at each other, the lantern in the middle and the glimmering gems below, as though we were conspirators about to commit a crime, instead of being, as we thought, the most fortunate men on earth.

'*Hee! hee! hee!*' cackled old Gagool as she flitted about like a vampire bat behind us. 'There are the bright stones ye love, white men, as many as ye will; take them, run them through your fingers, *eat* of them, *hee! hee! drink* of them, *ha! ha!*'

At that moment there was something so ridiculous to my mind in the idea of eating and drinking diamonds, that I began to laugh outrageously, an example which the others followed, without knowing why. There we stood and shrieked with laughter over the gems that were *ours*, which had been found for *us* thousands of years ago by the patient delvers in the great hole yonder, and stored for *us* by Solomon's long-dead overseer, whose name, perchance, was written in the characters stamped on the faded wax that yet adhered to the lids of the chests. Solomon never got them, nor David, nor da Silvestra, nor anybody else. *We* had got them: there before us were millions of pounds' worth of diamonds, and tens of thousands of pounds' worth of gold and ivory only wanting to be taken away.

Suddenly the fit passed off, and we stopped laughing.

'Open the other chests, white men,' croaked Gagool, 'there are surely more therein. Take your fill, white lords! *Ha! ha!* take your fill.'

Thus adjured, we set to work to pull up the stone lids on the other two, first – not without a feeling of sacrilege – breaking the seals that fastened them.

Hurrah! they were full too, full to the brim; at least the second one was; no wretched, burglarious da Silvestra had been filling goat-skins out of that. As for the third chest, it was only about a fourth full, but the stones were all picked ones; none less than twenty carats, and some of them as large as pigeon-eggs. A good many of these bigger ones, however, we could see by holding them up to the light, were a little yellow, 'off coloured,' as they call it at Kimberley. Some, too, were black.

What we did *not* note, however, was the look of fearful malev-olence that old Gagool favoured us with as she crept, crept like a snake, out of the treasure chamber and down the passage towards the door of solid rock.

Hark! Cry upon cry comes ringing up the vaulted path. It is Foulata's voice!

'*Oh, Bougwan! help! help! the stone falls!*'

'Leave go, girl! Then –'

'*Help! help! she has stabbed me!*'

By now we are running down the passage, and this is what the light from the lamp shows us. The door of rock is closing down slowly; it is not three feet from the floor. Near it struggle Foulata and Gagool. The red blood of Foulata runs to her knee, but still the brave girl holds the old witch, who fights like a wild cat. Look! she is free! Foulata falls, and Gagool throws herself on the ground, to twist like a snake beneath the lip of the closing stone. She is under – ah! God! too late! too late! The stone nips her, and she yells in agony. Down, down, it comes, all the thirty tons of it, slowly pressing her old body against the rock below. Shriek upon shriek, such as we had never heard, then a long sickening *crunch*, and the door is shut just as, rushing down the passage, we hurl ourselves against its mass.

It was all done in four seconds.

Then we turned to Foulata. The poor girl was stabbed in the body, and I saw that she could not live for long.

'Ah! Bougwan, I die!' gasped the beautiful creature. 'She crept out – Gagool; I did not see her, I was faint – and the door began to fall. Then she came back, and was looking up the path – I saw her come in through the slowly falling door, and caught her and held her, and she stabbed me, and *I die*, Bougwan!'

'Poor girl! poor girl!' Good cried in his distress. Then, as he could do nothing else, he fell to kissing her.

'Bougwan,' she said, after a pause, 'is Macumazahn there? It grows so dark – I cannot see.'

'Here I am, Foulata.'

'Macumazahn, be my tongue for a moment, I pray thee, for Bougwan cannot understand me, and before I go into the night I would speak a word to him.'

'Say on, Foulata, I will render it.'

'Say to my lord, Bougwan, that – I love him, and that I am glad to die because I know that he cannot cumber his life with such as I am, for the sun may not mate with the moon, nor the white with the black.

'Say that, since I saw him, at times I have felt as though there were a bird in my bosom, which would one day fly hence and sing elsewhere. Even now, though I cannot lift my hand, and my brain grows cold, I do not feel as though my heart were dying; it is so full of love that it could live ten thousand years, and yet be young. Say that if I live again, mayhap I shall see him in the Stars, and that – I will search them all, though perchance there I must still be black and he will – still be white. Say – nay, Macumazahn, say no more, save that I love – Oh, hold me closer, Bougwan, I cannot feel thine arms – *oh! oh!*'

'She is dead – she is dead!' muttered Good presently, as he rose, the tears of grief running down his honest face.

'You need not let that trouble you, old fellow,' said Sir Henry.

'Eh!' exclaimed Good; 'what do you mean?'

'I mean that you will soon be in a position to join her. *Man, don't you see that we are buried alive?*'

Until Sir Henry uttered these words I do not think that the full horror of what had happened came home to us, preoccupied as we were with the sight of poor Foulata's end. But now we understood. The ponderous mass of rock had closed, probably for ever, for the only brain which knew its secret was crushed to powder beneath its weight. This was a door that none could hope to force with anything short of dynamite in large quantities. And we were on its wrong side!

For a few minutes we stood horrified, there over the corpse of Foulata. All the manhood seemed to have gone out of us. The first shock of the knowledge of the slow and miserable end that awaited us was overpowering. We saw it all now; that fiend Gagool had planned this snare for us from the first.

It must have been exactly the jest that her evil mind would have rejoiced in, this idea of the three white men whom, for some reason of her own, she had always hated, slowly perishing of thirst and hunger in the company of the treasure they had coveted. Now I saw the point of that sneer of hers about our eating and drinking the diamonds. Probably somebody had tried to serve the poor old Dom in the same way, when he abandoned the skin full of jewels. And who was that somebody?

'This will never do,' said Sir Henry hoarsely; 'the lamp will soon go out. Let us see if we can't find the spring that works the rock.'

We sprang forward with desperate energy, and, standing in a bloody ooze, began to feel up and down the door and the sides of the passage. But no knob or spring could we discover.

'Depend on it,' I said, 'it does not work from the inside; if it did, Gagool would not have risked trying to crawl underneath the stone. It was this knowledge that made her try to escape at all hazards, curse her.'

'At any rate,' answered Sir Henry with a hard little laugh, 'retribution was swift; hers was almost as awful an end as ours is likely to be. We can do nothing with the door; let us go back to the treasure room.'

We turned and went, and as we passed it I perceived by the unfinished wall across the passage the basket of food which poor Foulata had carried. I took it up, and brought it with me to the accursed treasure chamber that was to be our grave. Then we returned and reverently bore in Foulata's corpse, laying it on the floor by the boxes of coin.

Next we seated ourselves, leaning our backs against the three stone chests which contained the priceless treasure.

'Let us divide the food,' said Sir Henry, 'so as to make it last as long as possible.'

Accordingly we did so. It would, we reckoned, make four infinitesimally small meals for each of us, enough, say, to support life for a couple of days. Besides the 'biltong,' or dried game-flesh, there were two gourds of water, each of which held not more than a quart.

'Now,' said Sir Henry grimly, 'let us eat and drink, for tomorrow we die.'

We each ate a small portion of the 'biltong,' and drank a sip of water. Needless to say, we had but little appetite, though we were sadly in need of food, and felt better after swallowing it. Then we got up and made a systematic examination of the walls of our prison-house, in the faint hope of finding some means of exit, sounding them and the floor carefully.

There was none. It was not probable that there would be any to a treasure chamber.

Our lamp began to burn dim. The fat was nearly exhausted.

'Quatermain,' said Sir Henry, 'what is the time – your watch goes?'

I drew it out, and looked at it. It was six o'clock; we had entered the cave at eleven.

'Infadoos will miss us,' I suggested. 'If we do not return tonight he will search for us in the morning, Curtis.'

'He may search in vain. He does not know the secret of the door, nor even where it is. No living person knew it yesterday, except Gagool. To-day no one knows it. Even if he found the door he could not break it down. All the Kukuana army could not break through five feet of living rock. My friends, I see nothing for it but to bow ourselves to the will of the Almighty. The search for treasure has brought many to a bad end; we shall go to swell their number.'

The lamp grew dimmer yet.

Presently it flared up and showed the whole scene in strong relief, the great mass of white tusks, the boxes of gold, the corpse of poor Foulata stretched before them, the goat-skin full of treasure, the dim glimmer of the diamonds, and the wild, wan faces of us three white men seated there awaiting death by starvation.

Then the flame sank and expired.

CHAPTER 18

We Abandon Hope

I can give no adequate description of the horrors of the night which followed. Mercifully these were to some extent mitigated by sleep, for even in such a position as ours wearied nature will sometimes assert itself. But I, at any rate, found it impossible to sleep much. Putting aside the terrifying thought of our impending doom – for the bravest man on earth might well quail from such a fate as awaited us, and I never made any pretensions to be brave – the *silence* itself was too great to allow of it. Reader, you may have lain awake at night and thought the quiet oppressive, but I say with confidence that you can have no idea what a vivid, tangible thing is perfect stillness. On the surface of the earth there is always some sound or motion, and though it may in itself be imperceptible, yet it deadens the sharp edge of absolute silence. But here there was none. We were buried in the bowels of a huge snow-clad peak. Thousands of feet above us the fresh air rushed over the white snow, but no sound of it reached us. We were separated by a long tunnel and five feet of rock even from the awful Chamber of the Dead; and the dead make no noise. Did we not know it who lay by poor Foulata's side? The crashing of all the artillery of earth and heaven could not have come to our ears in that living tomb. We were cut off from every echo of the world – we were as men already in the grave.

Then the irony of the situation forced itself upon me. There around us lay treasures enough to pay off a moderate national debt, or to build a fleet of ironclads, and yet we would have bartered them all gladly for the faintest chance of escape. Soon, doubtless, we should be rejoiced to exchange them for a bit of food or a cup of water, and, after that, even for the privilege of a speedy close to our sufferings. Truly wealth, which men spend their lives in acquiring, is a valueless thing at the last.

And so the night wore on.

'Good,' said Sir Henry's voice at last, and it sounded awful in the intense stillness, 'how many matches have you in the box?'

'Eight, Curtis.'

'Strike one and let us see the time.'

He did so, and in contrast to the dense darkness the flame nearly blinded us. It was five o'clock by my watch. The beautiful dawn was now blushing on the snow-wreaths far over our heads, and the breeze would be stirring the night mists in the hollows.

'We had better eat something and keep up our strength,' I suggested.

'What is the good of eating?' answered Good; 'the sooner we die and get it over the better.'

'While there is life there is hope,' said Sir Henry.

Accordingly we ate and sipped some water, and another period of time passed. Then Sir Henry suggested that it might be well to get as near the door as possible and halloa, on the faint chance of somebody catching a sound outside. Accordingly Good, who, from long practice at sea, has a fine piercing note, groped his way down the passage and set to work. I must say that he made a most diabolical noise. I never heard such yells; but it might have been a mosquito buzzing for all the effect they produced.

After a while he gave it up and came back very thirsty, and had to drink. Then we stopped yelling, as it encroached on the supply of water.

So we sat down once more against the chests of useless diamonds in that dreadful inaction which was one of the hardest circumstances of our fate; and I am bound to say that, for my part, I gave way to despair. Laying my head against Sir Henry's broad shoulder I burst into tears; and I think that I heard Good gulping away on the other side, and swearing hoarsely at himself for doing so.

Ah, how good and brave that great man was! Had we been two frightened children, and he our nurse, he could not have treated us more tenderly. Forgetting his own share of miseries, he did all he could to soothe our broken nerves, telling stories of men who had been in somewhat similar circumstances, and miraculously escaped; and when these failed to cheer us, pointing out how, after all, it was only anticipating an end which must come to us all; that it would soon be over, and that death from exhaustion was a merciful one (which is not true). Then, in a different sort of way, as once before I had heard him do, he suggested that we should throw ourselves on the mercy of a higher Power, which for my part I did with great vigour.

His is a beautiful character, very quiet, but very strong.

And so somehow the day went as the night had gone, if, indeed, one can use these terms where all was densest night, and when I lit a match to see the time it was seven o'clock.

Once more we ate and drank, and as we did so an idea occurred to me.

'How is it,' said I, 'that the air in this place keeps fresh? It is thick and heavy, but it is perfectly fresh.'

'Great heavens!' said Good, starting up, 'I never thought of that. It can't come through the stone door, for it's air-tight, if ever a door was. It must come from somewhere. If there were no current of air in the place we should have been stifled or poisoned when we first came in. Let us have a look.'

It was wonderful what a change this mere spark of hope wrought in us. In a moment we were all three groping about on our hands and knees, feeling for the slightest indication of a draught. Presently my ardour received a check. I put my hand on something cold. It was dead Foulata's face!

For an hour or more we went on feeling about, till at last Sir

Henry and I gave it up in despair, having been considerably hurt by constantly knocking our heads against tusks, chests, and the sides of the chamber. But Good still persevered, saying, with an approach to cheerfulness, that it was better than doing nothing.

'I say, you fellows,' he said presently, in a constrained sort of voice, 'come here.'

Needless to say we scrambled towards him quickly enough.

'Quatermain, put your hand here, where mine is. Now do you feel anything?'

'I *think* I feel air coming up.'

'Now listen.' He rose and stamped upon the place, and a flame of hope shot up in our hearts. *It rang hollow.*

With trembling hands I lit a match. I had only three left, and we saw that we were in the angle of the far corner of the chamber, a fact that accounted for our not having noticed the hollow sound of the place during our former exhaustive examination. As the match burnt we scrutinised the spot. There was a join in the solid rock floor, and, great heavens! there, let in level with the rock, was a stone ring. We said no word, we were too excited, and our hearts beat too wildly with hope to allow us to speak. Good had a knife, at the back of which was one of those hooks that are made to extract stones from horses' hoofs. He opened it, and with it scratched round the ring. Finally he worked it under, and levered away gently for fear of breaking the hook. The ring began to move. Being of stone it had not rusted fast in all the centuries it had lain there, as would have been the case had it been of iron. Presently the ring was upright. Then he thrust his hands into it and tugged with all his force, but nothing budged.

'Let me try,' I said impatiently, for the situation of the stone, right in the angle of the corner, was such that it was impossible for two to pull at once. I took hold and strained away, but no results.

Next Sir Henry tried and failed.

Taking the hook again, Good scratched all round the crack where we felt the air coming up.

'Now, Curtis,' he said, 'tackle on, and put your back into it;

you are as strong as two. Stop,' and he took off a stout, black silk handkerchief, which, true to his habits of neatness, he still wore, and ran it through the ring. 'Quatermain, get Curtis round the middle and pull for dear life when I give the word. *Now!*'

Sir Henry put out all his enormous strength, and Good and I did the same, with such power as nature had given us.

'Heave! heave! it's giving,' gasped Sir Henry; and I heard the muscles of his great back cracking. Suddenly there was a grating sound, then a rush of air, and we were all on our backs on the floor with a heavy flag-stone lying upon the top of us. Sir Henry's strength had done it, and never did muscular power stand a man in better stead.

'Light a match, Quatermain,' he said, so soon as we had picked ourselves up and got our breath; 'carefully, now.'

I did so, and there before us, Heaven be praised! was the *first step of a stone stair.*

'Now what is to be done?' asked Good.

'Follow the stair, of course, and trust to Providence.'

'Stop!' said Sir Henry; 'Quatermain, get the bit of biltong and the water that are left; we may want them.'

I went creeping back to our place by the chests for that purpose, and as I was coming away an idea struck me. We had not thought much of the diamonds for the last twenty-four hours or so; indeed, the very idea of diamonds was nauseous, seeing what they had entailed upon us; but, reflected I, I may as well pocket some in case we ever should get out of this ghastly hole. So I just put my fist into the first chest and filled all the available pockets of my old shooting-coat and trousers, topping up – this was a happy notion – with a few handfuls of big ones out of the third chest. Also, by an afterthought, I stuffed Foulata's basket, which, except for one water-gourd and a little biltong, was empty now, with great quantities of the stones.

'I say, you fellows,' I sang out, 'won't you take some diamonds with you? I've filled my pockets and the basket.'

'Oh, come on, Quatermain! and hang the diamonds!' said Sir Henry. 'I hope that I may never see another.'

As for Good, he made no answer. He was, I think, taking his last farewell of all that was left of the poor girl who had loved him so well.

Curious as it may seem to you, my reader, sitting at home at ease and reflecting on the vast, indeed the immeasurable wealth which we were thus abandoning, I can assure you that if you had passed some twenty-eight hours with next to nothing to eat and drink in that place, *you* would not have cared to cumber yourself with diamonds whilst plunging down into the unknown bowels of the earth, in the wild hope of escape from an agonizing death. If, from the habits of a life-time, it had not become a sort of second nature with me never to leave anything worth having behind if there was the slightest chance of my being able to carry it away, I am sure that I should not have bothered to fill my pockets and that basket.

'Come on, Quatermain,' repeated Sir Henry, who was already standing on the first step of the stone stair. 'Steady, I will go first.'

'Mind where you put your feet, there may be some awful hole underneath,' I answered.

'Much more likely to be another room,' said Sir Henry, while he descended slowly, counting the steps as he went.

When he got to 'fifteen' he stopped. 'Here's the bottom,' he said. 'Thank goodness! I think it's a passage. Follow me down.'

Good went next, and I came last, carrying the basket, and on reaching the bottom lit one of the two remaining matches. By its light we could just see that we were standing in a narrow tunnel, which ran right and left at right angles to the staircase we had descended. Before we could make out any more, the match burnt my fingers and went out. Then arose the delicate question of which way to go. Of course, it was impossible to know what the tunnel was, or where it led to, and yet to turn one way might lead us to safety, and to turn the other, to destruction. We were utterly perplexed, till suddenly it struck Good that when I had lit the match the draught of the passage blew the flame to the left.

'Let us go against the draught,' he said; 'air draws inwards, not outwards.'

We took this suggestion, and feeling along the wall with our hands, whilst trying the ground before us at every step, we departed from that accursed treasure chamber on our terrible quest for life. If ever it should be entered again by living man, which I do not think probable, he will find tokens of our visit in the open chests of jewels, the empty lamp, and the white bones of poor Foulata.

When we had groped our way for about a quarter of an hour along the passage, suddenly it took a sharp twist, or else was bisected by another, which we followed, only in the course of time to be led into a third. And so it went on for some hours. We seemed to be in a stone labyrinth which led nowhere. What all these passages are, of course I cannot say, but we thought that they must be the ancient workings of a mine, of which the various shafts and adits travelled hither and thither as the ore chutes led them. This is the only way in which we could account for such a multitude of galleries.

At length we halted, thoroughly worn out with fatigue and with that hope deferred which maketh the heart sick, and ate up our poor remaining piece of biltong and drank our last sup of water, for our throats were like lime-kilns. It seemed to us that we had escaped Death in the darkness of the treasure chamber only to meet him in the darkness of the tunnels.

As we stood, once more utterly depressed, I thought that I caught a sound, to which I called the attention of the others. It was very faint and very far off, but it *was* a sound, a faint murmuring sound, for the others heard it too, and no words can describe the blessedness of it after all those hours of utter, awful stillness.

'By heaven! it's running water,' said Good. 'Come on.'

Off we started again in the direction from which the faint murmur seemed to come, groping our way as before along the rocky walls. I remember that I laid down the basket full of diamonds, wishing to be rid of its weight, but on second thoughts took it up again. One might as well die rich as poor, I reflected. As we went the sound became more and more audible, till at last it seemed quite loud in the quiet. On, yet on; now we could distinctly make out the unmistakable swirl of rushing water. And yet how could there be running water in the bowels of the earth? Now we were quite near it, and Good, who was leading, swore that he could smell it.

'Go gently, Good,' said Sir Henry, 'we must be close.' *Splash!* and a cry from Good.

He had fallen in.

'Good! Good! where are you?' we shouted, in terrified distress. To our intense relief an answer came back in a choky voice:

'All right; I've got hold of a rock. Strike a light to show me where you are.'

Hastily I lit the last remaining match. Its faint gleam discovered to us a dark mass of water running at our feet. How wide it was we could not see, but there, some way out, was the dark form of our companion hanging on to a projecting rock.

'Stand clear to catch me,' sung out Good. 'I must swim for it.'

Then we heard a splash, and a great struggle. Another minute and he had grabbed at and caught Sir Henry's outstretched hand, and we had pulled him up high and dry into the tunnel.

'My word!' he said, between his gasps, 'that was touch and go. If I hadn't managed to catch that rock, and known how to swim, I should have been done. It runs like a mill-race, and I could feel no bottom.'

We dared not follow the banks of the subterranean river for fear lest we should fall into it again in the darkness. So after Good had rested a while, and we had drunk our fill of the water, which was sweet and fresh, and washed our faces, that needed it sadly, as well as we could, we started from the banks of this African Styx, and began to retrace our steps along the tunnel, Good dripping unpleasantly in front of us. At length we came to another gallery leading to our right.

'We may as well take it,' said Sir Henry wearily; 'all roads are alike here; we can only go on till we drop.'

Slowly, for a long, long while, we stumbled, utterly exhausted, along this new tunnel, Sir Henry now leading the way. Again I thought of abandoning that basket, but did not.

Suddenly he stopped, and we bumped up against him.

'Look!' he whispered, 'is my brain going, or is that light?'

We stared with all our eyes, and there, yes there, far ahead of us, was a faint, glimmering spot, no larger than a cottage window pane. It was so faint that I doubt if any eyes, except those which, like ours, had for days seen nothing but blackness, could have perceived it at all.

With a gasp of hope we pushed on. In five minutes there was no longer any doubt; it *was* a patch of faint light. A minute more and a breath of real live air was fanning us. On we struggled. All at once the tunnel narrowed. Sir Henry went on his knees. Smaller yet it grew, till it was only the size of a large fox's earth – it was *earth* now, mind you; the rock had ceased.

A squeeze, a struggle, and Sir Henry was out, and so was Good, and so was I, dragging Foulata's basket after me; and there above us were the blessed stars, and in our nostrils was the sweet air. Then suddenly something gave, and we were all rolling over and over through grass and bushes and soft, wet soil.

The basket caught in something and I stopped. Sitting up I halloaed lustily. An answering shout came from just below, where Sir Henry's wild career had been checked by some level ground. I scrambled to him, and found him unhurt, though breathless. Then we looked for Good. A little way off we discovered him also, jammed in a forked root. He was a good deal knocked about, but soon came to himself.

We sat down together, there on the grass, and the revulsion of feeling was so great that really I think we cried with joy. We had escaped from that awful dungeon, which was so near to becoming our grave. Surely some merciful Power guided our footsteps to the jackal hole, for that is what it must have been, at the termination of the tunnel. And see, yonder on the mountains the dawn we had never thought to look upon again was blushing rosy red.

Presently the grey light stole down the slopes, and we saw that we were at the bottom, or rather, nearly at the bottom, of the vast pit in front of the entrance to the cave. Now we could make out the dim forms of the three Colossi who sat upon its verge. Doubtless those awful passages, along which we had wandered the live-long night, had been originally in some way connected with the great diamond mine. As for the subterranean river in the bowels of the mountain, Heaven only knows what it is, or whence it flows, or whither it goes. I, for one, have no anxiety to trace its course.

Lighter it grew, and lighter yet. We could see each other now, and such a sight as we presented I have never set eyes on before or since. Gaunt-cheeked, hollow-eyed wretches, smeared all over with dust and mud, bruised, bleeding, the long fear of imminent death yet written on our countenances, we were, indeed, a spectacle to frighten the daylight. And yet it is a solemn fact that Good's eye-glass was still fixed in Good's eye. I doubt whether he had ever taken it out at all. Neither the darkness, nor the plunge in the subterranean river, nor the roll down the slope, had been able to separate Good and his eye-glass.

Presently we rose, fearing that our limbs would stiffen if we stopped there longer, and commenced with slow and painful steps to struggle up the sloping sides of the great pit. For an hour or more we toiled steadfastly over the blue clay, dragging ourselves on by the help of roots and grasses with which it was clothed. But now I had no more thought of leaving the basket; indeed, nothing but death would have parted us.

At last it was done, and we stood by the great road, on that side of the pit which is opposite to the Colossi.

At the side of the road, a hundred yards off, a fire was burning in front of some huts, and round the fire were figures. We staggered towards them, supporting one another, and halting every few paces. Presently one of the figures rose, saw us and fell on to the ground, crying out for fear.

'Infadoos, Infadoos! it is we, thy friends.'

He rose; he ran to us, staring wildly, and still shaking with fear.

'Oh, my lords, my lords, it is indeed you come back from the dead! – come back from the dead!'

And the old warrior flung himself down before us, and clasping Sir Henry's knees, he wept aloud for joy.

CHAPTER 19

Ignosi's Farewell

Ten days from that eventful morning found us once more in our old quarters at Loo; and, strange to say, but little the worse for our terrible experience, except that my stubbly hair came out of the treasure cave about three shades greyer than it went in, and that Good never was quite the same after Foulata's death, which seemed to move him very greatly. I am bound to say, looking at the thing from the point of view of an oldish man of the world, that I consider her removal was a fortunate occurrence, since, otherwise, complications would have been sure to ensue. The poor creature was no ordinary native girl, but a person of great, I had almost said stately, beauty, and of considerable refinement of mind. But no amount of beauty or refinement could have made an entanglement between Good and herself a desirable occurrence; for, as she herself put it, 'Can the sun mate with the moon, or the white with the black?'

I need hardly state that we never again penetrated into Solomon's treasure chamber. After we had recovered from our fatigue, a process which took us forty-eight hours, we descended into the great pit in the hope of finding the hole by which we had crept out of the mountain, but with no success. To begin with, rain had fallen, and obliterated our spoor; and what is more, the sides of the vast pit were full of ant-bear and other holes. It was impossible to say to which of these we owed our salvation.

Also, on the day before we started back to Loo, we made a further examination of the wonders of the stalactite cave, and, drawn by a kind of restless feeling, even penetrated once more into the Chamber of the Dead. Passing beneath the spear of the White Death we gazed, with sensations which it would be quite impossible for me to describe, at the mass of rock hat had shut us off from escape, thinking the while of the priceless treasures beyond, of the mysterious old hag whose flattened fragments lay crushed beneath it, and of the fair girl of whose tomb it was the portal. I say gazed at the 'rock,' for, examine as we would, we could find no traces of the join of the sliding door; nor, indeed, could we hit upon the secret, now utterly lost, that worked it, though we tried for an hour or more. It is certainly a marvellous bit of mechanism, characteristic, in its massive and yet inscrutable simplicity, of the age which produced it; and I doubt if the world has such another to show.

At last we gave it up in disgust; though, if the mass had suddenly risen before our eyes, I doubt if we should have screwed up courage to step over Gagool's mangled remains, and once more enter the treasure chamber, even in the sure and certain hope of unlimited diamonds. And yet I could have cried at the idea of leaving all that treasure, the biggest treasure probably that in the world's history has ever been accumulated in one spot. But there was no help for it. Only dynamite could force its way through five feet of solid rock.

So we left it. Perhaps, in some remote unborn century, a more fortunate explorer may hit upon the 'Open Sesame,' and flood the world with gems. But, myself, I doubt it. Somehow, I seem to feel that the tens of millions of pounds' worth of jewels which lie in the three stone coffers will never shine round the neck of an earthly beauty. They and Foulata's bones will keep cold company to the end of all things. And yet who can tell?

With a sigh of disappointment we made our way back, and next day started for Loo. Still it was really very ungrateful of us to be disappointed; for, as the reader will remember, by a lucky thought I had taken the precaution to fill the wide pockets of my old shooting coat and trousers with gems before we left our prison-house, also Foulata's basket, which held twice as many more, notwithstanding that the water-bottle had occupied some of its space. A good many of these fell out in the course of our roll down the side of the pit, including several of the big ones, which I had crammed in on the top of my coat pockets. But, comparatively speaking, an enormous quantity still remained, including ninety-three large stones ranging from over two hundred to seventy carats in weight. My old shooting coat and the basket still held sufficient treasure to make us all, if not millionaires as the term is understood in America, at least exceedingly wealthy men, and yet to keep enough stones each to form the three finest sets of gems in Europe. So we had not done so badly.

On arriving at Loo we were most cordially received by Ignosi, whom we found well, and busily engaged in consolidating his power and reorganising the regiments which had suffered most in the great struggle with Twala.

He listened with intense interest to our wonderful story; but when we told him of old Gagool's frightful end he grew thoughtful.

'Come hither,' he called to a very old Induna, or councillor, who was sitting with others in a circle round the king, but out of earshot. The ancient man rose, approached, saluted, and seated himself.

'Thou art aged,' said Ignosi.

'Ay, my lord the king! Thy father's father and I were born on the same day.'

'Tell me, when thou wast little, didst thou know Gagool the witch doctress?'

'Ay, my lord the king!'

'How was she then – young, like thee?'

'Not so, my lord the king! She was even as she is now and as she was in the days of my great grandfather before me; old and dried, very ugly, and full of wickedness.'

'She is no more; she is dead.'

'So, O king! then is an ancient curse taken from the land.'

'Go!'

'*Koom!* I go, Black Puppy, who tore out the old dog's throat. *Koom!*'

'Ye see, my brothers,' said Ignosi, 'this was a strange woman, and I rejoice that she is dead. She would have let you die in the dark place, and mayhap afterwards she had found a way to slay me, as she found a way to slay my father and to set up Twala, whom her black heart loved, in his place. Now go on with the tale; surely there never was its like!'

After I had narrated all the story of our escape, as we had agreed between ourselves that I should, I took the opportunity to address Ignosi on the matter of our departure from Kukuanaland.

'And now, Ignosi,' I said, 'the time has come for us to bid thee farewell, and start to see our own land once more. Behold, Ignosi, thou camest with us as a servant, and now we leave thee a mighty king. If thou art grateful to us, remember to do even as thou didst promise: to rule justly, to respect the law, and to put none to death without a cause. So shalt thou prosper. To-morrow, at break of day, Ignosi, thou wilt give us an escort who shall lead us across the mountains. Is it not so, O king?'

Ignosi covered his face with his hands for a while before answering.

'My heart is sore,' he said at last; 'your words split my heart in twain. What have I done to you, Incubu, Macumazahn, and Bougwan, that ye should leave me desolate? Ye who stood by me in rebellion and in battle, will ye leave me in the day of peace and victory? What will ye – wives? Choose from among the maidens! A place to live in? Behold, the land is yours as far as ye can see. The white man's houses? Ye shall teach my people how to build them. Cattle for beef and milk? Every married man shall bring you an ox or a cow. Wild game to hunt? Does not the elephant walk through my forests, and the river-horse sleep in the reeds? Would ye make war? My Impis wait your word. If there is anything more which I can give, that will I give you.'

'Nay, Ignosi, we want none of these things,' I answered; 'we would seek our own place.'

'Now do I learn,' said Ignosi bitterly, and with flashing eyes, 'that ye love the bright stones more than me, your friend. Ye have the stones; now ye would go to Natal and across the moving black water and sell them, and be rich, as it is the desire of a white man's heart to be. Cursed for your sake be the white stones, and cursed he who seeks them. Death shall it be to him who sets foot in the place of Death to find them. For they are yours, and yours alone. I have spoken. White men, ye can go.'

I laid my hand upon his arm. 'Ignosi,' I said, 'tell us, when thou didst wander in Zululand, and among the white people of Natal, did not thine heart turn to the land thy mother told thee of, thy native land, where thou didst see the light, and play when thou wast little, the land where thy place was?'

'It was even so, Macumazahn.'

'In like manner, Ignosi, do our hearts turn to our land and to our own place.'

Then came a silence. When Ignosi broke it, it was in a different voice.

'I perceive that now, as ever, thy words are wise and full of reason, Macumazahn; that which flies in the air loves not to run along the ground; the white man loves not to live on the level of the black or to house among his kraals. Well, ye must go, and leave my heart sore, because ye will be as dead to me, since from where ye are no tidings can come to me.

'But listen, and let all your brothers know my words. No other white man shall cross the mountains, even if any man live to come so far. I will see no traders with their guns and gin. My people shall fight with the spear, and drink water, like their forefathers before them. I will have no praying-men to put a fear of death into men's hearts, to stir them up against the law of the king, and make a path for the white folk who follow to run on. If a white man comes to my gates I will send him back; if a hundred come I will push them back; if armies come I will make war on them with all my strength, and they shall not prevail against me. None shall ever seek for the shining stones; no, not an army, for if they come I will send a regiment and fill up the pit, and break down the white columns in the caves and choke them with rocks, so that none can reach even to that door of which ye speak, whereof the way to move it is lost. But for you three, Incubu, Macumazahn, and Bougwan, the path is always open; for, behold, ye are dearer to me than aught that breathes.

'So ye would go. Infadoos, my uncle, and my Induna, shall take you by the hand and guide you with a regiment. There is, as I have learned, another way across the mountains that he shall show you. Farewell, my brothers, brave white men. See me no more, for I have no heart to bear it. Behold! I make a decree, and it shall be published from the mountains to the mountains; your names, Incubu, Macumazahn, and Bougwan, shall be "*hlonipa*" even as the names of dead kings, and he who speaks them shall die.[1] So shall your memory be preserved in the land for ever.

'Go now, ere my eyes rain tears like a woman's. At times as ye look back down the path of life, or when ye are old and gather yourselves together to crouch before the fire, because for you the sun has no more heat, ye will think of how we stood shoulder to shoulder, in that great battle which thy wise words planned, Macumazahn; of how thou wast the point of the horn that galled Twala's flank, Bougwan; whilst thou stoodst in the ring of the Greys, Incubu, and men went down before thine axe like corn before a sickle; ay, and of how thou didst break that wild bull Twala's strength, and bring his pride to dust. Fare ye well, perchance for ever, Incubu, Macumazahn, and Bougwan, my lords and my friends.'

Ignosi rose and looked earnestly at us for a few seconds. Then he threw the corner of his karross over his head, so as to cover his face from us.

We went in silence.

Next day at dawn we left Loo, escorted by our old friend

---

[1] This extraordinary and negative way of showing intense respect is by no means unknown among African people, and the result is that if, as is usual, the name in question has a significance, the meaning must be expressed by an idiom or another word. In this way a memory is preserved for generations, or until the new word utterly supplants the old one. – A.Q.

Infadoos, who was heart-broken at our departure, and by the regiment of Buffaloes. Early as was the hour, we found the main street of the town lined with multitudes of people, who gave us the royal salute as we passed at the head of the regiment, while the women blessed us for having rid the land of Twala, throwing flowers before us as we went. It was really very affecting, and not the sort of thing one is accustomed to meet with from natives.

One ludicrous incident occurred, however, which I rather welcomed, as it gave us something to laugh at.

Just before we reached the confines of the town, a pretty young girl, with some lovely lilies in her hand, ran forward and presented them to Good – somehow they all seemed to like Good; I think his eye-glass and solitary whisker gave him a fictitious value – and then said that she had a boon to ask.

'Speak on,' he answered.

'Let my lord show his servant his beautiful white legs, that his servant may look on them and remember them all her days, and tell of them to her children; his servant has travelled four days' journey to see them, for the fame of them has gone throughout the land.'

'I'll be hanged if I do!' exclaimed Good excitedly.

'Come, come, my dear fellow,' said Sir Henry, 'you can't refuse to oblige a lady.'

'I won't,' replied Good obstinately; 'it is positively indecent.'

However, in the end he consented to draw up his trousers to the knee, amidst notes of rapturous admiration from all the women present, especially the gratified young lady, and in this guise he had to walk till we got clear of the town.

Good's legs, I fear, will never be so greatly admired again. Of his melting teeth, and even of his 'transparent eye,' the Kukuanas wearied more or less, but of his legs, never.

As we travelled, Infadoos told us that there was another pass over the mountains to the North of the one followed by Solomon's Great Road, or rather that there was a place where it is possible to climb down the wall of cliff which separates Kukuanaland from the desert, and is broken by the towering shapes of Sheba's Breasts.

It appeared, also, that rather more than two years previously a party of Kukuana hunters had descended this path into the desert in search of ostriches, whose plumes are much prized among them for war head-dresses, and that in the course of their hunt they had been led far from the mountains and were much troubled by thirst. Seeing trees on the horizon, however, they walked towards them and discovered a large and fertile oasis some miles in extent, and plentifully watered. It was by way of this oasis that Infadoos suggested we should return, and the idea seemed to us a good one, for it appeared that we should thus escape the rigours of the mountain pass. Also some of the hunters were in attendance to guide us to the oasis, from which, they stated, they could perceive other fertile spots far away in the desert.[2]

Travelling easily, on the night of the fourth day's journey we found ourselves once more on the crest of the mountains that separate Kukuanaland from the desert which rolled away in sandy billows at our feet, and about twenty-five miles to the north of Sheba's Breasts.

At dawn on the following day, we were led to the edge of a very precipitous chasm, by which we were to descend the precipice, and gain the plain two thousand or more feet below.

Here we bade farewell to that true friend and sturdy old warrior, Infadoos, who solemnly wished all good upon us, and nearly wept with grief. 'Never, my lords,' he said, 'shall mine old eyes see the like of you again. Ah! the way that Incubu cut his men down in the battle! Ah! for the sight of that stroke with which he swept off my brother Twala's head! It was beautiful – beautiful!

---

[2]It often puzzled all of us to understand how it was possible that Ignosi's mother, bearing the child with her, should have survived the dangers of her journey across the mountains and the desert, dangers which so nearly proved fatal to ourselves. It has since occurred to me, and I give the idea to the reader for what it is worth, that she must have taken this second route, and wandered out like Hagar into the wilderness. If she did so, there is no longer anything inexplicable about the story, since, as Ignosi himself related, she may well have been picked up by some ostrich hunters before she or the child was exhausted, and led by them to the oasis. Thence she may have travelled by stages to the fertile country, and so on by slow degrees southwards to Zululand. – A.Q.

I may never hope to see such another, except perchance in happy dreams.'

We were very sorry to part from; indeed, Good was so moved that he gave him as a souvenir – what do you think? – an *eye-glass;* afterwards we discovered that it was a spare one. Infadoos was delighted, foreseeing that the possession of such an article would increase his prestige enormously, and after several vain attempts he actually succeeded in screwing it into his own eye. Anything more incongruous than the old warrior looked with an eye-glass I never saw. Eye-glasses do not go well with leopard-skin cloaks and black ostrich plumes.

Then, after seeing that our guides were well laden with water and provisions, and having received a thundering farewell salute from the Buffaloes, we wrung Infadoos by the hand, and began our downward climb. A very arduous business it proved to be, but somehow that evening we found ourselves at the bottom without accident.

'Do you know,' said Sir Henry that night, as we sat by our fire and gazed up at the beetling cliffs above us, 'I think that there are worse places than Kukuanaland in the world, and that I have known unhappier times than the last month or two, though I have never spent such queer ones. Eh! you fellows?'

'I almost wish I were back,' said Good with a sigh.

As for myself, I reflected that all's well that ends well; but that in the course of a long life of peril, I never had such shaves as those which I had recently experienced. The thought of that battle still makes me feel cold all over, and as for our experience in the treasure chamber – !

Next morning we started on a toilsome trudge across the desert, having with us a good supply of water carried by our five guides, and camped that night in the open, marching again at dawn on the morrow.

By noon of the third day's journey we could see the trees of the oasis of which the guides spoke, and within an hour of sundown we were walking once more upon grass and listening to the sound of running water.

CHAPTER 20

Found

And now I come to perhaps the strangest adventure that happened to us in all this strange business; one, too, which shows how wonderfully things are brought about.

I was walking along quietly, some way in front of the other two, down the banks of the stream which runs from the oasis till it is swallowed up in the hungry desert sands, when suddenly I stopped and rubbed my eyes, as well I might. There, not twenty yards in front of me, placed in a charming situation, under the shade of a species of figtree, and facing to the stream, was a cosy hut, built more or less on the Kafir principle with grass and withes, but having a full-length door instead of a bee-hole.

'What the dickens,' said I to myself, 'can a hut be doing here?' Even as I said it the door of the hut opened, and there limped out of it a *white man* clothed in skins and an enormous black beard. I thought that I must have got a touch of the sun. It was impossible. No hunter ever came to such a place as this. Certainly no hunter would ever settle in it. I stared and stared, and so did the other man, and just at that juncture Sir Henry and Good walked up.

'Look here, you fellows,' I said, 'is that a white man, or am I mad?'

Sir Henry looked, and Good looked, and then all of a sudden the lame white man with a black beard uttered a great cry, and began hobbling towards us. When he was close he fell down in a sort of faint.

With a spring Sir Henry was by his side.

'Great Powers!' he cried, '*it is my brother George!*'

At the sound of the disturbance, another figure, also clad in skins, a gun in his hand, and ran towards us. On seeing me he too gave a cry.

'Macumazahn,' he halloed, 'don't you know me, Baas? I'm Jim the hunter. I lost the note you gave me to give to the Baas, and we have been here nearly two years.' And the fellow fell at my feet, and rolled over and over, weeping for joy.

'You careless scoundrel!' I said; 'you ought to be well *sjam-bocked*' – that is hided.

Meanwhile the man with the black beard had recovered and risen, and he and Sir Henry were pump-handling away at each other apparently without a word to say. But whatever they had quarrelled about in the past – I suspect it was a lady, though I never asked – it was evidently forgotten now.

'My dear old fellow,' burst out Sir Henry at last, 'I thought that you were dead. I have been over Solomon's Mountains to find you. I had given up all hope of ever seeing you again, and now I come across you perched in the desert, like an old *aasvögel*.'[1]

'I tried to cross Solomon's Mountains nearly two years ago,' was the answer, spoken in the hesitating voice of a man who has had little recent opportunity of using his tongue, 'but when I reached here a boulder fell on my leg and crushed it, and I have been able to go neither forward nor back.'

Then I came up. 'How do you do, Mr Neville?' I said; 'do you remember me?'

'Why,' he said, 'isn't it Hunter Quatermain, eh, and Good too? Hold on a minute, you fellows, I am getting dizzy again. It is all so very strange, and, when a man has ceased to hope, so very happy!'

That evening, over the camp fire, George Curtis told us his story, which, in its way, was almost as eventful as our own, and, put

[1] Vulture.

shortly, amounted to this. A little less than two years before, he had started from Sitanda's Kraal, to try to reach Suliman's Berg. As for the note I had sent him by Jim, that worthy lost it, and he had never heard of it till to-day. But, acting upon information he received from the natives, he headed not for Sheba's Breasts, but for the ladder-like descent of the mountains down which we had just come, clearly a much better route than that marked out in old Dom Silvestra's plan. In the desert he and Jim suffered great hardships, but finally they reached this oasis, where a terrible accident befell George Curtis. On the day of their arrival he was sitting by the stream, and Jim was extracting the honey from the nest of a stingless bee which is to be found in the desert, on the top of a bank immediately above him. In so doing he loosened a great boulder of rock, which fell upon George Curtis's right leg, crushing it frightfully. From that day he had been so lame that he found it impossible to go either forward or back, and had preferred to take the chance of dying on the oasis to the certainty of perishing in the desert.

As for food, however, they got on pretty well, for they had a good supply of ammunition, and the oasis was frequented, especially at night, by large quantities of game, which came thither for water. These they shot, or trapped in pitfalls, using the flesh to eat, and, after their clothes wore out, the hides for clothing.

'And so,' George Curtis ended, 'we have lived for nearly two years, like a second Robinson Crusoe and his man Friday, hoping against hope that some natives might come here to help us away, but none have come. Only last night we settled that Jim should leave me, and try to reach Sitanda's Kraal to get assistance. He was to go to-morrow, but I had little hope of ever seeing him back again. And now *you*, of all people in the world, *you*, who, as I fancied, had long ago forgotten all about me, and were living comfortably in old England, turn up in a promiscuous way and find me where you least expected. It is the most wonderful thing that I have ever heard of, and the most merciful too.'

Then Sir Henry set to work and told him the main facts of

our adventures, sitting till late into the night to do so.

'By Jove!' said George Curtis, when I showed him some of the diamonds: 'well, at least you have got something for your pains, besides my worthless self.'

Sir Henry laughed. 'They belong to Quatermain and Good. It was a part of the bargain that they should divide any spoils there might be.'

This remark set me thinking, and having spoken to Good, I told Sir Henry that it was our joint wish that he should take a third portion of the diamonds, or, if he would not, that his share should be handed to his brother, who had suffered even more than ourselves on the chance of getting them. Finally, we prevailed upon him to consent to this arrangement, but George Curtis did not know of it until some time afterwards.

Here, at this point, I think that I shall end my history. Our journey across the desert back to Sitanda's Kraal was most arduous, especially as we had to support George Curtis, whose right leg was very weak indeed, and continually threw out splinters of bone. But we did accomplish it somehow, and to give its details would only be to reproduce much of what happened to us on the former occasion.

Six months from the date of re-arrival at Sitanda's, where we found our guns and other goods quite safe, though the old rascal in charge was much disgusted at our survival to claim them, saw us all once more safe and sound at my little place in the Berea, near Durban, where I am now writing. Thence I bid farewell to all who have accompanied me throughout the strangest trip I ever made in the course of a long and varied experience.

P.S. – Just as I had written the last word, a Kafir came up my avenue of orange trees, carrying a letter in a cleft stick, which he had brought from the post. It turned out to be from Sir Henry, and as it speaks for itself I give it in full.

'October I, 1880.

'Brayley Hall, Yorkshire.

'My dear Quatermain,

'I sent you a line a few mails back to say that the three of us, George, Good, and myself, fetched up all right in England. We got off the boat at Southampton, and went up to town. You should have seen what a swell Good turned out the very next day, beautifully shaved, frock coat fitting like a glove, brand new eye-glass, etc., etc. I went for a walk in the park with him, where I met some people I know, and at once told them the story of his "beautiful white legs."

'He is furious, especially as an ill-natured person has printed it in a Society paper.

'To come to business, Good and I took the diamonds to Streeter's to be valued, as we arranged, and really I am afraid to tell you what they put them at, it seems so enormous. They say that of course it is more or less guess-work, as such stones have never to their knowledge been put on the market in anything like such quantities. It appears that (with the exception of one or two of the largest) they are of the finest water, and equal in every way to the best Brazilian stones. I asked them if they would buy them, but they said that it was beyond their power to do so, and recommended us to sell by degrees, over a period of years indeed, for fear lest we should flood the market. They offer, however, a hundred and eighty thousand pounds for a very small portion of them.

'You must come home, Quatermain, and see about these things, especially if you insist upon making the magnificent present of the third share, which does *not* belong to me, to my brother George. As for Good he is *no good*. His time is too much occupied in shaving, and other matters connected with the vain adorning of the body. But I think he is still down on his luck about

Foulata. He told me that since he had been home he hadn't seen a woman to touch her, either as regards her figure or the sweetness of her expression.

'I want you to come home, my dear old comrade, and to buy a house near here. You have done your day's work, and have lots of money now, and there is a place for sale quite close which would suit you admirably. Do come; the sooner the better; you can finish writing the story of our adventures on board ship. We have refused to tell the tale till it is written by you, for fear lest we shall not be believed. If you start on receipt of this you will reach here by Christmas, and I book you to stay with me for that. Good is coming, and George; and so, by the way, is your boy Harry (there's a bribe for you). I have had him down for a week's shooting, and like him. He is a cool young hand; he shot me in the leg, cut out the pellets, and then remarked upon the advantages of having a medical student with every shooting party!

'Good-bye, old boy; I can't say any more, but I know that you will come, if it is only to oblige,

'Your sincere friend,
'Henry Curtis.

'P. S. – The tusks of the great bull that killed poor Khiva have now been put up in the hall here, over the pair of buffalo horns you gave me, and look magnificent; and the axe with which I chopped off Twala's head is fixed above my writing-table. I wish that we could have managed to bring away the coats of chain armour. Don't lose poor Foulata's basket in which you carried off the diamonds.

'H. C.'

To-day is Tuesday. There is a steamer going on Friday, and I really think that I must take Curtis at his word, and sail by her for England, if it is only to see you, Harry, my boy, and to look after the printing of this history, which is a task that I do not like to trust to anybody else.

Allan Quatermain

CLASSIC LITERATURE: WORDS AND PHRASES
adapted from the Collins English Dictionary

Accoucheur NOUN a male midwife or doctor ❑ *I think my sister must have had some general idea that I was a young offender whom an Accoucheur Policemen had taken up (on my birthday) and delivered over to her* (*Great Expectations* by Charles Dickens)

addled ADJ confused and unable to think properly ❑ *But she counted and counted till she got that addled* (*The Adventures of Huckleberry Finn* by Mark Twain)

admiration NOUN amazement or wonder ❑ *lifting up his hands and eyes by way of admiration* (*Gulliver's Travels* by Jonathan Swift)

afeard ADJ afeard means afraid ❑ *shake it – and don't be afeard* (*The Adventures of Huckleberry Finn* by Mark Twain)

affected VERB affected means followed ❑ *Hadst thou affected sweet divinity* (*Doctor Faustus 5.2* by Christopher Marlowe)

aground ADV when a boat runs aground, it touches the ground in a shallow part of the water and gets stuck ❑ *what kep' you? – boat get aground?* (*The Adventures of Huckleberry Finn* by Mark Twain)

ague NOUN a fever in which the patient has alternate hot and cold shivering fits ❑ *his exposure to the wet and cold had brought on fever and ague* (*Oliver Twist* by Charles Dickens)

alchemy ADJ false or worthless ❑ *all wealth alchemy* (*The Sun Rising* by John Donne)

all alike phrase the same all the time ❑ *Love, all alike* (*The Sun Rising* by John Donne)

alow and aloft phrase alow means in the lower part or bottom, and aloft means on the top, so alow and aloft means on the top and in the bottom or throughout ❑ *Someone's turned the chest out alow and aloft* (*Treasure Island* by Robert Louis Stevenson)

ambuscade NOUN ambuscade is not a proper word. Tom means an ambush, which is when a group of people attack their enemies, after hiding and waiting for them ❑ *and so we would lie in ambuscade, as he called it* (*The Adventures of Huckleberry Finn* by Mark Twain)

amiable ADJ likeable or pleasant ❑ *Such amiable qualities must speak for themselves* (*Pride and Prejudice* by Jane Austen)

amulet NOUN an amulet is a charm thought to drive away evil spirits. ❑ *uttered phrases at once occult and familiar, like the amulet worn on the heart* (*Silas Marner* by George Eliot)

amusement NOUN here amusement means a strange and disturbing puzzle ❑ *this was an amusement the other way* (*Robinson Crusoe* by Daniel Defoe)

ancient NOUN an ancient was the flag displayed on a ship to show which country it belongs to. It is also called the ensign ❑ *her ancient and pendants out* (*Robinson Crusoe* by Daniel Defoe)

antic ADJ here antic means horrible or grotesque ❑ *armed and dressed after a very antic manner* (*Gulliver's Travels* by Jonathan Swift)

antics NOUN antics is an old word meaning clowns, or people who do silly things to make other people laugh ❑ *And point like antics at his triple crown* (*Doctor Faustus 3.2* by Christopher Marlowe)

appanage NOUN an appanage is a living allowance ❑ *As if loveliness were not the special prerogative of woman*

– *her legitimate appanage and heritage!* (*Jane Eyre* by Charlotte Brontë)

appended VERB appended means attached or added to ❑ *and these words appended* (*Treasure Island* by Robert Louis Stevenson)

approver NOUN an approver is someone who gives evidence against someone he used to work with ❑ *Mr. Noah Claypole: receiving a free pardon from the Crown in consequence of being admitted approver against Fagin* (*Oliver Twist* by Charles Dickens)

areas NOUN the areas is the space, below street level, in front of the basement of a house ❑ *The Dodger had a vicious propensity, too, of pulling the caps from the heads of small boys and tossing them down areas* (*Oliver Twist* by Charles Dickens)

argument NOUN theme or important idea or subject which runs through a piece of writing ❑ *Thrice needful to the argument which now* (*The Prelude* by William Wordsworth)

artificially ADJ artfully or cleverly ❑ *and he with a sharp flint sharpened very artificially* (*Gulliver's Travels* by Jonathan Swift)

artist NOUN here artist means a skilled workman ❑ *This man was a most ingenious artist* (*Gulliver's Travels* by Jonathan Swift)

assizes NOUN assizes were regular court sessions which a visiting judge was in charge of ❑ *you shall hang at the next assizes* (*Treasure Island* by Robert Louis Stevenson)

attraction NOUN gravitation, or Newton's theory of gravitation ❑ *he predicted the same fate to attraction* (*Gulliver's Travels* by Jonathan Swift)

aver VERB to aver is to claim something strongly ❑ *for Jem Rodney, the mole catcher, averred that one evening as he was returning homeward* (*Silas Marner* by George Eliot)

baby NOUN here baby means doll, which is a child's toy that looks like a small person ❑ *and skilful dressing her baby* (*Gulliver's Travels* by Jonathan Swift)

bagatelle NOUN bagatelle is a game rather like billiards and pool ❑ *Breakfast had been ordered at a pleasant little tavern, a mile or so away upon the rising ground beyond the green; and there was a bagatelle board in the room, in case we should desire to unbend our minds after the solemnity.* (*Great Expectations* by Charles Dickens)

bah EXCLAM Bah is an exclamation of frustration or anger ❑ *"Bah," said Scrooge.* (*A Christmas Carol* by Charles Dickens)

bairn NOUN a northern word for child ❑ *Who has taught you those fine words, my bairn?* (*Wuthering Heights* by Emily Brontë)

bait VERB to bait means to stop on a journey to take refreshment ❑ *So, when they stopped to bait the horse, and ate and drank and enjoyed themselves, I could touch nothing that they touched, but kept my fast unbroken.* (*David Copperfield* by Charles Dickens)

balustrade NOUN a balustrade is a row of vertical columns that form railings ❑ *but I mean to say you might have got a hearse up that staircase, and taken it broadwise, with the splinter-bar towards the wall, and the door towards the balustrades: and done it easy* (*A Christmas Carol* by Charles Dickens)

bandbox NOUN a large lightweight box for carrying bonnets or hats ❑ *I am glad I bought my bonnet, if it is only for the fun of having another bandbox* (*Pride and Prejudice* by Jane Austen)

barren NOUN a barren here is a stretch or expanse of barren land ❑ *a line of upright stones, continued the length of the barren* (*Wuthering Heights* by Emily Brontë)

basin NOUN a basin was a cup without a handle ❑ *who is drinking his tea* *out of a basin* (*Wuthering Heights* by Emily Brontë)

battalia NOUN the order of battle ❑ *till I saw part of his army in battalia* (*Gulliver's Travels* by Jonathan Swift)

battery NOUN a Battery is a fort or a place where guns are positioned ❑ *You bring the lot to me, at that old Battery over yonder* (*Great Expectations* by Charles Dickens)

battledore and shuttlecock NOUN The game battledore and shuttlecock was an early version of the game now known as badminton. The aim of the early game was simply to keep the shuttlecock from hitting the ground. ❑ *Battledore and shuttlecock's a wery good game vhen you an't the shuttlecock and two lawyers the battledores, in which case it gets too excitin' to be pleasant* (*Pickwick Papers* by Charles Dickens)

beadle NOUN a beadle was a local official who had power over the poor ❑ *But these impertinences were speedily checked by the evidence of the surgeon, and the testimony of the beadle* (*Oliver Twist* by Charles Dickens)

bearings NOUN the bearings of a place are the measurements or directions that are used to find or locate it ❑ *the bearings of the island* (*Treasure Island* by Robert Louis Stevenson)

beaufet NOUN a beaufet was a sideboard ❑ *and sweet-cake from the beaufet* (*Emma* by Jane Austen)

beck NOUN a beck is a small stream ❑ *a beck which follows the bend of the glen* (*Wuthering Heights* by Emily Brontë)

bedight VERB decorated ❑ *and bedight with Christmas holly stuck into the top.* (*A Christmas Carol* by Charles Dickens)

Bedlam NOUN Bedlam was a lunatic asylum in London which had statues carved by Caius Gabriel Cibber at its entrance ❑ *Bedlam, and those carved maniacs at the gates* (*The Prelude* by William Wordsworth)

beeves NOUN oxen or castrated bulls which are animals used for pulling vehicles or carrying things ❑ *to deliver in every morning six beeves* (*Gulliver's Travels* by Jonathan Swift)

begot VERB created or caused ❑ *Begot in thee* (*On His Mistress* by John Donne)

behoof NOUN behoof means benefit ❑ *"Yes, young man," said he, releasing the handle of the article in question, retiring a step or two from my table, and speaking for the behoof of the landlord and waiter at the door* (*Great Expectations* by Charles Dickens)

berth NOUN a berth is a bed on a boat ❑ *this is the berth for me* (*Treasure Island* by Robert Louis Stevenson)

bevers NOUN a bever was a snack, or small portion of food, eaten between main meals ❑ *that buys me thirty meals a day and ten bevers* (*Doctor Faustus 2.1* by Christopher Marlowe)

bilge water NOUN the bilge is the widest part of a ship's bottom, and the bilge water is the dirty water that collects there ❑ *no gush of bilge-water had turned it to fetid puddle* (*Jane Eyre* by Charlotte Brontë)

bills NOUN bills is an old term meaning prescription. A prescription is the piece of paper on which your doctor writes an order for medicine and which you give to a chemist to get the medicine ❑ *Are not thy bills hung up as monuments* (*Doctor Faustus 1.1* by Christopher Marlowe)

black cap NOUN a judge wore a black cap when he was about to sentence a prisoner to death ❑ *The judge assumed the black cap, and the prisoner still stood with the same air and gesture.* (*Oliver Twist* by Charles Dickens)

black gentleman NOUN this was another word for the devil ❑ *for she is as impatient as the black gentleman* (*Emma* by Jane Austen)

boot-jack NOUN a wooden device to help take boots off ❑ *The speaker appeared to throw a boot-jack, or some such article, at the person he addressed* (Oliver Twist by Charles Dickens)

booty NOUN booty means treasure or prizes ❑ *would be inclined to give up their booty in payment of the dead man's debts* (Treasure Island by Robert Louis Stevenson)

Bow Street runner PHRASE Bow Street runners were the first British police force, set up by the author Henry Fielding in the eighteenth century ❑ *as would have convinced a judge or a Bow Street runner* (Treasure Island by Robert Louis Stevenson)

brawn NOUN brawn is a dish of meat which is set in jelly ❑ *Heaped up upon the floor, to form a kind of throne, were turkeys, geese, game, poultry, brawn, great joints of meat, sucking-pigs* (A Christmas Carol by Charles Dickens)

bray VERB when a donkey brays, it makes a loud, harsh sound ❑ *and she doesn't bray like a jackass* (The Adventures of Huckleberry Finn by Mark Twain)

break VERB in order to train a horse you first have to break it ❑ *"If a high-mettled creature like this," said he, "can't be broken by fair means, she will never be good for anything"* (Black Beauty by Anna Sewell)

bullyragging VERB bullyragging is an old word which means bullying. To bullyrag someone is to threaten or force someone to do something they don't want to do ❑ *and a lot of loafers bullyragging him for sport* (The Adventures of Huckleberry Finn by Mark Twain)

but PREP except for (this) ❑ *but this, all pleasures fancies be* (The Good-Morrow by John Donne)

by hand PHRASE by hand was a common expression of the time meaning that baby had been fed either using a spoon or a bottle rather than by breast-feeding ❑ *My sister, Mrs. Joe Gargery, was more than twenty years older than I, and had established a great reputation with herself . . . because she had bought me up 'by hand'* (Great Expectations by Charles Dickens)

bye-spots NOUN bye-spots are lonely places ❑ *and bye-spots of tales rich with indigenous produce* (The Prelude by William Wordsworth)

calico NOUN calico is plain white fabric made from cotton ❑ *There was two old dirty calico dresses* (The Adventures of Huckleberry Finn by Mark Twain)

camp-fever NOUN camp-fever was another word for the disease typhus ❑ *during a severe camp-fever* (Emma by Jane Austen)

cant NOUN cant is insincere or empty talk ❑ *"Man," said the Ghost, "if man you be in heart, not adamant, forbear that wicked cant until you have discovered What the surplus is, and Where it is."* (A Christmas Carol by Charles Dickens)

canty ADJ canty means lively, full of life ❑ *My mother lived til eighty, a canty dame to the last* (Wuthering Heights by Emily Brontë)

canvas VERB to canvas is to discuss ❑ *We think so very differently on this point Mr Knightley, that there can be no use in canvassing it* (Emma by Jane Austen)

capital ADJ capital means excellent or extremely good ❑ *for it's capital, so shady, light, and big* (Little Women by Louisa May Alcott)

capstan NOUN a capstan is a device used on a ship to lift sails and anchors ❑ *capstans going, ships going out to sea, and unintelligible sea creatures roaring curses over the bulwarks at respondent lightermen* (Great Expectations by Charles Dickens)

case-bottle NOUN a square bottle designed to fit with others into a case ❑ *The spirit being set before him in a huge case-bottle, which had originally come out of some ship's* locker (*The Old Curiosity Shop* by Charles Dickens)

casement NOUN casement is a word meaning window. The teacher in Nicholas Nickleby misspells window showing what a bad teacher he is ❏ *W-i-n, win, d-e-r, der, winder, a casement.'* (*Nicholas Nickleby* by Charles Dickens)

cataleptic ADJ a cataleptic fit is one in which the victim goes into a trancelike state and remains still for a long time ❏ *It was at this point in their history that Silas's cataleptic fit occurred during the prayer-meeting* (*Silas Marner* by George Eliot)

cauldron NOUN a cauldron is a large cooking pot made of metal ❏ *stirring a large cauldron which seemed to be full of soup* (*Alice's Adventures in Wonderland* by Lewis Carroll)

cephalic ADJ cephalic means to do with the head ❏ *with ink composed of a cephalic tincture* (*Gulliver's Travels* by Jonathan Swift)

chaise and four NOUN a closed four-wheel carriage pulled by four horses ❏ *he came down on Monday in a chaise and four to see the place* (*Pride and Prejudice* by Jane Austen)

chamberlain NOUN the main servant in a household ❏ *In those times a bed was always to be got there at any hour of the night, and the chamberlain, letting me in at his ready wicket, lighted the candle next in order on his shelf* (*Great Expectations* by Charles Dickens)

characters NOUN distinguishing marks ❏ *Impressed upon all forms the characters* (*The Prelude* by William Wordsworth)

chary ADJ cautious ❏ *I should have been chary of discussing my guardian too freely even with her* (*Great Expectations* by Charles Dickens)

cherishes VERB here cherishes means cheers or brightens ❏ *some*

philosophic song of Truth that cherishes our daily life (*The Prelude* by William Wordsworth)

chickens' meat PHRASE chickens' meat is an old term which means chickens' feed or food ❏ *I had shook a bag of chickens' meat out in that place* (*Robinson Crusoe* by Daniel Defoe)

chimeras NOUN a chimera is an unrealistic idea or a wish which is unlikely to be fulfilled ❏ *with many other wild impossible chimeras* (*Gulliver's Travels* by Jonathan Swift)

chines NOUN chine is a cut of meat that includes part or all of the backbone of the animal ❏ *and they found hams and chines uncut* (*Silas Marner* by George Eliot)

chits NOUN chits is a slang word which means girls ❏ *I hate affected, niminy-piminy chits!* (*Little Women* by Louisa May Alcott)

chopped VERB chopped means come suddenly or accidentally ❏ *if I had chopped upon them* (*Robinson Crusoe* by Daniel Defoe)

chute NOUN a narrow channel ❏ *One morning about day-break, I found a canoe and crossed over a chute to the main shore* (*The Adventures of Huckleberry Finn* by Mark Twain)

circumspection NOUN careful observation of events and circumstances; caution ❏ *I honour your circumspection* (*Pride and Prejudice* by Jane Austen)

clambered VERB clambered means to climb somewhere with difficulty, usually using your hands and your feet ❏ *he clambered up and down stairs* (*Treasure Island* by Robert Louis Stevenson)

clime NOUN climate ❏ *no season knows nor clime* (*The Sun Rising* by John Donne)

clinched VERB clenched ❏ *the tops whereof I could but just reach with my fist clinched* (*Gulliver's Travels* by Jonathan Swift)

close chair NOUN a close chair is a sedan chair, which is an covered chair which has room for one person. The sedan chair is carried on two poles by two men, one in front and one behind ❑ *persuaded even the Empress herself to let me hold her in her close chair* (*Gulliver's Travels* by Jonathan Swift)

clown NOUN clown here means peasant or person who lives off the land ❑ *In ancient days by emperor and clown* (*Ode on a Nightingale* by John Keats)

coalheaver NOUN a coalheaver loaded coal onto ships using a spade ❑ *Good, strong, wholesome medicine, as was given with great success to two Irish labourers and a coalheaver* (*Oliver Twist* by Charles Dickens)

coal-whippers NOUN men who worked at docks using machines to load coal onto ships ❑ *here, were colliers by the score and score, with the coal-whippers plunging off stages on deck* (*Great Expectations* by Charles Dickens)

cobweb NOUN a cobweb is the net which a spider makes for catching insects ❑ *the walls and ceilings were all hung round with cobwebs* (*Gulliver's Travels* by Jonathan Swift)

coddling VERB coddling means to treat someone too kindly or protect them too much ❑ *and I've been coddling the fellow as if I'd been his grandmother* (*Little Women* by Louisa May Alcott)

coil NOUN coil means noise or fuss or disturbance ❑ *What a coil is there?* (*Doctor Faustus 4.7* by Christopher Marlowe)

collared VERB to collar something is a slang term which means to capture. In this sentence, it means he stole it [the money] ❑ *he collared it* (*The Adventures of Huckleberry Finn* by Mark Twain)

colling VERB colling is an old word which means to embrace and kiss ❑ *and no clasping and colling at all* (*Tess of the D'Urbervilles* by Thomas Hardy)

colloquies NOUN colloquy is a formal conversation or dialogue ❑ *Such colloquies have occupied many a pair of pale-faced weavers* (*Silas Marner* by George Eliot)

comfit NOUN sugar-covered pieces of fruit or nut eaten as sweets ❑ *and pulled out a box of comfits* (*Alice's Adventures in Wonderland* by Lewis Carroll)

coming out VERB when a girl came out in society it meant she was of marriageable age. In order to 'come out' girls were expecting to attend balls and other parties during a season ❑ *The younger girls formed hopes of coming out a year or two sooner than they might otherwise have done* (*Pride and Prejudice* by Jane Austen)

commit VERB commit means arrest or stop ❑ *Commit the rascals* (*Doctor Faustus 4.7* by Christopher Marlowe)

commodious ADJ commodious means convenient ❑ *the most commodious and effectual ways* (*Gulliver's Travels* by Jonathan Swift)

commons NOUN commons is an old term meaning food shared with others ❑ *his pauper assistants ranged themselves behind him; the gruel was served out; and a long grace was said over the short commons.* (*Oliver Twist* by Charles Dickens)

complacency NOUN here complacency means a desire to please others. Today complacency means feeling pleased with oneself without good reason. ❑ *Twas thy power that raised the first complacency in me* (*The Prelude* by William Wordsworth)

complaisance NOUN complaisance was eagerness to please ❑ *we cannot wonder at his complaisance* (*Pride and Prejudice* by Jane Austen)

complaisant ADJ complaisant means polite ❑ *extremely cheerful and* complaisant to their guest (*Gulliver's Travels* by Jonathan Swift)

conning VERB conning means learning by heart ❑ *Or conning more* (*The Prelude* by William Wordsworth)

consequent NOUN consequence ❑ *as avarice is the necessary consequent of old age* (*Gulliver's Travels* by Jonathan Swift)

consorts NOUN concerts ❑ *The King, who delighted in music, had frequent consorts at Court* (*Gulliver's Travels* by Jonathan Swift)

conversible ADJ conversible meant easy to talk to, companionable ❑ *He can be a conversible companion* (*Pride and Prejudice* by Jane Austen)

copper NOUN a copper is a large pot that can be heated directly over a fire ❑ *He gazed in stupefied astonishment on the small rebel for some seconds, and then clung for support to the copper* (*Oliver Twist* by Charles Dickens)

copper-stick NOUN a copper-stick is the long piece of wood used to stir washing in the copper (or boiler) which was usually the biggest cooking pot in the house ❑ *It was Christmas Eve, and I had to stir the pudding for next day, with a copper-stick, from seven to eight by the Dutch clock* (*Great Expectations* by Charles Dickens)

counting-house NOUN a counting house is a place where accountants work ❑ *Once upon a time – of all the good days in the year, on Christmas Eve – old Scrooge sat busy in his countinghouse* (*A Christmas Carol* by Charles Dickens)

courtier NOUN a courtier is someone who attends the king or queen – a member of the court ❑ *next the ten courtiers;* (*Alice's Adventures in Wonderland* by Lewis Carroll)

covies NOUN covies were flocks of partridges ❑ *and will save all of the best covies for you* (*Pride and Prejudice* by Jane Austen)

cowed VERB cowed means frightened or intimidated ❑ *it cowed me more than the pain* (*Treasure Island* by Robert Louis Stevenson)

cozened VERB cozened means tricked or deceived ❑ *Do you remember, sir, how you cozened me* (*Doctor Faustus 4.7* by Christopher Marlowe)

cravats NOUN a cravat is a folded cloth that a man wears wrapped around his neck as a decorative item of clothing ❑ *we'd a' slept in our cravats to-night* (*The Adventures of Huckleberry Finn* by Mark Twain)

crock and dirt PHRASE crock and dirt is an old expression meaning soot and dirt ❑ *and the mare catching cold at the door, and the boy grimed with crock and dirt* (*Great Expectations* by Charles Dickens)

crockery NOUN here crockery means pottery ❑ *By one of the parrots was a cat made of crockery* (*The Adventures of Huckleberry Finn* by Mark Twain)

crooked sixpence PHRASE it was considered unlucky to have a bent sixpence ❑ *You've got the beauty, you see, and I've got the luck, so you must keep me by you for your crooked sixpence* (*Silas Marner* by George Eliot)

croquet NOUN croquet is a traditional English summer game in which players try to hit wooden balls through hoops ❑ *and once she remembered trying to box her own ears for having cheated herself in a game of croquet* (*Alice's Adventures in Wonderland* by Lewis Carroll)

cross PREP across ❑ *The two great streets, which run cross and divide it into four quarters* (*Gulliver's Travels* by Jonathan Swift)

culpable ADJ if you are culpable for something it means you are to blame ❑ *deep are the sorrows that spring from false ideas for which no man is culpable.* (*Silas Marner* by George Eliot)

241

cultured ADJ cultivated ❑ *Nor less when spring had warmed the cultured Vale* (*The Prelude* by William Wordsworth)

cupidity NOUN cupidity is greed ❑ *These people hated me with the hatred of cupidity and disappointment.* (*Great Expectations* by Charles Dickens)

curricle NOUN an open two-wheeled carriage with one seat for the driver and space for a single passenger ❑ *and they saw a lady and a gentleman in a curricle* (*Pride and Prejudice* by Jane Austen)

cynosure NOUN a cynosure is something that strongly attracts attention or admiration ❑ *Then I thought of Eliza and Georgiana; I beheld one the cynosure of a ballroom, the other the inmate of a convent cell* (*Jane Eyre* by Charlotte Brontë)

dalliance NOUN someone's dalliance with something is a brief involvement with it ❑ *nor sporting in the dalliance of love* (*Doctor Faustus Chorus* by Christopher Marlowe)

darkling ADV darkling is an archaic way of saying in the dark ❑ *Darkling I listen* (*Ode on a Nightingale* by John Keats)

delf-case NOUN a sideboard for holding dishes and crockery ❑ *at the pewter dishes and delf-case* (*Wuthering Heights* by Emily Brontë)

determined ■ VERB here determined means ended ❑ *and be out of vogue when that was determined* (*Gulliver's Travels* by Jonathan Swift) ■ VERB determined can mean to have been learned or found especially by investigation or experience ❑ *All the sensitive feelings it wounded so cruelly, all the shame and misery it kept alive within my breast, became more poignant as I thought of this; and I determined that the life was unendurable* (*David Copperfield* by Charles Dickens)

Deuce NOUN a slang term for the Devil ❑ *Ah, I dare say I did. Deuce take me, he added suddenly, I know I did. I find I am not quite unscrewed yet.* (*Great Expectations* by Charles Dickens)

diabolical ADJ diabolical means devilish or evil ❑ *and with a thousand diabolical expressions* (*Treasure Island* by Robert Louis Stevenson)

direction NOUN here direction means address ❑ *Elizabeth was not surprised at it, as Jane had written the direction remarkably ill* (*Pride and Prejudice* by Jane Austen)

discover VERB to make known or announce ❑ *the Emperor would discover the secret while I was out of his power* (*Gulliver's Travels* by Jonathan Swift)

dissemble VERB hide or conceal ❑ *Dissemble nothing* (*On His Mistress* by John Donne)

dissolve VERB dissolve here means to release from life, to die ❑ *Fade far away, dissolve, and quite forget* (*Ode on a Nightingale* by John Keats)

distrain VERB to distrain is to seize the property of someone who is in debt in compensation for the money owed ❑ *for he's threatening to distrain for it* (*Silas Marner* by George Eliot)

Divan NOUN a Divan was originally a Turkish council of state – the name was transferred to the couches they sat on and is used to mean this in English ❑ *Mr Brass applauded this picture very much, and the bed being soft and comfortable, Mr Quilp determined to use it, both as a sleeping place by night and as a kind of Divan by day.* (*The Old Curiosity Shop* by Charles Dickens)

divorcement NOUN separation ❑ *By all pains which want and divorcement hath* (*On His Mistress* by John Donne)

dog in the manger, PHRASE this phrase describes someone who prevents you from enjoying something that they themselves have no need for

❑ *You are a dog in the manger, Cathy, and desire no one to be loved but yourself* (Wuthering Heights by Emily Brontë)

dolorifuge NOUN dolorifuge is a word which Thomas Hardy invented. It means pain-killer or comfort ❑ *as a species of dolorifuge* (Tess of the D'Urbervilles by Thomas Hardy)

dome NOUN building ❑ *that river and that mouldering dome* (The Prelude by William Wordsworth)

domestic PHRASE here domestic means a person's management of the house ❑ *to give some account of my domestic* (Gulliver's Travels by Jonathan Swift)

dunce NOUN a dunce is another word for idiot ❑ *Do you take me for a dunce? Go on?* (Alice's Adventures in Wonderland by Lewis Carroll)

Ecod EXCLAM a slang exclamation meaning 'oh God!' ❑ *"Ecod,"* replied Wemmick, shaking his head, *"that's not my trade."* (Great Expectations by Charles Dickens)

egg-hot NOUN an egg-hot (see also 'flip' and 'negus') was a hot drink made from beer and eggs, sweetened with nutmeg ❑ *She fainted when she saw me return, and made a little jug of egg-hot afterwards to console us while we talked it over.* (David Copperfield by Charles Dickens)

encores NOUN an encore is a short extra performance at the end of a longer one, which the entertainer gives because the audience has enthusiastically asked for it ❑ *we want a little something to answer encores with, anyway* (The Adventures of Huckleberry Finn by Mark Twain)

equipage NOUN an elegant and impressive carriage ❑ *and besides, the equipage did not answer to any of their neighbours* (Pride and Prejudice by Jane Austen)

exordium NOUN an exordium is the opening part of a speech ❑ *"Now, Handel,"* as if it were the grave beginning of a portentous business exordium, he had suddenly given up that tone (Great Expectations by Charles Dickens)

expect VERB here expect means to wait for ❑ *to expect his farther commands* (Gulliver's Travels by Jonathan Swift)

familiars NOUN familiars means spirits or devils who come to someone when they are called ❑ *I'll turn all the lice about thee into familiars* (Doctor Faustus 1.4 by Christopher Marlowe)

fantods NOUN a fantod is a person who fidgets or can't stop moving nervously ❑ *It most give me the fantods* (The Adventures of Huckleberry Finn by Mark Twain)

farthing NOUN a farthing is an old unit of British currency which was worth a quarter of a penny ❑ *Not a farthing less. A great many back-payments are included in it, I assure you.* (A Christmas Carol by Charles Dickens)

farthingale NOUN a hoop worn under a skirt to extend it ❑ *A bell with an old voice – which I dare say in its time had often said to the house, Here is the green farthingale* (Great Expectations by Charles Dickens)

favours NOUN here favours is an old word which means ribbons ❑ *A group of humble mourners entered the gate: wearing white favours* (Oliver Twist by Charles Dickens)

feigned VERB pretend or pretending ❑ *not my feigned page* (On His Mistress by John Donne)

fence ◼ NOUN a fence is someone who receives and sells stolen goods ❑ *What are you up to? Ill-treating the boys, you covetous, avaricious, in-sa-ti-a-ble old fence?* (Oliver Twist by Charles Dickens) ◻ NOUN defence or protection ❑ *but honesty hath no fence against superior cunning* (Gulliver's Travels by Jonathan Swift)

fess ADJ fess is an old word which means pleased or proud ❑ *You'll be* *fess enough, my poppet* (*Tess of the D'Urbervilles* by Thomas Hardy)

fettered ADJ fettered means bound in chains or chained ❑ *"You are fettered," said Scrooge, trembling. "Tell me why?"* (*A Christmas Carol* by Charles Dickens)

fidges VERB fidges means fidgets, which is to keep moving your hands slightly because you are nervous or excited ❑ *Look, Jim, how my fingers fidges* (*Treasure Island* by Robert Louis Stevenson)

finger-post NOUN a finger-post is a sign-post showing the direction to different places ❑ *"The gallows," continued Fagin, "the gallows, my dear, is an ugly finger-post, which points out a very short and sharp turning that has stopped many a bold fellow's career on the broad highway."* (*Oliver Twist* by Charles Dickens)

fire-irons NOUN fire-irons are tools kept by the side of the fire to either cook with or look after the fire ❑ *the fire-irons came first* (*Alice's Adventures in Wonderland* by Lewis Carroll)

fire-plug NOUN a fire-plug is another word for a fire hydrant ❑ *The pony looked with great attention into a fire-plug, which was near him, and appeared to be quite absorbed in contemplating it* (*The Old Curiosity Shop* by Charles Dickens)

flank NOUN flank is the side of an animal ❑ *And all her silken flanks with garlands dressed* (*Ode on a Grecian Urn* by John Keats)

flip NOUN a flip is a drink made from warmed ale, sugar, spice and beaten egg ❑ *The events of the day, in combination with the twins, if not with the flip, had made Mrs. Micawber hysterical, and she shed tears as she replied* (*David Copperfield* by Charles Dickens)

flit VERB flit means to move quickly ❑ *and if he had meant to flit to Thrushcross Grange* (*Wuthering Heights* by Emily Brontë)

floorcloth NOUN a floorcloth was a hard-wearing piece of canvas used instead of carpet ❑ *This avenging phantom was ordered to be on duty at eight on Tuesday morning in the hall (it was two feet square, as charged for floorcloth)* (*Great Expectations* by Charles Dickens)

fly-driver NOUN a fly-driver is a carriage drawn by a single horse ❑ *The fly-drivers, among whom I inquired next, were equally jocose and equally disrespectful* (*David Copperfield* by Charles Dickens)

fob NOUN a small pocket in which a watch is kept ❑ *"Certain," replied the man, drawing a gold watch from his fob* (*Oliver Twist* by Charles Dickens)

folly NOUN folly means foolishness or stupidity ❑ *the folly of beginning a work* (*Robinson Crusoe* by Daniel Defoe)

fond ADJ fond means foolish ❑ *Fond worldling* (*Doctor Faustus 5.2* by Christopher Marlowe)

fondness NOUN silly or foolish affection ❑ *They have no fondness for their colts or foals* (*Gulliver's Travels* by Jonathan Swift)

for his fancy PHRASE for his fancy means for his liking or as he wanted ❑ *and as I did not obey quick enough for his fancy* (*Treasure Island* by Robert Louis Stevenson)

forlorn ADJ lost or very upset ❑ *you are from that day forlorn* (*Gulliver's Travels* by Jonathan Swift)

foster-sister NOUN a foster-sister was someone brought up by the same nurse or in the same household ❑ *I had been his foster-sister* (*Wuthering Heights* by Emily Brontë)

fox-fire NOUN fox-fire is a weak glow that is given off by decaying, rotten wood ❑ *what we must have was a lot of them rotten chunks that's called fox-fire* (*The Adventures of Huckleberry Finn* by Mark Twain)

frozen sea PHRASE the Arctic Ocean ❑ *into the frozen sea* (*Gulliver's Travels* by Jonathan Swift)

gainsay VERB to gainsay something is to say it isn't true or to deny it ❏ *"So she had," cried Scrooge. "You're right. I'll not gainsay it, Spirit. God forbid!"* (*A Christmas Carol* by Charles Dickens)

gaiters NOUN gaiters were leggings made of a cloth or piece of leather which covered the leg from the knee to the ankle ❏ *Mr Knightley was hard at work upon the lower buttons of his thick leather gaiters* (*Emma* by Jane Austen)

galluses NOUN galluses is an old spelling of gallows, and here means suspenders. Suspenders are straps worn over someone's shoulders and fastened to their trousers to prevent the trousers falling down ❏ *and home-knit galluses* (*The Adventures of Huckleberry Finn* by Mark Twain)

galoot NOUN a sailor but also a clumsy person ❏ *and maybe a galoot on it chopping* (*The Adventures of Huckleberry Finn* by Mark Twain)

gayest ADJ gayest means the most lively and bright or merry ❏ *Beth played her gayest march* (*Little Women* by Louisa May Alcott)

gem NOUN here gem means jewellery ❏ *the mountain shook off turf and flower, had only heath for raiment and crag for gem* (*Jane Eyre* by Charlotte Brontë)

giddy ADJ giddy means dizzy ❏ *and I wish you wouldn't keep appearing and vanishing so suddenly; you make one quite giddy.* (*Alice's Adventures in Wonderland* by Lewis Carroll)

gig NOUN a light two-wheeled carriage ❏ *when a gig drove up to the garden gate: out of which there jumped a fat gentleman* (*Oliver Twist* by Charles Dickens)

gladsome ADJ gladsome is an old word meaning glad or happy ❏ *Nobody ever stopped him in the street to say, with gladsome looks* (*A Christmas Carol* by Charles Dickens)

glen NOUN a glen is a small valley; the word is used commonly in Scotland ❏ *a beck which follows the bend of the glen* (*Wuthering Heights* by Emily Brontë)

gravelled VERB gravelled is an old term which means to baffle or defeat someone ❏ *Gravelled the pastors of the German Church* (*Doctor Faustus 1.1* by Christopher Marlowe)

grinder NOUN a grinder was a private tutor ❏ *but that when he had had the happiness of marrying Mrs Pocket very early in his life, he had impaired his prospects and taken up the calling of a Grinder* (*Great Expectations* by Charles Dickens)

gruel NOUN gruel is a thin, watery cornmeal or oatmeal soup ❏ *and the little saucepan of gruel (Scrooge had a cold in his head) upon the hob.* (*A Christmas Carol* by Charles Dickens)

guinea, half a NOUN a half guinea was ten shillings and sixpence ❏ *but lay out half a guinea at Ford's* (*Emma* by Jane Austen)

gull VERB gull is an old term which means to fool or deceive someone ❏ *Hush, I'll gull him supernaturally* (*Doctor Faustus 3.4* by Christopher Marlowe)

gunnel NOUN the gunnel, or gunwhale, is the upper edge of a boat's side ❏ *But he put his foot on the gunnel and rocked her* (*The Adventures of Huckleberry Finn* by Mark Twain)

gunwale NOUN the side of a ship ❏ *He dipped his hand in the water over the boat's gunwale* (*Great Expectations* by Charles Dickens)

Gytrash NOUN a Gytrash is an omen of misfortune to the superstitious, usually taking the form of a hound ❏ *I remembered certain of Bessie's tales, wherein figured a North-of-England spirit, called a 'Gytrash'* (*Jane Eyre* by Charlotte Brontë)

hackney-cabriolet NOUN a two-wheeled carriage with four seats for hire and pulled by a horse ❑ *A hackney-cabriolet was in waiting; with the same vehemence which she had exhibited in addressing Oliver, the girl pulled him in with her, and drew the curtains close.* (*Oliver Twist* by Charles Dickens)

hackney-coach NOUN a four-wheeled horse-drawn vehicle for hire ❑ *The twilight was beginning to close in, when Mr. Brownlow alighted from a hackney-coach at his own door, and knocked softly.* (*Oliver Twist* by Charles Dickens)

haggler NOUN a haggler is someone who travels from place to place selling small goods and items ❑ *when I be plain Jack Durbeyfield, the haggler* (*Tess of the D'Urbervilles* by Thomas Hardy)

halter NOUN a halter is a rope or strap used to lead an animal or to tie it up ❑ *I had of course long been used to a halter and a headstall* (*Black Beauty* by Anna Sewell)

hamlet NOUN a hamlet is a small village or a group of houses in the countryside ❑ *down from the hamlet* (*Treasure Island* by Robert Louis Stevenson)

hand-barrow NOUN a hand-barrow is a device for carrying heavy objects. It is like a wheelbarrow except that it has handles, rather than wheels, for moving the barrow ❑ *his sea chest following behind him in a hand-barrow* (*Treasure Island* by Robert Louis Stevenson)

handspike NOUN a handspike was a stick which was used as a lever ❑ *a bit of stick like a handspike* (*Treasure Island* by Robert Louis Stevenson)

haply ADV haply means by chance or perhaps ❑ *And haply the Queen-Moon is on her throne* (*Ode on a Nightingale* by John Keats)

harem NOUN the harem was the part of the house where the women lived ❑ *mostly they hang round the harem* (*The Adventures of Huckleberry Finn* by Mark Twain)

hautboys NOUN hautboys are oboes ❑ *sausages and puddings resembling flutes and hautboys* (*Gulliver's Travels* by Jonathan Swift)

hawker NOUN a hawker is someone who sells goods to people as he travels rather than from a fixed place like a shop ❑ *to buy some stockings from a hawker* (*Treasure Island* by Robert Louis Stevenson)

hawser NOUN a hawser is a rope used to tie up or tow a ship or boat ❑ *Again among the tiers of shipping, in and out, avoiding rusty chain-cables, frayed hempen hawsers* (*Great Expectations* by Charles Dickens)

headstall NOUN the headstall is the part of the bridle or halter that goes around a horse's head ❑ *I had of course long been used to a halter and a headstall* (*Black Beauty* by Anna Sewell)

hearken VERB hearken means to listen ❑ *though we sometimes stopped to lay hold of each other and hearken* (*Treasure Island* by Robert Louis Stevenson)

heartless ADJ here heartless means without heart or dejected ❑ *I am not heartless* (*The Prelude* by William Wordsworth)

hebdomadal ADJ hebdomadal means weekly ❑ *It was the hebdomadal treat to which we all looked forward from Sabbath to Sabbath* (*Jane Eyre* by Charlotte Brontë)

highwaymen NOUN highwaymen were people who stopped travellers and robbed them ❑ *We are highwaymen* (*The Adventures of Huckleberry Finn* by Mark Twain)

hinds NOUN hinds means farm hands, or people who work on a farm ❑ *He called his hinds about him* (*Gulliver's Travels* by Jonathan Swift)

histrionic ADJ if you refer to someone's behaviour as histrionic, you are being critical of it because it is dramatic and exaggerated

❏ *But the histrionic muse is the darling* (*The Adventures of Huckleberry Finn* by Mark Twain)

hogs NOUN hogs is another word for pigs ❏ *Tom called the hogs 'ingots'* (*The Adventures of Huckleberry Finn* by Mark Twain)

horrors NOUN the horrors are a fit, called delirium tremens, which is caused by drinking too much alcohol ❏ *I'll have the horrors* (*Treasure Island* by Robert Louis Stevenson)

huffy ADJ huffy means to be obviously annoyed or offended about something ❏ *They will feel that more than angry speeches or huffy actions* (*Little Women* by Louisa May Alcott)

hulks NOUN hulks were prison-ships ❏ *The miserable companion of thieves and ruffians, the fallen outcast of low haunts, the associate of the scourings of the jails and hulks* (*Oliver Twist* by Charles Dickens)

humbug NOUN humbug means nonsense or rubbish ❏ *"Bah," said Scrooge. "Humbug!"* (*A Christmas Carol* by Charles Dickens)

humours NOUN it was believed that there were four fluids in the body called humours which decided the temperament of a person depending on how much of each fluid was present ❏ *other peccant humours* (*Gulliver's Travels* by Jonathan Swift)

husbandry NOUN husbandry is farming animals ❏ *bad husbandry were plentifully anointing their wheels* (*Silas Marner* by George Eliot)

huswife NOUN a huswife was a small sewing kit ❏ *but I had put my huswife on it* (*Emma* by Jane Austen)

ideal ADJ ideal in this context means imaginary ❏ *I discovered the yell was not ideal* (*Wuthering Heights* by Emily Brontë)

If our two PHRASE if both our ❏ *If*

our two loves be one (*The Good-Morrow* by John Donne)

ignis-fatuus NOUN ignis-fatuus is the light given out by burning marsh gases, which lead careless travellers into danger ❏ *it is madness in all women to let a secret love kindle within them, which, if unreturned and unknown, must devour the life that feeds it; and, if discovered and responded to, must lead ignis-fatuus-like, into miry wilds whence there is no extrication.* (*Jane Eyre* by Charlotte Brontë)

imaginations NOUN here imaginations means schemes or plans ❏ *soon drove out those imaginations* (*Gulliver's Travels* by Jonathan Swift)

impressible ADJ impressible means open or impressionable ❏ *for Marner had one of those impressible, self-doubting natures* (*Silas Marner* by George Eliot)

in good intelligence PHRASE friendly with each other ❏ *that these two persons were in good intelligence with each other* (*Gulliver's Travels* by Jonathan Swift)

inanity NOUN inanity is silliness or dull stupidity ❏ *Do we not wile away moments of inanity* (*Silas Marner* by George Eliot)

incivility NOUN incivility means rudeness or impoliteness ❏ *if it's only for a piece of incivility like to-night's* (*Treasure Island* by Robert Louis Stevenson)

indigenae NOUN indigenae means natives or people from that area ❏ *an exotic that the surly indigenae will not recognise for kin* (*Wuthering Heights* by Emily Brontë)

indocible ADJ unteachable ❏ *so they were the most restive and indocible* (*Gulliver's Travels* by Jonathan Swift)

ingenuity NOUN inventiveness ❏ *entreated me to give him something as an encouragement to ingenuity* (*Gulliver's Travels* by Jonathan Swift)

ingots NOUN an ingot is a lump of a valuable metal like gold, usually shaped like a brick ❑ *Tom called the hogs 'ingots'* (*The Adventures of Huckleberry Finn* by Mark Twain)

inkstand NOUN an inkstand is a pot which was put on a desk to contain either ink or pencils and pens ❑ *throwing an inkstand at the Lizard as spoke* (*Alice's Adventures in Wonderland* by Lewis Carroll)

inordinate ADJ without order. Today inordinate means 'excessive'. ❑ *Though yet untutored and inordinate* (*The Prelude* by William Wordsworth)

intellectuals NOUN here intellectuals means the minds (of the workmen) ❑ *those instructions they give being too refined for the intellectuals of their workmen* (*Gulliver's Travels* by Jonathan Swift)

interview NOUN meeting ❑ *By our first strange and fatal interview* (*On His Mistress* by John Donne)

jacks NOUN jacks are rods for turning a spit over a fire ❑ *It was a small bit of pork suspended from the kettle hanger by a string passed through a large door key, in a way known to primitive housekeepers unpossessed of jacks* (*Silas Marner* by George Eliot)

jews-harp NOUN a jews-harp is a small, metal, musical instrument that is played by the mouth ❑ *A jews-harp's plenty good enough for a rat* (*The Adventures of Huckleberry Finn* by Mark Twain)

jorum NOUN a large bowl ❑ *while Miss Skiffins brewed such a jorum of tea, that the pig in the back premises became strongly excited* (*Great Expectations* by Charles Dickens)

jostled VERB jostled means bumped or pushed by someone or some people ❑ *being jostled himself into the kennel* (*Gulliver's Travels* by Jonathan Swift)

keepsake NOUN a keepsake is a gift which reminds someone of an

event or of the person who gave it to them. ❑ *books and ornaments they had in their boudoirs at home: keepsakes that different relations had presented to them* (*Jane Eyre* by Charlotte Brontë)

kenned VERB kenned means knew ❑ *though little kenned the lamplighter that he had any company but Christmas!* (*A Christmas Carol* by Charles Dickens)

kennel NOUN kennel means gutter, which is the edge of a road next to the pavement, where rain water collects and flows away ❑ *being jostled himself into the kennel* (*Gulliver's Travels* by Jonathan Swift)

knock-knee ADJ knock-knee means slanted, at an angle. ❑ *LOT 1 was marked in whitewashed knock-knee letters on the brewhouse* (*Great Expectations* by Charles Dickens)

ladylike ADJ to be ladylike is to behave in a polite, dignified and graceful way ❑ *No, winking isn't ladylike* (*Little Women* by Louisa May Alcott)

lapse NOUN flow ❑ *Stealing with silent lapse to join the brook* (*The Prelude* by William Wordsworth)

larry NOUN larry is an old word which means commotion or noisy celebration ❑ *That was all a part of the larry!* (*Tess of the D'Urbervilles* by Thomas Hardy)

laths NOUN laths are strips of wood ❑ *The panels shrunk, the windows cracked; fragments of plaster fell out of the ceiling, and the naked laths were shown instead* (*A Christmas Carol* by Charles Dickens)

leer NOUN a leer is an unpleasant smile ❑ *with a kind of leer* (*Treasure Island* by Robert Louis Stevenson)

lenitives NOUN these are different kinds of drugs or medicines: lenitives and palliatives were pain relievers; aperitives were laxatives; abstersives caused vomiting; corrosives destroyed human tissue; restringents caused constipation; cephalalgics stopped headaches;

icterics were used as medicine for jaundice; apophlegmatics were cough medicine, and acoustics were cures for the loss of hearing ❑ *lenitives, aperitives, abstersives, corrosives, restringents, palliatives, laxatives, cephalalgics, icterics, apophlegmatics, acoustics* (*Gulliver's Travels* by Jonathan Swift)

lest CONJ in case. If you do something lest something (usually) unpleasant happens you do it to try to prevent it happening ❑ *She went in without knocking, and hurried upstairs, in great fear lest she should meet the real Mary Ann* (*Alice's Adventures in Wonderland* by Lewis Carroll)

levee NOUN a levee is an old term for a meeting held in the morning, shortly after the person holding the meeting has got out of bed ❑ *I used to attend the King's levee once or twice a week* (*Gulliver's Travels* by Jonathan Swift)

life-preserver NOUN a club which had lead inside it to make it heavier and therefore more dangerous ❑ *and with no more suspicious articles displayed to view than two or three heavy bludgeons which stood in a corner, and a 'life-preserver' that hung over the chimney-piece.* (*Oliver Twist* by Charles Dickens)

lighterman NOUN a lighterman is another word for sailor ❑ *in and out, hammers going in ship-builders' yards, saws going at timber, clashing engines going at things unknown, pumps going in leaky ships, capstans going, ships going out to sea, and unintelligible sea creatures roaring curses over the bulwarks at respondent lightermen* (*Great Expectations* by Charles Dickens)

livery NOUN servants often wore a uniform known as a livery ❑ *suddenly a footman in livery came running out of the wood* (*Alice's Adventures in Wonderland* by Lewis Carroll)

livid ADJ livid means pale or ash coloured. Livid also means very angry ❑ *a dirty, livid white*

(*Treasure Island* by Robert Louis Stevenson)

lottery-tickets NOUN a popular card game ❑ *and Mrs. Philips protested that they would have a nice comfortable noisy game of lottery tickets* (*Pride and Prejudice* by Jane Austen)

lower and upper world PHRASE the earth and the heavens are the lower and upper worlds ❑ *the changes in the lower and upper world* (*Gulliver's Travels* by Jonathan Swift)

lustres NOUN lustres are chandeliers. A chandelier is a large, decorative frame which holds light bulbs or candles and hangs from the ceiling ❑ *the lustres, lights, the carving and the guilding* (*The Prelude* by William Wordsworth)

lynched VERB killed without a criminal trial by a crowd of people ❑ *He'll never know how nigh he come to getting lynched* (*The Adventures of Huckleberry Finn* by Mark Twain)

malingering VERB if someone is malingering they are pretending to be ill to avoid working ❑ *And you stand there malingering* (*Treasure Island* by Robert Louis Stevenson)

managing PHRASE treating with consideration ❑ *to think the honour of my own kind not worth managing* (*Gulliver's Travels* by Jonathan Swift)

manhood PHRASE manhood means human nature ❑ *concerning the nature of manhood* (*Gulliver's Travels* by Jonathan Swift)

man-trap NOUN a man-trap is a set of steel jaws that snap shut when trodden on and trap a person's leg ❑ *"Don't go to him," I called out of the window, "he's an assassin! A man-trap!"* (*Oliver Twist* by Charles Dickens)

maps NOUN charts of the night sky ❑ *Let maps to others, worlds on worlds have shown* (*The Good-Morrow* by John Donne)

mark VERB look at or notice ❑ Mark but this flea, and mark in this (*The Flea* by John Donne)

maroons NOUN A maroon is someone who has been left in a place which it is difficult for them to escape from, like a small island ❑ *if schooners, islands, and maroons* (*Treasure Island* by Robert Louis Stevenson)

mast NOUN here mast means the fruit of forest trees ❑ *a quantity of acorns, dates, chestnuts, and other mast* (*Gulliver's Travels* by Jonathan Swift)

mate VERB defeat ❑ *Where Mars did mate the warlike Carthigens* (*Doctor Faustus Chorus* by Christopher Marlowe)

mealy ADJ Mealy when used to describe a face meant palid, pale or colourless ❑ *I only know two sorts of boys. Mealy boys, and beef-faced boys* (*Oliver Twist* by Charles Dickens)

middling ADJ fairly or moderately ❑ *she worked me middling hard for about an hour* (*The Adventures of Huckleberry Finn* by Mark Twain)

mill NOUN a mill, or treadmill, was a device for hard labour or punishment in prison ❑ *Was you never on the mill?* (*Oliver Twist* by Charles Dickens)

milliner's shop NOUN a milliner's sold fabrics, clothing, lace and accessories; as time went on they specialized more and more in hats ❑ *to pay their duty to their aunt and to a milliner's shop just over the way* (*Pride and Prejudice* by Jane Austen)

minching un' munching PHRASE how people in the north of England used to describe the way people from the south speak ❑ *Minching un' munching!* (*Wuthering Heights* by Emily Brontë)

mine NOUN gold ❑ *Whether both th'Indias of spice and mine* (*The Sun Rising* by John Donne)

mire NOUN mud ❑ *Tis my fate to be always ground into the mire under the iron heel of oppression* (*The Adventures of Huckleberry Finn* by Mark Twain)

miscellany NOUN a miscellany is a collection of many different kinds of things ❑ *under that, the miscellany began* (*Treasure Island* by Robert Louis Stevenson)

mistarshers NOUN mistarshers means moustache, which is the hair that grows on a man's upper lip ❑ *when he put his hand up to his mistarshers* (*Tess of the D'Urbervilles* by Thomas Hardy)

morrow NOUN here good-morrow means tomorrow and a new and better life ❑ *And now good-morrow to our waking souls* (*The Good-Morrow* by John Donne)

mortification NOUN mortification is an old word for gangrene which is when part of the body decays or 'dies' because of disease ❑ *Yes, it was a mortification – that was it* (*The Adventures of Huckleberry Finn* by Mark Twain)

mought PARTICIPLE mought is an old spelling of might ❑ *what you mought call me? You mought call me captain* (*Treasure Island* by Robert Louis Stevenson)

move VERB move me not means do not make me angry ❑ *Move me not, Faustus* (*Doctor Faustus 2.1* by Christopher Marlowe)

muffin-cap NOUN a muffin cap is a flat cap made from wool ❑ *the old one, remained stationary in the muffin-cap and leathers* (*Oliver Twist* by Charles Dickens)

mulatter NOUN a mulatter was another word for mulatto, which is a person with parents who are from different races ❑ *a mulatter, most as white as a white man* (*The Adventures of Huckleberry Finn* by Mark Twain)

mummery NOUN mummery is an old word that meant meaningless (or pretentious) ceremony ❑ *When they were all gone, and when Trabb and his men – but not his boy: I* looked for him – had crammed their mummery into bags, and were gone too, the house felt wholesomer. (*Great Expectations* by Charles Dickens)

nap NOUN the nap is the woolly surface on a new item of clothing. Here the surface has been worn away so it looks bare ❏ *like an old hat with the nap rubbed off* (*The Adventures of Huckleberry Finn* by Mark Twain)

natural ① NOUN a natural is a person born with learning difficulties ❏ *though he had been left to his particular care by their deceased father, who thought him almost a natural.* (*David Copperfield* by Charles Dickens) ② ADJ natural meant illegitimate ❏ *Harriet Smith was the natural daughter of somebody* (*Emma* by Jane Austen)

navigator NOUN a navigator was originally someone employed to dig canals. It is the origin of the word 'navvy' meaning a labourer ❏ *She ascertained from me in a few words what it was all about, comforted Dora, and gradually convinced her that I was not a labourer – from my manner of stating the case I believe Dora concluded that I was a navigator, and went balancing myself up and down a plank all day with a wheelbarrow – and so brought us together in peace.* (*David Copperfield* by Charles Dickens)

necromancy NOUN necromancy means a kind of magic where the magician speaks to spirits or ghosts to find out what will happen in the future ❏ *He surfeits upon cursed necromancy* (*Doctor Faustus chorus* by Christopher Marlowe)

negus NOUN a negus is a hot drink made from sweetened wine and water ❏ *He sat placidly perusing the newspaper, with his little head on one side, and a glass of warm sherry negus at his elbow.* (*David Copperfield* by Charles Dickens)

nice ADJ discriminating. Able to make good judgements or choices ❏

consequently a claim to be nice (*Emma* by Jane Austen)

nigh ADV nigh means near ❏ *He'll never know how nigh he come to getting lynched* (*The Adventures of Huckleberry Finn* by Mark Twain)

nimbleness NOUN nimbleness means being able to move very quickly or skillfully ❏ *and with incredible accuracy and nimbleness* (*Treasure Island* by Robert Louis Stevenson)

noggin NOUN a noggin is a small mug or a wooden cup ❏ *you'll bring me one noggin of rum* (*Treasure Island* by Robert Louis Stevenson)

none ADJ neither ❏ *none can die* (*The Good-Morrow* by John Donne)

notices NOUN observations ❏ *Arch are his notices* (*The Prelude* by William Wordsworth)

occiput NOUN occiput means the back of the head ❏ *saw off the occiput of each couple* (*Gulliver's Travels* by Jonathan Swift)

officiously ADJ kindly ❏ *the governess who attended Glumdalclitch very officiously lifted me up* (*Gulliver's Travels* by Jonathan Swift)

old salt PHRASE old salt is a slang term for an experienced sailor ❏ *a 'true sea-dog', and a 'real old salt'* (*Treasure Island* by Robert Louis Stevenson)

or ere PHRASE before ❏ *or ere the Hall was built* (*The Prelude* by William Wordsworth)

ostler NOUN one who looks after horses at an inn ❏ *The bill paid, and the waiter remembered, and the ostler not forgotten, and the chambermaid taken into consideration* (*Great Expectations* by Charles Dickens)

ostry NOUN an ostry is an old word for a pub or hotel ❏ *lest I send you into the ostry with a vengeance* (*Doctor Faustus 2.2* by Christopher Marlowe)

outrunning the constable PHRASE outrunning the constable meant spending more than you earn ❏ *but I shall by this means be able to* *check your bills and to pull you up if I find you outrunning the constable.* (*Great Expectations* by Charles Dickens)

over ADJ across ❏ *It is in length six yards, and in the thickest part at least three yards over* (*Gulliver's Travels* by Jonathan Swift)

over the broomstick PHRASE this is a phrase meaning 'getting married without a formal ceremony' ❏ *They both led tramping lives, and this woman in Gerrard-street here, had been married very young, over the broomstick (as we say), to a tramping man, and was a perfect fury in point of jealousy.* (*Great Expectations* by Charles Dickens)

own VERB own means to admit or to acknowledge ❏ *It's my old girl that advises. She has the head. But I never own to it before her. Discipline must be maintained* (*Bleak House* by Charles Dickens)

page NOUN here page means a boy employed to run errands ❏ *not my feigned page* (*On His Mistress* by John Donne)

paid pretty dear PHRASE paid pretty dear means paid a high price or suffered quite a lot ❏ *I paid pretty dear for my monthly fourpenny piece* (*Treasure Island* by Robert Louis Stevenson)

pannikins NOUN pannikins were small tin cups ❏ *of lifting light glasses and cups to his lips, as if they were clumsy pannikins* (*Great Expectations* by Charles Dickens)

pards NOUN pards are leopards ❏ *Not charioted by Bacchus and his pards* (*Ode on a Nightingale* by John Keats)

parlour boarder NOUN a pupil who lived with the family ❏ *and somebody had lately raised her from the condition of scholar to parlour boarder* (*Emma* by Jane Austen)

particular, a London PHRASE London in Victorian times and up to the 1950s was famous for having very dense fog – which was a combination of real fog and the

smog of pollution from factories ❏ *This is a London particular . . . A fog, miss'* (*Bleak House* by Charles Dickens)

patten NOUN pattens were wooden soles which were fixed to shoes by straps to protect the shoes in wet weather ❏ *carrying a basket like the Great Seal of England in plaited straw, a pair of pattens, a spare shawl, and an umbrella, though it was a fine bright day* (*Great Expectations* by Charles Dickens)

paviour NOUN a paviour was a labourer who worked on the street pavement ❏ *the paviour his pickaxe* (*Oliver Twist* by Charles Dickens)

peccant ADJ peccant means unhealthy ❏ *other peccant humours* (*Gulliver's Travels* by Jonathan Swift)

penetralium NOUN penetralium is a word used to describe the inner rooms of the house ❏ *and I had no desire to aggravate his impatience previous to inspecting the penetralium* (*Wuthering Heights* by Emily Brontë)

pensive ADV pensive means deep in thought or thinking seriously about something ❏ *and she was leaning pensive on a tomb-stone on her right elbow* (*The Adventures of Huckleberry Finn* by Mark Twain)

penury NOUN penury is the state of being extremely poor ❏ *Distress, if not penury, loomed in the distance* (*Tess of the D'Urbervilles* by Thomas Hardy)

perspective NOUN telescope ❏ *a pocket perspective* (*Gulliver's Travels* by Jonathan Swift)

phaeton NOUN a phaeton was an open carriage for four people ❏ *often condescends to drive by my humble abode in her little phaeton and ponies* (*Pride and Prejudice* by Jane Austen)

phantasm NOUN a phantasm is an illusion, something that is not real. It is sometimes used to mean ghost ❏ *Experience had bred no fancies in* him that could raise the phantasm of appetite (*Silas Marner* by George Eliot)

physic NOUN here physic means medicine ❑ *there I studied physic two years and seven months* (*Gulliver's Travels* by Jonathan Swift)

pinioned VERB to pinion is to hold both arms so that a person cannot move them ❑ *But the relentless Ghost pinioned him in both his arms, and forced him to observe what happened next.* (*A Christmas Carol* by Charles Dickens)

piquet NOUN piquet was a popular card game in the C18th ❑ *Mr Hurst and Mr Bingley were at piquet* (*Pride and Prejudice* by Jane Austen)

plaister NOUN a plaister is a piece of cloth on which an apothecary (or pharmacist) would spread ointment. The cloth is then applied to wounds or bruises to treat them ❑ *Then, she gave the knife a final smart wipe on the edge of the plaister, and then sawed a very thick round off the loaf: which she finally, before separating from the loaf, hewed into two halves, of which Joe got one, and I the other.* (*Great Expectations* by Charles Dickens)

plantations NOUN here plantations means colonies, which are countries controlled by a more powerful country ❑ *besides our plantations in America* (*Gulliver's Travels* by Jonathan Swift)

plastic ADV here plastic is an old term meaning shaping or a power that was forming ❑ *A plastic power abode with me* (*The Prelude* by William Wordsworth)

players NOUN actors ❑ *of players which upon the world's stage be* (*On His Mistress* by John Donne)

plump ADV all at once, suddenly ❑ *But it took a bit of time to get it well round, the change come so uncommon plump, didn't it?* (*Great Expectations* by Charles Dickens)

plundered VERB to plunder is to rob or steal from ❑ *These crosses stand for the names of ships or towns that they sank or plundered* (*Treasure Island* by Robert Louis Stevenson)

pommel ❶ VERB to pommel someone is to hit them repeatedly with your fists ❑ *hug him round the neck, pommel his back, and kick his legs in irrepressible affection!* (*A Christmas Carol* by Charles Dickens) ❷ NOUN a pommel is the part of a saddle that rises up at the front ❑ *He had his gun across his pommel* (*The Adventures of Huckleberry Finn* by Mark Twain)

poor's rates NOUN poor's rates were property taxes which were used to support the poor ❑ *"Oh!" replied the undertaker; "why, you know, Mr. Bumble, I pay a good deal towards the poor's rates."* (*Oliver Twist* by Charles Dickens)

popular ADJ popular means ruled by the people, or Republican, rather than ruled by a monarch ❑ *With those of Greece compared and popular Rome* (*The Prelude* by William Wordsworth)

porringer NOUN a porringer is a small bowl ❑ *Of this festive composition each boy had one porringer, and no more* (*Oliver Twist* by Charles Dickens)

postboy NOUN a postboy was the driver of a horse-drawn carriage ❑ *He spoke to a postboy who was dozing under the gateway* (*Oliver Twist* by Charles Dickens)

post-chaise NOUN a fast carriage for two or four passengers ❑ *Looking round, he saw that it was a post-chaise, driven at great speed* (*Oliver Twist* by Charles Dickens)

postern NOUN a small gate usually at the back of a building ❑ *The little servant happening to be entering the fortress with two hot rolls, I passed through the postern and crossed the drawbridge, in her company* (*Great Expectations* by Charles Dickens)

pottle NOUN a pottle was a small basket ❑ *He had a paper-bag under each arm and a pottle of* strawberries in one hand . . . (*Great Expectations* by Charles Dickens)

pounce NOUN pounce is a fine powder used to prevent ink spreading on untreated paper ❏ *in that grim atmosphere of pounce and parchment, red-tape, dusty wafers, ink-jars, brief and draft paper, law reports, writs, declarations, and bills of costs* (*David Copperfield* by Charles Dickens)

pox NOUN pox means sexually transmitted diseases like syphilis ❏ *how the pox in all its consequences and denominations* (*Gulliver's Travels* by Jonathan Swift)

prelibation NOUN prelibation means a foretaste of or an example of something to come ❏ *A prelibation to the mower's scythe* (*The Prelude* by William Wordsworth)

prentice NOUN an apprentice ❏ *and Joe, sitting on an old gun, had told me that when I was 'prentice to him regularly bound, we would have such Larks there!* (*Great Expectations* by Charles Dickens)

presently ADV immediately ❏ *I presently knew what they meant* (*Gulliver's Travels* by Jonathan Swift)

pumpion NOUN pumpkin ❏ *for it was almost as large as a small pumpion* (*Gulliver's Travels* by Jonathan Swift)

punctual ADJ kept in one place ❏ *was not a punctual presence, but a spirit* (*The Prelude* by William Wordsworth)

quadrille ■ NOUN a quadrille is a dance invented in France which is usually performed by four couples ❏ *However, Mr Swiveller had Miss Sophy's hand for the first quadrille (country-dances being low, were utterly proscribed)* (*The Old Curiosity Shop* by Charles Dickens) ■ NOUN quadrille was a card game for four people ❏ *to make up her pool of quadrille in the evening* (*Pride and Prejudice* by Jane Austen)

quality NOUN gentry or upper-class people ❏ *if you are with the quality*

(*The Adventures of Huckleberry Finn* by Mark Twain)

quick parts PHRASE quick-witted ❏ *Mr Bennet was so odd a mixture of quick parts* (*Pride and Prejudice* by Jane Austen)

quid NOUN a quid is something chewed or kept in the mouth, like a piece of tobacco ❏ *rolling his quid* (*Treasure Island* by Robert Louis Stevenson)

quit VERB quit means to avenge or to make even ❏ *But Faustus's death shall quit my infamy* (*Doctor Faustus 4.3* by Christopher Marlowe)

rags NOUN divisions ❏ *Nor hours, days, months, which are the rags of time* (*The Sun Rising* by John Donne)

raiment NOUN raiment means clothing ❏ *the mountain shook off turf and flower, had only heath for raiment and crag for gem* (*Jane Eyre* by Charlotte Brontë)

rain cats and dogs PHRASE an expression meaning rain heavily. The origin of the expression is unclear ❏ *But it'll perhaps rain cats and dogs to-morrow* (*Silas Marner* by George Eliot)

raised Cain PHRASE raised Cain means caused a lot of trouble. Cain is a character in the Bible who killed his brother Abel ❏ *and every time he got drunk he raised Cain around town* (*The Adventures of Huckleberry Finn* by Mark Twain)

rambling ADJ rambling means confused and not very clear ❏ *my head began to be filled very early with rambling thoughts* (*Robinson Crusoe* by Daniel Defoe)

raree-show NOUN a raree-show is an old term for a peep-show or a fairground entertainment ❏ *A raree-show is here, with children gathered round* (*The Prelude* by William Wordsworth)

recusants NOUN people who resisted authority ❏ *hardy recusants* (*The Prelude* by William Wordsworth)

redounding VERB eddying. An eddy is a movement in water or air which goes round and round instead of flowing in one direction ❑ *mists and steam-like fogs redounding everywhere* (*The Prelude* by William Wordsworth)

redundant ADJ here redundant means overflowing but Wordsworth also uses it to mean excessively large or too big ❑ *A tempest, a redundant energy* (*The Prelude* by William Wordsworth)

reflex NOUN reflex is a shortened version of reflexion, which is an alternative spelling of reflection ❑ *To cut across the reflex of a star* (*The Prelude* by William Wordsworth)

Reformatory NOUN a prison for young offenders/criminals ❑ *Even when I was taken to have a new suit of clothes, the tailor had orders to make them like a kind of Reformatory, and on no account to let me have the free use of my limbs.* (*Great Expectations* by Charles Dickens)

remorse NOUN pity or compassion ❑ *by that remorse* (*On His Mistress* by John Donne)

render VERB in this context render means give. ❑ *and Sarah could render no reason that would be sanctioned by the feeling of the community.* (*Silas Marner* by George Eliot)

repeater NOUN a repeater was a watch that chimed the last hour when a button was pressed – as a result it was useful in the dark ❑ *And his watch is a gold repeater, and worth a hundred pound if it's worth a penny.* (*Great Expectations* by Charles Dickens)

repugnance NOUN repugnance means a strong dislike of something or someone ❑ *overcoming a strong repugnance* (*Treasure Island* by Robert Louis Stevenson)

reverence NOUN reverence means bow. When you bow to someone, you briefly bend your body towards them as a formal way of showing them respect ❑ *made my reverence* (*Gulliver's Travels* by Jonathan Swift)

reverie NOUN a reverie is a day dream ❑ *I can guess the subject of your reverie* (*Pride and Prejudice* by Jane Austen)

revival NOUN a religious meeting held in public ❑ *well I'd ben a-running' a little temperance revival thar' bout a week* (*The Adventures of Huckleberry Finn* by Mark Twain)

revolt VERB revolt means turn back or stop your present course of action and go back to what you were doing before ❑ *Revolt, or I'll in piecemeal tear thy flesh* (*Doctor Faustus 5.1* by Christopher Marlowe)

rheumatics/rheumatism NOUN rheumatics [rheumatism] is an illness that makes your joints or muscles stiff and painful ❑ *a new cure for the rheumatics* (*Treasure Island* by Robert Louis Stevenson)

riddance NOUN riddance is usually used in the form good riddance which you say when you are pleased that something has gone or been left behind ❑ *I'd better go into the house, and die and be a riddance* (*David Copperfield* by Charles Dickens)

rimy ADJ rimy is an ADJECTIVE which means covered in ice or frost ❑ *It was a rimy morning, and very damp* (*Great Expectations* by Charles Dickens)

riper ADJ riper means more mature or older ❑ *At riper years to Wittenberg he went* (*Doctor Faustus chorus* by Christopher Marlowe)

rubber NOUN a set of games in whist or backgammon ❑ *her father was sure of his rubber* (*Emma* by Jane Austen)

ruffian NOUN a ruffian is a person who behaves violently ❑ *and when the ruffian had told him* (*Treasure Island* by Robert Louis Stevenson)

sadness NOUN sadness is an old term meaning seriousness ❑ *But I* *prithee tell me, in good sadness* (*Doctor Faustus* 2.2 by Christopher Marlowe)

sailed before the mast PHRASE this phrase meant someone who did not look like a sailor ❑ *he had none of the appearance of a man that sailed before the mast* (*Treasure Island* by Robert Louis Stevenson)

scabbard NOUN a scabbard is the covering for a sword or dagger ❑ *Girded round its middle was an antique scabbard; but no sword was in it, and the ancient sheath was eaten up with rust* (*A Christmas Carol* by Charles Dickens)

schooners NOUN A schooner is a fast, medium-sized sailing ship ❑ *if schooners, islands, and maroons* (*Treasure Island* by Robert Louis Stevenson)

science NOUN learning or knowledge ❑ *Even Science, too, at hand* (*The Prelude* by William Wordsworth)

scrouge VERB to scrouge means to squeeze or to crowd ❑ *to scrouge in and get a sight* (*The Adventures of Huckleberry Finn* by Mark Twain)

scrutore NOUN a scrutore, or escritoire, was a writing table ❑ *set me gently on my feet upon the scrutore* (*Gulliver's Travels* by Jonathan Swift)

scutcheon/escutcheon NOUN an escutcheon is a shield with a coat of arms, or the symbols of a family name, engraved on it ❑ *On the scutcheon we'll have a bend* (*The Adventures of Huckleberry Finn* by Mark Twain)

sea-dog PHRASE sea-dog is a slang term for an experienced sailor or pirate ❑ *a 'true sea-dog', and a 'real old salt,'* (*Treasure Island* by Robert Louis Stevenson)

see the lions PHRASE to see the lions was to go and see the sights of London. Originally the phrase referred to the menagerie in the Tower of London and later in Regent's Park ❑ *We will go and see the lions for an hour or two*

– it's something to have a fresh fellow like you to show them to, Copperfield (*David Copperfield* by Charles Dickens)

self-conceit NOUN self-conceit is an old term which means having too high an opinion of oneself, or deceiving yourself ❑ *Till swollen with cunning, of a self-conceit* (*Doctor Faustus chorus* by Christopher Marlowe)

seneschal NOUN a steward ❑ *where a grey-headed seneschal sings a funny chorus with a funnier body of vassals* (*Oliver Twist* by Charles Dickens)

sensible ADJ if you were sensible of something you are aware or conscious of something ❑ *If my children are silly I must hope to be always sensible of it* (*Pride and Prejudice* by Jane Austen)

sessions NOUN court cases were heard at specific times of the year called sessions ❑ *He lay in prison very ill, during the whole interval between his committal for trial, and the coming round of the Sessions.* (*Great Expectations* by Charles Dickens)

shabby ADJ shabby places look old and in bad condition ❑ *a little bit of a shabby village named Pikesville* (*The Adventures of Huckleberry Finn* by Mark Twain)

shay-cart NOUN a shay-cart was a small cart drawn by one horse ❑ *"I were at the Bargemen t'other night, Pip;" whenever he subsided into affection, he called me Pip, and whenever he relapsed into politeness he called me Sir; "when there come up in his shay-cart Pumblechook:"* (*Great Expectations* by Charles Dickens)

shilling NOUN a shilling is an old unit of currency. There were twenty shillings in every British pound ❑ *"Ten shillings too much," said the gentleman in the white waistcoat.* (*Oliver Twist* by Charles Dickens)

shines NOUN tricks or games ❑ *well, it would make a cow laugh to see the* shines that old idiot cut (*The Adventures of Huckleberry Finn* by Mark Twain)

shirking VERB shirking means not doing what you are meant to be doing, or evading your duties ❑ *some of you shirking lubbers* (*Treasure Island* by Robert Louis Stevenson)

shiver my timbers PHRASE shiver my timbers is an expression which was used by sailors and pirates to express surprise ❑ *why, shiver my timbers, if I hadn't forgotten my score!* (*Treasure Island* by Robert Louis Stevenson)

shoe-roses NOUN shoe-roses were roses made from ribbons which were stuck on to shoes as decoration ❑ *the very shoe-roses for Netherfield were got by proxy* (*Pride and Prejudice* by Jane Austen)

singular ADJ singular means very great and remarkable or strange ❑ *"Singular dream," he says* (*The Adventures of Huckleberry Finn* by Mark Twain)

sire NOUN sire is an old word which means lord or master or elder ❑ *She also defied her sire* (*Little Women* by Louisa May Alcott)

sixpence NOUN a sixpence was half of a shilling ❑ *if she had only a shilling in the world, she would be very lilkely to give away sixpence of it* (*Emma* by Jane Austen)

slavey NOUN the word slavey was used when there was only one servant in a house or boarding-house – so she had to perform all the duties of a larger staff ❑ *Two distinct knocks, sir, will produce the slavey at any time* (*The Old Curiosity Shop* by Charles Dickens)

slender ADJ weak ❑ *In slender accents of sweet verse* (*The Prelude* by William Wordsworth)

slop-shops NOUN slop-shops were shops where cheap ready-made clothes were sold. They mainly sold clothes to sailors ❑ *Accordingly, I took the jacket off, that I might*

learn to do without it; and carrying it under my arm, began a tour of inspection of the various slop-shops. (*David Copperfield* by Charles Dickens)

sluggard NOUN a lazy person ❑ *"Stand up and repeat 'Tis the voice of the sluggard,'"* said the Gryphon. (*Alice's Adventures in Wonderland* by Lewis Carroll)

smallpox NOUN smallpox is a serious infectious disease ❑ *by telling the men we had smallpox aboard* (*The Adventures of Huckleberry Finn* by Mark Twain)

smalls NOUN smalls are short trousers ❑ *It is difficult for a large-headed, small-eyed youth, of lumbering make and heavy countenance, to look dignified under any circumstances; but it is more especially so, when superadded to these personal attractions are a red nose and yellow smalls* (*Oliver Twist* by Charles Dickens)

sneeze-box NOUN a box for snuff was called a sneeze-box because sniffing snuff makes the user sneeze ❑ *To think of Jack Dawkins – lummy Jack – the Dodger – the Artful Dodger – going abroad for a common twopenny-halfpenny sneeze-box!* (*Oliver Twist* by Charles Dickens)

snorted VERB slept ❑ *Or snorted we in the Seven Sleepers' den?* (*The Good-Morrow* by John Donne)

snuff NOUN snuff is tobacco in powder form which is taken by sniffing ❑ *as he thrust his thumb and forefinger into the proffered snuff-box of the undertaker: which was an ingenious little model of a patent coffin.* (*Oliver Twist* by Charles Dickens)

soliloquized VERB to soliloquize is when an actor in a play speaks to himself or herself rather than to another actor ❑ *"A new servitude! There is something in that," I soliloquized (mentally, be it understood; I did not talk aloud)* (*Jane Eyre* by Charlotte Brontë)

sough NOUN a sough is a drain or a ditch ❏ *as you may have noticed the sough that runs from the marshes* (*Wuthering Heights* by Emily Brontë)

spirits NOUN a spirit is the nonphysical part of a person which is believed to remain alive after their death ❏ *that I might raise up spirits when I please* (*Doctor Faustus* 1.5 by Christopher Marlowe)

spleen **1** NOUN here spleen means a type of sadness or depression which was thought to only affect the wealthy ❏ *yet here I could plainly discover the true seeds of spleen* (*Gulliver's Travels* by Jonathan Swift) **2** NOUN irritability and low spirits ❏ *Adieu to disappointment and spleen* (*Pride and Prejudice* by Jane Austen)

spondulicks NOUN spondulicks is a slang word which means money ❏ *not for all his spondulicks and as much more on top of it* (*The Adventures of Huckleberry Finn* by Mark Twain)

stalled of VERB to be stalled of something is to be bored with it ❏ *I'm stalled of doing naught* (*Wuthering Heights* by Emily Brontë)

stanchion NOUN a stanchion is a pole or bar that stands upright and is used as a buidling support ❏ *and slid down a stanchion* (*The Adventures of Huckleberry Finn* by Mark Twain)

stang NOUN stang is another word for pole which was an old measurement ❏ *These fields were intermingled with woods of half a stang* (*Gulliver's Travels* by Jonathan Swift)

starlings NOUN a starling is a wall built around the pillars that support a bridge to protect the pillars ❏ *There were states of the tide when, having been down the river, I could not get back through the eddy-chafed arches and starlings of old London Bridge* (*Great Expectations* by Charles Dickens)

startings NOUN twitching or night-time movements of the body ❏ *with midnight's startings* (*On His Mistress* by John Donne)

stomacher NOUN a panel at the front of a dress ❏ *but send her aunt the pattern of a stomacher* (*Emma* by Jane Austen)

stoop VERB swoop ❏ *Once a kite hovering over the garden made a swoop at me* (*Gulliver's Travels* by Jonathan Swift)

succedaneum NOUN a succedaneum is a substitute ❏ *But as a succedaneum* (*The Prelude* by William Wordsworth)

suet NOUN a hard animal fat used in cooking ❏ *and your jaws are too weak For anything tougher than suet* (*Alice's Adventures in Wonderland* by Lewis Carroll)

sultry ADJ sultry weather is hot and damp. Here sultry means unpleasant or risky ❏ *for it was getting pretty sultry for us* (*The Adventures of Huckleberry Finn* by Mark Twain)

summerset NOUN summerset is an old spelling of somersault. If someone does a somersault, they turn over completely in the air ❏ *I have seen him do the summerset* (*Gulliver's Travels* by Jonathan Swift)

supper NOUN supper was a light meal taken late in the evening. The main meal was dinner which was eaten at four or five in the afternoon ❏ *and the supper table was all set out* (*Emma* by Jane Austen)

surfeits VERB to surfeit in something is to have far too much of it, or to overindulge in it to an unhealthy degree ❏ *He surfeits upon cursed necromancy* (*Doctor Faustus* chorus by Christopher Marlowe)

surtout NOUN a surtout is a long close-fitting overcoat ❏ *He wore a long black surtout reaching nearly to his ankles* (*The Old Curiosity Shop* by Charles Dickens)

swath NOUN swath is the width of corn cut by a scythe ❏ *while thy* hook Spares the next swath (*Ode to Autumn* by John Keats)

sylvan ADJ sylvan means belonging to the woods ❏ *Sylvan historian* (*Ode on a Grecian Urn* by John Keats)

taction NOUN taction means touch. This means that the people had to be touched on the mouth or the ears to get their attention ❏ *without being roused by some external taction upon the organs of speech and hearing* (*Gulliver's Travels* by Jonathan Swift)

Tag and Rag and Bobtail PHRASE the riff-raff, or lower classes. Used in an insulting way ❏ *"No," said he; "not till it got about that there was no protection on the premises, and it come to be considered dangerous, with convicts and Tag and Rag and Bobtail going up and down."* (*Great Expectations* by Charles Dickens)

tallow NOUN tallow is hard animal fat that is used to make candles and soap ❏ *and a lot of tallow candles* (*The Adventures of Huckleberry Finn* by Mark Twain)

tan VERB to tan means to beat or whip ❏ *and if I catch you about that school I'll tan you good* (*The Adventures of Huckleberry Finn* by Mark Twain)

tanyard NOUN the tanyard is part of a tannery, which is a place where leather is made from animal skins ❏ *hid in the old tanyard* (*The Adventures of Huckleberry Finn* by Mark Twain)

tarry ADJ tarry means the colour of tar or black ❏ *his tarry pig-tail* (*Treasure Island* by Robert Louis Stevenson)

thereof PHRASE from there ❏ *By all desires which thereof did ensue* (*On His Mistress* by John Donne)

thick with, be PHRASE if you are 'thick with someone' you are very close, sharing secrets – it is often used to describe people who are planning something secret ❏ *Hasn't he been thick with Mr*

Heathcliff lately? (*Wuthering Heights* by Emily Brontë)

thimble NOUN a thimble is a small cover used to protect the finger while sewing ❏ *The paper had been sealed in several places by a thimble* (*Treasure Island* by Robert Louis Stevenson)

thirtover ADJ thirtover is an old word which means obstinate or that someone is very determined to do want they want and can not be persuaded to do something in another way ❏ *I have been living on in a thirtover, lackadaisical way* (*Tess of the D'Urbervilles* by Thomas Hardy)

timbrel NOUN timbrel is a tambourine ❏ *What pipes and timbrels?* (*Ode on a Grecian Urn* by John Keats)

tin NOUN tin is slang for money/cash ❏ *Then the plain question is, an't it a pity that this state of things should continue, and how much better would it be for the old gentleman to hand over a reasonable amount of tin, and make it all right and comfortable* (*The Old Curiosity Shop* by Charles Dickens)

tincture NOUN a tincture is a medicine made with alcohol and a small amount of a drug ❏ *with ink composed of a cephalic tincture* (*Gulliver's Travels* by Jonathan Swift)

tithe NOUN a tithe is a tax paid to the church ❏ *and held farms which, speaking from a spiritual point of view, paid highly-desirable tithes* (*Silas Marner* by George Eliot)

towardly ADJ a towardly child is dutiful or obedient ❏ *and a towardly child* (*Gulliver's Travels* by Jonathan Swift)

toys NOUN trifles are things which are considered to have little importance, value, or significance ❏ *purchase my life from them bysome bracelets, glass rings, and other toys* (*Gulliver's Travels* by Jonathan Swift)

tract NOUN a tract is a religious pamphlet or leaflet ❏ *and Joe*

Harper got a hymn-book and a tract (*The Adventures of Huckleberry Finn* by Mark Twain)

train-oil NOUN train-oil is oil from whale blubber ❑ *The train-oil and gunpowder were shoved out of sight in a minute* (*Wuthering Heights* by Emily Brontë)

tribulation NOUN tribulation means the suffering or difficulty you experience in a particular situation ❑ *Amy was learning this distinction through much tribulation* (*Little Women* by Louisa May Alcott)

trivet NOUN a trivet is a three-legged stand for resting a pot or kettle ❑ *a pocket-knife in his right; and a pewter pot on the trivet* (*Oliver Twist* by Charles Dickens)

trot line NOUN a trot line is a fishing line to which a row of smaller fishing lines are attached ❑ *when he got along I was hard at it taking up a trot line* (*The Adventures of Huckleberry Finn* by Mark Twain)

troth NOUN oath or pledge ❑ *I wonder, by my troth* (*The Good-Morrow* by John Donne)

truckle NOUN a truckle bedstead is a bed that is on wheels and can be slid under another bed to save space ❑ *It rose under my hand, and the door yielded. Looking in, I saw a lighted candle on a table, a bench, and a mattress on a truckle bedstead.* (*Great Expectations* by Charles Dickens)

trump NOUN a trump is a good, reliable person wo can be trusted ❑ *This lad Hawkins is a trump, I perceive* (*Treasure Island* by Robert Louis Stevenson)

tucker NOUN a tucker is a frilly lace collar which is worn around the neck ❑ *Whereat Scrooge's niece's sister the plump one with the lace tucker: not the one with the roses blushed.* (*A Christmas Carol* by Charles Dickens)

tureen NOUN a large bowl with a lid from which soup or vegetables are served ❑ *Waiting in a hot tureen!*

(*Alice's Adventures in Wonderland* by Lewis Carroll)

turnkey NOUN a prison officer; jailer ❑ *As we came out of the prison through the lodge, I found that the great importance of my guardian was appreciated by the turnkeys, no less than by those whom they held in charge.* (*Great Expectations* by Charles Dickens)

turnpike NOUN the upkeep of many roads of the time was paid for by tolls (fees) collected at posts along the road. There was a gate to prevent people travelling further along the road until the toll had been paid. ❑ *Traddles, whom I have taken up by appointment at the turnpike, presents a dazzling combination of cream colour and light blue; and both he and Mr. Dick have a general effect about them of being all gloves.* (*David Copperfield* by Charles Dickens)

twas PHRASE it was ❑ *twas but a dream of thee* (*The Good-Morrow* by John Donne)

tyrannized VERB tyrannized means bullied or forced to do things against their will ❑ *for people would soon cease coming there to be tyrannized over and put down* (*Treasure Island* by Robert Louis Stevenson)

'un NOUN 'un is a slang term for one – usually used to refer to a person ❑ *She's been thinking the old 'un* (*David Copperfield* by Charles Dickens)

undistinguished ADJ undiscriminating or incapable of making a distinction between good and bad things ❑ *their undistinguished appetite to devour everything* (*Gulliver's Travels* by Jonathan Swift)

use NOUN habit ❑ *Though use make you apt to kill me* (*The Flea* by John Donne)

vacant ADJ vacant usually means empty, but here Wordsworth uses it to mean carefree ❑ *To vacant musing, unreproved neglect* (*The Prelude* by William Wordsworth)

valetudinarian NOUN one too concerned with his or her own health. ❏ *for having been a valetudinarian all his life* (*Emma* by Jane Austen)

vamp VERB vamp means to walk or tramp to somewhere ❏ *Well, vamp on to Marlott, will 'ee* (*Tess of the D'Urbervilles* by Thomas Hardy)

vapours NOUN the vapours is an old term which means unpleasant and strange thoughts, which make the person feel nervous and unhappy ❏ *and my head was full of vapours* (*Robinson Crusoe* by Daniel Defoe)

vegetables NOUN here vegetables means plants ❏ *the other vegetables are in the same proportion* (*Gulliver's Travels* by Jonathan Swift)

venturesome ADJ if you are venturesome you are willing to take risks ❏ *he must be either hopelessly stupid or a venturesome fool* (*Wuthering Heights* by Emily Brontë)

verily ADJ verily means really or truly ❏ *though I believe verily* (*Robinson Crusoe* by Daniel Defoe)

vicinage NOUN vicinage is an area or the residents of an area ❏ *and to his thought the whole vicinage was haunted by her.* (*Silas Marner* by George Eliot)

victuals NOUN victuals means food ❏ *grumble a little over the victuals* (*The Adventures of Huckleberry Finn* by Mark Twain)

vintage NOUN vintage in this context means wine ❏ *Oh, for a draught of vintage!* (*Ode on a Nightingale* by John Keats)

virtual ADJ here virtual means powerful or strong ❏ *had virtual faith* (*The Prelude* by William Wordsworth)

vittles NOUN vittles is a slang word which means food ❏ *There never was such a woman for givin' away vittles and drink* (*Little Women* by Louisa May Alcott)

voided straight PHRASE voided straight is an old expression which means emptied immediately ❏ *see the rooms be voided straight* (*Doctor Faustus 4.1* by Christopher Marlowe)

wainscot NOUN wainscot is wood panel lining in a room so wainscoted means a room lined with wooden panels ❏ *in the dark wainscoted parlor* (*Silas Marner* by George Eliot)

walking the plank PHRASE walking the plank was a punishment in which a prisoner would be made to walk along a plank on the side of the ship and fall into the sea, where they would be abandoned ❏ *about hanging, and walking the plank* (*Treasure Island* by Robert Louis Stevenson)

want VERB want means to be lacking or short of ❏ *The next thing wanted was to get the picture framed* (*Emma* by Jane Austen)

wanting ADJ wanting means lacking or missing ❏ *wanting two fingers of the left hand* (*Treasure Island* by Robert Louis Stevenson)

wanting, I was not PHRASE I was not wanting means I did not fail ❏ *I was not wanting to lay a foundation of religious knowledge in his mind* (*Robinson Crusoe* by Daniel Defoe)

ward NOUN a ward is, usually, a child who has been put under the protection of the court or a guardian for his or her protection ❏ *I call the Wards in Jarndyce. The are caged up with all the others.* (*Bleak House* by Charles Dickens)

waylay VERB to waylay someone is to lie in wait for them or to intercept them ❏ *I must go up the road and waylay him* (*The Adventures of Huckleberry Finn* by Mark Twain)

weazen NOUN weazen is a slang word for throat. It actually means shrivelled ❏ *You with a uncle too! Why, I knowed you at Gargery's when you was so small a wolf that I could have took your weazen betwixt this finger and thumb and chucked* *you away dead* (*Great Expectations* by Charles Dickens)

wery ■ ADV very ❑ *Be wery careful o' vidders all your life* (*Pickwick Papers* by Charles Dickens) ■ *See* wibrated

wherry NOUN wherry is a small swift rowing boat for one person ❑ *It was flood tide when Daniel Quilp sat himself down in the wherry to cross to the opposite shore.* (*The Old Curiosity Shop* by Charles Dickens)

whether PREP whether means which of the two in this example ❑ *we came in full view of a great island or continent (for we knew not whether)* (*Gulliver's Travels* by Jonathan Swift)

whetstone NOUN a whetstone is a stone used to sharpen knives and other tools ❑ *I dropped pap's whetstone there too* (*The Adventures of Huckleberry Finn* by Mark Twain)

wibrated VERB in Dickens's use of the English language 'w' often replaces 'v' when he is reporting speech. So here 'wibrated' means 'vibrated'. In Pickwick Papers a judge asks Sam Weller (who constantly confuses the two letters) 'Do you spell it with a 'v' or a 'w'?' to which Weller replies 'That depends upon the taste and fancy of the speller, my Lord' ❑ *There are strings . . . in the human heart that had better not be wibrated* (*Barnaby Rudge* by Charles Dickens)

wicket NOUN a wicket is a little door in a larger entrance ❑ *Having rested here, for a minute or so, to collect a good burst of sobs and an imposing show of tears and terror, he knocked loudly at the wicket;* (*Oliver Twist* by Charles Dickens)

without CONJ without means unless ❑ *You don't know about me, without you have read a book by the name of The Adventures of Tom Sawyer* (*The Adventures of Huckleberry Finn* by Mark Twain)

wittles ■ NOUN vittles is a slang word which means food ❑ *I live on broken wittles – and I sleep on the coals* (*David Copperfield* by Charles Dickens) ■ *See* wibrated

woo VERB courts or forms a proper relationship with ❑ *before it woo* (*The Flea* by John Donne)

words, to have PHRASE if you have words with someone you have a disagreement or an argument ❑ *I do not want to have words with a young thing like you.* (*Black Beauty* by Emily Brontë)

workhouse NOUN workhouses were places where the homeless were given food and a place to live in return for doing very hard work ❑ *And the Union workhouses? demanded Scrooge. Are they still in operation?* (*A Christmas Carol* by Charles Dickens)

yawl NOUN a yawl is a small boat kept on a bigger boat for short trips. Yawl is also the name for a small fishing boat ❑ *She sent out her yawl, and we went aboard* (*The Adventures of Huckleberry Finn* by Mark Twain)

yeomanry NOUN the yeomanry was a collective term for the middle classes involved in agriculture ❑ *The yeomanry are precisely the order of people with whom I feel I can have nothing to do* (*Emma* by Jane Austen)

yonder ADV yonder means over there ❑ *all in the same second we seem to hear low voices in yonder!* (*The Adventures of Huckleberry Finn* by Mark Twain)